P9-CBA-070

The Hunt for the Eye of Ogin

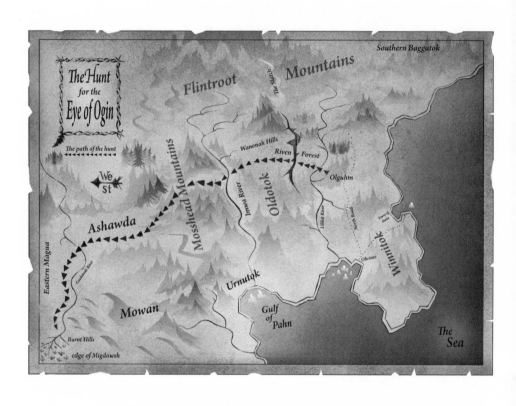

Southern Baggatok

Flintroot   Mountains

The Slatch

Wanonah Hills
Riven   Forest
Oldotok
Olguhin

Mosshead Mountains

The path of the hunt

West

Ashawda

Inuwa River
Lilikit River
North Basid

Winnitok

Eastern Magua
Guskovak River

Urnutok

Mowan

Gulf
of
Pahn

Ohrima

The
Sea

Burnt Hills
edge of Migdowsh

THE WINNITOK TALES

THE HUNT FOR THE EYE OF OGIN

PATRICK DOUD

North Atlantic Books
Berkeley, California

Published by
North Atlantic Books   Cover art by August Hall
P.O. Box 12327   Cover and book design by Paula Morrison
Berkeley, California 94712   Printed in the United States of America

The Hunt for the Eye of Ogin is sponsored by the Society for the Study of Native Arts and Sciences, a nonprofit educational corporation whose goals are to develop an educational and cross-cultural perspective linking various scientific, social, and artistic fields; to nurture a holistic view of arts, sciences, humanities, and healing; and to publish and distribute literature on the relationship of mind, body, and nature.

North Atlantic Books' publications are available through most bookstores. For further information, visit our Web site at www.northatlanticbooks.com or call 800-733-3000.

Hardcover Library Binding Edition: ISBN 978-1-55643-917-9

Library of Congress Cataloging-in-Publication Data

Doud, Patrick.
    The hunt for the Eye of Ogin / Patrick Doud.
        p. cm. — (The Winnitok tales ; [1])
    Summary: Thirteen-year-old Elwood Pitch mysteriously enters the far-off land of Winnitok, where he, his dog Slukee, warrior Drallah Wehr, and her talking raven Booj set out to find the Eye of Ogin, an ancient turtle shell with the power to find the missing immortal, Granashon, and restore peace to the land.
        ISBN 978-1-55643-822-6 (alk. paper)
    [1. Fantasy.] I. Title.
    PZ7.D74424Hun 2010
    [Fic]—dc22
                                                            2009048205

CPSIA Tracking Label
Printer: Sheridan Books   Printer Location: Chelsea, Michigan, USA
Date Printed: January 2010   Printing Number: 531453

1 2 3 4 5 6 7 8 9 SHERIDAN 16 15 14 13 12 11 10

CONTENTS

THE PATH TO THE GLADE

On a bright Saturday morning in October, a few minutes after breakfast and about an hour before he and the
world would part ways, Elwood Pitch sat in the front hall
tying his boots. Lying in her habitual place by the door, his dog,
Slukee, was giving his progress her whole attention. His older sister,
Ellen, was calling to him from another room.

"You'd better be back by four o'clock!"

A short, slight boy of thirteen, Elwood sat on the step a moment
longer. Then, not dignifying his sister's half-made threat with a reply,
he got up and quietly opened the door. Slukee shot out first, and he
followed. Linked by a leash on the dog's collar, the pair walked
quickly down to the road. There they waited for a break in the cars
roaring by, and crossed.

The Pitches had only recently moved into this neighborhood near
the city of Boston, and though it was a dull sort of place, it did lie
along the edge of a large and wild wooded park. Elwood bitterly
opposed the move, but the company his father worked for had offered
Mr. Pitch an opportunity to make more money at another office, and
there was nothing the boy could do to stop it. He had been obliged
to leave his home and friends hundreds of miles to the west, where
there were green hills and lake valleys, where he had lived since he was
born, all for a strange house, neighborhood, and school. Of these,

he despised the school the most: self-conscious of his country upbringing, and out of loyalty to his old life, Elwood made sure he had no friends there. He spent the long days at school alone among many, comforted by the thought of Slukee waiting for him at home.

The woods were another consolation, and the boy and the dog went walking in them whenever they were able. Across the busy road from the Pitches' house they lay: miles of hills, or fells as they sometimes call them in that part of the world, which had once been cleared for fields and pastures but had long since been reclaimed by trees. Elwood could see them out his bedroom window. From his front door it was a two-minute walk up the road to the nearest path into the woods, and it was toward that path, and the many other paths with which it joined, that he and Slukee were heading.

Reaching their aim, they stepped off the roadside and into the woods. The trees had on their autumn colors and had begun to strew the ground with fragrant leaves. Their scent filling the air reminded Elwood of his old home.

He unfastened the leash, and Slukee busied herself with seeing and smelling everything. She was neither big nor small, with fur of deep red and golden brown that was long in front and bushy behind, and a cascade of perfect white that began at the top of her throat and flowed down her chest. She had only a nub of a tail, and she could stand her lively tufty ears straight up.

They walked quickly, and the roar of cars faded. The ground began to rise steadily. Elwood was heading for a spot three quarters of a mile away, a windswept place they had found two weeks earlier on top of a high, rocky fell. From there he had been able to see the woods stretching away on all sides, right to the edge of the world of buildings and streets. He had even seen the skyscrapers of Boston standing like angular glass and metal mountains in the south. But Elwood was not climbing the fell to see them. He wanted to look down from that high place at the woods all around, to see where in them he had been and where he had not, and to choose an unknown area to explore.

The day grew warmer. The path wound and climbed. After walking a while they turned off it to the left, where the ground sank into a pebbly hollow overarched by a pair of spreading oak trees. In the deep shade at the bottom they found a pool fed by a little waterfall of recent rain. Elwood pushed up the sleeves of his sweater, dipped his hands in, and drew up some water. It was as colorless and clear as a polished window, and cold. After taking a drink he let the rest fall through his fingers, and pressed his wet palms to his warm forehead and cheeks. Then he sat down in a drift of leaves with his back against a large exposed root, and began to think.

He thought of how his life had changed since he and his family left their home, and the thought was bitter. It was not just leaving the people and places he had known all his life he resented, but that his family had made him do it. He felt betrayed. They had given him so much, and then simply took it all away. What is a job worth, he wondered, compared to a home? As a result, he had begun to regard change of any kind with suspicion. Wistfully he thought of the mustache and beard his father had worn since Elwood was an infant, but had shaved off when he took the new job. Mr. Pitch's face still looked strange to his son.

Not hiding his unhappiness, Elwood had been sullen and silent with both his father and his sister, and even his mother, for months. But his resentment was complicated by a growing feeling he was still only vaguely aware of, a feeling that there was much more to his misery than leaving home. After all, life there had not been perfect either. What he was slowly coming to realize was this: he was not only a part of his family, but his own person as well. It was a sure sign of this change when, for the first time in Elwood's life, his wishes and the wishes of his family parted ways on an important matter: the move from their old home. So, much of his anguish was not caused by what he thought it was, as the pain of leaving home and the pain of growing up were confused.

His thoughts turned to two old friends, Ed Marchfield and Kevin

Fishlock. It was a Saturday, which meant they were probably together doing something; maybe shooting at cans with Ed's BB gun in the fields behind Mason's Dairy, or if it was raining, playing a game of *Ghost* in the Fishlocks' old barn. The barn was an amazing place, where no one but the boys ever seemed to go. The three of them had spent countless afternoons under its high peaked roof, sometimes playing games, sometimes digging through the fascinating old junk deposited there by generations of Kevin's family. Often the boys would just sit in the hayloft and talk for hours on end. Elwood sighed; the boys in his new school, when they talked to him at all, mostly only did so to make fun of his name or his clothes.

Looking around him, he tried to reconcile the beautiful hollow with the place where he and his family now lived. A feeling he knew well was coming over him, one he had often had in these woods and around his old home, and which seemed to emanate from those places. It was the start of a certainty that future and past, earth and heavens were welcoming and good, filled with interest and pleasures and possibility; utterly opposite the dull, gray, hopeless world of his school and his family. The two kinds of places seemed so at odds that he sometimes thought he must be caught in some kind of between-world. It had not yet occurred to Elwood that such a contradiction might exist within himself as well; that he too might be composed of multiple, seemingly incongruous selves.

However, with its plashing little waterfall, the hollow soon lulled his thoughts far away from his troubles. He forgot they were less than a mile from their house, and many other houses, and the rest of the whole world, amidst which the woods were only a tiny island. But as he wriggled deeper down into this pleasant sense of solitude, a sudden thrill ran down his spine, and he felt with a strange certainty that someone had joined them in the hollow. Looking quickly around he could see no one, but still the feeling persisted. Slukee, her tufted ears cocked and her golden-green eyes blazing, made a querying sound in her throat. She felt it too.

"Weird," muttered Elwood, jumping up.

They climbed out of the hollow and walked on. In a few minutes Elwood saw a path branching off to the left that, for a reason he could only guess, ended abruptly after cutting straight into the trees for just a few yards. He thought maybe the wider paths were plowed in winter, and this might be a place for piling snow. Whatever its purpose, he had been watching for it: it was his landmark for finding the next path they were to take, which was narrow and hard to spot, and wound up the fell to the glade they were heading for. Elwood remembered it was on their right just past the strange path going nowhere. It began beside a boulder, and was half hidden by the green cat briar that grew thickly there.

He stopped. The sense of another presence had returned, and it was stronger than it was in the hollow. Scanning the trees, he saw something inexplicable: the very short path branching off to the left was no longer very short. Instead of ending after several yards, as it had a moment before, it now appeared to continue on indefinitely.

With Slukee beside him, he stepped uncertainly onto this path that had not been there before. It was narrow, and the trees stood densely on either side. Elwood felt alarm in the pit of his stomach, like he was looking down from a great height. The back of his neck tingled, and there was a lump in his throat. Thrilled and terrified at the uncanny path's beginning, Elwood began to force his feet forward.

The trees began to change. They seemed to Elwood to be dissolving, liquefying, yet still keeping their shapes. The change spread in waves from the tips of the branches into the air all around the boy and the dog, though they could still breathe, and from the roots into the ground beneath them, though they did not sink into the earth. They did not walk faster, but they seemed to begin to move faster; they stopped walking, but more and more rapidly the trees continued to slide by. While they remained still, all the leaves on the trees and on the ground melted together into a maelstrom of scarlet, orange, emerald, and gold rushing and swirling around them. There were extraordinary sounds in the liquid air, like far-off thunder joining in the song of a thousand birds, their harmonies now and then jarred by the strident notes of a great horn. Elwood felt a pressure on his left shoulder, as though a hand were guiding him through the chaos, but could see no one. Looking at Slukee, he saw her fur was blowing as it would in a tempest. For reasons he did not know or even wonder about, his fear was gone.

* * *

Like he had risen suddenly to the surface of a bottomless sleep, he found they were standing in a silent, sunny glade. It was speckled with a wild diversity of bright flowers, and ringed all around by the tallest of pine trees.

Elwood did not recognize this part of the woods at all, and was at a loss to explain how they had gotten there. "Did I hit my head?" he asked himself aloud, but a quick search of his skull told him he had not. Reaching into the big front pockets of his corduroy pants, he found the items he had filled them with that morning: a peanut butter and potato chip sandwich wrapped in a paper bag, three dog biscuits, Slukee's leash, his house key, and his wallet.

The sun was shining in dappled patches on the floor of the glade, and the world was very still. The warmth and silence, mixed with the fragrances of evergreens and flowers, suggested sleep. Wondering in which direction their house lay, Elwood stood at the glade's edge and peered into the trees. Since their boughs did not begin until high up their boles, and only short ferns grew in the thick covering of pine needles on the ground, he could see for some distance in the brown shade beneath them. They stretched out of sight in all directions, and there was no path to be seen.

Time did not feel like it was passing in the glade, and the temptation to linger was like a magic spell. Still, the strangeness of it all nagged at Elwood. Since he did not know where in the woods they were, he chose a direction at random and called to Slukee. As he took a step, a shadow crossed his path. Looking up, he saw a very large black bird hovering over the glade. It must have been afloat on a current of air, for it hung in the sky without flapping its wide wings. Elwood felt sure it was watching them. He hurried into the trees, Slukee following, and the bird uttered a long, harsh *cra-a-ark!* that resounded far and wide through the wood.

The silence beneath the trees was deep; the crunch of boots and paws on the carpet of pine needles filled the air. The absence of time, or at least Elwood's sense that time was not passing, lasted until they came to a place where the pines lessened in girth and stature, and mingled with other kinds of trees. Birds began to sing. As the wood changed, the calm the boy had felt in the glade was roiled by waves of anxiety. The farther they put the glade's sleepy stillness behind them, the more afraid he became that something terrible had happened.

Shortly they were confronted with an impenetrable wall of briar. There was no question of trying to pass through it, so the boy and the dog changed direction and walked along its edge. The dense green tangle of thorny vegetation went on and on. Just as Elwood was ready to give up hope of ever getting around it, the briar-wall was prevented from continuing by the base of a steep and rocky hill. Here they discovered a narrow, seldom-used-looking path, a trail penetrating the trees off to their left and proceeding windingly up the hill to their right.

Hoping to see some landmark he could recognize from its top, or at least the nearest house or road, Elwood decided to climb the hill. The way was so steep that at times he pulled himself up by trees growing beside the path. As they climbed, he looked to gaps in the leaves and branches for a sight of something that might tell him where they were, but these were too small and too few to allow more than glimpses of other hills and more trees.

In a quarter of an hour they reached the top. The ground leveled suddenly, and the path melted into the grass- and rock-covered floor of a thin windswept grove. There was a big boulder to their right. Clambering up and looking about, they saw that they were no longer in the woods across the road from their house. Here, hilly woods filled all the land, from where the boy and the dog stood to the far away round of the horizon. None of it was at all familiar to Elwood, and there were no signs of other people to be seen anywhere.

THE PLUM TREE

S itting on the boulder overlooking that vast forest, Elwood struggled to grasp what had happened to them and what to do about it. He had no idea where they were, how they had gotten there, or how they could get back to where they should be. He did not have a mobile phone, and even if he did it would be of no use so far from civilization. There was no one to ask for help. They could not be more lost.

At that moment Elwood was suffering the greatest fear of his life, with the exception perhaps of the inexpressible terrors that traumatized him in his dreams when he was a little boy. He wished that, like when he was little, he would now wake up screaming, his mother there instantly to soothe him back to sleep. Finally he turned to Slukee standing on the rock beside him, and the sight of her reassured him enough that he could think of their immediate needs.

The sun would go down in several hours, and it would be a cold night. There was the question of food. He was getting hungry, and all they had to eat between them was one sandwich and three dog biscuits. Though he loved to walk in the woods, he had no experience of living in them and off them. He thought of stories he had read, seen, and heard; of nuts and berries, of hunting and traps. But those were just stories. Elwood knew they had to find people—if there were any in that wilderness—before they used all their strength.

He thought the path they climbed up by was probably the quickest way to shelter and food, but he wondered if they could reach those things before they starved, or froze, or both. Still, a path meant people, and he could only hope that this one would lead to some before it was too late.

His high vantage and utterly forlorn state reminded him of an incident when he was small. Elwood and his mother were at a shopping mall, and he slipped off while she was trying on clothes in a department store changing room. He had wandered out into the mall's wide, busy corridors, quickly forgetting the way back to the place where he had left his mother. Too proud to ask for help, and noticing a high vacant throne surrounded by red velvet rope—it was the Christmas shopping season, and though he was not there that day, this was the grand chair of Santa Claus himself—Elwood had sat down upon it. A kind old woman soon noticed him, coaxed him down from the throne with red licorice, and helped him find his mother. In spite of everything, a smile twitched around the corners of Elwood's mouth at the memory.

They climbed back down the hill. Elwood set a fast pace, panic at the thought of the coming dark driving his feet. The path, though winding, tended southward. After an hour they reluctantly paused, and Elwood squatted down to dole out rations. Slukee had a biscuit, and he had a quarter of the peanut butter and potato chip sandwich. The rest he wrapped up again and put back in his pocket. As he ate his meager meal, he wondered how he would ever explain to his mother, father, and sister what had happened—and if he would ever get the chance.

They walked on. The shadows beneath the trees began to deepen. Elwood was startled by the sound of a fair-sized creature scurrying through the leaves. He thought he caught a glimpse of some dark thing just a few feet away, but it was lost in the shadows before he was sure. Once he thought for certain he saw a furry half-human face peep from a gap in a briar-tangle, but instantly it disappeared again. Soon he was seeing things out of the corner of his eye all around, and the trees and brush were full of the sounds of furtive movement. Though she pricked up her ears and pointed her nose at these disturbances, Slukee did not run off to investigate them. Side by side the boy and the dog hurried on, Elwood's stomach sour with fear of the coming dark.

They came to the bottom of a gradual slope. Elwood saw a place of fewer boughs and leaves at its top, and the late sun collecting there. The path was plain for a little way, and so he began to jog up the hill to see what was to be seen while there was still light.

Halfway up he was halted by the sudden startling appearance of a tall female figure, dark against the red sunlight on the hilltop, a dozen yards above them. Though Elwood stopped, Slukee barked once and ran on. The figure stood motionless, awaiting her. Elwood called her back, but she ignored him, instead gamboling and dancing around the stranger. He saw by the dimming glow that the girl or woman bent to pat the dog, and he thought he heard kindly spoken words. Full of hope and uncertainty, he walked up to join them.

The stranger was four or five years older than Elwood, he guessed, and very tall. Her hair was black and gleaming and fell down well past her shoulders, and in the light of the setting sun her skin shone like burnished red bronze. Her clothes struck Elwood as very odd, in that they made her look like someone out of a book or a film about some distant past: she wore a green-dyed buckskin shirt, green britches, and moccasins that reached her knees. She carried a tall narrow pack on her back, and other gear. There was a strange intense look in her dark eyes as she stared at Elwood, though the strong lines of her cheeks and mouth were forming an expression that was unmistakably friendly. He was also encouraged by Slukee, who was leaning a shoulder against the girl's leg and gazing up into her face through half-closed eyes. Resting a hand in the thick fur of the dog's shoulders, the girl spoke.

"*Ei dor erfol-ia dua. Ei od* Drallah Wehr." So saying, she held out her hands to Elwood, palms upward. Confused, he hesitated a moment, then held out his own hands. She clasped them warmly.

"I can't understand you," he said, shaking his head and wondering anew just how far from home they were. He could see by her puzzled expression that the girl did not understand him either. When she spoke again her words had a different sound.

"Ellu tengon Winnitoke?" Elwood shook his head again. At that she shrugged, pointed at herself and said, "Drallah; *Ei od* Drallah."

"I'm Elwood Pitch. And this is Slukee."

Suddenly great wings beat the air overhead, and a big black shape flew at them. Elwood ducked and threw up his arms to ward it off, but the bird only landed on top of Drallah's pack, drew in its wings, and shook itself so that the feathers of its throat and head bristled. It stood over two feet tall, had a huge beak, and looked down at Elwood and Slukee first with one glaring amber eye, then the other. Elwood slowly straightened again as he stared at the bird in amazement.

"Ind-lo Booj," said Drallah. *"Ind-lo* Elwood *oll ind-lo* Slukee." The bird bowed to the boy and the dog, then straightened again and uttered a sound like one Elwood had heard before: *"Ca-a-a-rork!"*

"Hello," he answered, wondering if this was the same bird that had been watching them in the glade. He noticed that half-buried in the black of Booj's feathers were faint shimmering hues of green, blue, and purple, and that thin feathers like whiskers or lashes sprouted between his beak and eyes.

Drallah gestured at the path behind her. *"Ind-orr!"* she said as she turned and began to walk up the hill, the bird still perching on her pack. Elwood and Slukee followed.

At the top of the slope the trees thinned, and they could see that the path descended into a shallow, narrow valley curving out of sight into the south. The treetops bathed in the light of the low sun, while all beneath them was growing dark. There were no signs of any other humans to be seen, but for the moment Elwood did not care. He was so relieved they had met Drallah—despite what her foreignness seemed to indicate about where they might be—that he felt like skipping. The noises and glimpses of mysterious creatures had ceased. He guessed she must have something to eat in her pack, something to start a fire with, and maybe a spare blanket. She must know where they were, and the way to the nearest civilized place. Looking more closely at all she carried, he saw for the first time that what had appeared to be a pole tied to Drallah's back was actually an unstrung bow of dark wood nearly as tall as her. There was also a lidded case on a strap he guessed was a quiver of arrows, a tomahawk in a sheath tied to her pack, and a long knife in her belt.

As they walked down into the vale a murmur of flowing water could be heard, and they came in the red dimness to a wide, deep creek. The path, broadening into a lane, took to its eastern bank. In the Y where the water and the path met stood an old stone cottage. The tile roof that once covered its one story was mostly gone, the doorway lacked a door, and tall reeds grew wild all around. A little plum tree still bearing purple fruit stood beside it.

Booj flapped over to the plum tree and landed on a branch. After leaning her pack and bow against the cottage, Drallah went to the tree, picked a plum, and brought it to Elwood, who was standing in the dooryard looking hungry and lost. Recalling his hunger, he thanked her, admiring the fruit's dusky purple skin for a moment before taking a deep bite. It was deliciously sweet and juicy, but his pleasure quickly ended: the first bite had barely been swallowed when the rest of the plum slipped from his fingers. At the same time his legs buckled, and he would have fallen if Drallah had not been there to catch and lay him gently down.

It did not seem so to Elwood. For him, the cottage and the plum tree were forgotten the moment he swallowed the fruit. Instead, he sat alone in a desert of white rock and dust. Bodiless voices gibbering words he could not understand floated in the void overhead. There was nothing to do, and he was there such an immeasurably long time that he came to believe he always had been.

However long it was, eventually an object appeared in the desolate white distance. From so far away, he could be sure only that it was brilliant red in color, and that it was not moving. He began to walk toward it. This took a long time, during much of which he seemed to make no progress at all. Then abruptly his walking brought him to his goal: a giant flower of fiery red growing up out of the floor of the waste. The stem was so bowed by the flower's weight that the ends of two long curving petals touched the dust of the ground. Like stairs, he climbed the petals into the flower's heart.

Within the flower was a land where—he knew it immediately—nothing ever died, or quite lived either. Walking beside an endless stream that wound among trees as tall as mountains, he realized it was always twilight in that land, and he wondered where the light came from. Following a sound of women and men singing, he found in a glade carpeted in purple flowers four people who fairly shone with their own light. They welcomed Elwood by name, though not one he recognized, and spoke to him for a long time before finally wandering away. When they left, they took Elwood's memories of them, and the desert of white rock, and the land inside the red flower. In place of these, they gave him knowledge he had not had before.

He was back at the creek again, looking down at himself lying on the ground. Drallah was kneeling over him and calling his name, and Slukee was vigorously licking his very white, peaceful face. *So I'm dead,* he thought, but the next moment the color rushed back into his cheeks. His eyes opened, and he was back behind them, staring out. Looking up at the faces of the girl and the dog, he became aware that Drallah was saying something in an urgent tone.

"What's wrong? Are you sick?"

"No, I'm all right, I think," he replied. Then he realized that she had spoken in her strange language, and he had not only understood her perfectly, but answered her as well.

Drallah sat back on her heels and stared at him, amazed. "You do know Winnitoke! Why didn't you say so?"

"I didn't know it, not till now. The plum is the first food I've had from . . . How long have I been like this?" he asked as he sat up and pushed away Slukee, who was licking his face with even greater vigor.

"A minute or so."

Elwood shook his head. It felt like a thousand years.

"I left my body. It seems like a long time ago. I don't know where I went, but I learned things. . . ." He took a deep breath. "You probably won't believe me, but we're not from here. I mean, from this world." He could hardly believe it himself, but he knew it was so. He could not remember the shining people he had met in the twilit land, but this awareness they had given him remained.

Drallah's eyes widened and she asked simply, "How?"

"I have no idea. Slukee and I were in the woods by our house, and all of a sudden the trees got weird. It was like they were melting. And I knew there was someone else there, but I never saw them. Then the trees went back to normal, and we were in this place I'd never seen before. . . ."

"The Glade of Granashon."

The name was familiar to Elwood, and he understood it belonged to the beautiful place among the tall pines where he and Slukee had arrived from their world.

"I have something strange to tell too," Drallah continued. "This morning we were miles to the south, by a creek. I stopped to drink from a little waterfall. As I did, the pool below became completely still, even though the water kept pouring down. Vision came to me. I saw the Glade of Granashon in that water.

"Granashon is the great friend and protector of this land, the land of Winnitok. She is not human like you and I, but of the immortal Noharn, the Sky People, who are few but mighty, and wisest of all the races. They wander the world, lending their power to those in need.

"But Granashon has not been seen or heard of in Winnitok, or anywhere else, for more than a year, and the power with which she's

15

always protected the land is fading. The Glade is her most sacred place, where she goes to rest from her labors when she needs to.

"I saw the Glade so clearly, and then it was gone. I didn't know what we would find, but I knew we should go there. Booj flew ahead; the paths of the sky are a lot straighter than the paths of the woods."

"I saw him watching me," said Elwood.

"He guided me to you. Now, if only someone would guide us to Granashon." Then she rose and said, "Let's have a fire and food while we talk." She picked up her pack and entered the old cottage, Elwood and Slukee following.

The floor was of worn stone. There was a pile of wood in a corner, and a fireplace in the wall. "It was abandoned a long time ago, but sometimes people still stop here on their way through the woods," said Drallah as she began to build a fire. "The walls don't keep out the rain, but they do keep out some of the wind, though there won't be either tonight. Still, you'll be more comfortable here than in the open."

The last of the twilight faded beneath a host of glimmering stars. Drallah took a small tinderbox out of her pack, and in a few moments there was a blaze in the grate. Then she went out to the creek and filled a waterskin. Returning, she spread a blanket on the floor in front of the fire, and they sat down. Booj landed on top of the wall, then glided to the floor. He strutted around and around the boy and the dog, examining them closely and making them self-conscious.

"All I have is cornbread and dried venison, but they're not so bad after a long walk," said Drallah, bringing out two bundles neatly wrapped in cloth. Eating hungrily, Elwood found the bread had been baked with walnuts and honey, and the meat well seasoned with herbs and salt. Though Slukee was quite content with her meal, she did not turn up her nose at the rest of the peanut butter and potato chip sandwich when Elwood offered it to her for dessert. Booj had given up his study of them for a strip of venison, but the sandwich revived his curiosity. When Elwood tossed the last morsel to the dog, Booj intercepted it deftly in his beak. Slukee's jaws snapped shut on nothing, and Drallah laughed as the bird swaggered off with his loot.

"Serves us right for not sharing," said Elwood, laughing too. "It's just not very good, compared to your food, and it's been in my pocket all day. How did you make friends with a crow, anyway?"

"*Crow!*" screamed a voice in the corner.

Elwood jumped. "Who was that?" he cried, looking wildly around the cottage. All he could see was Booj, his amber eyes glaring.

"Booj isn't a crow, Booj is a raven. He doesn't like being called a crow, just as you wouldn't like being called a woogan."

"But he talks!"

"Of course I talk," croaked Booj indignantly, and this time Elwood saw his beak open and close as he spoke.

"He speaks Winnitoke and Wohmog—that's the common language in this part of the world—and others too."

"Are there no ravens in your world?" asked Booj.

"Yes, but they don't talk. Some birds do, but it's more like they're . . . mimicking."

"Oh, Booj is a masterful mimic, like most ravens. It's one of their gifts," said Drallah.

"Well, I'm sorry, Booj."

Their hunger satisfied, the talk turned to what to do next. Elwood was intensely anxious about his family and what they must be going through: he had always been a fairly obedient son, and though he would sometimes be a little late, he had never in his life failed to return to the house at approximately the time he had been told to. By now, he thought, they had probably called the police. A lot of people would be searching the woods, and his mother . . . he quailed at the thought of how she must feel as hour followed hour and he did not come home. Lately, she had been worried about her children's safety in a way she never had before they moved from their tiny rural town to the big city suburb. He knew that as he sat in

comfort and safety by a fire some unknown and unimaginable distance from her, his mother was terrified that her worst fears may
have come true.

"I've got to get back somehow," he said, failing to suppress the
quaver in his voice. "My mom and dad must be going crazy."

Drallah nodded and said, "Granashon the Nohar would help you,
if we could find her. You should understand how important it is that
you came first to her sacred place, to the Glade. People do not visit
there, not without some very special reason. I don't know how, but
you and Granashon are connected in some way. Granashon must
be the answer."

"Have you ever seen her? I mean—is she your god, or something?" It seemed like a strangely forward question, but Elwood felt
he should know.

Drallah smiled and shook her head. "We don't worship her, no.
And though she is immortal, she too was created along with the rest
of Ehm—our name for this world.

"I saw her once, when I was a little girl," she continued thoughtfully. "She was passing through Ohrimo, where my family and I live,
in the south of Winnitok. A lot of people came out to see her, as
they always do. She looked down as she walked by, and smiled at
me. She glowed. And she was so tall. . . . I guess it's true my memory
of her *is* a little like that—like a god."

"But how can I find her?"

"I could take you to ask my uncle, Mithloo. He's been seeking
news of Granashon; maybe he's learned something. He has Vision."

"Vision?"

"Those with Vision see more of the world around them than the
rest of us. Maybe I'll grow to have it too—though seeing the Glade
in the pool was the first time anything like it has happened to me.
But my Uncle Mithloo sees much. He may even see a way for you
to go home."

"How far is your uncle's place?"

"Not far: three days or so north and west. I know the way well."

Elwood's hopes plummeted. "You call three days not far?" he asked, his disappointment sounding more like ungratefulness.

Drallah raised an eyebrow. "What do you call not far?"

Elwood regretted his words. She was, after all, offering help they desperately needed. "I'm sorry," he said. "It's just that I'm worried about being gone so long."

"I understand. But you have to be prepared: you may not be able to return to your world for a long time."

"Or ever," he replied, trying to sound ready for the worst. In truth, however, the possibility he might never see his family again was not something he was ready to accept.

* * *

Elwood was soon overwhelmed by weariness, and so they agreed to put off further talk until morning. Drallah loaned him her blanket, assuring him the night was warm enough and she could do without. Booj glided off to perch in a nearby tree. Slukee curled up beside Elwood, who was asleep almost before his head touched the sack Drallah had stuffed with leaves for his pillow.

In the middle of the night he was disturbed by a brightness falling on his eyelids. Squinting up into the light, he saw a big blue and green moon riding in the sky above the old roofless cottage. Upon its face he could see continents and oceans.

"Worlds on top of worlds," he said to himself, and lay awake for a time wondering how far they had come from their own, and what had brought them to this one.

IN THE WOODS OF WINNITOK

He woke an hour after dawn to the sound of Booj railing at a gang of impudent young blue jays. His first thought was that he had spent a whole night away from his family, and that they had no way of knowing what had become of him. But his worry was soon blunted by the thrill of discovery: he had often daydreamed about finding other worlds, but never thought it might actually happen.

Rising and stepping outside, the boy and the dog found Booj preening himself after driving off the blue jays, and Drallah picking plums. With some of these, some cornbread, and some venison for Slukee, they sat down under a willow tree by the creek's edge. Elwood draped Drallah's blanket over his shoulders against the chill morning air. As they ate, Drallah spoke more of Granashon the Nohar.

"Long before we began counting the days," she said, "and long before the Lindilish and Ringish came here from across the Sea, our grandmothers and grandfathers, the uprooted families that became my people, the Winharn, found their way into these woods. They were fleeing lands far to the west, which the hordes of the god Tehm's brother, the one we call the Other Twin, were conquering and laying waste. My people had wandered a long time, and of all the lands they'd seen, this one seemed best. Still, they feared they had not fled far enough, and would have soon moved on.

"But then one day they met Granashon the Nohar hunting the giant buck with her wolves. The people were afraid: they'd never met any of the immortal race of the Noharn, and she and her pack were fierce with the chase. But she gave up the hunt, and reassured them. She saw they loved the land, and because of that a great friendship grew between them and her. My people settled here, and Granashon named them the Winharn, the people of Winnitok.

"To help protect them from the Other Twin, Granashon gave the land some of her power. By sowing her magic Dread among the roots of the trees all along the Lilikit River to the west, and in the woods of the north, and between the great rocks down the shore of the Sea to the east and south, Granashon made certain the Other Twin's servants could not enter Winnitok. Any who came to the borders with ill will for the land in their hearts, any who saw Winnitok through hateful eyes, would see only a land of hate; a nightmare-country so terrible they would not dare set foot within. Such was the power of the Dread of Granashon."

Drallah paused, and trouble clouded her face as she continued. "But as I said last night, for more than a year now there's been bad news, and fear for our land. There have been strange signs the Dread of Granashon is failing—or has already failed. In the spring, two yugs were found crossing *back* over the River. The scouts who tracked them found the yugs had crept miles into Winnitok before turning around again."

"What're yugs?" asked Elwood.

"A cruel race created by the Other Twin long ago, to fight the war he makes on his brother Tehm. Yugs are hole-dwelling, green-skinned people who live by murder, theft, and war."

Elwood shook his head and told her there was nothing of the kind in his world.

"Your world is lucky," she said, then continued. "After the yugs were discovered in our land, we became more vigilant. The villages and towns along the shore of the Sea watch for sails on the horizon, and many more scouts guard the woods all along the River."

"What were you doing in the woods, Drallah? Before you saw the Glade in the water?"

"Just wandering," she answered. "I love to explore the woods, especially in places I only know from maps. The waterfall where the vision came to me is in the Valley of Moths, a place I'd never been before yesterday."

"I love exploring too."

"But also, I'm training to be a scout. When I'm old enough, Booj and I will guard the land. If we lose the Dread of Granashon, the Winharn will have a lot of work to keep foes out of Winnitok."

* * *

It took Drallah only a few moments to get her pack in order, and as she was finishing, Booj returned from a flight around the neighborhood. "Nothing stranger than a late badger," he told her in his harsh croak of a voice. Their preparations made, the four left the creek, the old cottage, and the plum tree behind, taking the path back the way they had come the night before.

It was a fine morning for walking, and soon it grew warm. Since the way was narrow, Drallah walked in front and Elwood behind. Slukee ranged here and there, or trotted between them. Booj rode on Drallah's pack, sometimes taking to the air to see the lay of the land, or to stretch his wings.

In less than an hour they turned left onto another path, little more than a deer trail, which Elwood had not noticed when he passed that way the evening before.

"It isn't the smoothest way, but it's the most direct. We're making for the North Road. We should reach it before sunset," said Drallah.

The trees and undergrowth were dense, and crowded in on either side of the trail. Elwood was impressed by the way Drallah, Booj ducking and swaying atop her pack, seemed to glide without effort through the branches and brambles in her way. It was difficult for

Elwood to keep up, but she noticed he was lagging and adjusted her pace.

They stopped to rest a little before noon. The humans sat, their backs against a golden-leaved chestnut tree, eating cornbread and drinking water from the skin. After she too had some water, Slukee settled at Elwood's feet to chew a piece of venison. Booj perched on a branch above, making low burbling sounds in his throat.

"You never told me how you and Booj met," said Elwood.

"Ah! Well, my mother, father, and I rescued him from an old sorcerer. It was in Oldotok, the land west of ours, three years ago. We were sailing along the coast on our way to visit friends, and camped one night on the beach. We heard someone crying in the middle of the night, and found it was coming from an old castle on the cliff above the shore. A petty sorcerer called Ustane, an old Ringishman, lived there. He had caught poor Booj in a trap and put him in a cage with no food. I've never heard a sadder sound than the cry of a starving raven."

Booj flapped down to the ground beside Drallah. "Oh, Booj, you were pitiful!" she chuckled, placing a morsel of bread in the raven's big beak. He blinked, and for the first time Elwood noticed the raven's eyelids were a strange opalescent white.

"Ustane wanted to make Booj his slave, and was trying to starve a magic oath of service out of him. We put a stop to it, or my parents did. They make dangerous enemies, both my mother and my father. When we left—me carrying Booj, who was too weak to fly—old Ustane was glad to get off as lightly as he did. I cared for Booj till he was healthy again, and we've been together ever since."

* * *

Just as Drallah had said, they reached the Road a little while before sunset. Suddenly the faint path they had been following most of the day was crossed by a dusty wide way through the woods. They turned onto it to their right and headed north.

24

"If you aren't too tired, there is a village two miles from here where we could spend the night," said Drallah. Though Elwood was very tired, he steeled himself to go a little farther and agreed.

They came upon a herd of deer browsing in the grasses along the roadside. A huge buck among them was aware of the four travelers before they came close. He stamped a hoof, and as the others fled into the trees flashing their white tails, the buck raised his antlered head and belled a warning like a trumpet call to arms.

"Peace, Lord of the Woods! We aren't hunting," said Drallah.

The buck snorted and glared at them with wild eyes. Then he leapt into the trees after the already disappeared herd, his call still ringing through the woods.

They had not been on the Road long when they heard the thud of a different kind of hoof, and the sound of a wagon trundling up behind them.

"Ah! We can get a ride," Drallah said, slapping Elwood's back.

It was a wide, open wagon drawn by two big shambling horses. On the bench sat an old man nonchalantly holding the reins, and a little girl. Like Drallah, they both had ruddy burnished-looking skin. The old man wore a wide-brimmed farmer's hat, and he had thrown a green and yellow-striped blanket over his shoulders. The girl was wrapped in a corner of the same blanket, and set in her black hair was a little blue feather.

"You have come from far away," the man said to Elwood, eyeing the boy's clothes. "Would you like a ride?"

Gratefully they clambered, leapt, and flapped into the wagon. While Drallah and the old man traded news, Booj entertained his granddaughter with voices and antics. Happy to be off his feet, Elwood scratched Slukee's head and watched the woods roll by.

He soon noticed a change happening on either side of the Road: they had come to a place where the trees were enormous, and the spaces between them were as green and open as in a park. They began to pass leafy lanes leading off from the main way, and more and more frequently, houses and barns. These were made chiefly of logs, but there was also stone, tile, and thatch. Around and amidst the homes and ancient trees were half-harvested fields of corn, apple trees dangling bright fruit, and gatherings of fat pumpkins. People were in abundance as well. In most every dooryard, neighbors and families were working, or visiting, or both, and the evening air resonated with the voices of children playing the last games of the day.

They soon came to the center of the village. There, in the middle of the road, stood a big oak tree with lanterns in its lower branches. These were already lit, as were other lights around the village square, one whole side of which was occupied by a two-story log-and-stone inn. The inn's many windows were aglow with orange light.

The old man and his granddaughter, who were continuing on to their home farther up the Road, dropped them off beneath the big oak. The sun was setting as the wagon drove away.

"Don't worry about money, Elwood," said Drallah as they walked up to the inn. "I've got enough for us. And tomorrow we can find you a blanket, and a pack, and everything else you'll need."

The double front doors opened into a broad rectangular hall stretching lengthwise away from the road. Lanterns hung from the rafters, and a fire blazed in a big stone hearth opposite the entrance. The atmosphere was delicious with aromas of cooking and pipe smoke. To the left and right the walls were lined with tables and benches, most of them occupied by villagers and guests staying at the inn. All nodded and smiled as the four young travelers passed on their way to a table near the fire. There Slukee lay down under the bench where Elwood sat across from Drallah, and Booj paced back and forth on the tabletop.

"We'll get hot food, and then soft beds," said Drallah.

Elwood opened his mouth to voice enthusiasm for this plan, but gasped instead. A person very thick in trunk and limb, and covered head to toe in fur, had just come shuffling into the room. It was,

Elwood would have believed, a giant badger; but he walked on his hind legs, wore a loose leather tunic, and carried a sack slung over his shoulder. Fascinated and frightened, the boy watched the creature move quickly past the fire and into the kitchen.

"What's—that?" he asked.

Drallah leaned across the table and softly answered, "He's a badger truan. There are a lot of different truan races, each kin to a different four-legged creature of Ehm. They're magic, mysterious peoples. Our kinds mostly avoid each other, but we have dealings, even friendship sometimes."

A round woman bearing a big tray of mugs came to ask them what they would like to eat. Elwood and Drallah had golden-crusted pies filled with bits of turkey, green snap beans, corn, and potatoes, and a jug of cool water. For Slukee and Booj there were bowls of various morsels aswim in gravy. Once their hunger was satisfied, the humans had mugs of warm cider.

Content and sleepy, Elwood sat back in his chair. Looking around, he wondered aloud about the origin of some of their hosts, most of whom were blond or brown-haired, with pale-pink skin like his own. Also, unlike any of the Winharn men he had seen, some of the men from the inn wore beards.

"They're Lindilish," explained Drallah. "Humans from the country Lindilune, who first came to the western shores many years ago. They were soon followed by the other light-skinned humans from beyond the Sea: the Ringish. Most of the Lindilish live in their great stone towns on the Bay. When they landed on the shores of Winnitok, and other lands of Pahn—that's what this whole region of Ehm is called—they came only to live beside those who were already here, as equals. But when the Ringish came, with their soldiers in their gray cloaks, they came to conquer all the peoples, to possess all the lands for themselves."

They were interrupted then by the round woman who brought them their meal. "Mish is going to sing for us!" she announced. All turned toward an aged woman sitting on a bench near the hearth, and as she began to hum the room grew quiet. Then she sang,

Departed!
Return well before winter,
before time to gather
the soft-haired cobs
beside the home we made together
east of the River
west of the Sea.

If you cannot come home
because your path sleeps
beneath the snow
never mind.
All are warmed again in spring
east of the River
west of the Sea.

Before summer is in the woods
we want you with us,
chanting planting songs,
laying seeds
in new mounds for autumn
east of the River
west of the Sea.

Elwood listened as the woman's strong old voice rose and fell, and something about her song moved him like a long-forgotten lull-aby. The words and melody reminded him of his old home, his old friends, his mother and father and sister—the whole of the life and world he was cut off from.

Thinking of these things, he was visited by a memory of one morning in the first grade. He and his sister, Ellen, had almost missed the bus to school. Because Ellen rushed them out the door so quickly, he had forgotten to get the usual good-bye hug and kiss from his mother. Elwood had begun to cry before they were even halfway to the bus stop, and continued to do so all the way to school. Almost unforgivably, Ellen had told the other children what was the matter, and some of them had teased him with names like "momma's boy." They were not wrong: his mother had always been his chief comfort, dearest friend, and the one person Elwood loved more than any other.

Listening to the old woman's song, thinking how he had failed once again to say good-bye to his mother, the wells of his life's sorrow and joy were plumbed. Tears filled his eyes and began to run down his cheeks. Embarrassed and surprised at himself, Elwood quickly wiped his face with his sleeve and turned away from the bright fire. Noticing him weeping, Drallah considerately looked the other way, and when the song ended she spoke cheerfully of other things.

Shortly the four tired travelers gathered themselves and went up to their rooms. Their windows looked out on the square and the ancient tree, its lanterns now extinguished, and let in the blue-green light of the moon through gauzy drapes. The leaf mattresses on their beds were freshly stuffed, jugs had been filled with water for washing, and their hosts had thoughtfully put a blanket rack in Drallah and Booj's room for the raven to perch on.

They wished each other a good night and retired. Late in the night, Elwood began to dream that he was walking with Slukee in the green hills around their old home. Always as they walked he was seeking a particular way to a certain house. He searched and searched, but did not find either before the morning light woke him, and the dream was gone.

WINDOW LIGHT

The morning was chill and gray. A blustering wind rattled the travelers' windowpanes as they washed and dressed. Downstairs, the innkeepers brought breakfast and chatted with them while they ate. For Elwood and Drallah there were apple pancakes and maple syrup, and the dog and the raven again had bowls of tidbits in gravy. When the meal was finished, Drallah paid their bill with coins she carried in her pack. Then, with thanks to their hosts, they departed to provision themselves before setting out.

In one stall in the square they found a thick brown blanket for Elwood, as well as a roomy but small pack to carry things in. "You're going to need this today," said Drallah as she showed him how to wear the blanket. She also bought him a waterskin and a tinderbox like her own, "in case we get separated somehow." For Slukee, they found a pair of carved wooden bowls, one fitting neatly inside the other, and for her coat, a wooden comb. Elsewhere they replenished and increased their supply of bread and meat, adding to it walnuts, chestnuts, and red apples.

Soon they were ready, and walked once again up the North Road. The wind blew cold in their faces.

"A storm is coming, probably after noon. We'll find shelter then and wait it out," said Drallah, eyeing the sky through the treetops.

By noon they had left farms and lanes far behind and had seen no other travelers on the Road for a long while. They had spent most of the morning passing through a pleasant country of maples and oaks, but now came to a lofty and dim hemlock wood. Here the Road began to curve, and Drallah led them into the trees.

"We're avoiding a big loop," she said. "The Road goes miles out of our way to the east. We'll strike it again in half the time it would take to go the long way around."

They had come to a part of the woods dominated by elms when, noticing something off to their right, Drallah and Booj went to investigate. They had not yet gone out of Elwood and Slukee's sight when the girl called back to them. They caught up with her standing in a road overgrown with cat briar and saplings that ran north and south through the trees.

"I don't know what road this is," she said. "But for now it goes our way." After a brief halt to rest and eat they went on, following the strange road north, but Drallah soon stopped and stood still, listening.

"The storm is coming."

Even as she said it, the wind increased with a roar, causing the trees to sway and ripping showers of leaves from their boughs. Through the turbulent foliage they glimpsed ragged black clouds flying toward them from the north. The woods grew darker, lightning flashed, and there was a long roll of thunder. Raindrops began to patter down. The four travelers hurried on, and as they went Drallah kept an eye out for some kind of shelter. Booj shot into the air to see if he could spot anything from above.

The wind swirled around them in little cyclones that threw dust and leaves in their faces. Worrying that it might bring a branch or a whole tree down on top of them, Elwood told Slukee to stay close.

Drallah discovered a hollow unoccupied elm just off the road that was big enough for them all to squeeze into. "This will do," she called, motioning Elwood and Slukee toward a wide hole in the base of its trunk. It was raining much harder. Booj returned and lit on a branch over Drallah's head.

"There's a big house not far up the road," he croaked.

"Well, there's this elm here we could stay dry in," said Drallah, practically shouting in order to be heard above the rising storm, "but not so comfortably as in a house. And this rain's going to be falling for a long time. What do you think, Elwood?" asked Drallah.

"I don't mind a little rain, if there's a house to dry off in."

"Then we'll go to the house."

Elwood pulled his blanket tighter around him, and they all went on. The thunder clapped and the lightning flashed with growing frequency. The rain fell faster than the earth could take it in.

They came to an iron-barred gate on the right-hand side of the road. It was shut, and rusting, and beside it hung a bell. The lane beyond was straight, but so long its end was lost in shadows. It was thick with fallen leaves.

"This is the way," said Booj.

"It doesn't look like anyone's been here for a long time," said Elwood.

Drallah found the bell was cracked, so they stepped into the trees, bypassed the gate, and started down the lane through the thick cover of old leaves. The trees lining the way hunched over the travelers, the low branches so densely entwined that little of the wind, rain, and what light there was could pierce them.

After a quarter mile the way ended in a wide cleared place. The travelers stood in the shelter just within the lane's mouth and looked out. Through the torrent they saw long-untended grounds and gardens gone wild around a sprawling old house, much of which was obscured by pointed fir trees standing close beside it. A flash of lightning showed that, though certainly once a proud place, the house too was in a state of neglect: the wood of its upper parts had weathered as gray as its stone foundation, and many shutters were gone. One shutter closed over an upstairs window was missing a slat, and through that opening could be seen a pale yellow light.

"Someone's there," said Drallah, pointing at it.

They ran through the pouring rain to the tall twin front doors of the house. Partially sheltered by an overhanging roof, they waited while Drallah knocked on the doors repeatedly. There was no response. Flying up to the window where they had seen the light, Booj rapped on the shutter with his beak. Still no one came, and when he flew back down to them he reported seeing no movement through the gap.

"Quoth the Raven, 'Nevermore,'" said Elwood loudly, competing with the rain beating over their heads.

Booj cocked his head to one side and looked at him.

"It's from a poem, from my world," the boy explained.

The bird impatiently shook the rain from his beak. "'Quoth?' I thought you said the ravens in your world don't talk."

"This is a raven in a poem, not a real one."

"They must not be able to hear over the storm," said Drallah. She tried to turn a doorknob, but the doors were locked. "That's strange. You all stay here; I'll look for another way in." Running back out into the rain, she quickly disappeared around the house's northwest corner.

She returned several minutes later from the opposite direction, having made a full circuit of the house. Motioning to the others to follow, Drallah led them around the back. She stopped at one of the fir trees growing next to the house, slipping between it and the wall. The tree concealed a shutterless four-paned window. One of the lower panes was missing, and the opening was wide enough to climb through.

Elwood went first, with a hoist from Drallah. Crouching on the windowsill he peered in, but it was too dark to see. Turning his back on the interior and keeping a tight grip on the sill, he cautiously lowered himself into the house. Next, Booj hopped onto the sill and inside. Drallah picked up Slukee and passed her through to Elwood, then climbed in herself.

It was a musty place, that much they could tell in the dark.

Drallah took off her pack and fished within for a candlestick. Finding one, she lit it with flint, steel, and wood shavings from her tinderbox. By the little circle of light it produced, they saw they were in a long-forsaken room cramped with worn cupboards, chairs, couches, and tables, all covered in a thick layer of dust. There were two doors, both shut. The way they had come in was the only window.

Trying the doors, Drallah found that one led to a second, similar room, and the other to a passageway. Dripping a trail of water on its once-rich red carpet, and showered by Slukee shaking her sodden coat, Elwood followed Drallah into the passageway. Her candle shone on walls draped with faded tapestries, depictions of shadowy figures in odd bleak landscapes. The way often turned and divided, so that Elwood soon lost his sense of direction.

After several minutes of wandering they came to a lofty, murky hall. From outside, only a feeble light came through where a shutter was missing from one high window. Elwood discerned a wide staircase at one end of the hall, and at the other a tall pair of doors: the front entrance, where Drallah had knocked in vain.

"Hello!" Drallah called from the foot of the stairs, and though the storm still roared outside, her voice seemed unnaturally loud. She waited and tried again, but there was no reply.

Drallah crossed the hall and looked through a wide entry into a large room. Inside was an immense fireplace, a store of old wood, and several couches and chairs. Along the walls reared tall cabinets, and above these hung weapons and armor of black steel: broad-bladed swords, great round shields, and long-faced war helmets. A pair of poleaxes made an X over the mantel.

"I'll build a fire. Once we're warmed up and our things are drying, we'll look for our hosts," said Drallah.

Elwood was uneasy. "Shouldn't we get permission first?" he asked.

"No one refuses travelers shelter in weather like this!" exclaimed Drallah.

Shaking his head, Elwood began to carry wood over to the hearth.

Once Drallah had a fire going, they hung their blankets from the mantel. Elwood shook the dust from an old tablecloth and did his best to dry Slukee with it. Booj perched on a chandelier and settled into ruffling and preening. The humans pulled a couch up to the fire, and Slukee stretched out at their feet.

Outside the rain was still beating down, and thunder still accompanied the lightning that filled the room with flashes of brilliant white. Expecting the inhabitants of the house to appear at any moment, Elwood sat sideways to the fire with his back against the couch's armrest. In this way he kept one eye on the room's entrance, and with the other watched the firelight dance on the walls and ceiling.

"I haven't seen a house in Winnitok so ill cared for in all my life," said Drallah in a low voice. "Whoever lives here hasn't used this part of it for a long time. Maybe they've grown old, without anyone to help with things."

"Maybe they're deaf too," Elwood said, thinking of all her knocking and calling. "Do we have to find them? Let's wait in here till the storm's over, then go."

"They might need help. Booj and I will look upstairs, but you don't have to. You and Slukee stay here. We won't be long."

"No, no, we'll come too," said Elwood, noticing that a trick of the firelight made the mouth-guards of the helmets on the walls seem to move, and the empty holes of their eyes to flicker.

"These arms are Ringish," said Drallah with distaste. She rose to study them more closely.

"Are the Ringish really that bad?" asked Elwood. "You said they're human, but you talk about them like they're evil."

"Well ... I don't think they're made that way, like the yugs."

"They turned bad?"

"It's not true of every Ringishman, I've been told, but most of them. They fell whole forests. They take fish from the lakes till the fish are gone. They raise creatures to slaughter, and sometimes hunt and kill just for pleasure. They take more than they need, and ruin what's left.

"This is one of the worst things about their way: they imagine they've cut the land in pieces. They say 'This piece is this man's, and that piece is that man's.' They even say the creatures that live in or wander onto a piece of land, and the water in the lakes and streams, and the trees and everything else that grows there, all belong to them."

"It sounds like my world," interrupted Elwood. "People own the land their house is on, or their business, or whatever. Like the Mason family: they have a dairy by my old house; they own acres and acres."

Drallah looked at him, wondering what she would think about his world. "In Ringish countries," she continued, "most people have no land, but are the slaves of the ones who do. And for some reason women almost never 'own' land.

"So to them, the lands across the Sea are cut up like flesh of the hunt. They've tried to have their way here in Pahn, in lands like Oldotok. The Ringish soldiers, the Graycloaks, killed most of the Oldharn trying to remake the land in their way. But there was a terrible war eighty years ago, and they were driven from Pahn."

Elwood waved his hand at the hanging weaponry. "And these are from that war?"

"Even before. The fashion is old, but definitely Ringish. But how strange, displaying them like this."

* * *

Once their clothes, hair, fur, and feathers were mostly dry, they gathered themselves to find the people of the house. Drallah lit two candlesticks in the fire, put them in holders she found on the mantel, and gave one to Elwood. They passed through the hall and started up the creaking stairs, Slukee walking a little in front, Drallah and Elwood side by side. Booj glided ahead to perch on one of the worn cobwebbed banisters. There was a wide landing halfway up, and from it the staircase divided in two to the left and right, each branch continuing up to second floor galleries overlooking the central hall. Over the landing hung a dark blue banner, upon which was embroidered a golden star cupped in a golden hand.

"I don't know this device," said Drallah.

It was very quiet, and Elwood realized the thunder and lightning had moved away. Drallah called out another strident "Hello," making him jump.

"Warn me when you're going to do that," he whispered fiercely. His nerves were stretched taut: he did not want to meet anyone who lived in such a place, and would have preferred it out in the rain.

"Sorry," she grinned, and pointed to the left-hand way. "The light we saw was on that side of the house."

The gallery at the top of the stairs was also carpeted in worn red, and there were several doors in its one wall. Drallah led them past these to the last door, which opened into a hallway. This too had many doors, now on one side and now on the other.

The hallway turned toward the front of the house. Rounding the corner, they saw a line of pale yellow light shining through the crack under a door. Drallah strode up to it. Slukee stopped, ears high and head cocked to one side, staring at the light. Elwood hung back with her, wishing they were somewhere else. Just as Drallah was about to knock, Booj, who was right beside her, softly but urgently said, *"uk!"* and she stayed her hand. Drallah questioned the raven with a look, and then put an ear to the door.

There was a voice speaking on the other side. It sounded impossibly far away, yet at the same time as close as the buzz of a fly settling in her ear. There was a strange echo to it, as though the person speaking were hollow, empty.

It was saying, "We dare not leave the Glass. We are weak yet."

Another, similar voice angrily replied, "Gah! Raukbug. You heard them. You feel the beating of their hearts. The bloodbags are near. Do you want them to find the Glass?"

Drallah peered through the keyhole. She could see part of a long chamber filled with chaotically stacked papers and books awash in an eldritch yellow glow, but there was no one in her narrow line of sight.

A third voice entered the conversation like icy water flooding a lightless cavern. "Aufgawl is right . . . foolish to wander so far from the Glass . . . foolish to wander in the cursed wood . . . but bloodbags in the house must be found. . . ."

Slukee's hackles rose all along her back, and she growled a low, deep growl. Elwood, who could not hear the voices where they were standing, knelt beside her, held her muzzle, and whispered, "Quiet!" in her ear.

Drallah turned her head at the sound. Elwood could see by the candlelight that her eyes were wide with fear. He mouthed the question, "What is it?" but she only put her finger to her lips for silence and returned to the keyhole. The discussion within was continuing.

"There, Raukbug. Hear the words of Latchfowell. We will not wait to spill the blood. Not since that squealer there have I."

". . . none may escape . . . tell others of us . . . none may escape . . ."

"It will be back to Wuth for us, like as not," muttered the one called Raukbug.

Then, at the other end of the chamber, a vaporous purple-black figure came into Drallah's view through the keyhole. Its shape was like that of a stretched, gangling man's, the outline vague except for its long thin fingers that tapered into sharp points. The lower half was to Drallah's eyes more blurred than the rest, so that it seemed to float in a gown of dark purple mist. The face was completely featureless, blank. It was rapidly approaching the door.

"Run!" hissed Drallah.

"Hide!" choked Booj.

In her panic, Drallah bolted farther down the passage rather than back the way they had come, and the others followed hard on her heels. The way turned almost immediately. Around the corner, it came abruptly to a dead end.

They stood and stared for a moment at the wall in their way. It was covered with a dreary tapestry like those they had seen in other parts of the house. However poor a hiding place it would make (it did not even quite touch the floor, so their feet would be exposed to view), it was the only one to be had: they did not dare turn back and pass by that dreadful door again so soon. But when Drallah lifted up a bottom corner for them to slip between the heavy cloth and the wall, it revealed a small door underneath. She yanked it open with a loud creak of dry hinges. Beyond was a steep narrow staircase going up. They all started up it as quietly and quickly as they could. Elwood closed the door behind them, the tapestry fell back in place, and they stopped to listen. The house was silent.

"What is it?" whispered Elwood to Drallah, setting his candle-stick, which had gone out, down on a step.

"Wuth-wigs!" she whispered back. The light from her candle showed her face was rigid with fright. "They know we're here; they're searching. If they find us, we're lost."

"What-wigs? What are they?"

"Devils!"

"Devils! What—"

"No time! We must get away from here." Saying this she took a step up, and winced at the creak it made. She looked back expect-ing to see grim shapes coming after them through the door below, but for the moment none appeared.

At the top of the stairs they came to another passageway, lower-ceilinged and narrower than those below.

"Follow me, and no one make a sound," whispered Drallah, and led the way down the long straight hallway with her little circle of candlelight. Ignoring doors and other hallways they passed on either side, they followed it to its end at another staircase, this one lead-ing down.

As Drallah took the first step, a near-paralyzing dread came over each of them, and they knew they were being pursued. The next moment a long unearthly howl sounded from back down the passageway. Bumping and jostling each other, they flung themselves pell-mell down the stairs. At the bottom they burst through another little door with a crash, tearing down the tapestry that covered it. The candle went out as they tumbled into the passage beyond.

Feeling their way in the dark, they found a door that opened on the gallery overlooking the house's central hall. There Drallah stopped and blurted out, "We can't outrun them! Try to get away, and I'll delay them as long as—"

"*Crurk!* The Glass, try and get the Glass," cried Booj. "I will draw them."

"The Glass," said Drallah, reining in her wits. "You two hide downstairs, quick! Be careful, Booj!" Without another word or a look back to see if the boy and the dog did as she told them, Drallah ran off down the gallery.

Booj lit on the railing facing the door, which they had closed behind them, and ruffled his feathers up. "Hide," he croaked at Elwood, who was standing and staring stupidly after Drallah. Slukee whined softly. Coming back to his senses with a jolt, Elwood ran to the stairs and down them, the dog following.

Downstairs he automatically ran for the room where their fire was still burning, but halfway there realized the fire was sure to attract the wuth-wigs' attention. Frantically searching the murky hall, he found a small door under the stairs. Pulling it open, his nostrils met with a smell like a tomb that had not been disturbed for years, and he could just make out the beginning of a flight of stone stairs going down. They went through the door and stood on the top steps. Elwood shut the door not quite tight, leaving just a crack through which to peer out into the hall.

Upstairs, Drallah was again entering the hallway they had taken minutes earlier, the one that led to the source of the light. As she cautiously retraced their steps, the silence of the house was broken by a terrible cry from Booj. She could barely restrain herself from running back to him. Instead, she abandoned caution and dashed for the yellow-lit room.

Booj had perched waiting on the banister, tensed for the moment a pursuer came through the door. Though fear threatened to reduce him to a shivering pile of feathers, he remained resolute through what seemed, though it was less than a minute, an interminable wait, and he was staring hard at the closed door when a purple form passed through its very substance like a fish through water.

With a cry the raven spread his wings and leapt backward, just avoiding a great raking sweep of the wuth-wig's claws. Booj had heard stories of the devils of Wuth, and knew that though they moved through solid objects as easily as through air, their claws became quite substantial when the time came for rending flesh. He winged off into the more open central hall. The wuth-wig, who was the one called Aufgawl, ascended from the floor of the gallery and glided through the air after the raven. Looking out from his hiding place behind the cellar door, Elwood cried aloud when he saw the figure of dark purple mist flying overhead.

Latchfowell was entering the central hall when Elwood cried out. Hearing him, the wuth-wig glided silently toward the cellar door. Elwood was unaware of his approach, concentrating as he was on the aerial chase going on above him. Though Booj was swift, Aufgawl was swifter still, and it was only by deftly executed maneuvers—breakneck dives, sudden turns, corkscrew rolls—that the raven was keeping himself from the wuth-wig's cruel claws.

Elwood was watching breathlessly, wondering how long Booj could keep it up and what he could do to help him, when the cellar door was suddenly wrenched wide open from without. Latchfowell towered over him. Elwood took a step backward, tripped over Slukee, and with a cry tumbled down the cold stone stairs. Cowering and stunned, he came to rest on a narrow landing. Barking savagely,

Slukee crouched between Elwood and the ghostly wuth-wig, her every hair on end.

"Bird ... dog ... boy ... " moaned Latchfowell, drifting down a step. "Pleasant making hearts cease ... " Slukee stopped barking and set herself to spring.

On the second floor, Drallah returned to the door leaking yellow light into the passageway. She grasped the knob and tried to turn it, but it was locked. Desperately she threw all her weight into the door, striking with her shoulder near the frame on the side opposite the hinges. Again and again she struck, and finally the old wood began to give. With one more mighty effort, it splintered, the lock broke free of the frame, and the door swung wide open with a strange rattling sound so suddenly that Drallah almost fell headlong into the room. The first thing she saw was a skeleton on the floor, the arrangement of which the violently opening door had upset. The finger bones of one hand still clutched a key, though, and it wore shredded crimson robes. There was a large black stain on the carpet beside it.

The room was a long rectangle, and seemed brilliantly lit. There were three shuttered windows along one wall, and Drallah saw that one of these was missing a slat. Many books and papers were stacked and strewn about. On a table in the middle of the room was a small globe of pale yellow flame.

"The Glass," she breathed, and rushed to the table.

Setting the candle down, she held her hand over the Glass, but it gave off no heat. Taking it up in her palm it did not burn but felt cool. She looked into its core. Beautiful pale-yellow flames struggled and writhed there like tiny trapped serpents. Despite the urgency of her errand, she was entranced.

As she gazed into the glass, the vaporous purple-black figure of Raukbug rose up through the floor at her feet. Drallah was so hypnotized by the flames she did not see the wuth-wig before her; but as the long fingers reached for her throat, he uttered a whimpering sigh of anticipation.

43

Hearing it, she leapt backward and to one side, and Raukbug shrieked in anger. Arms outstretched, he glided after her. Raising the little globe high over her head, Drallah hurled it at the wall with all her might. The glass shattered into pieces, the flames within were extinguished, and Raukbug disappeared with a wail that lingered a moment longer than he did.

In the central hall, Booj had reached the limits of his skill, strength, and wits. He was flying as he never had before, yet Aufgawl was ever at his tail feathers. The raven was desperately reversing direction in a loop-the-loop when the wuth-wig abruptly vanished. Booj dropped down to a gallery-banister and called out to the others with a long, loud *Cra-a-ark!*

Slukee answered from the cellar stairs with a bark: Latchfowell had disappeared even as he lunged at her, and she at him. She and Elwood, who was dazedly rubbing a bump on the back of his head, stepped out into the hall and began to climb the staircase. Drallah could be heard calling out for some moments before she appeared, running to them, in the gallery above. They all met at the top of the stairs.

"Is everyone all right? Oh, I'm so glad everyone's all right," said Drallah, hugging each of them repeatedly.

"What happened? Were they ghosts?" gasped Elwood as Drallah squeezed the breath out of him.

"No, not ghosts; wuth-wigs aren't the spirits of the dead. They're devils of Wuth, a spirit-land beyond the lands of earth, air, and water. But come on, I'll show you."

After getting fresh candles from her pack and assuring Elwood they were now quite safe, Drallah once again led the way to the room of the glass globe. Pointing to the skeleton on the floor, she said, "I believe that unfortunate person summoned the wigs from Wuth, and used that," here she let her candle shine over the remains of the little globe, "to do it. He could not master them, I guess. Wuth-wigs are hate itself, and will not suffer anything they can slay to live. I doubt there are any creatures living near this house."

Elwood stood gaping at the skeleton, horrified. "But what was this glass?" he finally asked. "How did he summon them?"

"It had magic flames trapped inside. That was the light we saw. Booj and I heard the wuth-wigs talking about it through the door; a glass they didn't want anyone else to find, that they'd been away from too long. Booj had the sense to realize that finding and breaking it might save us."

"Sorcerer's Glass," said Booj.

"Yes. They're difficult to make, and can be very powerful—powerful enough to call devils from Wuth, powerful enough to do all kinds of things." Drallah gestured at the skeleton. "Maybe he wanted them for some service, but was too weak to command them when they came. Anyhow, once he was dead, they wouldn't have returned to Wuth even if they could. Wigs kill for pleasure, they say, and killing is their only pleasure, and the spirits of Wuth can't kill each other. So, when they come to the lands of flesh and blood, they'll do anything to stay.

"But as I said, they couldn't have left, even if they wanted to. They were summoned by the Glass, and so they were bound to it—until it gave another command or was broken." Deeply troubled, Drallah sighed. "I should have seen something was wrong here, even if I couldn't feel it. I just didn't believe such things could come to Winnitok. The Dread of Granashon should have kept them out. The power of the Nohar—it's gone."

Elwood did not know how to respond, and so remained silent while Drallah scanned the books and papers on the table where she had found the glass globe. An old leather-bound notebook caught her eye. She read a little, shuddered, and turned away.

"Yes, that's a summoning ritual. It would be safe enough to sleep here tonight, but if you don't mind, I'd rather not."

When the rain stopped in the late afternoon, they were quickly on their way, blankets still wet, down the leaf-covered lane. Looking back, they saw the house framed like a picture by the hunching trees. Through the breaking clouds, late sunlight glittered on the rain-washed roof, but all supporting it was robed in shadow. The companions hurried away.

OLGUHM

They passed the night wrapped in their blankets beneath a wide-spreading fir tree. It was not dry, by any means, but it was the driest patch of ground they could find before dark. The clouds had rolled away in the night, and in the bright morning the memory of the previous afternoon was like that of a bad dream. Waking from a fitful sleep with an aching back and stiff limbs, Elwood was glad to rise and move on.

The travelers struck the Road before the morning's end, reaching it near the point where it veered off north again after its long curve to the east. As they walked, Drallah taught Elwood the names and natures of the trees, plants, and creatures they passed. She also told tales of the woods, and of people like her Uncle Mithloo. Occasionally they met travelers heading south, sometimes driving carts or wagons, but usually on foot.

In the mid-afternoon they turned left off the North Road and descended a gradual slope to a broad brown creek. Several long canoes with high curving prows and sterns were lying upside down on the near bank.

"This is Engo," said Drallah as she surveyed the water. "It meets the River south and west of here, and on the way flows right past Mithloo's door—I hope not through it! The creek's really swollen from the storm. Can you paddle?"

"Sure," answered Elwood, delighted at the prospect. His father used to take him canoeing on a little lake near their old home. "Are these your uncle's?" he asked.

"Yes, he always keeps a few canoes here for travelers coming up the Road on foot. There's another way farther north for horses and wagons."

Together Drallah and Elwood carried a canoe down to the water. They loaded their gear on board, and Elwood and Slukee climbed in. Drallah pushed them off, then nimbly climbed in herself. Taking up the oars they had found lying beneath the overturned boat, they paddled out into midstream. The water flowed west, and this was the direction in which Drallah, seated on the aft bench, pointed them. Slukee stood at the prow sniffing the air, and Booj flew ahead to scout the creek and its banks.

They had walked a long way, so the gliding canoe and the gently plashing oars were a welcome change. The swollen current and their paddling carried them quickly along, and the banks on either side began to rise. Eventually they were floating down a ravine some thirty feet deep, with walls of rough granite topped with tough little pines.

The sun had sunk low, and it had become cool and shadowy down on the stream, when Drallah set her oar down in the bottom of the canoe.

"Let's switch, Elwood. I want to see if we can bring Mithloo some meat for his table."

Carefully they traded places. From a watertight compartment in her quiver Drallah took a coil of bowstring, one end of which she hooked to the bottom end of her bow. Then, while Elwood looked on with trepidation, she stood up in the canoe's center, wrapped her left leg around the bow for leverage, and bending it with her left hand, hooked the other end of the bowstring to the top end of the bow with her right. Despite Elwood's fear she would capsize them, the canoe did not rock even a little before the bow was strung and Drallah was again sitting on the fore bench.

She was inspecting a long red-and-white-feathered arrow when Booj returned and lit on the prow of the canoe.

"Have you seen any creatures?" the girl asked the raven.

"There are turkeys up there," croaked Booj. "And deer are stirring."

Drallah drew a second arrow from the quiver and laid it on the bench beside her. Then she stood up again and fitted the first arrow to the string. Holding it loosely in place but ready to be drawn, she watched the sky, cliff tops, and water. Elwood paddled as quietly as he could, and none of them spoke. Drallah remained standing a long time, motionless except for her searching eyes and slightly turning head, her balance perfect.

The peace and quiet down on the creek was disrupted suddenly by a ferocious yowl from the woods above. Tensing, Elwood and Slukee stared at the cliff tops. A long answering meowl went up from the canoe. It was Booj, his voice marvelously altered to sound like a big cat's. Glancing back, Drallah saw the boy and the dog's anxious faces.

"Don't worry. It's only a cougar letting us know she's here."

"A cougar! What did Booj say to her?"

"That we hear her."

Elwood was not entirely reassured, and more than half expected a lithe tawny shape to pounce from above at any moment. However, Drallah still stood in the fore of the canoe, obviously unconcerned, so he tried not to be concerned either.

He was still nervously watching the cliff tops a few minutes later when Drallah spied ducks floating on the creek ahead of them. She signaled Elwood to stop paddling, then slowly raised and bent her bow. They drifted closer, letting the current carry them. Then the bowstring hummed, and the ravine filled with the flapping and quacking of flying ducks. With a fluid motion that was almost too swift to be seen, Drallah swept up the second arrow, fit it to the string, drew, and let go. A duck dropped from the air to the water with a splash. The flapping and quacking faded in the distance and was gone.

Elwood paddled slowly ahead. Leaning over the prow, Drallah searched the darkening creek. Soon two fat brown-speckled dabblers were lying in the bottom of the canoe: her first shot had found its duck also. "Thank you," she said softly as she laid them out. She removed and cleaned the arrows, setting them on the bench to dry. Then she covered the ducks with a special cloth of green which she carried for that purpose alone.

Elwood had anticipated the moment when he would at last see Drallah use her bow, and was not disappointed: in fact he was awed, and filled with desire some day to rival her with skill of his own.

The sun set, and clusters of bright stars soon filled the sky as they paddled down the ravine of Engo Creek. As he looked up and wondered if one of them might be the sun of his own world, Elwood became aware of a deep sound in the near distance that was like the steady thunder of a waterfall.

"Do you hear the drums? They're holding a feast," said Drallah.

They passed beneath a log bridge, and beyond it the stream widened. The granite wall on their right sank, and by the light of the rising moon they saw woods and fields sloping down to the northwest. On their left the cliffs continued to form a high wall along the creek, and now Elwood could hear it was from the tops of these that the drums were sounding. Then he saw light-filled windows in the rock and heard talk and laughter.

They came to a granite landing, over which stood a tall woodbine-covered house carved out of the rock, its upper stories reaching above the level of the cliff top. Paddling to a set of stairs that rose up out of the creek, they moored the canoe among many others.

In a few moments Elwood found himself rubbing his eyes in a grand hall lit by dozens of carved-pumpkin lamps, where many were gathered around a long table laden with food and drink. As his eyes adjusted to the light, he saw with a thrill that among the gathering were several who were not human. There were three who stood quite a bit shorter than Elwood, though they were four or five times his age. He knew from all Drallah had told him that these were people of the woogan race, who in appearance were much like humans except for their stature. Also seated among the rest were a pair of big raccoon creatures, their little ring-masked eyes blinking at the brightness of the hall. *Truans,* he thought.

A tall human of majestic bearing and frame rose from his place at the table to welcome the companions. His silver-streaked hair hung down to his belt, he wore a thin leather band set with emerald-green beads across his brow, and he was dressed in a blanket of fine white. Three sleepy, wolfish dogs trotted after him, and on each of his shoulders perched a long-tailed magpie. This, Elwood rightly guessed, was Mithloo. Drallah and her uncle met with joy, and once she had given him the ducks, and after the magpies and Booj had traded greetings in a bizarre-sounding language, and when Slukee and the other dogs were wagging their tails pleasantly at one another, the girl explained why they had come.

There was wonder and keen interest in the tall man's eyes as he listened and regarded the boy and the dog. With a kindly smile he said, "You are welcome in Olguhm, Elwood Pitch. We are honored by your company. Join our feast tonight, and in the morning we will talk."

Deeply weary from his adventures, Elwood's first evening at Olguhm passed in a blur. Between arrival and bed, he ate a large and wonderful meal of freshly harvested food, met most every person in the house, and heard many songs sung. At last, rubbing eyes he could no longer keep open, he and Slukee were led to a little room to sleep. It was high on the creek side of the house, with an oval window looking out over the creek of Engo and the land beyond. It was a warm night, and the window had been left open. After he blew out the lamp and before he crawled into bed, Elwood paused a moment to look out. The moon had traveled far across the sky. The land fell away to the northwest in a series of shallow steps that the creek, turning sharply in its course a short way downstream from the house, flowed over in gentle waterfalls. Far away, across a moon-lit expanse of groves and meadows, a broken thread of sparkling blue could here and there be discerned. Elwood did not realize it at the time, but this was the moon reflecting off the Lilikit River, the western border of Winnitok.

* * *

Mithloo sent for them early the next morning. Once they were ready, Drallah led them up out of the house to a rocky way along the cliff tops. Soon they came to the bridge of logs they had passed under the night before. Across the bridge the road continued on through gardens and orchards, then turned off to the right. Leaving the road, they took a path up a rise, atop which they found the master of Olguhm, his dogs and his magpies looking out over the land. Also there were several men and women from Mithloo's house, and a few from other houses. Breakfast was laid out on a blanket.

After they had eaten, and the dogs were romping in the fields, and the birds were chasing one another around the sky, Mithloo looked first at Drallah and then at Elwood and said, "Now, tell us what is happening."

Elwood spoke first, telling the story of their strange arrival in Winnitok as best he could. Then Drallah told them of her vision in the pool, and of finding the boy and the dog in the woods. Elwood described what happened when he tasted the plum, and, after passing briefly over how they came there, Drallah told the tale of their encounter with the wuth-wigs in the house. Hearing this, their audience stirred uneasily. When the girl had finished, it was a long time before anyone else spoke.

"Wuth-wigs in the heart of our land," said Mithloo at last. "It is the surest sign yet: the protection Granashon gave us for so long is no more."

After another silence, Drallah asked, "Uncle, do you know the house where we found them?"

"I have heard of it, I think. The home of a family from both Lindilish and Ringish ancestors, called Baron. People say they are aloof and without friends. Maybe the bones you saw belonged to the last of that family." Then Mithloo gave his niece a pointed look and said, "I feel your mother and father will want you to stay close to home, once they know of these events.

"But the appearance of wuth-wigs in Winnitok is not the only news," he continued. "Why has Elwood Pitch come here from another world? Surely there is some tie between him and Granashon the Nohar. Why else would he appear in her sacred Glade? Something of great significance is happening. All this summer I spent up, down, and on either side of the River: it flows uncertainly, as if wary or afraid. And across the River, the trees of Oldotok are uneasy. There are rumors of woe in their roots. Amidst all this, where is the Nohar? No one knows. Those of us with Vision have not had any sign. She is hidden from us. We perceive she still lives, but where, we cannot say."

"Can't we go seeking her?" asked Drallah.

"Some of our scouts will soon try," answered Mithloo, "but the world is big. I do not put much hope in the attempt. Still, they will try. There has been word from other Houses, from Limith and Wahnta; they also send scouts to seek the Nohar. I am sure others around Winnitok are doing the same. We cannot spare many, though. Winnitok is vulnerable now, and we need our warriors here."

"I will go," Drallah blurted out. Booj, who had returned from play with the magpies and was perched on Drallah's shoulder, seconded her with a croak.

The adults all smiled, and Mithloo gently raised a halting hand. "No, niece," he said. "My sister and your father would not forgive me if I let you wander out of Winnitok at your age, and they would be right. And as I said, they will want you close to home in Ohrimo now that Winnitok is no longer protected by the Dread of Granashon. At home, or here with us at Olguhm."

"Pardon me," said Elwood. "But I was wondering . . . why didn't

Slukee faint the first time she ate food from this world, like I did?"

The master of Olguhm shrugged. "I cannot say. There are a thousand possible reasons why that was so."

"Some creatures grasp from birth matters that others never do," said a woman clad in a violet blanket, a friend of Mithloo's family visiting from the north. "Maybe the ties between worlds are not such a mystery to dogs as they are to us; maybe coming from your world to ours was not as strange for Slukee as it was for you. Or maybe humans have more to digest. Think of the knowledge you gained from the fruit: the plum gave you the language of Winnitok, which, like the plum, also sprang from this land."

Elwood pondered this, then asked what was most on his mind. "Does anyone know how I can get back?"

None answered, until finally Mithloo spoke. "Only gods have the ability to travel between worlds, and gods will not suffer to be sought out. If they desire contact with us, they seek it themselves. But the Noharn are, perhaps, an exception. I can at least see this: you appeared in the Glade of Granashon, and Granashon is your best hope of returning. If only you could speak with her, you might learn the secret of how you came to Ehm, and how to get back.

"My feeling is that you were brought to this world for a reason, and it will be discovered in time. I would gladly be of more help to you if I could, Elwood. But you are welcome in our house as long and as often as you wish."

Disappointed but unsurprised, the boy thanked him. While the talk turned to other matters, he thought distractedly of his family. Four nights had come and gone since he disappeared from the woods in the park. He wondered if they had given up searching for him yet. *If only they could see me right now,* he thought; *if only there was a way to let them know what happened to me, to tell them I am safe.* He decided he must find Granashon.

As he walked back to the house with Drallah, Slukee, and Booj, he told the Winharn girl of his determination to find the Nohar.

"I understand," she said, "but you can't go looking without any idea where to find her. Why don't you stay here at Olguhm, and wait for news from the scouts? They'll return here as soon as they learn anything of Granashon. I'm going to stay too, at least for a while. There's really nothing else we can do right now."

Hearing from Drallah that she intended to remain with him for some time pleased Elwood greatly. He had assumed she would leave him in the care of Mithloo now that she had brought him safely to Olguhm. She could not, after all, be expected to spend all her time with someone so much younger than herself. Still, at that moment he wished she was willing to go with him and Slukee in search of the Nohar. He decided to take her advice, though, and stay at Olguhm to wait for news.

*　*　*

The four friends spent many days roaming the woods around Olguhm. With Drallah as his teacher, Elwood began to learn what wild things were good to eat and where to find them, how to read a trail and how to conceal one, the way of the hunter and the hunted, and many other things. She and Booj also taught him Wohmog, the common language of the many peoples and races of Pahn, the region of Ehm that Winnitok was a part of. Elwood eagerly took in everything that was offered and more, and so learned a great deal in those days. But the lessons he loved best were in archery, which he practiced with a short bow loaned to him by another of Mithloo's nieces.

All Elwood's days were darkened by worry for his mother, father, and sister. He often confided in Drallah about this, and about the way his life had been ruined by the move from his old home. The calm, self-assured manner with which she faced the difficulties and uncertainties of life was comforting, and he began to try to emulate her in this and other ways. Spending as much time with her as he did, and being a young woman of such kindness, accomplishment, and pleasing looks, it was not surprising that Elwood quickly became, in a boyish way, infatuated with Drallah Wehr.

Word of Elwood's mysterious arrival in the Glade had soon spread through the woods. The people of Olguhm, who honored him like a hero returned from some great adventure, took to referring to him as Granashon's Scout. Whenever Elwood—more than a little embarrassed by what he saw as their unfounded regard for him—pointed out that he had never even met Granashon, the people of Olguhm would only smile and say, "Wait." Though at first he was content enough to do so, it was not long before Elwood got another idea.

THE TURTLE AND THE MAP

For three weeks, Elwood, Slukee, Drallah, and Booj lived in Olguhm as autumn carried on. During that time, as the leaves lost their colors and turned to brown, scouts went out in pairs seeking Granashon. None could say how long they would be gone, and though the hopes of many went with them, it was far from certain the scouts would bring back news of the Nohar when they returned.

One cold night after the evening meal, the four friends gathered in Mithloo's library. It was not Elwood's first visit: over the previous weeks, he had taken to spending more and more time among books. There, within walls lined with shelves overflowing with tomes, breathing air heavy with the perfumes of aged paper, he had read Lindilish poetry translated into Winnitoke, and fantastic tales of truans on Uhl, the Winharn name for Ehm's moon. He had read about the Ringish wars, and the subsequent founding of the Towns of Stone on Winnitok Bay. But wishing to learn all he could of Granashon, it was from tales and histories involving her that Elwood read the most.

On this particular night he and Drallah sat in deep, soft chairs by the fire. Slukee dozed at their feet, and Booj perched meditatively on a tall three-pronged candelabra. Elwood was reading from a tome called *The Noharitt,* a cycle of tales about Granashon's mysterious race, the Noharn. The atmosphere in the library was very warm, and except for the hissing and snapping of the fire, the room was silent. With the book on his lap, Elwood began to nod off.

As his chin dipped to his chest, he fell into a dream. The warm library became a cave. In the floor of the cave there was a pool, its depths aglow with the rainbow's share of color. Stepping to the pool's edge and looking down into its depths, he saw the source of the glowing light: a turtle with a shell of many hues floating far below.

Suddenly a powerful voice called Elwood's name, making him jump in his chair. The big leather-bound book fell to the floor with a bang.

"Better go to bed," said Drallah, without looking up from Gowich's *Mountain Hall,* the treatise on woogan architecture she was poring over. (Olguhm itself, Elwood learned soon after their arrival, had been built for Mithloo's ancestors by the diminutive woogans.)

"Did you call me?"

"No, you were dreaming."

Reaching down to retrieve it, Elwood found that the tome had fallen open to a tale he had not yet read. It was called *Nentop and the Eye of Ogin.* Despite his intention to go to bed, he found himself reading:

> One day Nentop the Nohar was fishing in the Southern Sea. The waves were still and the sun was high, and Nentop could see far into the waters below. As he gazed down from his canoe, he saw a light shine up from some bright thing in the deep. He dove and swam after it, down to the bottom of the Sea. Nentop found that the glowing dark-lighter was a turtle whose many-colored shell shone with its own light.

Elwood could not believe his eyes. He was sure he had not read this story before, and yet the turtle was straight out of his dream. He read on.

*The Nohar longed to possess the shell, but the turtle was aware
of him and strove to escape. For three days and nights he chased
the turtle through the Sea, until at last he caught the creature
in a cave beneath Ogin Island, and slew him with his knife.
But with his last breath the turtle said,*

> *I was Ogin*
> *and Ogin was me,*
> *since the beginning*
> *the Island's heart.*
> *Now, Nohar,*
> *you shall be.*

*and Nentop knew he had done an awful deed. In the earth
there was a trembling. A great rock barred the watery passage
between the cave and the Sea, imprisoning him in the heart of
the Island. Remorseful and lonely he took the wondrous shell,
aglow even in the lightless cave, and sang over it for many
days. He worked its magic with his own, and filled it with
water from the Sea. The water and the shell let him look beyond
the cave to see the rest of the world. So Nentop made of the
turtle shell an eye on Ehm, that he might at least watch the
other Nohars, and the rest of the world that concerned him,
through his long captivity.*

*After a hundred years passed Tehm took pity on him, and
with a spear cut open the cave over Nentop's head. He ascended
to the upper world, carrying the shell with him, to discover that
the Island he had dwelt in the heart of for so long was a par-
adise like no other in Ehm. Everywhere was the music of the
Island, and the Sea around it, in uncommon harmony. He saw
creatures and trees unlike any he had ever seen, and all was
full of health. However, Nentop was eager to depart after being
so long imprisoned, and he did not tarry. Away he swam with
the shell. Looking back, he saw that the cave had closed once*

again, and that all the Island's creatures, all its beauties, were withering and dying. When he reached land, Nentop wandered north. He made a gift of the Eye of Ogin to Mobb of Ashawda, in whose house it remained for many generations, until it was lost in the Battle of the Burnt Hills.

So the tale ended. Elwood's thoughts raced. "How was the Eye of Ogin lost?" he asked, turning to Drallah.

She looked up distractedly from *Mountain Hall.*

"The Eye of Ogin," he repeated. "This story says it was lost in a fight called the Battle of the Burnt Hills. Was it destroyed?"

"I don't know," answered Drallah. "That was many years ago. Why?"

"I just fell asleep and had a dream about a turtle with a glowing shell. And then the book fell open to this story about just that: the Eye of Ogin. It says Nentop the Nohar used the shell *to watch the other Nohars.* It's a vision, do you see? With the Eye of Ogin we could find Granashon!"

Drallah simply stared at him.

"Are there other books about the Eye here?" he asked.

Drallah jumped from her chair and, scanning the library's shelves, found the volume she was looking for.

"This history includes the Battle of the Burnt Hills," she said, laying it on a table beside a lamp and leafing through its pages. Booj dropped from his perch to the tabletop. "About two hundred and fifty years ago, a horde of yugs from the Burnt Hills raided Ashawda; those are lands far to the west and south of Winnitok. There were a lot of yugs in the Burnt Hills in those days. They sacked the House of Pruck—Mobb's descendant—then ran for it back to the Hills. The Ashaws chased them and eventually destroyed them." Finding mention of Pruck, she read aloud, "'The yugs plundered many heirlooms, most precious among them the Eye of Ogin, before fleeing into the Burnt Hills.' That's all there is about it here."

She returned to the shelf, and after a few moments' hunt pulled down another book. "This is a translation of an account of the Battle by the famous Ashaw scout Ingagil, who fought in it." She read the clear and flowing script for some time. Then, toward the end of the book, which told how the remnant of the weary and much-reduced yugs was surrounded near Migdowsh, the Great Swamp, she found something like what she had hoped she might.

"'After the last fight we could not find Mobb's treasures,'" she read, "'but discovered the trail of a dozen heavily burdened green-folk moving south into Migdowsh. We followed their trail through the Breathless Gate, and five miles south into Migdowsh—far enough to be certain they carried on into the heart of that cruel place, and did not double back, or hide near its edge—but Pruck bade us return, saying he would not have us die for the sake of his House's belongings, and surely the yugs would not escape. It grieved us especially to allow the Eye of Ogin, which doubtless was among the plunder they carried—for it was not among that left behind—to be swallowed by the Swamp.'"

Drallah groaned, snapped the book shut, and laid it on the table. "Lost, indeed! It would be easier to find at the bottom of the Sea."

"Why do you say that?" asked Elwood, snatching up the book and beginning to look through it.

"Migdowsh is not just any swamp. It's enormous. It sucks life. The lands around it are all dead. It's said to be a maze of bottomless slime pools and false paths, full of bugs as big as your hand. There are yugs, and the giant people called nahrwucks. But worst of all, there's—"

"What's this?" exclaimed Elwood. Turning to the last page of Ingagil's book, he had discovered the corner of a folded parchment just peeking out from a slit in the leather of the inside back cover. Carefully drawing it out of the pocket, he unfolded the old paper, revealing writing and drawing in faded red, black, and green inks.

"A map," croaked Booj, hopping to the edge of the tabletop so the boy had room to lay it out.

"It's all written in Wohmog," said Elwood.

"It's Ingagil's map!" cried Drallah, pointing to words written in the upper right-hand corner of the yellowing old parchment. "Look: he signed it. And there are the Burnt Hills, and there is Migdowsh. I wonder if Mithloo knows he has this?"

Squinting his eyes to discern its finer details, Elwood moved the lamp closer to the faded map. "Look at this," he said, pointing to a faint line of dashes. It started in the southernmost Hills at a place marked with crossed arrows to indicate a battlefield, wound south, and ended in Migdowsh, the Great Swamp.

"Yes," Drallah said, "you can just make out the note beside it. 'Yugs escaped this way with Mobb's magic shell.' It passes right between these two outer hills: Gutt and Gatt. That must be the 'Gate' he mentioned in the book: see how close together they stand."

"So that is the exact place where they entered the Swamp," said Elwood. "Knowing that might help a lot. Finding the Eye, I mean."

"Yes . . . but the trail is long dead after two and a half centuries. This map is very interesting, but it wouldn't be much help finding the Eye."

"But it's a start."

Drallah shook her head. "I haven't told you the worst thing about Migdowsh yet."

"What?"

"The Lord of the Swamp. The monster. He's like a frog, only bigger than a house, and so powerful the Swamp itself obeys him. Like Migdowsh he is always hungry, they say. The Ashaw people call him the Otguk."

"But in a place so big—"

"He is lord of it all. And Migdowsh itself is the most treacherous swamp in Ehm. Even Ingagil and Pruck would not venture far into it, long before the Otguk came there. And dangers aside, the Swamp is so vast it would take a lifetime just to begin looking for something so small as the Eye. That's assuming it's even there any more: anything

62

could have happened to it in two hundred and fifty years. Maybe the yugs *did* somehow get out again, and carried it far away."

Elwood thought about all of this as he studied the old map. Then he slowly said, "I saw the turtle of Ogin, and a voice called my name; this book fell open to the exact page the story's on. Then I found this hidden map. You can't believe it's not Granashon, Drallah. She's telling me how to find her."

"*Crork!*" exclaimed Booj, amazed by the turn the evening had taken. Slukee, sensing something serious was developing, sat watching and listening intently.

"Winnitok needs to find her, and I need to find her," Elwood continued. "The land needs her protection, and I need her help to get home. I arrived in her sacred Glade, and now she's showing me how to find her. She wants me to get the Eye of Ogin so I can see where she is. I know it's true."

Staring into the fire, Drallah said quietly, "I believe you. But you don't understand how difficult, how dangerous it would be."

"Granashon will guide me to the Eye—somehow," said Elwood. "She's already begun. And I could ask Mithloo for help."

"My uncle would not let you go to Migdowsh," said Drallah. "He would go himself, if you convinced him. But he'd lock you up if he knew you were planning to go there."

Elwood folded his arms across his chest. "Then I won't tell him I'm going. I don't know why, but Granashon is showing *me* the way. Slukee and I will leave tomorrow. Will you come with us?"

Drallah returned to her chair. She sat and stared into the fire, which had subsided; gentle flames were rising from the coal-red logs. It was a far worse predicament than any she had yet faced in her young life: Winnitok's need, and Elwood's too, were great, and it was clear that only Elwood could answer those needs. Yet to allow such an inexperienced boy to go into such terrible danger was unthinkable. Then again, she thought, he was not just any boy: he had come from another world, and there was some extraordinary tie between him and Granashon. Also, there was a powerful desire in her to help Elwood on his quest, to be bold and strong for her land and for the Nohar. She wished she could turn to someone older and wiser for council, but she knew already what their advice would be. Her uncle and the rest would put Elwood's safety before the chance he might find Granashon.

"I want to help you find the Eye of Ogin," she said. "But without Granashon's help, the hunt would almost certainly end in death."

"But she will help us, so it won't," said Elwood.

"You and the Nohar are tied together in some way, but just how, we don't understand. We don't know for certain that that connection to her can keep you from danger. If we went, your life would be my responsibility; if you were killed, it would be my fault."

This rankled Elwood, though he knew it was true. "Your responsibility? I'm responsible for myself."

"Yes, you are. But if the worst happened, it would be my shame for allowing it."

"Isn't Winnitok more important? Than us, I mean? Isn't Granashon more important?"

Drallah did not immediately answer. If they made the journey and failed, she thought, it was true that Winnitok and Granashon would be no worse off than they were now. But if they succeeded, much might be mended, and all her rashness and irresponsibility in taking them to the Great Swamp would be forgiven.

"We'll have to lie to Mithloo," she said finally.

"Of course!" said Elwood, overjoyed.

Rising from her chair, Drallah took a large rolled parchment down from a shelf and spread it across the table. It was a map of Winnitok and the lands around it. "It's a long way to Migdowsh," she said. "And there are many dangerous places between here and there. We cannot go south too soon; that would take us through lands around Urnutok, where Booj and I are known. We don't want my family getting word and coming after us, which they would certainly do if they found out we left Winnitok. Obviously then, the River and the Gulf of Pahn are no good. We'll have to pass through Oldotok, cross the Imwa River, and go over the Mosshead Mountains before turning south. Then down through the woods of Ashawda into the Burnt Hills, where we'll find the Breathless Gate into Migdowsh."

"How long do you think it will take us to get there?"

"I'm not sure. Five weeks, maybe, if all goes well. But we must reach the Swamp before winter ends: the ground will be firmer, and the bugs fewer. And . . . maybe the Otguk will be sleeping, or at least not as watchful. We should leave very soon."

"The sooner the better."

"Tomorrow morning, then. I'll make a copy of Ingagil's map and collect provisions. If you have to talk to anyone, tell them we've decided to go to my home and spend the winter with my parents. Best to talk as little as possible, though: if anyone suspects we're planning to leave Winnitok, Mithloo will start asking questions, and we won't be going anywhere."

* * *

Before dawn two mornings later, Elwood, Drallah, and Slukee stood in the overcast dark near the Lilikit River, many miles south of Olguhm. They had left the winter house of Drallah's uncle the previous morning, having quickly prepared for the journey and keeping their farewells brief. Both Elwood and Drallah regretted telling Mithloo the lie that they were going to the girl's home in Ohrimo, but their hearts were committed to what they were doing, and they presented the falsehood convincingly enough. Neither felt any hint of suspicion in Mithloo's warm good-byes as he stood on the granite landing watching them paddle off upstream.

There had been no question of going downstream, as if they were canoeing all the way to Drallah's distant home on the Lilikit River, though normally that would have been the best way from Olguhm. They could not go that way because, without the protection of the

Dread of Granashon, Drallah's family did not want her on or near the border of Winnitok. The Road through the heart of the land was considered much safer.

By mid-afternoon they had left the canoe and the creek behind and were walking south down the North Road. Once night had fallen, and Drallah was confident no late wanderer who might see them was near, she had led them west into the pathless trees. They had toiled a long time without light or a clear way to follow, but at last they had come near the Lilikit River and a place Drallah knew where a canoe was kept for crossing.

There was a flapping of wings over their heads, and Booj landed on a rock beside them.

"Any watchers between here and the canoe?" asked Drallah.

The raven shook his beak.

"Anywhere else?"

"Two scouts are camped near the bank a mile down the River," he answered, waving a wing in that direction. "They didn't see me."

"We must hurry, but with care," said Drallah. "The light is coming. Be as quiet as you can."

They started across the chain of grassy meadows that lay between them and the River, Booj gliding back and forth across their path. Before long they saw a line of trees rising out of the darkness, and came to the riverbank.

It was a deep, sluggish point in the River. In the overcast night they could not see the opposite bank. The water was a dull black, with fluffs of mist floating just above the surface. Drallah led them north along its edge for a little while, then stopped beneath a giant weeping willow's branches. Lying among the reeds was a small canoe, one of many in place up and down Lilikit's east bank for the use of any who wished to cross.

They quickly had the canoe in the water. Elwood and Slukee boarded it and sat down. Booj swooped in and landed beside them.

"Still clear," he croaked. "Better hurry!"

"Yes," said Drallah. "What about the other side?"

"Clear."

Drallah pushed them into the River and sprang lightly into the canoe. Gradually the near bank receded into the general darkness. All the world around them was the dark, and sounds in the dark. Holding his breath, Elwood listened to the water slap the sides of the canoe. Drallah's oar gently skimmed the surface of the water, and some sleepless river bird gave a lonely call.

Before long the far bank reared up out of the darkness. Another massive willow loomed before them, Drallah paddled one last stroke, and they grounded on the other side.

"Welcome to Oldotok," she whispered. "Wait here; I'll be right back." She threw her blanket and gear on the bank, Elwood and Slukee stepped ashore, and she pushed off once again. The boy and the dog sat down, and Elwood wrapped his blanket and arms around Slukee to keep them warm while they waited.

Twilight almost imperceptibly began to take the place of night. Soon Elwood could see the far bank, and Booj's black shape flying to and fro above it. He swerved off and flew across the water to them.

"Here she comes," he croaked, landing on the bank beside Slukee.

Elwood scanned the gray dimness, and in a few moments spotted something bobbing in the water. Soon he could make out Drallah's face moving just above the surface, her clothes and hair tied in a bundle on top of her head.

"You're going to freeze," he exclaimed as she reached dry land.

"Well! That was cold," she said through chattering teeth to Elwood's back, which he kept turned while she emerged from the water, dried herself with one side of her blanket, and dressed. "But now the watchers won't be asking themselves who crossed the River and didn't return—unless they study the signs closely."

Once she was ready to move again, they paused to look back across the water. The light was growing, and they could see a long stretch of the opposite bank. Sky and river both were a pale range of misty gray-blues, and the giant willows between the two seemed to raise their branches to the dawn. Thinking on how she did not know when or even if she would see her land again, Drallah said, "It's so strange that to some this is an awful sight—or it was, while the Dread of Granashon lasted. Imagine looking at Winnitok, but seeing a land of nightmare and madness."

As dawn came they moved away from the riverbank and into a brown frost-coated marsh country. The upper sky was divided from the earth by one great expanse of cloud, and throughout the morning they saw numerous long trailing V's of geese flying high against its endless gray.

"They'll be flying over Migdowsh before we've even reached the other side of Oldotok," said Drallah, watching another formation disappear into the south.

Cold and weary to the core, Elwood watched them also. For the first time, he had some real notion of the difficulty of what they had set out to do, of the hardships and dangers that surely lay ahead. He thought self-pityingly of his warm, soft bed back in Olguhm, and wondered if he was crazy to have come. But then he looked at Drallah studying the horizon, her back straight and her senses alert despite all the miles she had walked, and the thought was gone.

THE MOUTH OF THE SNAKE

After a day and a half in the marshes, during which they had rested little, they came to a place where the land swelled up to the edge of a thick forest. Its gnarled knotty trees were stooped with age, and hung with curtains of moss that swept down to the dark forest floor. Here and there a few brown leaves still clinging to their branches rattled in the cold north wind.

"That's Riven Forest. We'll rest there," said Drallah. Fearing they might be followed despite her precautions, or be sighted in the open marshes by Winharn scouts, since they had set out she had allowed them just enough rest to be able to continue putting one foot in front of the other. Elwood was tottering along in a daze, and even Drallah was tiring, but at last she reckoned the Forest was far enough away from Winnitok and the cover of its trees sufficient to take a real rest safely.

"In the morning we'll find an old path through the Forest. It's used far less than the main forest road, so it's not likely we'll run into any of our scouts. We shouldn't be too far from the path now, if I read the maps right," she said.

They climbed the rise and looked into the trees. There was very little underbrush, but the accumulation of leaves and fallen branches was ancient and deep. Wading in until they were well out of sight from without, they cleared a nest to lie down in, and slept. Not long before dark they rose again and prepared a fire, which Drallah lit as soon as night fell and smoke would be less visible. They ate, and talked a while, and slept some more. When dawn came the next morning they were well rested, had already had breakfast, and were ready to set out again.

Stepping out of the Forest, they hurried south along its edge looking for the path. It was clear and chill, and the rising sun shone brightly upon the trunks of the old outlying trees.

Well before the morning's end they found the start of a narrow, disused pathway that bored tunnellike into the Forest. "Here it is! In we go," said Drallah, relieved to be quitting the open country.

Though the path was easier to tread than the rest of the Forest by far, still it was encumbered with a litter of old branches and leaves that slowed them. Their progress through the debris was necessarily noisy, so that only when they stopped to listen could they hear the sounds of the Forest. After they had been on the path for several minutes, Elwood looked over his shoulder at the way they had come. Back at the path's beginning, sunbeams were shining like lamps at the end of a dim hallway. Within the Forest it was dusk even in the middle of the day, and after a time Elwood's head hurt from straining his eyes against the shadows beneath the trees.

"So why is it called Riven Forest?" he asked as they walked.

"A great gorge called Rosodruim cuts through the middle of it for many miles," answered Drallah. "Rosodruim, Gorge of the Flat Snake. There is a legend that hundreds of years ago, the gorge was the den of an ancient gigantic snake." Glancing back at him she noticed a look of consternation on Elwood's face and added, "She's been dead and gone for ages, if she existed at all. Anyway, you'll see the gorge for yourself soon: we should cross it sometime tomorrow morning. And we should reach the other side of the Forest tomorrow night."

When darkness came they camped right on the path. At one point in the night Slukee growled at the sound of something large moving slowly not far outside their fire's light. Drallah guessed it was a curious bear. Also that night, they heard a wolf pack howling to one another in some distant part of the Forest. At this Elwood wrapped an arm around Slukee and pulled her tight against him, and they remained that way until first light.

* * *

They reached the gorge the next day before noon. Their path ended abruptly at its edge, and smashed posts were all that was left where a rope bridge once had been. The distance to the other side of the gorge was a little farther than Elwood could throw a stone, and its depth was several times greater than its breadth. Its granite walls were jagged and steep, and would be torturous to climb. The openness of the great rift was startling after the closeness of the Forest, which crowded to the edge on both sides.

"This makes it difficult," said Drallah, studying the bridge posts.

Elwood, who disliked heights, lay on his stomach and peered over the edge. On the rocky bottom flowed a sickly narrow stream, choked with fallen leaves and branches. The air below seemed strangely dank. "Well," he said, "What now?"

Drallah frowned. "We'll have to find a place we can climb: to go all the way around—north or south—would take days and days. I'd like to know who wrecked the bridge."

She craned her neck to give Booj, who was perched on her pack, a querying look. "I'll find a place you can cross," he croaked, then spread his wings and took off. He swooped down into the gorge and began to follow it north, studying the walls on either side as he soared.

The two humans and the dog settled down near the edge to await the raven's return. They ate and talked, and as often happened, their conversation turned to Drallah's family and home far in the south of Winnitok. She and Booj lived in a log and shingle house on a hillside above the mouth of the Lilikit River, in Ohrimo, the beautiful country around Ohrimo Bay, where the River flowed into the Sea. There were many islands in the Bay, and many Winharn villages both on the islands and on the mainland. While most of the Winhars of Ohrimo worked at fishing the Sea, Drallah's mother, Shonah, was a renowned arrow-maker: her arrows were prized throughout Winnitok for their quickness and sureness in flight. It was her mother's artistry that filled Drallah's quiver. Her father, Moodin Wehr, was one of the finest bow-hunters in Winnitok. Though in most respects Drallah was more like her mother, in this she showed signs of taking after her father.

A name that often came up when Drallah spoke of her home was that of her friend Attidan, a young man who seemed to have spent a considerable amount of time hunting with Drallah, Booj, and Moodin—and often enough, it seemed, with just Drallah and Booj. Elwood had grown quite curious about the exact nature of Drallah's relationship with this young man. Feigning a nonchalant air, he asked, "Is Attidan more than just a good friend?"

Amused by the care with which he so carelessly put the question, Drallah smiled. She had long since realized Elwood wished the difference in their ages were not so great, that in his very young way he would like to approach her, as he put it, as "more than just a good friend." It did not trouble her, though. She knew it was common at Elwood's age to feel the beginnings of desire for someone older, and that such feelings were neither strong nor lasting.

"Once he was more to me, yes. But he met someone else, and now his heart is hers."

This shocked Elwood, who could not imagine choosing someone else over Drallah. He did not say as much, however: he understood that she could not, because of his age, have reciprocal feelings. It was similar to having a crush on a teacher at school, which had happened to him frequently ever since the fifth grade, or even earlier. He knew the feeling would not be returned, and so there was no desire to speak his desire.

They heard an excited croak up in the sky, and Booj dropped to the ground beside Drallah. "There are stairs," he said. "Down one side, up the other. It's not far."

"What luck!" said Elwood, jumping to his feet. Mindful that any delay in their journey put off whatever chance he had of getting home, the halt had made him anxious.

"What signs did you see?" asked Drallah.

"It's quiet that way," said Booj. "And the gorge has a smell."

"What kind of smell?"

"Old water and rot. Maybe a lot of creatures find the way down to the bottom, but never find the way back up."

Drallah wrinkled her nose and said, "Well, we won't linger down there."

Picking a path through the layer of dead tree matter on the ground, they headed north along the gorge's edge. After covering about two miles in this way they found what they sought: a flight of steep, narrow stairs roughly hewn out of the rock, descending all the way down to the gorge bottom. Looking to the other side, they could just make out the second stairway cut into the cliff a little farther to the north.

Booj led the way down, flitting from step to step. These were irregular and rough, and so large even Drallah had to hop from one down to the next. Taking care not look into the void yawning beside them, Elwood progressed by sitting and lowering himself from the edge of each new step. Since Slukee was built nearer to the ground she descended with ease, patiently following behind the slower-moving boy.

About halfway down they came to a wide landing where the stairs switched back and began to descend in the opposite direction. There they paused, crouching, to survey the boulder strewn gorge bottom. The afternoon sun was falling on the carpet of litter from the forest above, which in several places had dammed the narrow stream and created pools of black water. By this light Drallah saw that there were pathways through the debris: one connecting the two staircases, and another winding along the gorge bottom.

Pointing at the paths she said, "Someone lives here."

"Get down!" rasped Booj, who was looking south along the floor of the rift. They all dropped low on the rock of the landing and turned to see what had alarmed him.

An exceedingly tall figure had just emerged from the shadow at the base of the gorge wall below them, some hundred feet from the bottom of the stairs. He was taller than Drallah by more than half her height, with great thick limbs and a mottled yellowish hide, some of which he covered with a ragged black bearskin. His huge nose, chin, and brow protruded far beyond the rest of his face, and his sunken eyes were tiny. As they watched he shouldered a long stone-headed hammer and meandered away down the gorge, calling out crude syllables in a booming voice.

Elwood recognized what he was looking at by Drallah's descriptions: it was a nahrwuck, the race of primitive giants.

"He didn't see us," he breathed.

"No," whispered Drallah. "But if he looks up here, he can't miss us."

In answer to the nahrwuck's call, a second came into view farther down the gorge. They met by a pool of black water and began a heated conversation in a harsh, crude language, their voices echoing off the rocks. Shortly they seemed to come to some kind of agreement, and hunkered down by the water's edge.

"As long as they stay, we're stuck," said Drallah, continuing to whisper.

"They're hungry, I think," hissed Booj. "That gives me an idea. Wait till I've drawn them away, then hurry down and up the other side. I'll meet you at the top."

He spread his wings and stepped off the landing, gliding silently toward the nahrwucks. Just as he passed over their heads he called, "Come, hunters! I'll take you to the kill."

The giants cried out in surprise, leapt up, and jogged after Booj. Soon they were out of sight beyond a bend in the gorge.

Wary there might be other nahrwucks about, Drallah, Elwood, and Slukee started down the stairs once again. The dankness in the air increased as they descended. Reaching the bottom, they found the start of a path through the debris-covered floor of the rift. They followed this path toward the second set of stairs and the other side of Rosodruim.

The companions were nearing the second stairs when they saw something that made them stop short: in the gorge wall, very close to the bottom of the steeply ascending steps, was the dark mouth of a cave. The stone all around the opening had been roughly carved in the likeness of a snake's fanged and scaly face; the cave itself was the stone snake's gullet. Cast carelessly in piles at the cave-mouth were many blackened bones, and there were human skulls among them.

"Let's go back," whispered Elwood, horror-struck.

But Drallah did not hear him, for just as when she looked into the pool and saw the Glade of Granashon, a vision came to her when she looked into the stone snake's mouth.

She saw all at once the whole of the Gorge of Rosodruim, and a great span of days, seasons, and years that had passed there. She saw the Flat Snake had indeed existed, for slowly sinking into the gorge bottom were colossal bones. Over the bones, a spiritual remnant of the monster reared a ghostly head.

She saw a wandering band of nahrwucks come to the edge of the gorge, to the edge of the monster's ancient den. Their chieftain perceived the Flat Snake's spirit, and believed it spoke to him. He told his band they would stop their wandering, and worship the god he had found. So they remained in that great scar in the earth, cutting the stairs with their crude might, and carving the cave-mouth in the Flat Snake's likeness.

Soon all the nahrwucks could hear the voice of the Flat Snake.

"I am Komust," her spirit said, and those who worshipped her were convinced she was speaking to them. But the Flat Snake was not aware of the nahrwucks, for she was dead: only a trace, only a ghostly memory of the monster remained in the lands of flesh and blood.

Because they were certain the powerless spirit was a god, the nahrwucks would not abandon the idol they had made. Even after their enormous appetites had emptied the forest of meat for miles around, they continued to dwell there. Without enough food to sustain them, the band died away. Now their number had dwindled to two.

Drallah's vision of so much time and space came and went in an instant, and she was once again looking into the dark cave mouth. There was a snap of wings and a harsh raven whisper directly over her head. Booj had returned, diving straight down from high above. "They're coming back," he warned, hovering. From down the gorge came a shout of surprise and anger. The companions turned to face its source, and saw the two giants loping toward them.

"Run," breathed Drallah, grabbing Elwood by the arm and propelling him in the direction of the second stairs. Like those on the opposite side of the gorge, the steps were very high, and the humans had to use their hands as well as their feet to mount them. With her shorter legs, Slukee leaped from step to step. As the others climbed, Booj streaked back to harry the pursuing nahrwucks, swooping low over their misshapen heads. They cursed and swatted at the raven as he passed, but pressed on relentlessly after the boy, the girl, and the dog.

The giants reached the stairs and started up them without breaking their stride. The steps were cut to their size, and their ascent was rapid. Seeing his friends would be caught before they were even halfway up the side of the gorge, Booj began to target the nahrwucks' eyes. But they were so sunken and small, and the arms and hands that defended them were so large, the raven failed even to slow the giants.

Drallah stopped and let Elwood and Slukee pass her. The nahrwucks were so near now she could hear their brute panting breath. The giant in the lead was almost close enough to strike, and he was brandishing his stone-headed hammer as he bounded up the stairs. Drallah drew her long knife.

Even as she turned to fight, Drallah heard again the voice from her vision, the voice of the Flat Snake's spirit. Instead of attempting to strike under the giant's guard as she had planned, she threw up her arms in warning and cried out with all the force in her lungs:

"Komust! Komust! Komust will take you both!"

At the sound of that name, the nahrwucks seemed to run headlong into an invisible wall. The first crashed against the second, and both lost their footing. In a tangle of torsos and limbs, the giants fell from step to step, their descent ending at the carved mouth of the cave.

Drallah resumed her climb, urging Elwood and Slukee on as she did. Reaching the first landing, she told the boy and the dog to continue on to the top of the gorge. As she swiftly strung her bow, she looked down at the giants recovering from their fall. They seemed to be stunned, but not badly hurt. She nocked an arrow and watched as they stirred and slowly rose to their enormous bare feet.

Pain, fear, and bewilderment were plain on the nahrwucks' faces as they looked up at Drallah. One took a tentative step toward the stairs. Drallah instantly drew, aimed, and released her arrow. It struck him in the shin of the leg he had put forward. The arrowhead broke the thick skin, but only dented the rock-like bone. With a howl the giant yanked the arrow from his leg and sat down, holding his shin and cursing.

Drallah remained on the landing, another arrow nocked. Booj lit on her pack and struck his most threatening pose, feathers ruffled out and wings half-spread. Once they were satisfied the giants would not soon attempt to climb the stairs again, the girl and the raven turned and followed Elwood and Slukee. When they reached the top of the haunted gorge, the giants were still lingering in the shadows near the mouth of the cave, watching them go.

* * *

The companions spent the night well off the Forest path, without a fire, and miles from the Gorge of the Flat Snake. They huddled together amidst the dense trees, Slukee curled up against Elwood, Booj perching on a low branch over the others' heads. In a soft voice Drallah told them of all she had seen in the cave mouth. As she was explaining how the vision had saved them, Booj suddenly did a loud imitation of the nahrwucks' angry shouts.

"Quiet, Booj!" said Drallah. "They're still out there, remember?"

"Sorry, sorry," chuckled the raven.

"In the vision," Drallah continued, "I saw the nahrwucks worship the Flat Snake, and I heard the spirit of the Flat Snake speak her own name. I felt it was a name of power—or at least a name of power over the nahrwucks."

Elwood was not following Drallah's explanation. He could not stop thinking of the heaps of bones at the cave-mouth, and how close their own had come to joining them. "Those things wanted to kill us," he said, his voice shaking.

Drallah did not immediately reply. When she did, there was an edge of disappointment in her words. "I thought you understood the danger, Elwood," she said. "I told you in Olguhm we'd be risking our lives. The gorge was nothing compared to all that lies ahead. This is only the beginning."

Now Elwood was struck by another fear: that Drallah might think him unworthy of their quest—and her companionship. Trying to sound calm he said, "I know. There's much worse to come."

"And the vision in the gorge is a good sign for the hunt," Drallah continued. "We had help when we needed it most."

Elwood buried his hands in the thick fur of Slukee's neck. "Did the Other Twin create the nahrwucks, like he did the yugs?" he asked.

"No, they're natural beings, like humans or woogans. They're just stupid and backward," answered Drallah.

"In my world, they wouldn't let things like that just roam around."

"The Ringish invaders left Oldotok a lawless place, so it's no surprise there are lawless people here."

Drallah's features were hidden by the dark, but the sound of her voice allowed him to imagine the expression on her face: so self-assured and brave. These qualities were very attractive to him. Wistfully he imagined the day when his body, which was still growing, would catch up with his desires. But he was not confident that even then his own face would be found attractive by anyone.

Without thinking, he said out loud, "I wish I was older."

"Why do you say that?" asked Drallah.

"Well, I'd be more ... ready for this," he answered, taking care now not to say too much. "The danger. Going to Migdowsh, and finding the Eye of Ogin. I'd be more like you."

Though she guessed the true reason for Elwood's wish, Drallah did not acknowledge it in what she said next.

"Granashon is showing the way to you, not me," she said lightly. "And like my mother always says: don't be hasty, you'll be older soon enough."

Grateful for his friend's tact, Elwood changed the subject.

"Do you have Vision now, like your Uncle Mithloo? This is the second time it's happened: first the pool, then the cave."

"Not yet," answered Drallah. "People like my uncle can actually will themselves to see visions. I haven't been able to do that, though I haven't seriously tried. Those with Vision have to go off by themselves to learn how to use it. Mithloo did that when he was young: he spent a summer alone in the woods. Some day, I'll do that too."

There was a groan from the branch above where Booj was perched. The raven did not like the thought of being apart from Drallah for weeks and weeks.

"Don't worry, Booj," she said. "I won't seek Vision for a long time. Not till we get back home."

Envying Drallah for the confident way she spoke of returning to her land and family, Elwood wrapped himself in his blanket and lay down for the night. He could hardly believe that just a few days earlier, he had been positively certain they would find the Eye, the Nohar, and the way back to the world where he belonged. Now, lying in the dark and struggling with fear, the time of Elwood's faith in their quest seemed far in the past.

THE HERB WITCH

They reached the western edge of Riven Forest the next afternoon. Beyond lay a land of thickets and lesser woods stitched together by low crumbling walls of loose stone.

"Once the Forest covered the greater part of northern Oldotok, but when the Ringish came they felled and burned most of it," explained Drallah as they entered this new country. "They used some of the trees to build warships and wagons, and they farmed some of the land, but mostly they destroyed the Forest because the Oldharn were hiding deep inside, and the Ringish soldiers, the Graycloaks, couldn't find them."

"Who lives here now?" Elwood asked as he scanned the countryside. It struck him as a melancholy place, but beautiful.

"A few Oldhars still farm and hunt here; very few. There are bad people—like that petty-sorcerer Ustane I told you about—and sometimes yugs, nahrwucks, and other things. We have to be on guard."

Before dark they came upon a meandering road that had once been a broad way but now was half swallowed up by brush and trees. Since it tended generally westward they followed this road, and for two days it led them through a land where they saw no one but wild creatures. There were signs of past human occupation, however: ruined stone forts like the crumbling skulls of giants glowered down from some of the taller hills, grim remains of the Ringish conquest long years before. The friends avoided these, preferring instead to camp in the shelter of thickets and woods.

The morning of the third day after they left Riven Forest was bright, cold, and strangely still. The country had grown increasingly hilly, and their way now wound between high bluffs covered with pine trees.

"I smell snow," croaked Booj from his perch on Drallah's pack.

"Yes; maybe it will snow this afternoon," said Drallah. "Could that be why it's so still?"

"Look!" said Elwood, nodding at the way ahead. An old woman who had not been there a moment before was on the road, walking slowly toward them.

"Where did she come from?" rasped Booj.

"She must have been in the trees by the side of the road," said Elwood.

The old woman drew closer. Her gray hair was woven in two braids that hung down to her knees, and her red cheeks were almost translucent. Her garb was light despite the season: just a long buckskin dress, a woolen shawl, and moccasins. She carried a woven basket on her back. She was humming softly to herself, and did not seem to notice the companions.

"Good morning, Old Mother," said Drallah in Wohmog. "How are you?"

Seeming to notice the four friends for the first time, the woman stopped and looked each of them up and down. She lingered longest over Elwood.

"Why are *you* on this road?" she said in accented Winnitoke, squinting her right eye shut and glaring at them with her left.

"We are traveling west," said Drallah.

She squinted her left eye and glared at them with her right. "That is plain, girl, plain. *Why* are you traveling west?"

"Because we—are looking for something that way," she replied. She did not want to tell the stranger their purpose, but she did not want to lie to her either.

"Oh? Well, I know what you will find in that direction. But what you will find is not, I think, what you seek."

"What will we find?" asked Elwood.

The old woman stepped up and bent over him so quickly and suddenly he took a startled step back.

"You will find yourself in the pot!" she cried. "There is a camp of the cursed yuggies that way, hundreds of them. They have been here for weeks now, creeping all over these parts. Frightening off the creatures, and squashing the forage."

"Yugs!" said Drallah. "How far is the camp?"

"Three miles. Can you not smell them, girl?"

"No, not yet; and I don't want to. Thank you for warning us."

"Do you live around here? Shouldn't you hide?" said Elwood.

"Oh, the yuggies could not hurt me if they tried," the old woman said with a disdainful wave of her hand. "And nobody finds my place unless I take them there."

"We must leave this road now," said Drallah to Booj. "We'll have to cut south and west to one of the bridges to—"

"You could do that, but I would not," snapped the stranger. "Did I not just tell you the yuggies are crawling all over these hills?"

"What would you do, Old Mother?" asked Drallah.

"Tell me who you are; that is the first thing I would do," she said sternly.

"I am Drallah Wehr."

"I am Noshkwa," said the woman, taking Drallah's hands in her own. The girl noticed they were black in the creases with freshly turned earth, and surprisingly soft. Elwood, Slukee, and Booj introduced themselves, and Noshkwa continued.

"If you want to avoid the yuggies, I can show you a hidden way to the north that is best. But not today. I have been on an errand all the night, and must rest. You had better stay with me in my house. You will be safe there until tomorrow, and then I will show you."

Though the old woman's temper was prickly and strange, Drallah could see in Noshkwa's face that there was no guile or falseness about her.

"Thank you. We will come with you," she said.

"Good!" said the Oldharn woman. Then she practically sprang from the road, disappearing into a dense thicket.

"Come on," said Drallah, and they all plunged into the thicket after her.

Noshkwa led them in a northeasterly direction. She seemed to be in quite a hurry, and not hindered in the slightest by all the different sorts of pathless terrain she bustled through. Bushes and trees seemed to make way for her, then immediately close up again once she had passed. On bluff or in wood, through bog or thicket, Noshkwa pressed onward as though ever on a straight and level road. Elwood had an especially difficult time, and the old woman scowled very darkly indeed whenever she had to stop and wait for him to catch up.

They had been traveling in this way for a little more than an hour when Noshkwa halted, tilting her head as if to hear better. They were in the midst of a thick hawthorn brake, and could not see far in any direction. Elwood, Slukee, Drallah, and Booj all strained their ears, but could hear nothing.

"What is it?" asked Drallah after they had been standing silently among the hawthorns for some minutes.

"Shh!" answered Noshkwa. "This is the place."

Then they all began to hear the sound of something large moving through the trees not far away. Drallah quickly recognized that whatever it was, it went on two legs. She crouched and drew her knife, signaling Elwood to get down as well. The sound grew louder. Someone was crashing recklessly through the hawthorns, heading straight for them.

Presently a tall man who seemed on the verge of collapse listed and staggered into view. He was dressed in ragged mud-spattered buckskins, and clutching at his side. Noshkwa and Drallah rushed to help him.

"Ginnich Taw!" cried Drallah, recognizing him as one of the scouts who a month earlier had set out from Olguhm in search of Granashon. Plainly the scout's errand had gone wrong: his buckskin shirt was stiff with drying blood, the broken stump of a javelin was stuck in his side, and his wrists were raw and bloody. He stared at Drallah in wonder, but did not speak.

"No need to talk now, boy," said Noshkwa as they helped him lie down. Her tone was as soft and kind now as it had been hard and irritable before. "Save your strength, and we will make you well."

"How far is it to your house?" asked Drallah, lifting Ginnich's head and sliding her blanket underneath.

"Not so far, but we'll need a carrier all the same."

While Noshkwa knelt over Ginnich with her hand laid gently upon his forehead, Drallah and Elwood found and felled two straight-trunked saplings. They stripped them of branches, then tied a folded blanket between the hastily cut poles. As they were moving Ginnich onto it, Booj returned with a swoop from a flight over the neighborhood.

"Yugs are on his trail, a half mile behind," he said.

"How many?" asked Drallah.

"Twenty or more."

"Do not mind them," said Noshkwa, drawing a tiny jar out of a bag that hung around her neck. She moved slowly away in the direction Ginnich had come from, muttering words they could not catch and occasionally pouring something from the jar into her palm and sprinkling it on his trail. The four friends waited for her by the makeshift carrier.

"How did she know he was going to come this way?" whispered Elwood, staring at the bloody javelin stump in Ginnich's side. "Is she a witch?"

Drallah was carefully securing the wounded man to the carrier with cords Noshkwa had given her. "She must be something," she whispered back. "It was no chance that brought us to this spot." Then, though Ginnich seemed to be in a faint or asleep, she drew Elwood a few steps away to be sure he did not hear.

"He's badly hurt," she said. "I hope she knows more about healing than I do."

"There!" said Noshkwa, returning. "They shall lose the trail soon enough."

She and Drallah each took up one of the carrier poles at the end by Ginnich's head and began to drag him through the brake as quickly and gently as they could. Despite her age, the woman had ample strength for sharing the burden of the tall, powerfully built Winhar. She told Elwood which way to go, and he did his best to clear a path. Though they had been traveling in a straight line northeast before they found Ginnich, Noshkwa now led them in a westerly direction. In the course of a slow, difficult mile, their guide stopped to scatter the contents of her tiny jar upon their trail at several points.

"What are you doing?" asked Elwood as she finished her strange ritual for the third time.

"Throwing the yuggies off our trail," she replied, scowling.

"But how?" persisted Elwood.

Ignoring him, Noshkwa took up the carrier pole once again. Drallah gave Elwood a look of warning, and with a shrug he dropped the subject.

As tiny, nearly invisible flakes of snow began to flurry down, the Oldharn woman led them up a steep rise. Reaching the summit after a laborious climb, they found an oak wood half submerged in a green sea of briar, its great thorn-filled waves climbing tree trunks and flowing over lower branches.

"There is my home," cried the old woman with a sweep of her hand.

The four friends all looked at one another, and then looked again at the thorny green immensity before them. It was impassable, and there was no dwelling to be seen.

"I don't see—where is it? How will we get Ginnich through *that?*" said Drallah.

Noshkwa did not answer, but took a small twisted root from a bag tied to her belt. She lightly touched each of their brows with it, and softly whispered something in what Elwood guessed must be Oldotoke. When they looked again they saw a wide, clear path weaving through the briar to an enormous peaked rock rearing up above the treetops.

"It's like when we came from our world," gasped Elwood, remembering the sudden appearance of the path that led them to Ehm. He did not notice the sharp look Noshkwa gave him when he said it, but Drallah did.

They followed the broad path to the peaked rock, which was surrounded by smaller humps of stone rising out of the ground like a ring of foothills. The path ended in a hollow scooped out of the massive rock's base. At the back of the hollow, set in the very stone, was a sturdy wooden door painted a deep blue.

"Bring him inside," said Noshkwa, throwing it open.

Gently she spoke to Ginnich, who was only half conscious, and after the cords were untied she and Drallah helped him to his feet and through the doorway. Within was a pleasant, tidy room carved out of the rock. There was a table covered with a mustard-yellow cloth, a fireplace, an old black kettle, and several cupboards. To the ceiling were fastened numerous racks, from which a variety of herbs were hung to dry. There were several shafts cut through the walls and ceiling, which had been cleverly rigged with ropes and shutters to let in air and light, or to keep out rain and cold, depending on the need. At the back of the room was another opening leading deeper into the rock, across which was hung a heavy orange and green blanket woven in gorgeous patterned bands.

While Elwood held the blanket aside for them, the old woman

and the girl helped Ginnich through the opening. Beyond was a second room, which was very dark. Noshkwa directed them, and in a moment the Winharn man was lying on a low soft bed. Then she lit a lamp, and they saw that this room was a little smaller than the first. On the floor against the wall opposite the bed were two trunks of woven bark, and two little chairs. More herbs dangled from the ceiling, and in the far wall was another doorway. This one was hung with a blanket of purple and gold.

"I must have everything ready when the weapon is removed," said Noshkwa, kneeling and gathering items from one of the trunks. "It will take a little time. Sit with him, girl, while I prepare." Then she bustled into the kitchen to start a fire and heat water, brusquely ordering Elwood, Slukee, and Booj out of the room where the wounded man lay. Giving the boy a long-hafted tomahawk, she commanded him to go outside and split wood for the fire.

Drallah drew a chair to the bedside. When the water in the kettle was warm, she soaked a cloth and bathed Ginnich's brow. At first she ministered to him in silence, but after a while she softly sang:

> *If you cannot come home*
> *because your path sleeps*
> *beneath the snow*
> *never mind.*
> *All are warmed again in spring*
> *east of the River*
> *west of the Sea.*

Noshkwa came back from the kitchen bearing a tray filled with various covered dishes, stoppered bottles, and implements. Setting it on a stool, she bade Drallah get up and move the lamp to a niche in the rock above the bed. Then she sat in the chair and began carefully to cut away at Ginnich's shirt with a small, sharp knife.

"Can you help me, or does the wound frighten you?" she asked Drallah.

"I have seen wounds before. Not as bad as this one, but I will help."

"Good. Now lift his head so I can give him this," said Noshkwa, pulling the stopper out of a slender bottle she took from the tray.

Drallah lifted Ginnich's head, and Noshkwa poured a little of the bottle's contents down his throat. She watched the Winhar's face closely. Slowly the muscles in his brow, which had been knit tightly together since they found him, parted and smoothed. "Now he will be sure to sleep through our work," she said, removing the rest of his shirt. Then she laid a stack of white cloth beside him on the bed, and tentatively began to feel the area around the javelin-stump. After a few minutes of this she suddenly grabbed hold of it and, with a deft, forceful motion, yanked it out of his body. Blood came welling up. Ginnich shuddered, but did not wake.

While Drallah stemmed the flow of blood with cloth, Noshkwa examined the broken javelin. It had a small, simple head of black metal twined to a shaft of stout wood.

"Yuggish, of course," she muttered.

After studying it closely, she submerged the tip in a bowl filled with a milky liquid. The blood that remained on the javelin-head made a crimson cloud in the bowl, but there was no other change.

"No poison," she said, giving Drallah a twinkling little smile.

She then cleaned and searched the wound, frowning and muttering to herself and keeping her eyes closed as she worked. Seeming to come to a decision, she wiped her hands on a cloth and took a jar from the tray. The ointment she scooped from it and spread on the wound filled the room with a heady odor. She removed the lid from a dish, releasing a gush of steam into the air. Inside was a thick boiled slab of green-gray moss. She placed this over the wound, holding it there with long strips of cloth she tied around Ginnich's middle. When this was done, she lay her hand on his brow and softly chanted in Oldotoke for several minutes while Drallah washed and bandaged his wrists. Then she dimmed the lamp and moved it to the other side of the room, and she and Drallah quietly slipped out to the kitchen.

They found Booj preening on the blanket rack, and Elwood and Slukee seated on the floor, the boy plucking burrs from the dog's coat and tossing them into the fire. Noshkwa lowered herself wearily into a chair at the table.

"He will be well in time," she sighed. "The weapon came near the vitals, but did not find them."

"Was it the yugs who hurt him?" asked Elwood.

"It was."

"All the scouts from Olguhm went in pairs," said Drallah. "I wonder what's become of the other Winhar."

"I met the two of them on the road three weeks ago, not far from where we met this morning," said Noshkwa. "They were looking for Granashon the Nohar. I could not help: I have heard nothing of her for a long time. But I warned them of the yuggies' camp. They do not seem to have heeded me."

"How long do you think it will be before he's well enough to speak?" said Drallah.

"Tomorrow, I think. He is a strong one. But now, children, I must sleep. You are welcome to all you like, and can rest here by the fire without a worry for yourselves. I will be in the room beyond the next, and will know if he wakes."

*　*　*

Ginnich slept all through the afternoon, evening, and night, and the companions did not see Noshkwa again until the next morning just before sunrise. Elwood, Slukee, and Drallah were still asleep in their blankets on the floor before the fireplace, but Booj had already gone out through a shaft in the wall. Noshkwa's entrance woke the dog, who rose to greet her with a bowing stretch and wagging tail.

"Good morning, pup," answered Noshkwa, patting Slukee's head. "Well!" she said to Elwood and Drallah, who were beginning to stir.

"The Winhar has slept long and soundly. That is good. Maybe he will like a little breakfast."

She threw open the door. A thin veil of snow had fallen, and the twilit wood was a ghostly silver hue. Somehow the cold morning air did not cross the threshold into the kitchen, and Noshkwa left the door open while they prepared breakfast. The sun came up, making fierce rosy-orange blushes in the new white. Booj, who had found and breakfasted on the remains of a deer in the woods, came winging back, and he and Slukee rolled and played in the snowy dooryard.

As soon as it was hot, Noshkwa took a bowl of broth in to Ginnich, and when she returned it was empty. "He will sleep more now," she said. "Maybe when he wakes again he will be strong enough to tell his tale. In the meantime, I will show you something."

After they had had some of Noshkwa's corncakes and pumpkin stew, the Oldharn woman bade Elwood and Drallah put on their moccasins and blankets. Then she led the way, not out the kitchen door as they expected, but softly through the room where Ginnich slept. She carried a lantern in one hand, and with the other held aside the purple and gold curtain for them to pass through.

The room beyond was smaller than the one before it and had a cozy-looking bed set in a deep alcove. No shafts were cut in its walls; the only light came from Noshkwa's lantern. There was an ember oven in the middle of the room to warm it on cold days, and opposite the bed stood a big wooden cupboard exquisitely carved with flowering herb shapes. In the far wall was hung still another curtain, this one a blue so dark it was almost black. They passed through it and found a smooth-hewn staircase curving in a wide spiral upward into the rock.

With her lantern held high, Noshkwa led the way up. After several complete spirals, the stairs ended in a heavy wooden door that was like the kitchen's, but painted a dark green. She opened it, and they were all blinded for a moment by the sunlight that came streaming in. Stepping outside, they found themselves on a high natural terrace just below the great rock's peak. There were pockets of mossy soil here and there, and blueberry bushes, and a few small oaks and long-needled firs. The terrace commanded a wide view of the surrounding hills, their sides all white with the new snow. From a valley not far to the west, and from other parts of the woods in that direction, rose many thin black columns of smoke.

"There are more camps today than yesterday," said Noshkwa as she slowly searched the distant woods, a hand shading her eyes. "You can see by the way their fires smoke it is yuggies." She took up a straw broom from where it leaned at the top of the stair and began sweeping the snow from a raised part of the rock. "They are gathering, and that kind gathers for only one reason."

"To make war," said Drallah. She studied the smoke, fearing what it might mean. "Who will they attack, though?"

"I do not know who they will attack. Not the woogans on the other side of Imwa; the yuggies are coming down from the mountains in the north. Maybe they come to attack your land while the Nohar is gone, and it is vulnerable."

That was what Drallah was afraid of. If it were so, she knew, Winnitok must be warned. But how to know for certain? She wondered if Ginnich had learned what the yugs were planning, and resolved to ask him when he woke.

So as not to dwell on the sight of the camp smoke, the humans sat facing east on the rock Noshkwa had cleared of snow. The dog and the raven set about exploring the terrace. As he sat looking out on the world, Elwood worked up the courage to put the question he had been longing to ask since the previous morning. Though she was sharp-tongued, and her manner was sometimes odd, something comforting and sweet about Noshkwa's presence emboldened him.

"Noshkwa, how did you know about Ginnich? Are you a witch?"

"No, boy, no," she answered, staring up into the sky as though at something the others were not farsighted enough to see. "Or maybe

I am: I do not know. I just know herbs, and all things that grow around here, as my mother did, and my grandmother, and her mother too."

"You mean herbs told you Ginnich needed help, and where he would be, and when?"

"Elwood!" exclaimed Drallah.

"I suppose you could say that, Elwood Pitch," answered Noshkwa. "But maybe you do not know such secrets are just that: secret. Or do you wish to apprentice? Maybe you do not know that it is almost always the girls who have the skill, not the boys." She shot him a sudden shrewd look. "Maybe you are from somewhere very, very far away, somewhere people do not know about these matters." Then she gave him one of her rare twinkling smiles, took a stubby pipe out of the bag on her belt, and began to fill it.

"Look!" cried Drallah, leaping up. "Ginnich, wait!"

Down on the ground below, the wounded man was slowly making his way along the path away from the rock. He had wrapped a blanket around his shoulders, and walked almost doubled over. He stopped when he heard Drallah call, and turning looked up to the terrace. They all rushed down the stairs, through the three rooms, and out the kitchen door. The girl was the first to reach him.

"Drallah Wehr!" he gasped. "I thought I dreamed of you. Why are you here?"

"Never mind that! You should be in bed," she said, taking him by the arm and turning him back toward the rock.

"Winnitok must be warned," he cried, wrenching his arm from her grasp and drawing himself up. Then he grimaced, doubled over, and clutched at his side beneath the blanket. Noshkwa and Drallah once again took him gently by each arm, and led him back to bed.

When he was lying down again, Drallah—who had already guessed Ginnich's news, and was filled with trepidation—sat beside him and said, "We will get word to Winnitok, but you must stay here with Noshkwa until you're healed. Tell me: what has happened?"

"Wait," said Noshkwa. "First I must care for the wound."

She removed the blood-stained bandages and moss. Then she washed the wound, spread more ointment, and applied a fresh slab of moss, all the while scolding him for leaving his bed. She wound him in clean bandages, and warned him not to get up until she told him he may. Finally she turned to Drallah.

"You can talk to him now, if he wishes to talk," she said.

"I do indeed," said Ginnich weakly. "There is no time to lose." Then for the first time he was aware of Elwood, who was standing by the door. "Granashon's Scout is here," he said, amazed.

Kneeling beside him, Drallah asked again, "What happened?"

"The yugs are gathering—when we were taken they—" he choked out, struggling to speak.

"Take your time, Winhar," said Noshkwa, lowering a cup of water to his lips as Drallah helped him raise his head.

He took a deep breath after he drank and, speaking very slowly and with great effort, began again.

"The yugs are gathering to invade Winnitok. Searching for news of Granashon, Gulah and I were making for the lake country west of the Flintroots. We met Noshkwa—I don't know. Many days ago. What moon is it?"

"The ninth since the Mink's Moon," said Noshkwa.

Ginnich shook his head. "Then it was three weeks. We met Noshkwa, and she warned us that yugs were camped on the road to the west. When we went to investigate, we were ambushed." He groaned and turned his head to the wall.

"The yugs are led by Ringishmen clad in gray cloaks, like the ravagers of old. The Graycloaks have returned. They plot to destroy us. There is one Graycloak, the other men call him General. I do not know his name, but in their ugly speech the yugs call him *Vank-mul:* 'cunning bear.' He wears the skull of a strange creature on his head like a crown.

"They held us in a pit, and Vank-mul tortured us; questioned us about Winnitok, taunted us—he said small bands of yugs have been creeping down from the north for months. Once they are gathered there will be a horde of many thousands. The Graycloaks will then lead them swiftly east. The people must be warned."

The Winhar took another drink of water and a deep breath, then continued. "My companion, Gulah, was mighty. He did not falter, told them nothing—and two days ago Vank-mul the Graycloak murdered him. I knew he would kill me too. In the night I broke out of the pit. They saw me; alarm was sounded. I came against two yugs on watch. It was one of their javelins you took from my side. Now go, Drallah Wehr! Go and warn Winnitok."

"Rest now," said Noshkwa. "We will get word to your land. Rest, and do not worry."

"Yes, Ginnich Taw. We swear it," said Drallah, gripping his hand.

They left him then, and as the companions talked in the kitchen about what to do, the old woman watched Elwood intently.

"Booj can fly to Winnitok," said Drallah, the raven bobbing his head in agreement. "He can get there swiftly and warn them."

"Somebody has to warn Winnitok," said Elwood. "But where would we be now without Booj? We're going to need him, if we're ever going to get to . . . " he trailed off with a glance at Noshkwa.

"I have heard of you," she said. "You are the boy from another world. The boy who appeared in the sacred Glade of the Nohar."

"Yes," he said, taken aback.

"Why not tell me where you are going, and why?"

Elwood turned to Drallah, who nodded.

"We are going to the Great Swamp, to Migdowsh," he answered. "Granashon told me to go there, to get the Eye of Ogin. With the seeing power of the Eye we can find her; once she's found, she can help Winnitok, and help me find a way back home."

The woman's wrinkled round face had clouded over. "The Swamp, and the monster! The Eye of Ogin," she murmured, musing. Then she said, "I do not see how it might happen, but my Vision tells me if anyone can find Granashon the Nohar, it is this boy from another world. Winnitok is in great danger without the Dread of Granashon; you must find her, and find her soon.

"But Elwood should have what help he can get. Raven, go with him! Others can warn Winnitok: my grandson Buck will go. He is a masterful scout, and will not fail."

Moved and reassured by Noshkwa's belief in him, Elwood crouched at her feet and looked up into her face. "Please, tell us everything you see."

She smiled down at him and patted his shoulder. "I have, boy. To know more, you must find Granashon."

Drallah too moved close to the old woman. "Can you help us? Will you come with us?"

A look of pain traversed Noshkwa's face. "I am older than I seem. My bones are propped up by this place, and if I left it, they would slump. I cannot come."

The boy and the girl hung their heads, the raven sighed a long rasping sigh, and the dog looked anxiously from one face to another. "Do not worry," said the old woman with a soft laugh. Then she took Elwood and Drallah each by the hand. She began to whisper sweetly in her own language, and though they could not understand, their doubts and fears shrank from her words like shadows from noon's approach.

RUNNING

That afternoon, Noshkwa set out for the home of her grand-son Buck. He lived some miles to the south, and she would not return until the next morning. Since they were near the country where he was hatched, it was possible Booj might find a relation or an old friend who would be willing to bear news to Winnitok, and so off he flew. While they waited for Noshkwa and Booj to return, Drallah, Elwood, and Slukee cared for Ginnich.

The Winharn scout slept after he told his story, and did not wake again until the evening. As soon as he did, he asked to hear Elwood and Drallah's tale, and to know why they were so far from Winnitok. They told him of their adventures since they had left Olguhm, and the reasons they had set out. Shocked to learn they meant to go to Migdowsh, he started to beg them to turn back, but after a little consideration said, "Or at least wait until I have healed enough to guide you."

"Thank you, Ginnich, but we cannot wait," Drallah answered. "There's no time to waste, as Noshkwa said."

With Booj and Noshkwa away crossing yug-infested country, the companions did not rest well. When morning came, then mid-morning, and neither of them returned, they grew truly worried. Slukee kept watch from the high terrace, frequently joined by Elwood, or Drallah, or both. All three were looking out from atop the great rock when, not long before noon, the dog spotted wide black wings at last streaking toward them out of the south.

"I found my cousin Dar," croaked Booj as he landed among them. "At Thunder Bluff. He flies to Olguhm with the news."

"We were worried about you," said Elwood. "And Noshkwa's late too."

The terrace door swung open, and there the old woman stood at the top of the stair. She had approached and entered the rock undetected by any of them.

"What kept you?" laughed Drallah. "Or have you been back for a while, taking a nap in the bedroom?"

"I did not find Buck until after dawn this morning. The yuggies drove him from his house, and he was hiding. He is well enough, though, and already on his way to Winnitok. Now it is time for you to go also. I will show you the hidden road I told you of."

They made ready, and said farewell to Ginnich Taw.

"Winnitok will be warned the yugs are coming," Drallah said to him. "So don't leave here until Noshkwa has healed you."

"Take care, all of you," he replied, troubled and grave. "Be cautious at every turn."

"We shall, we shall," they promised.

Before they left the great rock, Noshkwa replenished their provisions. Among all she gave them was a small pot of blue clay, the raised center of its sealed lid molded in the shape of a dragonfly.

"Do not open this until you reach Migdowsh," she said. "It is a precious jelly. Dab it here and there on yourselves—just a dab, here and there—and you may walk the Swamp untroubled by bugs."

"Thank you," said Drallah, slipping the pot of jelly in her pack.

"You must beware the Swamp, children. The monster makes it wicked—though not *entirely* so, I think. Still, if it is aware you have come, it will not release you."

Elwood asked Noshkwa how they could avoid this, but she only scowled in reply.

* * *

When they were ready, Noshkwa led them out of the oak and briar wood, down the hill, and around to the north. In that direction the bluffs were soon left behind, their steep slopes giving way to a wide rust-brown flatland where little snow had fallen and autumn was not so advanced. After a pathless tramp of two miles they came to a beech wood. Vines wound all around the trees' slender trunks and crept thickly among their roots. The berries on these vines were small and white, and everywhere trios of flame-red leaves remained on their stems. Drallah recognized them immediately.

"Poison ivy!" she said, wrinkling her nose. "Is that the way we're going?"

"It is," answered Noshkwa, smiling.

"Look at your legs, Noshkwa; we're covered up, but you'll get the stuff on you. Are you leaving us now?"

"Soon," she said, and led on. Picking her way carefully so as to avoid touching the poisonous plant, Noshkwa took them to a big boulder standing not far from the edge of the beech wood. Beyond it they found a three-foot-tall circle of stones that looked like a well.

"This is the way," said Noshkwa, standing at the stone circle's edge. Joining her, the four friends saw that it was several feet around, only a few feet deep, and quite dry inside.

"There is an underground channel down there, big enough to creep through. It leads to a dried-up ditch the Ringish dug when they took our land — just over there," said Noshkwa, pointing through the trees. "The ditch runs many miles west and north. It ends in an empty reservoir. The ivy grows thick all along the length of the ditch, on both sides, but not inside. In it you should be safe from the yuggies. At the other end you will be well past their camps, and close by a place where the road bends north. But whatever you do, stay off the road. At least until you cross Imwa."

"This is perfect," grinned Drallah.

"But if the yugs have been around here for weeks, they must have found this ditch by now," said Elwood, puzzled.

"The ivy is much, much more poisonous to yugs than it is to us," said Drallah. "Its touch is death to them."

"It is a joke of the one who made them," said Noshkwa. "Like the yuggies' hatred of green growing things, though they are green and grow themselves: of all peoples, none delight in using poisons like the yuggies, yet by poisons are no people more quickly slain. That is why the Oldhars that remain have long nurtured the ivy, and kept the ditch clear, for such times as now. The yuggies will not go near this place, even in winter, while the ivy remains."

Though this was reassuring, the friends were loath to say good-bye to the herb witch. The brief time since they had met Noshkwa seemed like a sweet dream from which they felt themselves waking.

"Now go, children," said the old woman, embracing Elwood and Drallah and kissing each of them on the forehead. "Farewell, Booj Raven. Farewell, pup. I will hide our tracks on the way back home."

"We'll come back to see you when we can," said Drallah, feeling far less capable and confident than she usually did.

"Yes, we will . . . " muttered Elwood, glum and sorry for himself.

There was nothing left to say to her then but thank you; so they did, and Noshkwa watched as one by one they jumped out of sight down the well. When they were all gathered within they looked up and saw her round face smiling down at them.

"Remember, the road is dangerous! From the Whole, to the Whole, children," she said, and was gone.

There was an oval opening in the base of the shallow well that was tall enough for Slukee and Booj to walk through. Due to her height and her pack, Drallah had to creep on her belly, but Elwood was able to go on his hands and knees. The little granite tunnel was clear and dry, and it ended inside an ancient stone-lined ditch. Ten feet wide and as many feet deep, the ditch was overarched with beech branches, poison ivy vines, and occasionally a fallen tree trunk, but there was little debris within its walls. Every now and then there were worn steps climbing up to ground level, and small openings that led to other wells.

The friends set out along this sunken road, within which they were as hidden from sight as in a tunnel underground. They went quietly all the same, for the swath of poison ivy on either side of the ditch was not broad, and yugs were not the only people in Oldotok they wanted to avoid.

The ditch was also a creature haven and highway, as they could see by many tracks and signs. Shortly before dark they saw an inquisitive fox observing them pass by the mouth of her den, a sharp red face with glinty eyes peering out from a crack in the wall. A little later, they saw a shadowy shape disappear with a leap over the ditch's edge as they approached. "Bobcat," said Drallah, kneeling and pointing at a round paw print in a patch of leaf mold.

As the last of the dusk-light leaked away they halted. A fire was out of the question, so they wrapped up tight against the cold and munched their dinner in the dark. Though Slukee and Booj were naturally watchful—one or both would be roused even from sleep if so much as an opossum approached the camp—as an extra precaution Elwood and Drallah took turns at watch through the night. The hours of darkness passed quietly, though, and when the sun returned in the morning they had yet to hear or see any sign of the yugs they knew were not far away.

There had been a frost, and as the warm orange light slanted down into the ditch it found innumerable points of rime to sparkle upon and melt. Everything was lovely and still, and they hardly thought of the danger that lay all around them. But just as they were hoisting their packs onto their backs, a deep baying sounded from somewhere close by in the wood to the south, a call like the howl of some evil hound.

"What's that?" cried Elwood, terrified.

"A horn," exclaimed Booj, hopping with fright.

Another sounded in the north and was answered by several more, each calling from a different direction.

Booj shot into the air and up through the branches overhead. Tensed to move, the others waited and listened. The horns ceased. Drallah climbed a stair in the southern wall and cautiously looked over the edge of the ditch. Nothing moved in the trees immediately around them. Minutes passed. Then she saw something.

"Fire!" she whispered, sighting a black cloud of smoke rising through the trees to the southeast.

The raven returned from the direction of the smoke, whizzing back toward them between the walls of the ditch. "They're burning the wood, they're burning the ivy! They're all along both sides of the ditch!" he croaked, lighting on top of Drallah's pack.

"I know, I know! They must think Ginnich is down here; they're trying to smoke him out into the open. How is it that way?" she asked, pointing along the ditch to the northwest.

"Not so many fires yet. If we hurry!"

Without any more deliberation they set off at a cautious jog, their moccasins and paws barely making a sound on the stones. They could all smell the burning now. Booj flew ahead under cover of the tunnel-like ditch to scout the progress of the fires, and to see how far they had yet to go before they reached the reservoir Noshkwa had described.

Blown on the western wind, trails of black smoke began to appear overhead. Harsh, dreadful shouts in the trees beyond the ditch reached their ears, and the crackle of flames devouring wood. Forsaking caution for haste, in unison they broke into a wild run.

Elwood's stamina, though much increased in recent weeks, was not yet nearly as great as Drallah's, and after they had run a mile he was forced to stop and catch his breath. While he did, Drallah decided to get a look at what was going on in the woods. Since there were no stairs at hand she leapt, caught at the top of the southern wall, and hauled herself up. Crouching at the edge of the ditch she could see that, though they had left several fires behind, they were approaching more. There were no yugs in sight, but she knew they had placed themselves some distance back from the ivy and the fires all along both sides of the ditch, waiting and watching for whoever might be within to try to escape. She could well hear what sounded like a large mob of them whooping and hollering as they fed the flames not too far off. She could not see Booj anywhere.

As Drallah dropped back down into the ditch the wind shifted to the south. A shriek of pain rose up amidst the yugs' din, hung frightfully in the air for a moment, then faded and died.

"One got caught in the smoke," said Drallah. "It carries the burning ivy's poison; it's a good thing for us that we're down here, and smoke rises. Are you ready to move again?"

Still gasping, Elwood nodded.

On they ran. The western wind returned. They left the shouts of the yugs behind, but after running a little farther heard more. Here were massed a greater number, it seemed, and the tumult of so many ugly voices raised at once was terrifying. A cloud of black smoke blew overhead, darkening the ditch. There was a deep roar that was not that of the wind. Through the acrid reek they saw red flames licking trees along the top of the wall to their right. Down through the burning branches and ivy plunged Booj, turning sharply to glide past Drallah.

"Hurry; the reservoir is just ahead," he cried.

"Is it on fire?"

"Not yet!"

"But the yugs are sure to have surrounded it," she said, grasping the hilt of the long knife at her side as she ran.

With a crash the top of a young beech consumed by flames fell crosswise to the bottom of the ditch, almost at their feet. Elwood thought they were trapped, but then saw there was space enough between the fiery branches and the wall for him and Slukee to slip past. Drallah was long-legged enough to leap over it, and Booj simply flew. As they ran on, more burning wood and vine fell into the ditch around them.

"Keep away from the smoke if you can," cried Drallah.

In a hundred more yards they came to a place where the fire seemed to have burned itself out: the trees overhead were charred and smoking, but there were no flames to be seen. They halted, and Drallah and Elwood hastily strung their bows. When this was done they proceeded warily, eyeing the top of the ditch on either side as they went.

"You can see the end from here," croaked Booj. "There's ivy all around the reservoir, but cover beyond it—"

"For an ambush," finished Drallah. She and Elwood each drew an arrow from their quivers. With Drallah leading, they all approached the ditch's mouth.

Upon reaching it, Drallah looked out and saw that the old reservoir was a wide, deep bowl overgrown with trees and poison ivy. Around it stood a crumbling wall of stone, and through the branches she could see a half-ruined flight of stairs on the southern side that climbed to the top. The wall prevented her from seeing what lay beyond.

"I'm going to climb up," she whispered. "Wait for me by that oak at the bottom of the stairs. Now come on, and stick to the wall."

Glancing apprehensively at its rim some thirty feet above their heads, the companions hurried along the edge of the reservoir. They reached the oak tree, and there Elwood and Slukee, both of them panting, crouched and waited. The Winharn girl went swiftly and silently to the stairs, the raven perching tensely on her pack. Lightly they ascended, and when they neared the top Drallah got down and crept the rest of the way, Booj hopping up from step to step beside her.

Slowly the girl and the raven raised their heads just enough to look over the wall. They discovered the reservoir stood atop a long slope, upon which grew a stand of older oaks. Poison ivy was everywhere, and they saw no yugs. The slope ran down to a trickling streambed winding generally east and west, and on the other side the land sloped upward once again. A second flight of stairs descended the outside of the wall opposite the one they had climbed up.

"Where are they?" whispered Drallah. "Why aren't they burning the woods here?"

Still seeing nothing, they turned in the direction they had come from. The wind was blowing billows of smoke to the east, and they could see the top of a great pocket of flames in the woods not a quarter of a mile away. In places they thought they could see figures moving, but the view was too obscured by smoke to be certain. They looked again at the slopes below.

"I see nothing in the way," rasped Booj doubtfully.

"I don't believe it either, but it's no use waiting until we *do*," said Drallah, waving a signal to Elwood and Slukee.

The boy and the dog clambered up the crumbling stairs. "What do you see?" asked Elwood.

"Nothing," repeated Booj.

They climbed over the wall, descended the reservoir's outer stairs, and hurried down the slope. They did not dare take time to conceal their tracks, but made their way westward along the muddy streambed as quickly and cautiously as they could.

After the concealing shelter of the ditch they felt terribly exposed. As they jogged along, Elwood could not refrain from looking over his shoulder again and again. There was no sign of pursuit though, and for several elated moments he thought they had escaped the trap. But just as it occurred to him that there did not seem to be any more poison ivy around, a horn-blast called out from somewhere up the left-hand slope. Turning toward the sound, Elwood saw an ancient pasture-wall of piled stone along the slope's summit. A row of green faces was looking down over the wall at them.

The yugs jumped over the stones and charged, whooping and waving javelins festooned with red rags. Their hairless skin was a vegetal green; their bulging, red-irised eyes rolled in their sockets; their faces were grotesquely humanlike. Though they were bow-legged and hunchbacked, the yugs moved with maniacal swiftness.

At the sound of the horn the friends sprang forward with a desperate burst of speed, clods of mud flying from under their moccasins and paws. Booj flapped and darted about, begging them to run faster still. Drallah and Slukee could have, but they would not leave Elwood behind. Yet even though he was not as fast as they, for a boy his age he was a fleet runner, and the companions passed the cut off moments before the yugs did. The green soldiers fell in line behind them along the streambed, the horn blower blowing almost merrily.

For one long minute it seemed they would be caught right there. While their quarry had already run much and were burdened with packs, the yugs were fresh and carried only their weapons. However, once they lost the momentum given them by their charge down the slope, most of the yugs began to trail behind. Only the swiftest two remained in close pursuit, and ecstatic yells turned to cries of frustration.

Growing more and more exhausted, Elwood began to slow. The other three held back with him, and the distance between the companions and the two lead yugs narrowed.

"Keep going," Drallah ordered the others. Slowing a little, she allowed the yugs to gain on her. When they were just a few steps behind she suddenly stopped, wheeled around, and with a sweeping two-handed swing of her bow struck the foremost yug on the ear just below his iron cap. The blow connected with a sharp *crack*, and the yug fell stunned and senseless in the mud.

The second yug rushed up and attempted to knock Drallah down with the blunt end of his javelin. As she deflected it, Booj flew into the fight, beating his wings in the yug's face. Drallah dealt another sweeping blow, and the yug dropped to the trickling streambed. Seeing what happened to their fellows, the yugs who had trailed behind howled and drove their bowed legs harder, the horn blower sounding a note of urgency.

The girl and the raven quickly caught up with Elwood and Slukee, who had all but stopped to watch the fight. "Go on! Go on!" cried Drallah. The yugs were beginning to close in once again.

The slopes on either side leveled, and the streambed turned south. They came to a place where the little watercourse was lost under a windrow of giant trees. Some time earlier a storm out of the east had blown them down, and the great boles lay across their path.

"We won't find a better place to face them," said Drallah, springing atop one of the fallen boles and drawing an arrow from her quiver. Elwood and Slukee climbed up after her, and Booj lit on an upthrust branch at her side.

"But—can we beat that many?" said Elwood, swallowing hard amidst gasps for breath.

"Better to try here than on level ground," said Drallah, talking fast. "I don't know this country. Without a lead we can't lose them, and you're too tired to run. But listen: did you see how that yug used the blunt of his javelin? Remember what Ginnich said? Their orders are to take prisoners, not kill."

Elwood thought to tell her it would amount to the same thing, but the yugs were drawing close, and in a moment they would have a clear shot at them through the trees. As they waited with feet planted and arrows ready, they saw that not far behind the approaching yugs, clouds of smoke were rising over the woods.

"You take the ones in the middle, I'll take the ones at the front. When they reach us, fall back to the next tree and get another shot off as they climb up. Then run!" said Drallah, her bow creaking as she drew back her arrow and took aim.

Slukee barked a sharp warning. A second group was overtaking the first, racing toward them from the northeast: five more yugs and a tall human, the latter outstripping the others with long strides. On his shoulders was a gray cloak that flowed out behind him as he ran, and in his hand was a bright sword. His pale features strained toward them, ferocious and hard, the eyes overshadowed both by a heavy brow and the skull of a big reptile he wore on his head.

Recognizing the man the yugs called Vank-mul by Ginnich's description, Elwood gasped.

"I see him!" cried Drallah. Her bow twanged. There was a shriek, and the yug at the head of the first group fell on his face. "These are near enough; shoot them first."

Elwood drew and released, but the arrow went wild. Drallah shot another arrow, and another yug fell. Trying to hide behind each other from Drallah's deadly aim, the yugs jostled together as they ran, slowing their approach. Out of the corner of her eye Drallah saw that at least a dozen more yugs were answering the horn's summons, running through the trees from the east. Elwood let a second arrow fly, and a yug—though not the one he had been aiming for— stumbled and fell with it stuck in his leg.

Vank-mul the Graycloak had almost overtaken the first group of yugs. There was only time for one more arrow, or perhaps two, before they reached the companions. Drallah sent one glancing harmlessly off an iron cap, and Elwood's flew wide. As Elwood fumbled in his quiver for another, Drallah set a fourth to the string and drew it back, taking aim at the green throat of the nearest yug.

As she did, a sudden wind came tearing through the woods from the north, shaking the trees and nearly sweeping them off the dead trunk. Upon it was driven a great cloud of thick black smoke from the burning. Turning their heads in wonder, the yugs were seized with panic when they saw it. The first of them broke against the fallen tree and fled madly to either side, their quarry forgotten. The dense black cloud came on, gushing through the woods like a giant amorphous beast of prey. It caught the second group of yugs in its midst. Their cries ceased the moment the smoke obscured them from view. The yugs approaching from the east quailed, turned, and ran back the way they had come.

Not heeding the poison cloud, Vank-mul pressed on for the windrow. Drallah could see his eyes now, and there was murder in them. She took aim, hesitated, then let her arrow fly just as he was overtaken by the smoke and she could see him no more. Not waiting to learn whether she had hit the Graycloak general or not, she grabbed Elwood by the shoulder.

"Come on," she shouted. But he did not hear her, or feel her hand, transfixed as he was by what he saw: the figure of a warrior formed of smoke, and something more than smoke, towering above the black cloud's peak. Her eyes burned with green fire as she searched the earth below, stooping to smite the yugs with the tall spear she grasped in her hands.

"Granashon!" Elwood cried. The wind ceased as suddenly as it began. The smoke-cloud halted, hanging in the air just before the fallen tree they stood upon.

Drallah heard a booming cough amidst the smoke. "Come on," she repeated, dragging Elwood from where he stood. With a start he looked around him, and then back up into the smoke. The warrior was gone.

He stumbled back down to the ground with the others. Hastily the companions extricated themselves from the windrow, and ran west.

TUTHWOY GLIM
AND KWOG NIKWOG

While the raven kept watch from a branch high above, the boy, the girl, and the dog had hidden themselves in a hollow oak tree for a brief rest. It was early in the afternoon; they were a short distance north of the road, and about three miles west of the place where they had nearly been caught by Vank-mul and his yugs. Though Elwood's legs were like lead from running half the day, for the moment he hardly noticed. His thoughts were consumed by the towering shape in the smoke cloud.

"Drallah, didn't you see her?" he asked. "She was so tall...."

Filled with wonder and joy she replied, "No. But I could feel she was there the moment I saw that terrible cloud of smoke."

"I wish I knew why she can't tell us where to find her," said Elwood. "I mean, if she can save us from yugs, and she can give us visions, why can't Granashon just tell us where she is?"

"I don't know. But I'm sure the Nohar is doing everything she can."

"She was right there in front of us! Why didn't she just—"

"Elwood, listen. Rest while you can. We move again soon."

Guessing she had not killed him with her arrow, and certain that, being human, he was not killed by the smoke-borne poison ivy either, Drallah knew they must assume Vank-mul had gathered his yugs and was on their trail. Though it was an awful risk to stop at all, they had no choice: Elwood would collapse otherwise. She wondered how long he could go on without a real rest.

After a few minutes they set out again, following a line parallel to the road through a somber oak wood. Elwood's exhausted trudging set a painfully slow pace. As he was stepping over an old stone pasture-wall that lay across their path, he stumbled and nearly fell. Once he regained his balance he sat down heavily and rested his head in his hands.

"I'm sorry," he mumbled. "Can't we stop just a while? I can't go on."

"Not yet!" said Drallah, turning to haul him back to his feet.

Just as she was doing so, a woogan stepped out from behind an oak tree only a few feet from where they had stopped. "Hello," he said in Wohmog. "Are you pursued?"

Jumping to his feet again, Elwood studied him. The woogan was slightly under four feet tall, above the average for that race. His skin was dusky with a hint of ruddiness similar to the Winharn, but tougher in appearance, like soft leather. He had large hazel eyes, and his big nose was bent like an eagle's beak. He wore a roughly conical hat of faded sackcloth, a long tunic of the same material, and a rust-red buckskin jacket. At his side was a sword in a stained old leather scabbard, and across his back an unstrung bow. He was holding out his open empty hands in a gesture of peace.

Drallah looked at him warily. Like humans, not all woogans were to be trusted, at least not all those met in the woods of Oldotok. The fact that he had already perceived they were on the run, and so probably had been watching them for some time, made her even more suspicious of the stranger.

"Hello," she answered, no trace of friendliness in her tone. "We have been attacked by yugs, yes. I believe they are still on our trail."

He frowned and looked into the trees to the east. "How far

behind?" he asked. Unlike the steady pace of typical Winharn speech, the woogan's words skipped off his tongue somewhat unpredictably, like flat stones off the rippling surface of a lake.

"I'm not certain—half the morning, at most."

His frown deepened. "And what could bring young ones to such a place at such a time?" he said, half bemused, half scolding. "But I am not alone: my friend and I feared you might be alarmed if we both showed ourselves at once." The woogan then whistled a high, chirruping birdcall.

"We do not have time to stay and meet your friend," said Drallah, her hand moving to the hilt of her knife.

From behind another tree a little distance off in the wood, a man appeared and strode toward them. His frame was long and lank, and he was dressed and equipped much like the woogan. He did not wear a hat, though, and his unkempt brown hair was barely long enough to cover his ears. His weathered clean-shaven face was pale beneath a blush of health.

"This is Tuthwoy Glim, and I am Kwog NiKwog," said the woogan with a bow of the head as the man walked up to them.

Drallah's eyes narrowed. "Glim? That's a Ringish name," she said, taking a step to put herself between the two strangers and Elwood.

"That's right, it is that," said Tuthwoy Glim affably. "Though you won't find me furthering those wrongs that commenced long ago, if that's what you're thinking. I regret the connection—but you'll agree, I'd naught to do with its making." Then he smiled a kindly, disarming smile, and squatted down. "Ho, pup!" he said softly, holding out an open hand to the dog. "Ho, wush!"

Slukee trotted over, sniffed him here and there, and began to wiggle and wag in circles around Tuthwoy Glim, who chuckled and patted her. Elwood watched his dog and the man fawn over each other, then gave Drallah a questioning look. She shrugged.

"I am Drallah Wehr; this is Elwood Pitch, and Booj, and she is Slukee."

"The *grku* are on their trail, Glim," said Kwog NiKwog. "She thinks at most only half the morning behind."

"And I see the boy is weary. Devils—to waylay and hunt children," muttered Glim angrily. "How many?" he asked Drallah.

"I don't know," she answered curtly. "However many, you see we can't linger. Let's go, Elwood. Come on, Slukee."

The man and the woogan looked at one another for a moment. "We cannot leave you to fend for yourselves," said Glim. "And as NiKwog and I have some experience of yugs, it seems to me fine and propitious that we've met. You're trying to make your way back home to Winnitok?"

"That's kind of you," said Drallah, ignoring the question, "but we don't want help."

Booj murmured to himself, a little *ragh-agh-agh* sound in his throat. Slukee moved over to continue her circular dance around NiKwog. Elwood stared at the ground, where he longed to sit.

"But you see that you need it?" said the woogan, kindly slapping Slukee's flank. "And you see that we're not the sort to leave young ones to a bad end."

Elwood gave in to his longing and plunked down on the ground with a groan. In Winnitoke he said, "Drallah, I think can we trust them."

The Winharn girl looked at him and gritted her teeth. Then she turned her head to look back through the wood in the direction from which they had come. "We are traveling—west," she said.

The man and the woogan's faces showed their surprise. "I thought you were driven this way by the *grku*, not that you chose it yourselves," said NiKwog. "But I can see you don't want to say where you're heading. You don't have to, Drallah Wehr. Wherever it is, things are far safer on the other side of Imwa, which you must cross if you mean to go any distance into the west. Let us guide you to a crossing."

Drallah considered. She knew bandits sometimes put on masks of kindness, gaining their victims' trust in order to have an easier time murdering and robbing them later on. And Tuthwoy Glim was Ringish: tales of good deeds done by Ringishmen were rare. But why, she thought, did he use a Ringish name if his intentions were wicked? Would a false Lindilish name not suit the purpose better? And if the man and the woogan did mean them harm, would her denying their help stop them attempting it? And what chance had they of escaping Vank-mul by themselves, with Elwood unable to go on? They really had no choice, she reckoned. Putting guarded trust in these strangers was less perilous than trying to lose or outrun Vank-mul on their own.

"We will accept your help, and our thanks to you," she said. Then she put her hands on her hips and drew herself up proudly. "But if you are false, I warn you: we are not helpless. There are many yugs back that way who trail us no more."

"You are wise to be cautious, Drallah Wehr," said the woogan, plainly approving of her attitude.

"We'd never harm you; but showing bests saying, so we won't try to convince you with more words," said Tuthwoy Glim. "Now. Young Pitch, will you suffer me to carry you?"

Exhausted and relieved, Elwood simply nodded and took off his pack. Without any further discussion, the lank man picked the boy up and cradled him in his arms. Drallah threw Elwood's gear over her shoulder, and they were off. Glim's long legs setting the pace, they went in the same direction the four friends had been walking, always keeping plenty of trees between them and the road off to their left.

Though Booj was reluctant to leave his companions alone with their new guides, at the same time he was anxious to learn whether Vank-mul was on their trail or not. He fretted over it for a mile or so, then rasped a word in Drallah's ear, spread his wings, and took flight.

"Remember, they've seen you with us," she called after him.

"Tell me," NiKwog said to Drallah in a low voice, trotting in order to match her and his friend's long strides. "Do you come from the burning?"

"Yes."

"Was it the *grku* set the fires?"

"Yes—a trap."

"For the trappers and the trapped! There's a lot of poison ivy over that way . . . were you traveling the old ditch?"

Seeing no point in denying it, Drallah told him they were. "You know this country well," she said.

"I've spent my life here as a scout and a hunter. Here, and in other lands."

"Where is your home?"

"Anywhere there are woods," he said with a wave of his muscular little arms. "But I was born in the Mossheads, in Buru Vale on Mount Tonnetulk." After a moment's reflection he said, "It's a great shame the old ditch is secret and safe no more. But it could not remain so, with so many wicked folk come to stay."

Then the woogan asked Drallah about the trap, and what befell them, and she told the tale in full from when they first heard the yugs' hunting horns to their narrow escape from Vank-mul. She chose not to tell them of the magical nature of the cloud, or of Elwood's vision of Granashon in it. When she finished, Glim looked down at the boy in his arms with a furrowed brow. "These Graycloaks, they have more woodcraft than any yug," he said after a little.

"What do you know of them?" asked Drallah earnestly.

"Not as much as I would," answered Glim. "But theirs is Ringish blood, that's certain, and they all wear gray cloaks like the conquerors of old. They come up from far, far south-away—so NiKwog and I believe. Many of my people went to the distant south-lands after the wars. There's talk of a new leader among the Ringish of the south; a man called Egode Vallow. They say he's a sorcerer, and that he traded the heart in his chest for great power. Mayhap this Vallow sent the Graycloaks, but to what purpose I don't know.

"You've seen they ally with yugs. I've never known green-folk so clever in the woods as these; that's human learning, I'll warrant. We were obliged to skirmish with a band of yugs the day before yester, five leagues north-away, and one of these Graycloaks was there. They were wilier fighters than yugs are as a rule, and he their master was doughty all right—but no more." This last statement was made in a tone that somehow combined respect and moral indignation, as well as deep melancholy. "Bad men," he concluded, shaking his head.

"What has brought you here now?" said Drallah.

"We serve the House of Uginuptch as scouts," said NiKwog. "The woogans of Mount Kulenumpt, and the Mosshead Mountains in general, are alarmed by these yuggish doings, and want news."

"Well, you can tell them this," said Drallah, at last sure of the strangers. "The Graycloaks are gathering a horde of yugs to invade Winnitok."

"Winnitok? How do you know? Where did you learn it?" they asked, and Drallah told them of Ginnich Taw, how the Graycloaks held him prisoner and told him of their plans.

"What of the Dread of Granashon, then?" said Glim. "It's true that it's failed?"

"It's true."

"These Graycloaks," said NiKwog, "these masters of the *grku*—I think they would do much to keep news of this horde from travel-ing beyond Oldotok."

* * *

When Booj had left them a few minutes earlier, he ascended just above the treetops and began zigzagging his way eastward, passing back and forth across their trail. Off to the east and south he could see that a line of smoke miles long still fouled the otherwise clear sky. Carefully he searched the woods with his sharp eyes, and it was not long before he saw what he had expected, and feared: down in the trees below, dark figures were running.

He banked off to the right and flew in a long curve around behind them. When he caught them up, he saw through the branches that they were not yugs, but five Graycloaks running like wolves. At their head was Vank-mul. As Booj recognized him, the man, sensing eyes upon him, suddenly turned and looked up through the treetops. His face was growing as red as a cardinal's feathers with poison ivy rash. He saw the raven hovering overhead, and with a cry to the other four stopped, pointing at Booj. A volley of arrows tore through the air around him as the raven shot away westward.

Like an arrow himself, Booj shot back to his bobbing perch atop Drallah's pack. "Make haste!" he cried as he returned. "Vank-mul and four others with bows follow fast."

They began to run. Glim led, still cradling Elwood before him as he would a big rag doll. Slukee kept pace close beside them. Drallah and Booj followed, then NiKwog. Though the woogan's legs were much shorter than the others', they were powerful, propelling him forward with long leaping bounds. They ran until they reached the edge of a steep-banked gully a little more than ten feet deep. There they paused and caught their breath.

"We might await them there, on the other side," said NiKwog, studying the trees across the gully. "And set on them when they're below, climbing up."

Glim shook his head. "They can read the trail; they've seen our prints have joined their quarry's. They'll be expecting an ambush for certain."

"Let them! Then they won't follow our trail down into this gully. Two bows above with cover matches five below without."

"Three bows," exclaimed Drallah.

"Four," put in Elwood, standing and stretching on the spot where Glim had set him down.

Glim and NiKwog both grimaced. "I won't have children in the fray," said the lank Ringishman. "And 'specially when it's other humans to be fought."

Drallah drew herself up defiantly. "I am hardly a child anymore; I am nearly a woman. And besides: I've already killed yugs to defend our lives. I've dispelled wigs summoned from Wuth, and thrown nahrwucks to the bottom of Rosodruim. Should I do nothing while humans try to catch us, and probably kill us?"

The man and the woogan stared at her. Then NiKwog grinned and said, "I would like to hear about the nahrwucks and the wigs; but first, this tale." With that he plunged down into the gully. The rest followed, and they all climbed up the other side.

"You, at least, young Elwood, and Slukee and Booj as well, will keep out of the fight," said Glim when they reached the top. He led them to a fallen, rotting, moss-covered tree trunk some distance beyond the gully, where they could lie hidden on its western side. "But string your bow; mayhap you'll need it," he told the boy, and hurried back to where Drallah and NiKwog were choosing thick-boled oaks at the gully's edge to hide behind. Glim chose another tree a little to the north, where the gully bent eastward. The bend allowed him a clear view of the area where their trail crossed the gully bottom. Once they found their places, there was nothing to do but string their bows, ready their arrows, and wait.

"Keep your head down, or you'll give away the ambush," rasped Booj to Elwood. The boy was lying propped on one elbow, his head raised just enough for him to see over the decaying tree trunk. He ducked back down.

"Do you think we'll hear them coming?" he asked.

"Not if you're talking we won't," said Booj.

Elwood gripped his bow tighter, held his tongue, and listened. Except for the wind's fitful stirrings among the thick fall of leaves, the woods were silent. He tried to calm his thoughts. His legs still ached. He was famished, but even if he dared dig something to eat out of his pack, he was far too anxious and afraid to be able to get it down. He asked himself a dozen questions about Granashon he could not answer. His thoughts turned uncomfortably to his family: Elwood would not want his mother to see him now, lying in the woods awaiting bloody strife.

Noticing the light beginning to fail, he realized it would soon be night. He began picking a patch of moss off the old fallen tree. *What's taking them so long?* he wondered to himself. *Have they given up?* But he knew they had not.

Slukee heard it first. Lying on her belly by Elwood's side, suddenly she pricked up her ears and pointed her nose east. Soon Booj heard it too, and then Elwood: a sound of men running through dry, dead leaves. It drew nearer and grew louder, then abruptly ceased. Elwood wished he could raise himself up to see where their pursuers had halted, just enough to see what they were doing, but knew he must not. He held his breath and waited for the twanging of bowstrings and the cries of the wounded to begin, his knuckles white on the grip of his bow.

With her back pressed against the tree's western side Drallah could not see Vank-mul and his men, but she knew by the sound they had halted at the edge of the gully. *They're reading the signs,* she thought. *They know we're here.* Her heart was beating faster than she liked. She looked over to her right at NiKwog, who was also standing with his back against his tree, arrow set to bowstring. His expression was calm, and he gave her a comradely nod as their eyes met.

Then they both heard one of the men speak quietly to the others, followed by two pairs of footsteps moving away in opposite directions along the top of the gully. Drallah pressed closer to the tree: if the men went far enough in either direction, they would be able to see her and NiKwog. She was sorely tempted to get an arrow off then, before they were spotted, but restrained herself. Their plan was that Glim's would be the first arrow. Hopefully it would turn attention toward his position, and gain a momentary but critical advantage for NiKwog and Drallah. She waited.

But only for a moment longer: from off behind her and to her right she heard the sharp *fft* of an arrow's swift voyage through the air, and a grunt, and a thud. Even before she heard that last sound—that of a man hitting the ground with Glim's long yellow-feathered arrow in his chest—Drallah was leaning out from behind her tree and taking aim at the Graycloak moving south along the gully. But he too had heard, and dove to the earth as Drallah's bowstring twanged. Her arrow stuck deep in a tree just beyond where the man had been an instant earlier, and which he scrambled behind an instant later. At the same time there was another trio of sounds—*fft, grunt, thud*—as NiKwog loosed an arrow at a third Graycloak, one of three standing together on the opposite bank. Before they could get off another volley, the other two men—Vank-mul one of them—slipped out of sight behind an oak that split into two tall trees a few feet above the ground.

It was silent again. Elwood and Booj peeked over the top of the fallen tree. They saw that Drallah and NiKwog were unhurt, and were themselves warily peeking out from behind their cover. They could see neither Glim nor Vank-mul and his men, but Booj's far-reaching eyes could just make out the slain where they lay. "Two of the foe are fallen," he rasped as he ducked his glossy black head down again.

"So it's even now, if you don't count us," whispered Elwood.

"We must watch," said the raven. "One of them will try to sneak around behind." Then with a flap of his wings he was in the air, and Elwood and Slukee watched him fly up to a high branch that commanded a view of the woods for some distance all around. There he perched, big and black, motionless except for the turning of his glossy head and the darting of his amber eyes.

With a few gestures NiKwog and Drallah agreed he would attend the two Graycloaks directly across the gully, and she the one hidden a little farther down. She leaned on her left shoulder, her bow in her right hand hanging loose but ready by her side, her head tilted just enough to see with one eye past the tree. As she watched, the man stepped suddenly from his hiding place, and with a *thunk* his arrow struck the wood three inches from her head. She raised her bow, but he had already disappeared again behind another tree. Simultaneously, the other of Vank-mul's remaining men shot out from behind the split oak and ducked under cover again before the woogan could loose an arrow. They continued in this way, fanning out tree by tree, never exposing themselves long enough to give Drallah and NiKwog a target. Vank-mul remained out of sight behind the split oak.

Seeing they would soon be outflanked, NiKwog hissed a warning to Drallah.

"One of these is heading Glim's way—the other's still back of the twin oaks," he whispered.

"They're not taking prisoners anymore, by the way," said Drallah with a glance at the arrow that had pierced the tree by her head. So far she had lost several that day, and would have tried to pull it from the trunk were it not in full view of the men across the gully.

She looked again, but could no longer see her man dodging from tree to tree. "I'll catch this one up before he can get around behind you," she said to NiKwog, and darted off in Elwood's direction. She too moved from tree to tree, and soon turned southward, warily scanning the wood ahead for a glimpse of the Graycloak.

Elwood lay on his side, listening and looking up at Booj. Hearing light steps crunching in the leaves, he peeked over the trunk and saw that Drallah was moving south. Though he could not see it there surrounded by trees, as he watched her the sun dropped behind a low bank of clouds, and the wood grew darker. In the dimness he saw Drallah stop by the lightning-charred remains of an oak and crouch there, waiting.

From over in the direction of the gully came the ring of metal striking metal, the clash of swords. Seeing the woogan still in his place, Elwood knew one of the swordsmen must be Glim. There was a cry, and again silence. The boy bit his lip. "I hope that wasn't Tuthwoy," he whispered to Slukee.

He turned his eyes back to the burned tree where he had last seen Drallah. She was still there, motionless, watching. A part of the charred black wood at her side seemed to move slightly. Looking up, Elwood saw that Booj had left his perch, and realized he must have flown down to the girl.

He wondered what they would do when night fell. How would they find each other in the dark without betraying where they were to these men who wanted to kill them? He imagined him and Slukee running blindly through the woods, losing Drallah, losing Booj. He shuddered, and thought of Granashon. Then, casting about with his eyes to gauge how much light was left, Elwood glimpsed a movement in the shadows to Drallah's right. Squinting, he made out the form of a gray-cloaked man. He had crossed the gully farther down, and made his way back toward them so stealthily that the girl and the raven were unaware he had crept so close. His bow was raised, and he was drawing back an arrow aimed at Drallah.

"To your right!" the boy cried out, his voice squeaking with fear. Surprised by the sound, the man jerked his head toward it. Swiveling, Drallah saw him, and the next instant her arrow pierced his heart. Falling slowly to his knees, he loosed his arrow into the ground before him. His bow dropped from his grip. Trying to raise his arms, it seemed, he cried out a single word in Ringish, then fell backward and lay still.

*　*　*

When Tuthwoy Glim and Kwog NiKwog came cautiously through the trees in the twilight, they found Drallah kneeling on the ground beside the mortally wounded man. Booj, Elwood and Slukee were standing nearby, silent and still. Drallah's head was bowed, her face hidden behind her hair. The man was looking up at her with an expression unfathomable, his eyes wanly shining. A moment later the light left them, and he was dead.

Slowly Drallah rose, the look on her face mirroring the man's a moment before his death. "Such men must never come to Winni-tok," she said in a hoarse voice, and did not speak again for hours.

"That's the five accounted for," said Glim quietly. "I spied the last of them—by his hat, I'd say it was him you met earlier—running off east-away like a hare. All the same, we'll get from this place now."

NiKwog and Glim led them away through the dusk and dark to a deep hollow where they rested the night in safety, lulled by the song of a brook that flowed bubbling and murmuring through it. In the morning they pressed on through the Wanonah Hills, and late in the afternoon began the descent into the Imwa River Valley. The companions had left Oldotok, and passed into the lands beyond.

IN THE MOSSHEADS

ig, faintly luminous snowflakes were drifting gently down
to earth. The sun was sinking beyond the clouds. The companions and their guides were camped upon the knee of Mount
Kulenumpt, one of the sprawling round-peaked mountains called
the Mossheads that loomed over all the western rim of the Imwa
Valley. Their camp was a travelers' log lean-to at the bottom of a
cliff not far from the road. It was the only fairly commodious shelter to be had for miles, and so they had halted the day's march a
while before night began to fall. The six travelers were warming
themselves at a fire they had built just under the lean-to roof's edge,
leaving ample room within for all to sit or recline. The darkening
view was of the south: far below to the left was a woody dell like a
drained brown cup, with a dribble of dark drink still pooled in the
bottom; far, far below and beyond the dell could be seen a stretch
of the silvery gray Imwa River flowing through the Valley; rising up
farther and away to their right were the wild eastern slopes of Mount
Kulenumpt.

In the several days following the fight with Vank-mul and his
men, the four friends' tentative trust in the guidance and company
of Tuthwoy Glim and Kwog NiKwog had grown into friendship.
Despite that, or rather because of it, they had not told the man and
the woogan their ultimate goal, knowing that if they did, the scouts—

fearing for their young friends' lives—would try to stop them from going to Migdowsh. So Drallah simply told them she and Elwood had an urgent errand to do west of the Mosshead Mountains, an errand they could not, for the time being, reveal. Of Elwood's origin they said only that it was closely tied to their errand. Since the two scouts had decided to bear news of the gathering war clouds to their employers on Mount Kulenumpt in the Mosshead range without delay, for a while yet their path and that of the companions was the same.

To reach the Mossheads Mountains, NiKwog and Glim had chosen one of a number of narrow roads that crossed the Imwa Valley. The travelers followed it all the way to the Mountains without misadventure, but it was a strange journey. The road wound constantly off its westward course, occasionally even leading back eastward for miles before turning yet again. Sometimes the travelers heard the tromping feet of other walkers following close behind, but looking over their shoulders saw no one there. At other times they heard distant chanting in the woods, but whenever they stopped to listen closely, it was silenced. Here and there throughout the Valley the travelers saw great trees with trunks and limbs crazily contorted, as though frozen in the midst of a wild dance. Most disturbing, though, was the beating of a single drum that would begin suddenly and continue for hours. It sounded quite near, but as the travelers marched on the drumming would neither fade nor grow louder, until finally it ceased.

All of this had perpetually aroused the hair on the back of Elwood's neck, and filled him with a peculiar fear. The others had spoken quietly of the People of the Valley, explaining they were spirits with the power to pass back and forth freely between Wuth, the lands of flesh and stone, and other planes of Ehm. They had assured Elwood there was nothing to fear at all, so long as he and Slukee remained with them and did not wander from the road. So the travelers had pressed on through the haunted woods, occasionally sighting vistas of purple, brown, green, and snow-white through gaps in the trees, glimpses of the age-worn mountain vastnesses growing always larger as they moved toward them.

Elwood had become almost accustomed to the strange Valley by the time the travelers reached the Imwa River. While Drallah and Glim retrieved a canoe that the two scouts had hidden under a cover of leaves for their return, the rest looked out across the broad expanse of water to the mountains beyond. The Valley made Elwood feel like he had wandered into yet another world, and he had an idea that there, by the river, they were near the source of the Valley's mysteries. Trying to glimpse those mysteries as they made the crossing, he had clutched the canoe's edge and gazed down into the waters, but saw only the reflection of his own face and the cold sky above.

Outside the lean-to the snowfall was beginning to thicken. Inside, Glim, sitting with his back against the pack he had wedged between himself and the cliff, stretched his lank legs, filled a long-stemmed pipe of clay, and looked out at the snow with an appraising eye.

"This won't amount to much tonight, but we may wade through a fair bit of it before tomorrow's end."

"Not me," croaked Booj. To illustrate what he meant he spread his wings, of which he was very proud.

"You'll be in it anyway," said Drallah. "You never miss a chance to play in new snow." Slukee, pleased to hear her sounding cheerful for a change, wiggled over to where the girl was sitting and stood in her lap.

For a long time after killing the Graycloak, Drallah barely said a word, but in the past day or so she had begun once again to join in the others' talk. The deed of killing the man was always with her, though, darkening her thoughts and moods like a stain. She knew she had only done what she must; she had had no choice, she had been forced to kill or be killed. But for this, for trying to kill her—one of his own kind—and so forcing Drallah to kill him, she bitterly hated the dead man, and that hate was the heart of her trouble.

"Yes, there will be new snow on the Mountain," said NiKwog, spitting a bit of dried venison on a stick to roast over the fire. "We'll have to pick up our feet, and think of soft beds in Nuezer."

"But we'll still get there tomorrow night?" asked Elwood, who had already been thinking of soft beds for days.

"Oh, yes," Glim answered him. "It may slow us, but not enough to keep us from lodging with the Uginuptch tomorrow night."

Staring out into the failing light beyond the flames, Drallah said, "If the House of Uginuptch will aid Winnitok, how many warriors do you think will go?"

"Oh, they will come to help in the fight," said NiKwog. "The woogans of Kulenumpt won't forget their friendship with the peoples of Winnitok, or any other land. Besides, they won't allow the *grku* to have their way. Let me think ... many will wish to go, but they cannot leave the Mountain undefended. It's a guess, but I say two hundred will be sent. And others will come from other Houses too: Wanjutoln, Ulkinuptch, most of the rest. They will send all they can."

"The woogans may reach the yugs before the yugs reach Winnitok," said Glim, puffing on his pipe. "Considering that we don't know when the invaders will be marshaled and ready to move, it's hard saying. And the news may already have reached the Mountains: we weren't the only scouts afoot in Oldotok. We may find Nuezer stirring like a beehive in blossom time."

"And we will go back to Oldotok with them, brother," said NiKwog.

"Yes. We'll capture one of these south-land Ringishmen, these new Graycloaks, and learn something about them. They're no rambling bandits—that's certain."

"I wonder why the yugs have allied with Ringishmen?" said Drallah. "How did humans get the yugs to agree to fight their war?"

"It's a mystery," Glim said. "Mayhap they have something so dear to the yugs they'll soldier for it?"

"But what about the poison ivy?" said NiKwog. "They knew many of their number would be killed, yet they fired the woods around the old ditch anyway. Only *grku* in fear of far worse would risk burning poison ivy. The *grku* are in the power of some fear, or madness."

"True," said Glim. "A yug cares for no other, but his own life is precious enough."

Noticing Elwood irritably pushing the hair back from his forehead, NiKwog asked, "Hair bothering you?"

"Yes—I need to cut it," answered the boy, whose Wohmog had improved much while traveling with the scouts.

"Or I could sew you a cap to keep it up out of your way," said NiKwog. The companions had learned that the little woogan was not only a brilliant scout but also a skilled and resourceful crafter of all kinds of items. To replace some of those they had lost, NiKwog had improvised several excellent arrows for Elwood and Drallah with odds and ends he picked up on the trail as they walked each day. He had improved their packs with adjustments to their straps, as well as additional pockets. In the evenings when there was no other work to be done, he spent his time before sleep carving a set of small wooden pieces for a board game called zarum, which Elwood gathered was something like chess. The amount of minute detail in these amazed the companions, and they loved to watch him at his work: the tiny sharp knife he used seemed to become a part of NiKwog's long clever fingers.

Early on in their journey together he had told the companions, "When I was still young, the Uginuptch sent for me in our home in Buru Vale. She had seen some chairs I had made, and asked me to come and work for her. I did, for a little while. I did not like staying all the year under a roof, and missed the roaming life with Glim. So now we work for her as scouts, but I still turn out the occasional set of tableware, or ceremony dress."

Digging in his pack, NiKwog quickly produced a needle, stout thread, and a square of stiff gray-green cloth. "I carry this for patching holes, but I can get more at Nuezer."

Elwood thanked him, and as they talked the woogan set to work. Before they slept that night, he had fashioned a round cap for the boy. It was just a bit large when first he tried it on, but NiKwog explained that it would be better once he had sewn a thin strip of bark inside the brim, which he did in the morning. Then the cap fit well, and Elwood could keep his forelocks tucked up underneath it, away from his eyes.

The next day the road up the Mountain became steep. The trees on either side of the way were chiefly tall firs, and the earth at their roots was covered with a rich endless carpet of green moss and red needles faintly dusted with snow. Throughout the day the travelers saw many cold shady creeks rushing down the Mountain to join Imwa, many cataracts roaring over ledges of rock. They were eating their midday meal on the bank of one such flow when a chill wind came blowing down from the north, and again a light snow began to fall.

Soon after lunch they came to a long wide shelf in the mountainside, and the road leveled. Portions of the shelf had been cleared, and the flatness of the brown, lately harvested fields allowed the travelers a view of houses, barns, and other structures built into the mountainside. They were comfortable and solid-looking places; their fronts stone, wood, and thatch, their backs the mountain itself. There they met several woogans on the road, and the travelers learned that word of the horde gathering in Oldotok had come to them only as a dark rumor, a shadow of some kind of trouble in lands to the east. They spread the news and hurried on through the flurrying snow.

After passing several more gatherings of farms, NiKwog and Glim led them off the main road and onto a second, leveler way along the edge of one of Kulenumpt's northeastern shoulders. The trees were no longer numerous or tall, and there were vast fields of rough turf and heather. Despite the clouds and snow, the travelers could see herds of deer descending the mountainside as far as a mile away.

The road meandered along, following the shape of the mountain. As afternoon approached evening, the snow began to fall thick and fast, accumulating quickly on the cold ground. The limits of their vision shrank, and soon they could not see much beyond the road immediately before them. Elwood pulled part of his blanket up into a hood over his cap. As he squinted at the falling snow, a pair of figures shorter than him materialized out of it. They stepped nearer, and Elwood saw that they were woogan scouts in blankets and tunics the same green as the moss on the mountainside. They carried short bows, and in their belts were tomahawks with hafts intricately carved and richly painted.

"*Brnnchia Kwgoi, Glmoi,*" called one, thrusting his open right hand toward them. The other woogan made the same gesture and said in Wohmog, "Welcome, all! You have beaten the storm to the door of Nuezer, but not by much."

"The wind of another storm has blown us back, Bwon," answered NiKwog. "A *grkug* war is gathering in the Down Lands; we must see the Uginuptch as soon as she will."

"She is about to hold a council," said the woogan whom NiKwog called Bwon. "There has been word of yet another storm, coming up from Ashawda."

Hearing this, the travelers hurried on to the great stone-faced house of the Uginuptch. Elwood immediately recognized its style as distinctly wooganish, remembering Olguhm's front porch with its many doors, its oval windows, and its placement in the ravine of Engo Creek. Out of the mountainside on the house's left side protruded a giant A-frame of fir trunks, each nearly a hundred feet long. Its outward end was open, and inside four bonfires were burning. By their light many woogans could be seen gathering within.

After they shed their gear, warmed themselves, and had something to drink by a fire in the main house, the travelers joined the gathering in the A-frame hall. Elwood was amazed such little people had made something so large. Hundreds of woogans of all ages were seated on the ground under the giant fir trunks, radiating back toward the mountainside from the fire nearest the hall's open northeastern end. They sat facing a big carved stump, a high chair upholstered in thick moss with steps leading up to the seat, its back to the outer fire. Soon after the travelers arrived and took their places, an aged snowy-haired woogan woman rose from the crowd, slowly mounted the steps of the stump, and sat down. "The Uginuptch," said NiKwog to the companions. All talk ceased.

Bright flame and twilit snow behind her, the head of the House of Uginuptch sat in silence for several moments gazing about the hall at her people. Then she turned to the companions and said in Wohmog, "We bid our guests from Winnitok welcome, and ask their pardon for holding this council in our own tongue. It is important that all in this House hear and understand what is said, and that all speak who wish to. Glim or NiKwog will translate as we talk."

Then, speaking in Ukwchchia, the quick, agile language of the woogans of the central Mossheads, the Uginuptch asked Glim and NiKwog to tell the people their news. NiKwog stood up and did so, while Glim relayed to the companions in Wohmog all that was said. The woogan did not linger over a detailed account of the fight with Vank-mul and his Graycloak bowmen, but quickly related what Drallah had learned from Ginnich Taw of the coming invasion of Winnitok, as well as all the signs of war the scouts and the companions had seen themselves. He also told the gathering that the Dread of Granashon no longer protected Drallah's land, rumor of which had already come to them.

"Our friends to the east are in peril," said the Uginuptch when NiKwog had finished. "What shall we do, my people?"

A woogan nearing the end of his middle years rose and spoke. "Here is the worst news to come up the Mountain since Kutch cursed the Bears of Gumatulk. I say all warriors willing to go must ready themselves and depart immediately. If Oldotok and Winnitok are overrun, all Pahn will follow."

132

Scores called out in agreement, but a young woogan woman stood up and said, "There is trouble both to the east and the west. What of the threat from Ashawda, the purpose this council was called for?"

The Uginuptch bowed her head. "Yes, Yethonnie. For any who have not heard: hunters from Ashawda, humans of the Ashaw people, have come up the Mountain after beaver folk. Three days ago, two of our scouts found a party of them in Shadowy Vale. They were cleaning skins, and already the Ashaws had killed more than is well on one mountain in one year. The scouts demanded to know by what right they hunted so in our land, and the Ashaw hunters answered them it was by command of Ainathuai, the Girl Queen. The scouts bid them leave the remains of the creatures they had wrongfully taken and depart for their own land, but the Ashaws laughed, and mocked them, and refused to go. They said their Queen would take Kulenumpt for Ashawda if the woogans tried to prevent her people hunting there. There was a fight; one of our scouts and an Ashaw were badly hurt.

"I believe Ainathuai's threat is the idle talk of a child," continued the Uginuptch. "The Ashaws and the woogans have been enemies at times in the past, but it has been more than a hundred years since last there was war between us. There is no cause for us to have war again. Regardless, some among the Ashaws hunt unwelcome on the Mountain, and that cannot be."

A tiny and wrinkled woogan sitting with her back against the Uginuptch's chair said something in a frail voice only those immediately around her could hear. While she spoke, Glim told the companions, "That is Wothwing, the Uginuptch's spouse."

Leaning down from her high seat so she could catch her words, the Uginuptch related to the people what her wife had said. "Wothwing asks why the Ashaws hunt like Ringishmen, taking so many creatures at once with no thought of the future. And she says, perhaps it is because the Ashaw people allow their land to be ruled by kings and queens, as the Ringish do."

"If greed rules their hunt," called a woogan from the back of the hall, "why should they not strike rich neighbors?"

The woogan man who had spoken earlier spoke again. "But winter comes, and the Ashaws love their warm pine woods. Who can see them attacking before spring touches the sides of Kulenumpt? We cannot worry about the Ashaws for the moment. It is the yugs ready to cross Lilikit that concern us now."

NiKwog rose to speak again. "If the Ashaws knew of the yugs gathering, maybe they would also send warriors to fight the *grku*. A messenger should go down to Ashawda to tell them what is afoot."

Hearing this translated, Drallah rose and said in Wohmog, "We are going that way. The path my companions and I must take does not lead all the way to the Girl Queen's halls, but we can tell all Ashaws we meet the news of war."

"It is not safe in Ashawda now," said Glim. "Didn't I just tell you what the Uginuptch said?"

"We must go that way nevertheless."

"That would be good, Winhar," said the Uginuptch. "By doing so you will free one more warrior to go down into Oldotok. Or remain here to guard Nuezer; some must stay to defend the Mountain, should that be needed."

"We thank you for coming to the aid of our land," said Drallah, bowing her head.

Glim and NiKwog both regarded the Winharn girl, their faces full of annoyance and worry. "We will not be with you to help if you meet trouble, Drallah Wehr," said Glim as she sat down.

"Ashaws and Winhars have no quarrel."

"Neither did Ashaws and woogans, until three days ago."

It was agreed that the majority of the House's warriors would go down the Mountain as soon as they could gather and prepare, the rest remaining to protect the lands around Nuezer. Immediately the mountainside began to resound with the language of great drums, the ancient system by which the far-flung woogans of the Mossheads exchanged news. The council-gathering dispersed, and NiKwog and Glim showed the companions to a warm dining room in the main house. There they all sat down to a rich and satisfying meal of mysteriously stuffed breads, which they dipped in a thin golden soup. It was Elwood's first wooganish cooking; a tradition, he had been given to understand, that involved strange and wonderful magic. Tasting it, he did not doubt that that was true.

"If you must go to Ashawda, be wary," began Glim after they had eaten in silence a while. "Council is not taken there like it is in this House, or in Winnitok. In Ashawda, one soul rules over all the others. That soul is Ainathuai, daughter of Meituai. She rules the land as a child does her toys—though folk say her cousin has great influence. Her cousin's a witch."

"Well, something's wrong with her," said Elwood, pushing his empty plate and bowl away. "Unless the Ashaw hunters on the Mountain were liars."

"I advise you to avoid people altogether," said NiKwog. "Booj could fly to a house or a village to tell the Ashaws the news, then rejoin you. The risk for him alone would be small, unlike for the rest of you, earthbound in unfriendly country you do not know."

Glim sighed a long, troubled sigh and said, "I do hope one day we'll meet again. And that on that day you'll be able to tell us just *where* it is you have to get to and *why*, and what possible reason you could have for keeping it all from NiKwog and I—your friends."

"We hope so too," said Drallah.

* * *

It was nearly midnight, and Drallah was standing before a high window on the east, just down the darkened corridor from the bedchamber she and Booj had been given for the night. Unable to sleep she had wandered there, and for some time had been staring through the glass panes toward Winnitok. Not taking in the snowflakes swirling just outside the window, she focused instead upon a succession of images passing relentlessly before her imagination's eye. She was afraid for her land, and could not escape thoughts of its fall and ruin. Even now, she thought, Graycloaks might be stalking the woods of Winnitok, every one of their pale fell faces like that of the man she had killed. And even if they and their yug horde could be defeated, driven out again, how long would it take the scars of war, in a land that had never known war, to heal? Drallah thought of her own peace lost since slaying the Graycloak. A part of her longed to weep, but another part would not allow it.

"Can't sleep?" said a soft voice behind her. In stocking feet, Glim stepped silently to the window next to Drallah's. "It's hard for me as well, closing the eyes when there's so much to be done."

Drallah answered with a faint nod, but continued to stare sightlessly out the window. Glim did the same in silence for a time, but finally spoke again. "I believe I know why you've been fretting these past several days, though we only met the day your trouble began. I'd like to say some things about it, if you'll allow."

Drallah gave him permission with another nod, and Glim continued. "I'd wager that all your life your strength—both of limb and of will—have been a wonder to your people, and a cause of great pride. And I'd wager also that even when you were just a little girl you knew you'd be a scout.

"When I was a boy, I thought I'd be a farmer and a hunter, like my parents. Our home was at the foot of Mount Tonnetulk, and it was fair indeed. Ours was one of the richest apple orchards between the Mountains and the River, and just one of our pumpkins would fill a season's worth of pies for tables for miles around. Our place was hard by Buru Vale. Humans were scarce, but we Glims were friendly with our woogan neighbors. It was as bountiful and beautiful a home as a soul could wish for. All my young days, until I was about Elwood's age, I thought I would spend my life there.

"One early autumn day toward dark, at the table having our supper, we saw out the east window that the orchard was afire. We rushed from the house, and into a trap. It was a gang of marauders, and they were Ringishmen. They set the fire. They murdered my parents, two of their own people. Me they spared—to sell, I reckon.

"These Ringish marauders hated us so because they hated woogans, and we lived peacefully among our woogan neighbors. In their eyes we had betrayed our people, and were no better than those they despised. Hatred of all that's not Ringish—that about sums up my people's history.

"While the rest went in and looted the house, one stayed outside to guard me. He thought me too young to try anything bold, and dug in my father's pockets while I stood by weeping. He turned his back on me, and I brained him with a stone. It was easily done: I was overflowing with rage and despair and hatred.

"The rest of the men had found a barrel of my mother's good potent cider in the root cellar. While they enjoyed themselves below, I crept into the house. The cellar stairs were in the kitchen, in the back; they were gained by a heavy trapdoor, which opened upward on stout hinges. It was the only way in or out of the cellar. I closed the trapdoor, pushed a big cupboard over on top of it, and threw more heavy things over that. I made certain it would not be moved.

"I stuffed the kitchen with all the burnables at hand, and set fire to the house. The men cut at the trapdoor with their blades, but they did not have enough time. I dragged the man I'd killed into the house, and moved my mother and father farther away. Then I climbed up on the roof of the barn and watched the burning.

"That was how the woogans found me. They had seen the fires, and came to help. And help they did, though not in the way they expected. They buried my mother and father, and Kwog's mother and father took me in. So I became their son, and Kwog's brother.

"I'm telling you this because I know you're wretched about that skirmish back there in Oldotok, about the man you killed. Not that my tale is any comfort. But I wanted to show you I've some notion of how you feel. I'd never known real hatred before, until that day.

For a time afterward this life was so bitter to me it was almost beyond bearing. Bitter with that same accursed passion that moved the Ringishmen to murder my parents, that moved me to burn down our house with the Ringishmen within. That destroyed my family and home."

"How did you overcome it?"

"I cannot simply say. It happened little by little. I watched the world's things growing and passing, growing and passing all around, like apples on the apple tree. It occurred to me that hatred, though it's a part of the world as well, is different. More like fire, it can spread quickly if it's not minded, and then will go out when there's nothing left to burn. I decided I would mind my hatred.

"A warrior who is true must learn these things some day, Drallah. A pity you're made one so young. But you're wise beyond your years, as they say, and your very trouble these past days proves it."

"My greatest trouble is fear for Winnitok; that what happened to your family will happen to all my land. If that should be, I don't think any store of wisdom will stop me burning with the fire you talk of, as long as I live."

Glim nodded. "And the rest of us, likely. That's the way of it. But if you would deal the best blow, you will not strike in hatred. Good night to you, Drallah."

"And to you."

Glim retired, but Drallah continued to stare out the window, going to bed only after the snowflakes swirling beyond the glass found their way into the pictures in her mind, and finally covered them.

DOWN TO ASHAWDA

The House of Uginuptch was wide awake before dawn. The corridors and halls were alive with busy woogans, all helping the House's warriors prepare to depart for the Down Lands. Once they had risen, breakfasted, and readied themselves for their own journey, the companions went in search of Glim and NiKwog to say farewell. They found the scouts with many others in the enormous low-ceilinged kitchen, portioning out provisions for the warriors.

"We are nearly ready," said NiKwog. "Two hundred and eighteen of us are going down to Oldotok, and many more will join us from the other Mountain Houses. We will pass quickly through the woods by many paths, and harry the *grku* at many points."

"I'm sorry I cannot go with you," said Drallah.

Tying up two packets of provisions and giving them to Elwood and Drallah, Glim said, "Just go and accomplish whatever secret task you must—but on your way back home, stop on the Mountain to tell us about it. If we haven't yet returned, or have come and gone, leave word of yourselves. We'll be anxious for news."

"Here, take this," said NiKwog, drawing a cloth bag from a pocket and handing it to Elwood. Looking inside, the boy saw it was the set of intricately carved zarum pieces the woogan had been working on. "Along your road," he continued, "just on the other side of Kulenumpt, there is a woogan living in a hut of purple stone. His name is Menak. If you find him at home, he should be willing to trade these for a toboggan ride. Last I saw him, he was yearning for a new zarum set."

"Thanks," said Drallah. "That would shorten the way."

"I also have something for you," said Glim, picking up a large bag that had been sitting on the floor next to his trim pack. Taking it, Drallah found two pairs of sturdy-framed, tightly woven snow-shoes inside.

"Thanks," said Elwood, trying one for size. "I've been wondering how we were going to get through the snow."

"There are none for Slukee, but if she follows in your trail, it will be easier for her."

The companions thanked their friends for all they had done, and walking together to a front door of the House, they reluctantly said good-bye. Glim and NiKwog again warned them to take special care in Ashawda, and repeated advice they had already given them a dozen times. At last there was no more to be said. After a final farewell in the cave-like front porch, into which snow had drifted in the night and the rising sun was now pouring, they parted.

Set as it was high up the eastern side of Mount Kulenumpt, the House of Uginuptch looked out upon a wondrous vast prospect. To the north lay a great arm of the mountain the woogans called Gumat-ulk, to the south the one known as Vananumpt. Eastward, Mount Kulenumpt rolled down to the crowded humps of the foothills, and below them lay the long, wide Imwa Valley. As the companions set out, the view was of a new world: the snow had freshly fallen deep and white over all the Mossheads, and the Valley lay out of sight beneath a cold fog. Across the fog shone the new day's sun, the white of the mountainsides absorbing and returning its orange and crimson beams.

The companions were the first to tread the new snow. As Glim suggested, Elwood bade Slukee follow in his and Drallah's tracks, and doing so, the dog's slender legs seldom broke through the packed surface. The snowshoes soon carried them to the buried but recognizable way they had been directed to take: a narrow steep road curving around the Mountain.

It was by far the coldest day Elwood had yet experienced in Ehm, but he was protected by his warm Olguhm blanket and moccasins, as well as a resistance to the elements that had been growing since they began their journey. The labor of the march, though less difficult than it would have been without snowshoes, also helped ward off what harm there was in the bitter breath-taking air. Still, throughout the day his thoughts turned frequently to its end, and the warmth of a crackling campfire. When evening finally came, the companions stopped at a vacant hunter's lodge Booj found not far from the road. The day's walk had brought them around to the northwestern side of the Mountain, and the last of the setting sun shone on their faces as they watched it go down.

The next morning was calm, clear, and not far gone when, passing through a wood of snow-laden pines, the companions came to a cottage of purple-gray stone set back a little from the way. Its roof was covered in a heap of snow, and the many tiny panes of its oval windows were tinted with pale shades of blue, green, and red. From behind the cottage came the regular *whack* of someone chopping wood with a tomahawk.

Following the sound, the four friends walked around to the back of the house, where they found a brawny young woogan adding to an already tall stack of split logs. Despite the morning's cold he wore only slippers, britches, and a sleeveless tunic, and still he looked as though he thought the day too balmy for his taste. Seeing the companions approach, he left his tomahawk sunk halfway through a log (where it had been brought to rest with a single stroke) and extended an open hand to them.

"Welcome, travelers," he said in Wohmog.

"Thank you," replied Drallah, then introduced herself and the others. "Is this Menak's house?"

"It is, and I am Menak. What brings you over Kulenumpt? I heard the drums. Is there more news?"

"We are traveling west down the Mountain," said Drallah. "We left the House of Uginuptch yesterday morning, where warriors were readying to go down to Oldotok."

"Trouble in the Down Lands again," said the woogan, nodding gravely.

"Kwog NiKwog told us you might be able to give us a toboggan ride some way down the Mountain. He gave us a zarum set he carved to trade for it."

Menak brightened momentarily at the mention of the toboggan ride and the zarum set, but then he frowned. "It is a strange time for children to be traveling west unaccompanied," he said, looking at each of the friends in turn. "Why do your families allow it?"

"Our errand is urgent," answered Drallah. "We've come through great danger on our way already, and can take care of ourselves."

"Well—you at least are nearly grown up. You are large, Winhar, but I have a board long enough to carry us. The snow is the kind we call *bnnf;* not ideal for a run down the Mountain, but not bad either. When do you wish to go?"

"As soon as you're able, please," answered Elwood in his improving Wohmog. He offered Menak the bag of zarum pieces.

"Give it to me at the bottom. It is not for the ride down the Mountain that you trade; that is a pleasure. The work I require compensation for is the long climb back up!"

Menak disappeared within his house for a few minutes. When he reemerged, a satchel was slung over his shoulder, and on his head he carried a long toboggan with a curled front. He sat down in the snow and strapped snowshoes onto his feet, then rose and draped himself in a blanket. These simple preparations made, he waved to his passengers.

"It is three miles to the place where the run begins," he said. Without any further remarks Menak started out along the snowy road, one hand balancing the toboggan on top of his head.

As he led them around the Mountain, the last remaining shreds of cloud departed from the sky, and the day achieved the kind of azure and ivory brilliance that can only occur after a heavy snow. Elated, Booj spent the walk rolling in and sliding down the deep drifts, his shining black feathers in stunning contrast with the snow.

After a couple of miles, Menak took them off the little mountain road and onto a path along the edge of a mild descent. This way soon led to the top of a narrow cutting through the trees, a gently sloping road down the Mountain. Here Menak put down the toboggan and sat in the snow. He removed his snowshoes, and Elwood and Drallah did likewise.

"All you have to do is hold on to the grips, and I will do the rest," said Menak. "I will sit in front, and then the dog, and then you, little brother, and then you," he said, nodding to Drallah. "Raven can settle where he likes, so long as he does not perch on the front."

He situated the toboggan at the top of the slope and stood there, legs straddling either side of the board just behind the curled front. Elwood sat down behind him, and Slukee climbed on between the woogan and the boy. Drallah followed, Booj perched in his customary place atop her pack. The humans sat with their legs crossed in front of them, Elwood's wrapped around Slukee, and grasped the rope handles fastened on both sides of the sled.

The smoothly polished toboggan had been skillfully wrought from a single board of some exceedingly tough, flexible wood. All around its edge the board curved slightly upward, and at the curled front, inward, allowing both greater ease of motion and more stability for riders. It was the picture of simple grace, and as fine a conveyance as had ever gone down a hill.

Elwood loved the toboggan the moment he set eyes upon it. He thought of the sled he had shared with his sister, Ellen, and of the long slope above his old neighborhood in the country where all the children flocked whenever it snowed. He began to think of

winter afternoons returning home exhausted and cold from sled-
ding, when his mother would give him hot chocolate. But these
recollections pained him, and he quickly forced his thoughts back
to the present.

"Now hold fast, and don't roll out unless I do," said Menak over
his shoulder. "Don't lean to one side or the other. Just sit straight
and low, and leave the rest to me. Are you ready?"

Grabbing hold of the curled wood at the front, the woogan
pushed them forward. The toboggan passed over the border between
level and decline, and began to slide downhill. With a light step
Menak brought both feet up on the board beneath him, then
dropped into a ready crouch as they gathered speed. In that position he studied the way before them, still grasping the top of the
sled's prow-like front with both hands.

Though the run's curves were gentle, it was far from a straight
way. As they approached the first curve, which was to the right,
Menak threw his weight in that direction. He pushed himself away
from the board with planted feet, and held himself in place with
gripping hands, expertly maneuvering the toboggan so that it did
not fly off the run and into the trees. At times when he deemed their
progress too fast, Menak would thrust a heel into the snow to slow
them down.

But for Menak, too fast was fast indeed. At first their velocity
frightened Elwood, but after they had safely negotiated several tight
spots, he realized they were in very capable hands and began to
enjoy the ride. He looked back and smiled at Drallah, who he could
see was also exhilarated by their swift downhill flight. Just behind
and above her head, Booj, anchored to Drallah's pack by his toes,
swayed like a kite in the breeze.

"My family's house," called out Menak as they sped along,
waving an arm toward distant chimney-smoke rising over snowy
treetops.

As they approached a place where the run was broken by a drop of several feet, Menak admonished them all to hold tight. The toboggan sailed through the air. Booj involuntarily spread wide his wings, for a moment creating the illusion that the raven was bearing a remarkable burden up into the sky. They hit the snow again with a bump, and, with everyone still in their places and the toboggan's stride unbroken, raced on.

Three times during their toboggan ride Menak thrust both his heels into the snow, bringing them to a stop with his great strength. At these points the toboggan run ended, and they had to snowshoe some distance to where the next began. In this way they made swift progress down the Mountain, and late afternoon found Menak and the companions at the bottom of the last run. It was in a vale of ancient hemlocks, a concavity formed by the foot of Mount Kulenumpt and abutting hills where little snow had fallen. From there, a path made its way northward into the trees.

Elwood gave Menak the bag of zarum pieces, and thanked him.

"I'm glad you came," said the woogan. "I'd been wanting to take a run down Kulenumpt in the new snow." Then, gesturing at the path before them, he said, "This leads to the Wanjut Road. That is my way back home, and by it stands the house where I'll lodge tonight. Do you go that way?"

"No," answered Drallah. "We go south and west. I think we will make our own path."

"Whatever path you take in that direction, you must soon enter Ashawda. Be wary as you go! But now, walk with me up to the rim of this vale, and I will show you a line down through the hills you would be wise to follow."

The sun was nearing the western horizon when they stepped out upon a great ledge above the foothills, a promontory commanding an awesome sweep of Ashawda, the land beyond the Mountains. The hills dwindled and disappeared into a vast, flat pine forest, its dark green infused with the orange of the late sun. Here and there they could see where streams flowing down from the heights merged, together becoming rivers that flowed out of sight into the west.

Menak pointed to a long rocky slope that lay below them and said, "Begin there. When you reach the cliff, follow this line," here he pointed south-southeast, "out of the foothills. If your line strays to the west, you'll spend too much time going around impassable ridges and cliffs."

"I see it," said Drallah, studying the terrain along the route.

They gave the woogan their snowshoes, and questioned him about the nearest Ashaw villages. Then with thanks and handclasps they said good-bye.

"May your journey be good! Don't trust the Ashaws," said Menak. Balancing the toboggan on his head with one hand, he turned and walked with a brisk step toward the path to the Wanjut Road.

Since the daylight was all but gone, the companions decided to cast about for a sheltered place to spend the night. They found a suitable hollow, almost a shallow cave, beneath the very ledge where they parted with Menak. Having walked less that day than they were accustomed to, they were not as tired as they would have been otherwise, and stayed a long time awake talking by the light of their fire. After a while the conversation turned to Glim and NiKwog, whom they all sorely missed.

"I wish they could've come with us," said Elwood. "They would've been so much help...."

"If they knew we were going to Migdowsh," said Drallah, as she had more than once before, "they would've tied us up and dragged us back to Winnitok."

"I'm just glad we met them. And that they helped us as much as they did."

Thinking of what Glim had told her of his past the night they spent in Nuezer, Drallah agreed.

* * *

The end of the next day found the companions below the snow-line, but still struggling through the densely forested hills. Though the string of ridges Menak had shown them was easier going than the surrounding country, all the same there were no paths, and moving in a straight line for any distance was impossible. However, between Drallah's woodcraft and Booj's help scouting out the clearest ways forward, by nightfall they had managed to toil almost to the end of the high country that tumbled and rolled down from the Mountains. From their camp in the lee of one of the last hills they saw the sun set on the Mossheads' western faces, and thought with satisfaction of the sunrises they had seen lighting up the other side of the mountain range. Despite the day's slow going, they were making progress.

"Almost down," croaked Booj, returning from a sunset flight high over the neighborhood of their camp. His patience had been tested by his wingless friends' slow descent through the hills, especially after the swift toboggan ride of the previous day.

"We'll walk faster, Booj," said Drallah, "once we get down into the pines."

Before the sun had reached its zenith the following day, their struggling, as well as Booj's reconnoitering, brought them at last to a long downward slope. It was grassy with a scattering of very old hemlocks, broadening as it went and swallowed up finally by the forest of pines. With a last look back at the hills and the Mountains beyond, the companions walked down the long expanse of the slope and were themselves swallowed up among the tall trees.

Beneath them, depending on where one looked or stood, it was shadowy or light, the ground thick with sun-dappled pine needles. A woodpecker was knocking high above. No breezes stirred. Making their own path to the south and west they set out through the forest, the going much easier than it had been—except for the toboggan ride—for many days.

On the second afternoon in the forest, Booj, flying above the treetops with watchful eyes, spotted trails of smoke in the west. Instantly he dove to earth.

"There's a village or a big camp, five miles west and south," he crarked as he dropped onto Drallah's pack.

"Are we passing too near it?" asked the girl.

"A little. We should turn a bit more to the south. But first I'll fly to the village with the news."

"All right. We'll wait for you right here. Hurry! Dark's not far off."

"I'll be quick," he said, flexing his wings.

"And don't trust them," said Elwood. "Don't let them get too close. Call out from high in a tree, then come right back."

"Never fear, never fear," rasped Booj with a wink. Then with a single mighty beat of his wings he was up and away, and with another he was out of sight among the dark green boughs overhead.

"How does he ever find us again?" wondered Elwood. "This forest all looks the same."

"Some student!" cried Drallah, laughing. "Haven't you learned anything?"

They shed their gear and settled down to wait, Elwood and Drallah sitting cross-legged at the foot of a thick-girthed tree. Resting on the pine needles beside them, Slukee took the opportunity to examine the spaces between the pads of her paws, which she kept fastidiously clean. After a while Elwood rose, strung his bow, and began to practice with it. Drallah remained under the tree selecting targets for him.

Once he had hit a number of large close-at-hand marks, Drallah began to choose more difficult ones. "Do you see that mite-gnawed pine?" she said after several misses, pointing at a dead tree some distance off in the shadows of the forest. "Hit that big knot about five feet up the trunk."

Elwood turned and looked at her from under raised brows. "I'll lose the arrow," he objected. Already he had spent more time hunting and retrieving arrows than he had spent actually shooting.

"Try not to."

So Elwood turned back again, squinting at the proposed target. Then he planted his feet, drew back his arrow, and took aim.

"Elbow," muttered Drallah.

Hearing his teacher, Elwood adjusted his arm, took aim once again, and released. The arrow pierced its mark and stood fixed there, quivering. Elwood, beaming with pride, wheeled around to face Drallah.

"Good!" said she. "By far the hardest shot you've made yet."

"Fine shot," remarked a strange, soft voice on Elwood's left-hand. Slukee leapt up from her repose with a growl, and Drallah too sprang to her feet. Turning to see who had come so near unnoticed, Elwood found himself face-to-face with a rusty-furred fox.

Or, taken by surprise as he was, that is what Elwood for the first half-instant believed the creature to be: he had tall ears, a long sharp muzzle, and intelligent green eyes lined with black, the pupils cat-like slits. But then Elwood noticed the creature was standing upright on his hind legs, and was a little taller than him. Also, he was dressed in a jacket that seemed to be woven of pine boughs, and in one of his furry hands he held a short narrow-bladed sword. The boy was face to face not with a fox, he realized, but a truan.

"Who're you?" blurted Elwood. Though there was a slight current of air flowing in the direction from which the fox truan had come, they were standing so close that Elwood was able to catch a whiff of his musky smell. Then he realized the fox truan had intentionally approached them from downwind.

"Never mind that. Who are *you?*"

"Elwood. Elwood Pitch."

"And I am Drallah Wehr," said she, standing beside Elwood. Slukee too took her place beside him, her hackles up and a rumble sounding from deep down in the bottom of her throat.

The fox truan's eyes flashed as he looked down his long muzzle at the dog. Their eyes locked, and Slukee's growl deepened. The truan gave a short, fierce, fang-baring bark. Slukee's growl became a whimper, and she turned her face away.

"What do you want?" asked Drallah, a trace of the awful apprehension she was feeling finding its way into her voice.

Even as she spoke, tall shapes stepped into view from behind a number of the surrounding trees. They approached: a dozen human men armed with spear, tomahawk, sword, and bow. Their faces were striped and dotted with green, black, and red paint.

"What do you want?" repeated Drallah, trying to control her voice. The paint, she knew, signified the men and their people had committed themselves to the rule of war.

"Quiet," said the fox truan softly as a man took the knife from her belt, and another the bow from Elwood's hand. Others snatched up their gear. Commands were barked in a language they knew must be Ashawnk, and in moments four warriors were driving the companions westward at spear-point. The fox truan led them. They moved fast, and soon were far away from the place where the raven, returning, would seek them in vain.

THE GIRL QUEEN

ooj perched upon the highest bough of the tallest pine in the place where he had last seen his friends. Returning there and finding them gone, he had searched the surrounding area. They were nowhere to be found. The forest floor told him nothing: the carpet of pine needles bore little trace of feet, and Booj did not have the skill to read such a faint trail.

If only I had not gone to the Ashaw village, he thought. It had to be done, he knew, but he doubted any good would come of it. When he arrived the villagers had duly gathered to listen to his news, but hearing of the imminent invasion of Winnitok, had shown no concern whatsoever; at least not as far as he could tell. The raven realized he was not an authority on human behavior. He had done the best he could, begging them to send word to their Queen. Then he had sped back across the forest, only to find his friends gone.

Instinct and logic told Booj they were least likely to be heading back northeastward, or to the east at all. Most likely some danger had come to their meeting place, and to avoid it Drallah had led Elwood and Slukee away, probably in the same general direction they were traveling. So he spread his wide black wings, pointed his big beak south-southwest, and took to the air. He flew in zigzags just above the tops of the trees, now and then calling out a hopeful *crark*.

Little did the raven know that earlier, racing high on the wind from the Ashaw village, he had flown almost directly over his friends as they were driven, captive, through the forest far below.

* * *

After being run doggedly for some two miles, Elwood, who had been working twice as hard as his captors in order to keep pace with their long legs, stumbled and fell to the needle-carpeted ground. Instantly the four Ashaw warriors were looming all around him. Haunch pressed into Elwood's shoulder, body crouching low for a fight, Slukee snarled defiantly as they approached. Drallah stood over the boy and the dog, hands on hips.

"We will rest," said the fox truan in his soft voice, stepping in between two of the warriors and looking down at Elwood. The boy sat up and brushed away the pine needles covering his front.

"Where are you taking us?"

The fox truan turned away without answering. Studying him from behind, Elwood saw that, as well as the sword at his side, he bore a short bow and quiver on his back. His pine-bough jacket reached to his knees, and was tied close about his waist with a broad belt. Wide-spreading flaps in the jacket's back freed his bushy white-tipped tail to move as it pleased. Except for their dark fur, his nimble, paw-like feet were bare.

Talking among themselves in their own tongue, the Ashaw warriors withdrew a little, but remained arrayed around their prisoners. Elwood started to speak to Drallah, but she did not respond or even look at him. Realizing she did not mean to talk at all in the hearing of the Ashaws and the fox truan, he resigned himself to silence as well, joining her where she had settled at the base of a tree. She was gazing up into the boughs above with an unconcerned air, as though their predicament was beneath her notice. However, while Drallah seemed to be staring idly at nothing, she was in fact watching anxiously for Booj.

After just a few short minutes the fox truan gave the command,

and the Ashaw warriors and their prisoners were jogging west once again. They soon struck and began to follow a road winding through the forest in that direction. Considering the sure, straight route he had taken to this road without ever a pause to get his bearings, it was plain to Drallah that the fox truan knew the country intimately. Because they were heading west, and considering how Booj had described its location, she guessed they were going to the village the raven had flown off to visit earlier that afternoon. As they ran she speculated on the likelihood of Booj finding them again before dark, in what fashion they might be held overnight, and their chances of escape.

Now that their path was clear, Elwood found it is easier to keep up. In his thoughts he too speculated on how their misfortune might be reversed, but mostly he worried their capture would delay—or end—the journey to find the Eye of Ogin.

Arriving at dusk, they found the Ashaw village bright with crackling pine torches and fires. As the warriors and their prisoners approached, the village dogs began to bark. However, the moment they saw the fox truan at the front of the newcomers, they fell silent and skulked off into the deepening shadows. The people of the village dropped what they were doing to observe the warlike group's arrival, but it did not seem to surprise them. They were mostly hale, handsome people, forest farmers and hunters not unlike the Winharn. A gang of boys with toy bows, unawed by the truan and his entourage, launched a volley of blunt, harmless reed arrows at the prisoners. They were driven off scampering by several of their elders before a second round could be shot.

Directly following this assault, Elwood faced another in the form of three girls about his own age. As they discussed in Ashawnk what they saw, they stared and stared at him. All three were pretty, with wreaths of feathers crowning their raven-haired heads, and his face burned under their scrutiny. The girls giggled quietly together, and not unkindly; but in Elwood's ears, as if by malicious magic, that gentle sound was transformed into a flurry of derisive tittering. He turned his red face away, glowering fiercely at the ground.

With a gesture, the fox truan halted his followers and proceeded forward alone, stopping before a tall woman leaning on a carved staff in the center of the village. The pair exchanged words in low voices, and the Ashaw pointed to a small pavilion standing on the edge of the village. The three friends were taken there, a fire was built, and they were given blankets and bowls of stew. Their guard of four slept on the ground all around the pavilion, with two on watch by turns throughout the night. The fox truan was not seen again until morning. Elwood, Drallah, and Slukee slept little, and the night came and went without a sign of Booj.

They were on their way west again at first light. Though they spoke together in whispers when they got the chance, Elwood and Drallah remained otherwise mute. During the night they had agreed to speak to their captors as little as possible, and yield information only when some worthy advantage might be gained from it. By no means would they reveal that Elwood and Slukee were from another world, as this would likely increase their value in the eyes of their captors. In the meantime, they would remain alert and ready for any opportunity to escape.

The great pine forest stretched on and on, its eternal cover of brown needles dulling the monotonous rhythm of the company's footfalls as they jogged farther into the west. Twice they passed villages like the one where they had spent the night. At these the company stopped, and the fox truan spoke briefly with the village heads. Soon after midday a cold drizzle began to fall, and continued throughout the afternoon. The fox truan did not reduce their pace.

Two hours before sunset he led them off the road they had followed all day and onto a path that ages of passing feet had worn down to a point inches lower than the forest floor surrounding it. The gray light began to fail, and the rain ceased.

A welcome was called from somewhere high above the path.

The Ashaws, who at that moment were looking expectantly up into the lofty pines as they marched, waved greetings to a hidden sentry. The fox truan led them onward, and before they had walked another mile the path ended in a wide clearing bright with fires and busy with people.

Most of the clearing was occupied by an enormous pavilion, rectangular in shape, with a wall at the end facing northwest. Beneath its high peaked roof of pine trunks stood several domed tents of hide. Among the tents were Ashaw men and women who stopped what they were doing and crowded together to stare at the approaching warriors and their prisoners. Under and around the pavilion burned many campfires, and the scent of roasting venison filled the clearing.

The captives were herded to a little fire burning in the pavilion's southern corner. After a few words from their leader, two of the warrior-scouts walked off into the crowd, while two remained to stand guard over the prisoners. This arrangement made, the fox truan left them, talking as he went with two Ashaws who came to meet the group as they arrived. By their richly ornamented hair and blankets, the companions guessed these were men of high standing in Ashawda.

Elwood and Drallah sat on a log that had been dragged before the fire to serve as a bench, and Slukee curled up watchfully on the ground between them. A young man brought the friends a platter laden with corncakes and freshly roasted deer meat, which they quickly devoured. As they ate they looked about, trying to learn anything they could about their captors.

"I wish I knew what camp this is," whispered Drallah. "And why they're here."

"Don't the Ashaws winter indoors, like the Winharn?" asked Elwood.

"I think they do, but I . . ."

They were interrupted by the fox truan. Reappearing by the fire, he bade the prisoners and their guards follow him. The group wended their way through the tents and fire pits of the pavilion until they reached its northwestern end. There, in the shelter of roof and wall, stood a grand domed tent of countless deer hides sewn together, each cut in diamond shape and dyed a different and beautiful shade: cranberry, strawberry, mulberry, violet, and many others. Smoke from fires within the tent trailed from several openings. A triangular entrance, formed by the drawing back of two flaps, looked out upon the length of the pavilion. It was guarded by a quartet of lavishly armed warriors standing straight and still as statues. They moved, however, at the approach of the fox truan and his prisoners, stepping aside to allow them passage into the magnificent tent. The two guards who had accompanied them from the other end of the pavilion remained outside.

Within was brighter than without. The friends found themselves standing in the heat and light of a big fire burning in the center of the room, a space divided from the rest of the tent's interior by a wall of more diamond-shaped hides. Blankets were strewn on the ground a little distance from the fire, and upon these sat Ashaws at work with sewing, carving, and other tasks. As they took in the scene, a man slipped through an opening in the partition and made his way around the fire to them. He was in his middle years, and wrapped in a scarlet blanket.

"Children? They don't seem much, Tornonk," he said to the fox truan in Wohmog after he had looked over Elwood, Drallah, and Slukee.

"I was commanded to capture any and all strangers, Pennet, regardless of how they seemed."

Pennet turned to Elwood and Drallah. "Do they speak Wohmog?" Tornonk the truan nodded.

"Good. You will now enter the presence of Ainathuai, Queen of Ashawda. She has commanded it." For a moment Elwood's eyes widened, but Drallah made no sign. "Before we enter, what are your names?"

The girl quickly decided it was honorable enough, in this circumstance, to give their names. She had hoped, after all, that word of Winnitok's danger would reach the Queen. "I am Drallah Wehr, and this is Elwood Pitch. She is called Slukee."

"All right. Now be silent, and be still. Do not speak unless you are questioned. Do you understand? Come."

With the man leading and Tornonk following last, they filed through the second opening. The chamber beyond was larger than the first, and brighter. In addition to the great bonfire blazing in its center (which was also the center of the entire tent), tall pine torches were thrust in the ground around a circle of long slender poles supporting the dome. Many scouts and elders were sitting cross-legged around the central fire. All turned to watch the newcomers enter, and among them the companions saw several faces painted for war.

A couch heaped with pillows was set to one side of the fire, so the flames did not obstruct the line of sight between it and the chamber entrance. Half-sitting, half-reclining amidst the heaped pillows was a girl about his own age, Elwood guessed. She wore a dress of fine purple cloth, her brown eyes were dark and large, and her unbound hair fell into her lap. In one of her hands she held what appeared to be some kind of small doll.

On a blanket beside the couch sat a small plump woman who looked to be in her thirtieth year, and whose beauty seemed to extend mist-like into the air around her. Both the girl and the woman watched the prisoners with cold interest as they were led through the crowd and brought to stand before them. The hair on the back of Elwood's neck rose when the woman turned to stare at him. He took off his cap and pushed the hair from his eyes, but it quickly resettled on his brow.

"Drallah Wehr and Elwood Pitch, the Winhars that Tornonk captured, Queen," said Pennet, head bowed, before withdrawing to stand directly behind Elwood and Drallah. There was silence for a time, during which the girl and the woman continued to stare at the prisoners. Finally the woman spoke.

"Tornonk tells us you were traveling south through our land. Where were you going?"

"We bring word of Winnitok's peril to Ashawda," answered Drallah flatly, returning the woman's cold gaze.

"You have come a long way to do it. You are far, far from home, Winhar. Is there no other reason you are here?"

"Granashon the Nohar has disappeared, and her Dread no longer protects us. A horde of yugs is preparing to invade our land. They gather in secret, in Oldotok. The yugs are led by humans: Ringishmen who dress in gray cloaks, like the killers who ravaged Oldotok long ago."

"Yugs *and* Graycloaks, you say? Why would the two work together?"

"As I said, to invade our land."

Apparently skeptical of this news, the woman pursed her lips and raised her eyebrows. Then she said, "But you haven't answered my question. Is there no other reason you are here?"

"We have an errand that concerns only us. We are going south."

"Yes, well. Whether you do or not is for the Queen to decide."

Drallah turned to the Queen, half-sprawled among the pillows. The girl stared back at her with her big eyes, but did not speak. In the Queen's face Drallah thought she could see arrogance, vanity, and an inclination to be cruel, and as she met her eyes with her own, her anger at their captivity mounted. Moments passed, and the room filled with tension as all realized the pride of one girl was struggling with that of the other. The Ashaws knew their Queen, and feared what might follow if she lost.

They had been led to stand on a spot next to the fire, but that was not the only reason Elwood was beginning to feel intolerably hot. He could plainly see that each girl was determined to defeat the other; the look on the Queen's face was growing crueler and crueler, while Drallah's eyes flashed with anger. He realized that no matter who won this contest, the situation would worsen for the prisoners. Hardly knowing what he said, he addressed the Queen in a loud voice.

"We're on our way to the Great Swamp."

"Speak not unless you are told to!" cried Pennet, buffeting the side of Elwood's head with the flat of his hand. All eyes in the room turned toward them, including Drallah and the Queen's, and a murmur rose up among the elders and warriors.

"To Migdowsh? Why?" snorted the plump, beautiful woman sitting by the Queen.

"To see if the legends are true," answered Drallah quickly, while Elwood rubbed his head. The woman expressed more amusement and disbelief with another snort; but the Queen leaned forward, set one elbow on her knee, rested her chin on her knuckles, and looked closely at Elwood.

"*You* tell us why you seek the Great Swamp," she said. As he pieced together the words of his answer, Elwood studied her doll. Though it was only a dried cornhusk, it had been wonderfully stuffed, decorated and dressed: upon it skillful fingers had painted a beautiful and realistic face, it was clothed in a dress like the Queen's, and down past its waist hung shining black hair so real and soft-looking it must have been taken from a human head.

"That's right. We want to see if the legends are true," he answered.

"While your land, this girl says, awaits its doom. How strange. But I wonder which stories of the Swamp you are interested in. There are many, aren't there, Nemoor?"

"Just—you know, all of them," he answered weakly. Even without the audience of hostile strangers attending their every word, Elwood would have found his brain paralyzed and his tongue knotted in the presence of this cold, precocious, and pretty little Queen.

"What about the Lord of the Swamp? Do you mean to learn if the tales of him are true?"

Elwood stared at the ground and moved his head in a vague way that could have been taken for an affirmative nod, but might also have been interpreted as a negative shake.

"They are true," said the woman called Nemoor. "The Ashaws should know. Countless summers our people would travel to the Swamp's edge to gather certain herbs that can be found nowhere else. Then one year, when the Queen's grandfather was a child, the gatherers did not return. Scouts went seeking them. Only one came back, bearing news of grief and terror. The ravenous and invincible Otguk had awakened in the Great Swamp. He caught and devoured all the scouts but that one who escaped, and all the gatherers they were searching for also. For a time after that, now and again a brave warrior would go down to the Swamp to challenge the monster, but none ever returned. Neither would you, if you ventured there. None enter Migdowsh now—though Tornonk has gone in, and come out again." She turned to the fox truan, who stiffened slightly and met her eyes with an odd, quick glance.

This speech was followed by a silence which the Queen, leaning back into her pillows and turning again to Drallah, was the first to break. "You are bold adventurers," she said sarcastically. "Surely you must spring from mighty ancestors. But I wonder about something else. What have you to do with the little people of the Mountains?" The Winharn girl neither answered nor met the Queen's big eyes with her own, but stared at the ground before her. "The little people wounded one of my hunters a few days ago, and for that they will pay. By your silence we must assume you are their friends: you will pay also. I do not think you will go to the Great Swamp," she said, raising her voice declaratively. "Your lives will be much better spent with us, as our servants, until—and if—we decide to release you. The times are troubled enough without friends of our enemies roaming our lands. Now go away, until I summon you again. For now, Pennet will tell you what you must do. Tornonk, you remain."

160

Thus dismissed, Elwood, Drallah, and Slukee were ushered out of the Queen's tent into the cold air of nightfall, and back through the busy camp. "There is no room in the slaves' tent right now," said Pennet when they reached the little fire where they had been fed. "You will be shown where to get blankets and wood. Make certain this dog is no trouble, or she'll be turned out. You will not be under special guard, for the Queen's scouts are inescapable, and the punishment for running away is death. Tomorrow the slave master will teach you more. Serve the Queen well, and who can say? Perhaps some day she will release you. Until then, remember you are deep in Ashawda, and belong to her." Then, without another word, Pennet turned on his heel and strode off into the gathering dark, leaving the companions staring after him. Once he was gone they sat down on the log before the fire, threw more wood into the flames, and spoke Winnitoke to each other in hushed voices.

"What were you thinking?" said Drallah with real anger in her voice. "Why would you *tell* them we're going to Migdowsh?"

"Well, I had to say something," Elwood replied dejectedly. "That staring contest you got into with the Queen was about to end badly. Besides, they didn't believe us anyway."

"Did you forget about the copy of Ingagil's map? They've searched our packs by now. They're sure to find it."

Elwood did not respond to this; he had forgotten about the map Drallah carried.

Her anger cooling, Drallah said, "I guess it *is* true that no matter what we said, that little brat would've decided to make us her slaves."

Elwood groaned. "How're we going to get away?"

"I don't know yet. Hopefully Booj will find us soon."

"Then what? There's no chance of losing them in these woods. Especially that Tornonk! We'd never lose him."

"We'll lose him. Maybe if we can figure out what's happening here, it will help us escape. Now, that woman Nemoor has to be the Queen's cousin, the witch Tuthwoy mentioned. I can believe she has all the influence with Ainathuai, and the rest of these people. She's got so much magic you can *smell* it. We have to be wary of her."

"I'm wary of all of them. I wish we'd never come here."

"Don't waste your will on vain wishes," said Drallah cuttingly. "And don't talk as though we're beaten."

Badly stung, Elwood hung his head. Drallah rarely had cause to rebuke him, but he thought so highly of her—and wanted her to think likewise of him—that when she did say a sharp word, it pained him much more than it would otherwise. He would have spent the night tossing and turning in shame had she not nudged him with her elbow a moment later. "We've already come through a lot worse than this."

"That's true," he agreed, his face brightening briefly with gratitude.

A slave came and showed them where they were to fetch blankets and firewood from, and they passed the night comfortably enough in the shelter of the Queen's pavilion. In the morning they were awakened roughly by the slave master, a heavy sour-faced man called Tobb. Without offering anyone any breakfast, he put Drallah to work splitting logs and ordered Elwood to wait for a summons. The hungry boy and dog sat breathing the delicious atmosphere of the camp's morning meal as it warmed and bubbled over a score of fires. Elwood wondered what kind of summons he was waiting for, and hoped against hope it was to breakfast. When an hour later it finally came, it was borne by Pennet.

"The Queen calls for you, Elwood Pitch. Come."

The Queen? What could she want? thought Elwood to himself as he and Slukee rose to follow.

"Not the dog," said Pennet, glancing back.

Elwood and Slukee stopped. "She's a good dog; she won't cause trouble. And anyhow," he said, drawing himself up, "I'm not leaving her by herself with you people, no way."

The boy did not know it, but beneath his stern look Pennet suppressed an amused, approving grin. "I will see what the Queen says. Now, come!"

Once again Elwood and Slukee found themselves standing at the entrance to the Queen's magnificent domed tent. The guards stepped aside to allow Pennet in, and the boy and the dog waited to learn whether or not the Queen would permit Slukee to enter. After a few moments the Ashaw reappeared, and with a wave motioned them both into the tent. "Remember, do not speak unless you are questioned," he said over his shoulder as they followed him across the antechamber and into the huge central room.

Queen Ainathuai and her cousin Nemoor both occupied the same places they had the previous evening, but otherwise the room appeared to be empty. Elwood took off his cap. As they reached the Queen's couch, he noticed she again had her doll with her.

"Elwood Pitch, Queen," announced Pennet, taking his place directly behind the boy.

"What is your dog's name, Elwood Pitch?" asked the Queen.

"It's Slukee."

"Slukee. That's a sweet name." She turned to her cousin Nemoor, then back to Elwood. "It has a strange sound to it, not really like Winnitoke or Lindilish or Ringish at all. Where does it come from?"

"I made it up, from the name of a kind of dog I always wanted when I was a kid."

"Another kind of dog? And where does that dog come from?"

"Um, across the Sea. I've never really seen one—except in books."

"And where does 'Elwood' come from?" asked Nemoor. "It's an even stranger name than Slukee."

Again the hair on the back of Elwood's neck was standing on end. "It's an old Lindilish name," he lied. "I'm named after my great-uncle Elwood," he added, which was true.

"We are going to eat," said the Queen. "Are you hungry?"

"Yes, we are," answered Elwood with feeling. Nemoor waved to a servant who had been standing almost invisibly in the shadows at the edge of the room. In moments a blanket of pure white was spread on the ground, and its center covered with platters, bowls, and mugs filled with good things to eat and drink. Self-conscious in the presence of a queen, Elwood ate slowly and carefully, keeping a furtive eye on his hosts in order to imitate their manners. He placed Slukee's bowls on the ground directly behind his back, shielding the Queen from the sight of the dog devouring her food. Elwood got through the meal without committing any gaffes, at least as far as he knew. His relief was short-lived, though, for the Queen and her cousin almost immediately fell to questioning him again.

"What news from the little people of the Mountains?" asked Nemoor.

Elwood shrugged. "I don't know. We don't speak Ukwchchia, and we only saw a few woogans on our way."

The Ashaw witch raised a disbelieving eyebrow and said, "One of those few raided the kitchens of the Uginuptch, I guess. Your bags were full of supplies with the mark of her House."

Caught in his lie, Elwood tried to save face. "Oh, that stuff came from a storehouse where we stopped one night."

"Where were you born, Elwood?" asked Ainathuai, leaning forward and gazing with big eyes into his own. She appeared to be asking in earnest, without a trace of guile. In spite of what she was doing to him and to his friends, the boy wished he could tell her the truth.

"I don't exactly know. I lost my memory a while back."

"Oh!" she said, leaning closer still. "Don't you know your family? People who can tell you who you are?"

Something about the way she asked smote Elwood's heart. *Is this the same girl?* he wondered. Despite her haughty ways, despite the fact that she had enslaved him and his companions, she now seemed truly concerned. "No, I don't," he answered, returning her earnest gaze with one of his own.

"My parents died when I was very young. But at least I know who they were, and where I come from. And I have family yet," said Ainathuai, taking Nemoor's hand. After a thoughtful pause she continued, "But you are not friendless. How do you find the companionship of the Winharn girl?"

There was something different in the tone of this last question; something Elwood could not identify, but feared was scorn. Confused, he replied, "Good," and turned his eyes away from the Queen's.

Ainathuai withdrew her hand from her cousin's, and looked down at her doll. "I will meet with my council now," she said coldly. Not another word was said. With a gesture from Nemoor, Pennet led Elwood and Slukee from the Queen's tent.

* * *

"You did fine," said Drallah when Elwood finished recounting his interview with the Queen and her cousin. They were sitting by the fire that had become their new home, and the sun was going down. Since Drallah had been kept laboring elsewhere all day, it was the first chance they had had to talk since the morning.

"I don't know—I guess," said Elwood glumly. The memory troubled him.

"They found your wallet and the other things you carried from your world in your pack. And I bet the witch can see there's something unusual about you. That's why you were summoned, that's why they were asking you where you're from. We might turn her curiosity to our advantage somehow. Just be careful!"

* * *

The next day, the fourth since their capture, dawned on a heavy rain that had been falling half the night. The companions woke to the sound of it beating on the log roof overhead. They had barely stirred from their blankets when Tobb the slave master came around to give them orders. Drallah he sent to the cooking pots to help with breakfast, but Elwood was again commanded to stay and wait for a summons.

"You'll get to eat sooner than us, at least," said the boy to Drallah as she was about to go.

"Remember, be wary of Nemoor!" she whispered as she left.

After an hour or so, Pennet came to summon Elwood to the Queen's presence, and again the boy and the dog breakfasted with Ainathuai and Nemoor. The Queen did not appear interested in questioning her new slave as she had the day before, but instead was full of chat and jokes. Since he was not being pressed for information, Elwood became relaxed; so much so he forgot for the moment that he was forbidden to speak unless commanded to. Pennet did not reprimand him, though, and amidst their talk and laughter the presence of the adults, both Pennet and Nemoor, was all but forgotten. About halfway through breakfast it occurred to Elwood that Ainathuai was flirting with him.

When they finished eating, she rose from the blanket where the meal had been laid out, stretched lazily, and looked at Elwood.

"Would you like to see my dolls?"

"Sure," he answered, taken aback.

"Call for me if there is any news, Nemoor."

Indicating with a gesture that Elwood was to follow, Ainathuai led the way through a flapped opening at the back of the room. The room beyond was comparable in size to the great tent's antechamber, with a cheery little fire burning in a shallow pit in the middle of it. A strange but pretty perfume, mingled with the scent of wood smoke, filled the air. Between the fire and the entry were two beds made of many piled blankets and furs; noting the pair of them, Elwood surmised the Queen shared her sleeping quarters with her cousin the witch. Lining the semicircular outer wall was an array of racks on which were hung dozens of dresses, and tables covered with baskets and boxes of many descriptions. Elwood stood awkwardly looking about, wondering at his presence in the boudoir of a queen.

"No, Slukee!" he cried. Thinking they had left formalities in the other room with the human adults, the dog had begun exploring a tabletop with her nose.

"That's all right," laughed the Queen, standing very close to Elwood. She opened a little basket and offered him its contents. "Have some maple candy."

Once he had taken a cube of the sticky stuff, Ainathuai pointed Elwood to a short table standing at the head of one of the beds. On it was set a little cupboard with its doors standing open. Inside were shelves, and upon the shelves were rows of dolls. They were near in size to the one Ainathuai carried, and like that one had been fashioned with much craft and ingenuity. The boy and the girl knelt down beside the table, and Elwood looked at the dolls more closely. There were two men, mighty hunters standing at the ready with their deadly tools; a woman trailing a yellow, white, and red head-dress of minute feathers from the tiniest bird in the world; a big black bear rearing up on his hind legs; a stealthy cougar; a stag, a doe, and a fawn, all three bounding as if chased; a tall figure Elwood did not recognize with a golden-rayed head like a sun. Also there was a dog, and beside him a pale-skinned boy. Every respective detail of these two resembled Slukee and himself. The boy-doll even wore a cap like the one NiKwog had made him, and the dog-doll's fur, like most of Slukee's, was red. Stunned, Elwood picked them up, put them down, and picked them up again, but said nothing.

"Very good, don't you think? I had Nemoor make those two last night. She makes all my dolls," said Ainathuai, setting the doll she had been holding, which so resembled herself, on the shelf in the place of her two new ones.

Elwood was confused and worried. The little images of himself and Slukee had been fashioned by the Queen's cousin, a witch, and could be part of some magic that would mean trouble for the companions. But he was also flattered. It was as if the Queen had ordered his portrait painted. After all, she had wanted to see Elwood two mornings in a row. Still, he told himself, it couldn't be him the Queen was interested in. But what did interest her then? *What do you want these dolls for?* he longed to ask, but did not dare.

"Nemoor says I'm too old for dolls. Before long she won't make them for me anymore, and I will put these away."

"But you're Queen. Why can't you have your dolls as long as you want?"

"Oh, I could if I really wanted to. But I'm still too young to rule Ashawda alone. I trust cousin Nemoor's advice. She's very wise, you know." Then she gave Elwood a brilliant smile and said dramatically, "She says there's no one else like you in the whole world."

Even more confused, Elwood began to ask the Queen what she meant, but at that moment Nemoor appeared through the tent flaps. She looked at Elwood, who was kneeling on the floor holding the Elwood doll in his hands, and smiled.

"Queen, there is news."

"You may tell me now, unless it's very secret."

"Fienoth and six of his men have arrived unlooked-for. He travels south in haste, but begs an audience with you."

"He may have it—just him, of course. Bring him to the council chamber," commanded Ainathuai loftily. Rising, she turned to Elwood and ordered him to wait. "You may play with my dolls if you like," she added archly. "And there's more candy."

"I shall call for a servant to come and wait with him, Queen," said Nemoor, by which Elwood understood she did not want him left alone in the chamber. The girl and the witch exited the room as she was saying this, so he did not hear how or if the Queen responded.

Left suddenly alone together in the innermost recess of the Queen and her cousin's abode, the boy and the dog exchanged looks of surprise. Slukee placed herself on guard facing the doorway, and Elwood sat back on his heels to think about recent events.

He could not let himself believe what was happening. There was a smile in Ainathuai's big eyes when she looked into his own—and she was doing so constantly—that was more than just friendly. In spite of everything, Elwood could not resist. He returned her looks, and the feeling behind them, in earnest. But it must be some kind of mean joke, he told himself. He could not see a pretty girl like her, a Queen no less, being drawn to a plain, undersized boy like him. And then, what exactly had Nemoor meant by the remark Ainathuai had just repeated to him? Had the witch guessed he came from another world?

Too elated, worried, and baffled by the Queen's attentions to think clearly, he began to examine each of her dolls in turn, but quickly gave it up. He had a strange and disagreeable feeling they were somehow alive. Glancing around the room, he found nothing his agitated thoughts would focus their attention on. He became aware of a soft, distant drumming, and realized it was the rain falling on the timber roof of the pavilion, the sound muffled by the deerskin tent.

The minutes passed, but no servant came to wait with them. Guessing Nemoor had either changed her mind or forgotten her intention to send someone, Elwood decided to sneak a look at what was going forward in the council chamber. He walked over to the entry-flaps, gesturing to Slukee to remain still. The two hides that made the door overlapped, so with index finger and thumb he parted them just enough to peek with one eye into the room beyond.

He could see the Queen in profile, half-reclining in her usual place on the couch. On either side of her stood Nemoor and Tornonk, and cross-legged on the floor between the couch and the entrance sat several Ashaw warriors. The group was awaiting the arrival of the visitor. A moment later Pennet appeared through the opposite entry-way, followed by a tall cloaked man who appeared to be burdened with a bulbous, overlarge head.

Pennet strode to a spot a few paces from Ainathuai's couch. "Here is General Fienoth, Queen," he announced, then stepped back to stand directly behind the new arrival. The firelight splashed across Fienoth's front, and the boy could see that what had made his head appear too large was the ghastly skull of some long-mawed reptile, which he doffed to the Queen as he took his place with a short bow.

Elwood gasped. It was the Graycloak general, Vank-mul.

THE GREAT HUNT

Booj hunched down on the bough where he was perched and shook some of the water from his feathers. It had been raining since the middle of the night before, and the raven was soaked. He was also hungry. He had spent four days searching for lost his companions, and in that time had eaten almost nothing. But so far all his effort and sacrifice were to no avail: the girl, the boy, and the dog seemed to have disappeared from the lands of flesh and blood without a trace.

Farther than their legs ever could have carried them in four days, Booj had searched the pinewoods north and south without discovering any sign of his friends. He did see Ashaw scouts, their faces painted for war, moving swiftly and stealthily through the foothills, as well as Ashaw farmers who went about armed, glancing warily into the forest as they worked. He had hung around the several villages he came upon, each guarded as though an attack might be imminent, until he felt sure his friends were not hidden within a house. On a couple of occasions he resorted to questioning crows he encountered, but none had seen the young wanderers from Winnitok. In all his search he met no ravens, and he was beginning to think his kind had quit that land altogether.

Sometimes in wide high circles, sometimes skimming the tops of the pines, Booj flew west. Thick clouds spread to the horizon all around, and the view was much hindered by the soaking gloom. As he flew he regularly called out, listening carefully in case some answer should be returned.

Toward mid-morning, as he was wheeling high above the pinewoods, a movement in the trees caught his eye. He marked the spot in his head and dove, his heart hopping hopefully in his breast as it had many times before over the past four days. Mindful that whatever it was he had seen moving was more likely foe than friend, the raven flew down into the branches a short distance from the spot, choosing one with a somewhat clear view to light upon. From there he caught a glimpse of what looked to him like human shapes hurrying away to the west. He dropped from the branch and glided after them with caution, but full of hope.

The tips of his wings sometimes brushing their boles, Booj wove his way through the ancient pines in pursuit. Quickly he regained sight of the hurrying shapes, and his hopes plummeted. They were not his friends, but seven men in familiar gray cloaks and hoods running in single file. Disappointed again, Booj groaned a long, sad groan.

Amidst his disappointment, the raven felt a twinge of anxiety. What were Graycloaks doing here in Ashawda? Carefully he flew closer, following a line parallel to the one the humans were traveling. Then he saw something that made him stop in mid-flight and drop on the nearest branch: the lead Graycloak wore a big skull under his hood.

Filled with fear, wonder, and curiosity at finding the Graycloak general and his men so far from their army, Booj followed. He took care to keep as much distance as possible without losing them, remembering well that Vank-mul had eyes in the back of his head. Once he was certain of their westward course, the raven rose above the treetops for a look around. Through the rain he saw smoke rising over a village, or perhaps a big camp, not far to the west.

* * *

Horrified to see the Graycloak again, and especially there, with Ainathuai, Elwood let go of the door-flap and took a step backward. Seeing something was amiss, Slukee leapt up from the spot where she had been lying.

The boy desperately hoped the Graycloak general had not seen Drallah outside. He quickly rejected his fear that Vank-mul had followed the companions' trail and was hunting them still. Even if he was so determined to keep them from spreading news of the horde gathering in Oldotok, he must know it was too late to silence them now: there had been many chances to tell the world since their last encounter. No, Elwood thought, something else had brought him into Ashawda, but what? Had he come to see the Queen? Were they allies? Filled with apprehension, the boy returned to the flap and once again peeked out into the council chamber.

Nemoor was speaking, apparently questioning Vank-mul. Elwood could not quite catch her words across the wide space of the council chamber, but the big Ringishman's answer, which was given in Wohmog, he heard well enough.

"Hundreds of *dworkwoy* fighters have quit Kulenumpt. I heard their drums. They've gone to drive off the bands of yugs that have been raiding in the Imwa Valley and the foothills. Tonnetulk and Gumatulk have sent many fighters as well. I tell you, any inroads the Ashaws would make into the Mountains should be made now, while there are few woogans to resist."

The Queen answered him, and though Elwood strained his ears, he could not catch what she said. He could hear her tone however, and it was angry.

"You are Queen," resumed Vank-mul when she had finished. "But my master, Lord Egode Vallow, will be sorely disappointed the Ashaws did not take advantage of this opportunity. Perhaps he will no longer be willing to pay such a dear price for pelts."

Ainathuai answered him briefly, and then Nemoor spoke. Her tone was conciliatory and soothing, with a strong hint of something Elwood was sure was magic. When Vank-mul turned his fierce, crag-set eyes upon her, they were full of arrogant, unconcealed desire. The boy guessed from his expression that, though the Graycloak might not be under the spell of the witch's beauty, all the same he wanted it for his own.

"I will tell Lord Vallow as much," he answered. "But now, by your leave, Queen, I must continue on to New Efling immediately. I am required there." After a few more parting words he bowed to Ainathuai, called a patronizing farewell to "Mister" Tornonk, looked again with lusty arrogance at Nemoor, then turned and strode from the council chamber. A moment later he could be heard outside the tent calling stridently to his men, and Elwood listened as the tramp of their boots faded and was gone.

If he did see Drallah, he didn't do anything about it, he thought, much relieved.

As soon as Vank-mul departed, Tornonk dismissed the warriors, and Ainathuai and her cousin began an earnest discussion in Ashawnk. After taking several deep breaths, Elwood pushed aside the door-flaps and, followed closely by Slukee, strode quickly into the council chamber. Ainathuai and Nemoor looked up at him in surprise. From out of the shadows, Tornonk took a threatening step toward him.

The boy and the dog stopped. Speaking loudly to Ainathuai, Elwood said, "You didn't tell me you welcome the Graycloaks in your land."

Nemoor sat up and said in a voice louder still, "Simply because the Queen shows you favor, slave, does not mean you won't be given a beating!"

Tornonk took another step toward the boy.

"Wait," said Ainathuai, holding up a hand. "Why do you care, Elwood, whether or not we have dealings with the Ringish?"

"Drallah told you: they are getting ready to invade Winnitok. They are the enemies of all the lands of Pahn."

"And you are a slave with no right to speak here," said Nemoor, gesturing to Tornonk.

"Wait," the Queen repeated sternly. Her eyes met Elwood's, and she nodded for him to speak further.

"Don't you know what they're like?" he asked earnestly. "What they've done? I mean, they even join with yugs."

"You and your friend are not the first to mention this rumor to us," said Nemoor.

"It's not a rumor. I saw the General myself, in Oldotok. He tortured two of Drallah's people—he killed one of them. He was with a lot of yugs. We barely escaped from them. That's where the woogans are going, to Oldotok. Not the foothills. The General lied to you."

The Queen gave him a long look, which Elwood returned. "I believe you, Elwood Pitch," she said finally. "You're not a skilled liar—unlike General Fienoth.

"The horde you speak of is part of the same subject my cousin and I have been discussing. We trade with Fienoth's people, but we do not trust them. For a long time their leader, the Ringish sorcerer called Egode Vallow, has been trying to make a new war between us and the little people of the Mountains, though they think we are too stupid to see that's what they are doing."

"I've heard of him," said Elwood. "Why does he want your people to fight the woogans?"

"To weaken us both, so he can get a foothold in our lands," answered Ainathuai. "And take them entirely, as the Ringish have always desired. That will never happen. But there are advantages to be had, so we play a little at his war. If my scouts paint their faces and go armed into the hills, we are able to trade our pelts for more gold, and other precious things. But now Vallow would have us go too far—or that is what I say. Nemoor says the Ashaws could go into the Mountains, take lots of pelts, and not do the little people serious harm. But I say they would come down into Ashawda for vengeance, and that would be right. I would do the same if I were them.

"But the Ashaws do not deal with yugs, or those who deal with yugs—except in blows. We never forget the many harms that unnatural race have done our land over the ages. I believe what you say is true, Elwood, and I think I would like to have the General brought back to me hanging from a kill-pole."

"Unwise, Queen," said Nemoor. "Do you want the yugs to come to Ashawda after they have finished with Winnitok?"

"Allowing an ally of the yugs to walk our lands is the same as allowing a yug."

"It might be better in more ways than one not to interfere with General Fienoth," mused Nemoor. "He may well have been lying when he said he and his men are traveling to New Efling. Perhaps it is time to see if he will lead us to Egode Vallow.

"The sorcerer who is the Graycloak's master is very mysterious," she explained to Elwood. "No Ashaw has ever seen him. The Graycloaks claim he dwells in a Ringish town far to the south on the shore of the Sea, but whenever we propose sending an embassy to meet him, the Graycloaks give us excuses why Egode Vallow cannot receive it. I am suspicious that he is somewhere else, perhaps somewhere near. As I've counseled before, Queen, it would be to our advantage to learn where he dwells—or if he even exists. One day we may need to reach him."

"All right, cousin. I will take your counsel. Tornonk, I will put you on General Fienoth's trail."

"Not Tornonk, Queen," said Nemoor quickly, and Elwood noticed the fox truan once again glanced her way with strange eyes. "We need him here. Other scouts will do for this hunt."

Listening to all of this, Elwood thought about ways he might convince the Queen to help Winnitok in its peril. He decided to try Ainathuai's intolerance of yugs.

"The Ashaws would be a great help in the fight against the yugs," he said.

The Queen did not look at Elwood as she answered, "They are not threatening Ashawda."

"But they will. Like you said, the Ringish want to take Ashawda for themselves."

"Let them try! Ehm has never borne a people mightier than ours. The Ringish know it, so they try to weaken us by trickery and lies."

Though he was inexperienced at such things, Elwood was desperate enough to try to appeal to whatever feeling Ainathuai might have for him. Seeking out her big eyes, he softened his voice and inclined his head toward her. Nemoor did a poor job of suppressing a chuckle of wicked amusement as he said, "Ainathuai, Winnitok needs your help."

Blushing, he stumbled on, "Or we could help Winnitok ourselves. If you'd just let us go—"

Pennet, who had been away from the council chamber since leading Fienoth from the Queen's presence, suddenly rushed back in.

"*Mowa,* Pennet?" asked Nemoor.

"*Oso Bron,* Queen! *Oso Bron,*" he exclaimed.

Both Ainathuai and Nemoor leapt from the couch, and Tornonk stepped forward. The four had a heated exchange in Ashawnk, then Pennet turned and practically bolted from the chamber. From beyond the walls of the tent Elwood could hear people shouting, and the sound of many feet running here and there. Someone began to beat a drum.

"What's happening?" he asked.

"A *Bron,* a bear!" cried Nemoor happily. "A bear has come walking over the hills."

"So?"

"It is the way of the rulers of Ashawda to lead the *Suntawantus;* the Great Hunt. In the fall of each year the Queen seeks the *Bron.* If the Hunt is a success, it is well for the land until the next fall. If the

Queen slays no *Bron* ... things may go badly for the land. This year *Brondun* have been scarce in Ashawda, and people have been worried. Especially now that winter begins, and the bears are lying down for their long sleep. That is why we are encamped here, and haven't gone yet to the winter house."

Elwood was flabbergasted. "The Queen's supposed to kill a bear?"

Ainathuai grinned. "My best hunters will be with me, and Nemoor. They will help. And you too must join the *Suntawantus,* Elwood. Maybe it is you the bear follows, like good fortune."

Though he would have liked to speak up, Elwood refrained from pointing out that news of the bear had come closer to General Fienoth's arrival than to his own. Nor did he mention that, unlike the Graycloak, none of the names Elwood went by meant "bear." Instead, he wondered at this turn of events, and the Ashaws' priorities: a discussion that may ultimately have decided the fates of whole lands and peoples had been interrupted by a bear hunt. A bear hunt! He felt a little queasy at the thought. But if Ainathuai was going, he told himself, then he would too. Not that she gave him a choice.

The Queen commanded Elwood and Slukee to remain by the council fire, and she and Nemoor disappeared for a few minutes into their bedchamber. When they reemerged, they had exchanged the dresses Elwood was used to seeing them wear for tunics, britches, and moccasins of fur-lined buckskin. Suspended from a leathern necklace around Ainathuai's neck was a black bear's paw, hooked claws and cracked pads still intact, that was as big around as her head.

"To give me the bear's strength," she explained to Elwood, who was staring at it. Hanging so near her small, pretty face, the paw looked especially enormous and ugly.

Preceded by a pair of attendants and trailed by Elwood and Slukee, the Queen and her cousin left the council chamber, passed through the great tent's first room, and walked out into the more open shelter of the timber pavilion. Though the day was still gloomy and wet, it was bright enough outside to make Elwood blink. What looked like the entire camp had gathered in a semicircle around the tent's entrance. The moment the Queen appeared they all shouted as one, and then were silent. At the front of the crowd stood the Queen's hunters, intrepid-looking men leaning on bundles of tall spears. Tornonk stood in their midst. Behind the hunters were people of the Queen's House and council, lightly armed but otherwise without burdens. Back of these stood the attendants and slaves— the most numerous group by far—laden with packs and gear. All had been prepared in a matter of minutes, for the camp had been kept in a state of constant readiness.

Elwood searched the crowd, and with relief spotted Drallah standing near the back with a big pack on her shoulders. She appeared indifferent to the excitement of the people all around her, but her eyes were full of news and questions when they met Elwood's. *We've got a lot to talk about,* he thought.

Following the Queen out into the open of the clearing, the people formed a circle around her and Nemoor. Forgotten for the moment, Elwood and Slukee found themselves adrift on the inner edge of the crowd. Pennet and Tornonk brought forward a man, a hunter, and the Queen questioned him. As he answered, he waved a hand toward the southeast. It was he, Elwood gathered, who had discovered signs of the bear. Nemoor queried Tornonk on some matter, the truan briefly replied, and with that the consultation was at an end. Taking from an attendant a short spear to which were tied the glossy white and brown-barred feathers of a hawk, Nemoor passed it to the Queen, saying as she did, *"Ashawda arwu Bron obb."* Ainathuai took up the little weapon, and all were silent. She raised the spear ceremoniously with both hands to her mouth, and, much to Elwood's surprise, sank her teeth into it. She raised the spear with a flourish, and he saw that the bite had made indentations in the wooden haft. Again the people all shouted at once. Then Pennet began calling out commands, and the camp, which had been so still, went into motion.

Drallah too watched the ritual, and was stirred by it; every village in Winnitok had its own ancient and sacred traditions, some not unlike the Great Hunt. She had heard of the *Suntawantus* of the Ashaws since childhood, and after two days of slave work around the camp had been glad to learn she would be taking part. It was still slaving, but a ritual bear hunt could at least be interesting.

Not that it had been a dull morning. As Drallah was searching for dry kindling a half mile from the camp, Booj swept down from the sky and landed on her shoulder. Only briefly had they dared indulge their happiness at seeing one another again: there was a lot to tell and little time to tell it. With Booj perched in a tree over Drallah's head, he warned her that Vank-mul and his men were near, and she explained to him that she and Elwood were now slaves of the Queen. Quickly they made such plans as they could, and, proceeding with care—she did not want to find herself face to face with Vank-mul—Drallah had returned to the camp with her load of kindling. Having learned from his friend of a turkey that was killed and gutted near the camp that morning, hungry Booj had flown off in search of the remains.

Vank-mul and his men had arrived in the Queen's camp just minutes after Drallah returned from gathering kindling. Thanks to a large tent that stood between the wood piles and the campfire where he rested from his journey, the Graycloak did not see her. Using this cover to full advantage, the Winharn girl had taken a long time to finish her chore, exasperating the slave master to such a degree he threatened her with a beating. When she learned from another slave that the leader of the Graycloaks had gone in to see the Queen, and that Elwood and Slukee were still with her, Drallah had barely been able to keep herself from trying to enter the great tent as well. Never guessing that her friends were hidden from the Graycloak's sight in the Queen's bedchamber, her best hope had been that Ainathuai would protect them out of self-interest. She had been filled with relief and curiosity when Vank-mul reemerged, and he and his men departed. The scout had arrived with news of the bear shortly after, and all the camp had abandoned whatever they were doing to prepare for the Hunt.

Drallah looked up and spotted Booj. The raven glided from perch to perch, following the Great Hunt as it got underway. She wondered if Elwood and Slukee, walking near the head of the Hunt, had seen him. The Ashaws were not suspicious of Booj, assuming the raven came along hoping to get a bit of the kill.

For the rest of the day the long file of the Hunt moved snake-like through the pinewoods by various paths, always tending toward the south and east. The dense boughs thinned and softened the rain's fall, but nevertheless it was a wet march. Toward the end of the day the terrain began to roughen and rise as they drew nearer the Mountains. When darkness came, they spread out into the woods around the path to rest. The slaves were all directed to the same vicinity, which Pennet ringed with watchful scouts. Finding a place among but not too close to the rest, the companions made a tent for themselves with a blanket, and shared in whispers all that had happened that day. Before long Booj glided quietly down to them, and the four friends had a joyful though nearly silent reunion. When the Hunt began to stir and first light was not far off, the raven took to the trees once again.

They were nearing the area where they expected to find the bear, and so the majority of the Hunt kept camp where they had spent the night. Almost all the slaves remained, but a dozen of those who were strong and hale were chosen to follow the Queen. This was because, should the hunt be a success, they would be wanted to carry the slain bear back to the camp. Drallah was one of these. Elwood was also commanded to continue on with the Hunt, though he was not yet big enough to serve as a burden-bearer.

Now fewer than three dozen, the hunters set out again. The rain had stopped during the night, and on brief occasions throughout the morning the sun shone feebly through the clouds. Tornonk the truan led the way; Pennet, Nemoor, Ainathuai, Elwood, Slukee, and several scouts of Ainathuai's House, including the hunter who had found the bear signs, came after; Drallah and the rest of the slaves followed; the remaining scouts brought up the rear. The fox truan soon took them off the path they had been on, leading them up into an arm of hills that stretched out from the Mossheads for many miles to the west. As the morning advanced he paused often, turning his tall ears this way and that, and raising his long muzzle to sniff the air.

A little before noon they stopped on a blunt crag above a creek overflowing and fast with the previous day's rain. The hunters were excited, and Elwood guessed they had reached the place where the bear was thought to be. The country was uneven and rocky, and the towering pines had given way to smaller trees. Tornonk crouched at the crag's edge to study the terrain below, consulting with the man who had discovered the bear signs while the rest of the Hunt waited nearby. Quickly forming a plan, Tornonk spoke to Pennet, who relayed to Ainathuai and Nemoor what the fox truan had said. Then Pennet ordered the Hunt according to Tornonk's specifications. Dispersing across a wide area with the creek at its center, they began slowly and quietly to climb farther into the hills. The truan advanced along the northern bank of the creek, and the Queen and her cousin followed a short distance behind. Before they descended from the crag Ainathuai called Elwood to her, bidding him to follow her closely. Pennet, a stout spear resting on his shoulder, also remained close by the Queen. The rest of the Hunt—including the unarmed slaves—moved off into the folds of the hills, maintaining intervals of a few yards each between them. Tornonk's plan, Elwood gathered, was to drag a net of hunters along the banks of the creek, which they knew the bear had recently been haunting.

They had followed the creek for half a mile when they came upon signs so plain even Elwood could read them, inexperienced though he was. Four huge round paws had lately impressed a trail in the dead, muddied undergrowth. The trail crossed the hunters' path and disappeared into the brown water of the creek.

Tornonk dropped on all fours to examine the paw-prints, his long muzzle snuffling and searching. "Male, not old," Elwood heard him say softly to Pennet, who stood beside the fox truan. Rising, Tornonk pointed his nose at the sky and signaled the rest of the Hunt with a loud, short bark. Then, with startling suddenness, he launched himself up into the air and landed lightly on the opposite side of the creek. There he searched the far bank for more prints, soon finding they reemerged from the rushing water a few yards to the east and moved on up the creek. As he began to follow the trail, the rest walked along the northern bank until they came to a little fall of water, where they crossed and rejoined him.

Moving with great care, for the trail was very fresh, the Queen and her hunters followed the creek farther up the hill. With wide eyes, Elwood and Slukee watched the woods all around as they walked. Occasionally through the trees they caught sight of other members of the Hunt, and Booj flying to and fro above them. Drallah they did not see after descending from the crag. Glancing Ainathuai's way, Elwood saw she gripped her little spear resolutely, and as far as he could tell was unafraid.

The bear's trail continued alongside the creek for half a mile before it meandered away toward the south. Following it, their path soon intersected with that of a pair of hunters approaching on their right. Tornonk spoke with them quickly, redirecting them to a line parallel with that of the trail. Then he barked twice, signaling his and the Queen's position to the rest of the Hunt.

"Won't he warn the bear we're coming?" whispered Elwood to Ainathuai.

"The bear hears a fox, nothing more. Tornonk knows what he's doing."

Either reading in the trail that their quarry was very close, or sensing that it was so, Tornonk's posture shifted forward to such a degree he nearly walked on all fours. His big tail bristling, he followed the bear's trail to a point where it entered a dense stand of mountain laurel. The evergreen-leaved thicket grew beneath the curve of a low rocky cliff, a half-circle of stone thrust up from the earth directly before them. Searching the ground and studying the thicket, Tornonk determined that the bear was still within.

The fox truan and the adult humans spoke to each other briefly in low voices, and then Nemoor turned to Ainathuai. "The *Bron* is there, Queen," she whispered. Her eyes shone with excitement and magic, prickling the skin on the back of Elwood's neck.

"I will wait here," answered Ainathuai.

Nemoor nodded and, holding their spears ready before them, she, Pennet, and Tornonk stole softly into the thicket, quickly disappearing from the children's and the dog's view. Though still very tense, the boy was immensely relieved that Ainathuai was not actually going to confront the bear herself. Breathlessly the boy and the girl looked at one another. Then a movement in the trees behind the Queen caught Elwood's eye, and he saw Booj light on a low branch two dozen yards away. Perching there, the raven waved his wings, bobbed his head up and down, and silently opened and closed his beak. He was trying to tell the boy something, but what Elwood could not say. As he puzzled over Booj's antics, Ainathuai saw him looking elsewhere, and turned to see what had his attention. Booj ceased his efforts immediately and pretended to preen.

"Raven has come to bless the *Suntawantus,*" whispered the Queen.

"I'd better see what he wants," said Elwood hurriedly, as though he had not heard her. He walked quickly toward the tree where Booj was perched, Slukee trotting eagerly ahead. Ainathuai remained where she was. Just as Elwood reached the tree and opened his mouth to question Booj, a commotion erupted in the thicket. From deep within the mountain laurel's dense heart, Nemoor could be heard chanting in Ashawnk. At the same time, at a point near the laurel's edge, branches began to thrash and sway. The turmoil in the bush moved quickly away from the sound of Nemoor's chanting, and in moments its source—a huge form like an animate, furry black boulder—ambled out of the thicket not far from where Ainathuai stood.

The bear looked up with small, sleepy eyes, a very long, pink tongue dangling from his half-open jaws. He saw the girl before him. With the curve of the cliff behind, and beneath it a witch singing the bear's death song, she was standing in the one path by which he might escape. Taking just a moment to gather his enormous bulk, the bear charged.

Ainathuai watched the bear without moving, her spear forgotten in her hand. His appearance and charge had happened too quickly, and there was not time enough to run. The Queen depended entirely upon her three most capable and trusted servants, and was completely unprepared for their failure to protect her. So she just stood watching with wide eyes as the bear galloped toward her, his speed incredible for a creature so huge.

Though they could not possibly reach her before the bear did, Elwood, Slukee, and Booj rushed toward the Queen. As they ran and flew, a voice in the woods cried out in Winnitoke, *"Bombee calls you!"* and they caught sight of Drallah bounding swift as a cougar from the opposite direction. In her hand was a stout branch she had snatched up from the ground, and she was waving it over her head as she ran down the bear. Intercepting him moments before Ainathuai would have been crushed beneath his claws, Drallah broke the branch across his massive blunt muzzle. The bear stopped short and wheeled to face her, rearing up on his hind legs with a roar. Towering over Drallah and Ainathuai, he raised his great clawed forepaws to strike. Drallah too raised her arms, repeating and adding to the charm, *"Bombee calls you! Go and play!"* The bear stepped backward as if he had been pushed, dropped to all fours, and turned aside. With a snort he galloped around them, down the hill and away from Drallah, the Queen, and the thicket of mountain laurel.

When the boy, the dog, and the raven reached them a moment

later, Ainathuai was steadying herself with a hand clutching Drallah's tunic. Having emerged from the thicket just in time to witness Drallah turn the bear, Tornonk, Nemoor, and Pennet were also quickly at the Queen's side. The bear's roar brought the other hunters running to the spot as well. Catching sight of their fleeing prey, they began to chase him down the hill. Recovering a little from her fright, Ainathuai spoke.

"For saving my life, I free this Winhar from my service." She released her grip on Drallah's tunic and drew herself up. "And because I have been spared, I will end the *Suntawantus*. I will hunt the *Brondun* no more this winter. Ashawda will have a hard year, but Meituai's daughter will still live and rule. Tornonk, tell them."

The fox truan recalled the hunters with three short barks. They gathered again, and the party was soon heading back to the camp of the previous night. As they marched, the tale of how Drallah Wehr turned the bear and saved the Queen spread among the hunters and slaves, sowing a legend-seed in the memory of the Ashaw people.

TORNONK AND NEMOOR

Nemoor was ashamed of her part in the failed *Suntawantus*. When the Hunt returned to the pavilion the next day, she quickly retired to the chamber she shared with the Queen. Her fault lay in beginning her chant before Tornonk had discovered precisely where the bear lay hidden, thus warning the creature of their presence and placing Ainathuai in the gravest danger. She had not intended to do so, but, overconfident in her power, had acted too soon. When Nemoor, Pennet, and Tornonk heard the bear move and realized he was not, as they thought, between them and the cliff, but between them and Ainathuai, it was too late. The three freed themselves of the mountain laurel in time only to witness the bear's charge, and each knew that were it not for Drallah, the slave girl from Winnitok, the Queen would be dead.

From the time the Hunt reached the creek, Drallah had followed Elwood and Slukee as closely as she could without attracting the notice of the Queen and her people. Once they were commanded to fan out among the trees, no one seemed to watch the slaves, and so Drallah made her way where she would. She had hidden herself behind a tree when Tornonk, Pennet, and Nemoor followed the bear's trail into the mountain laurel, and from that vantage she had seen Booj land on the branch near Elwood, Ainathuai and Slukee.

She had understood the raven's gesticulations, though Elwood could not: Booj had seen the bear, and was trying to warn them he was very close. He did not simply fly to Elwood's ear and tell him plainly, because doing so might have drawn the bear's attention to the boy, the girl, and the dog. Also, the Queen's ignorance of her slaves' connection with the raven was an advantage he did not want to lose.

As Elwood and Slukee approached Booj, Nemoor had begun her Hunt-chant, which drove the bear from the thicket. Thanks to the raven, Drallah had already seen the Queen's danger, and using the cover of trees had begun to hurry toward her. Then the bear charged, and there was no further need for stealth. Bombee, the name Drallah had called, was the ancient bear truan who was lord—or father, as some said—of the bears of Pahn. It was a name of power, and did far more to turn the bear than the arm that wielded the branch.

As for Ainathuai, she either did not perceive or chose to overlook Nemoor's mistake. Her councilors muttered about the hard year that would come as a result of the Great Hunt's failure, and her cousin barely spoke to her for shame, but the Queen seemed too happy to be alive to care.

Since freeing Drallah, Ainathuai had done much to honor her. On the return journey to the pavilion, the Winharn girl (as well as Booj, who once again accompanied her openly) had walked with the Queen, Elwood, and Slukee at the head of the Hunt. Ainathuai tried to get Drallah to chat on the way, questioning her about her life and home. When they returned, the Queen offered Drallah a warm place in her own tent. She refused, preferring to stay with Elwood by their fire at the pavilion's edge.

Drallah pleaded with Ainathuai for Elwood's freedom, telling her their very land was at stake, but the Queen would not relinquish her claim on the boy. Instead she tried to tempt the Winharn girl with offers of high rank in her household. If she accepted, Ainathuai promised, Drallah could have most anything she desired. In answer she told the Queen that her house was in Winnitok, and that it was in danger. Ainathuai asked her what two so young, with only a raven and a dog, could do to save their land, but Drallah did not trust the Queen and her cousin, and would not answer.

Though a slave, Elwood was given no work other than keeping Ainathuai company. The day after they returned from the *Suntawantus* she called him to breakfast with her. He stayed until after the evening meal, which all four companions attended. As they ate there was much talk among the Ashaws of an impending journey: the Great Hunt was over, and the time had come to go to the Queen's winter house, which lay two days' walk north and west. Ainathuai, along with a dozen or so of her people, intended to depart in the morning. The rest would follow the next day, or the day after that. Elwood, the Queen told the companions, would be traveling with her, and Drallah was welcome to join them if she liked.

After dinner and before she dismissed him for the night, Ainathuai bade Elwood and Slukee come sit with her in her chamber at the back of the tent. With face aglow, the little monarch regaled the boy with a list of all the things they would do together at her winter house. They would lie upon mounds of the softest skins, she said, listening to the best singers, musicians, and storytellers in all Pahn and Magua; they would lead teams of slaves against each other in long games of *Catch the King,* the whole vast mansion of her ancestors theirs to use as they liked; and she would teach him the secret of her dolls.

Elwood sat beside her and listened sullenly. It was pleasant to imagine a life with Ainathuai, even as her slave. But he could not accept such a reality, he told himself: the only way into the future for him was the hunt for the Eye of Ogin, and Granashon, and a way back to his family. The longer she delayed Elwood from accomplishing these things, the harder it was to overlook how wrong she was to hold him against his will. He also blamed her—unjustly—for how little thought he had given to his mother, father, and sister recently.

"I see something is wrong," said Ainathuai, interrupting her catalogue of pleasures.

Elwood looked at her, resentment plain on his face. "How observant," he said.

Ainathuai narrowed her eyes and drew herself up. "Well?"

"What do you think? I'm a slave!"

"And you feel I do not treat you well?"

Elwood sighed in frustration. "That's not the point. Can't you see it's wrong?"

"I am Queen. I do no wrong." Despite the arrogance at the heart of this statement, Ainathuai sounded sad and hurt as she said it. Elwood melted. For all his determination to get away, he was irresistibly drawn to her. So moved was he that suddenly, recklessly, he began to pour out all the things he had kept inside for days.

"I would stay with you, Ainathuai—even as your slave. But I can't. If I tell you something that's hard to believe, will you try and believe me anyway?"

Her eyes grew enormous; she nodded her assent.

"I didn't lose my memory. I had to lie to you, I'm sorry. Ainathuai, I'm from another world, and I'm trying to get back."

Her eyes opened wider still, but not in disbelief. "So it *is* that," she said. "I told you Nemoor said there was no one else like you in the world; she sensed you come from somewhere—else."

"Please, Ainathuai: help me get back. Let me go, so I can find a way. My mother, my father, they don't know what happened to me. It's been months since I left." And then he told her the whole tale, from the walk in the wooded park in Massachusetts, to setting out on the hunt to find the Eye of Ogin, to being captured by Tornonk in the woods of Ashawda. She asked him many questions about his world, and as he told her of his life, and she told him of hers, Ainathuai moved close enough for their shoulders to touch, and took his hand and held it in her own.

They remained talking this way until the fire burned down to glowing coals. Finally Ainathuai turned her face to his, brushing his cheek with the tip of her nose. "I cannot release you," she said. "If you go, you will die. Or you will succeed, and return to your world forever. I don't want to be without you."

Overwhelmed by feelings intense and quite at odds with one another, for a moment Elwood was uncertain what to say or do. He had only dreamed of being so close to a girl, had only imagined hearing one speak such words. With newfound desire, tenderness, and pride hinting at the grown man he would eventually be, he felt he could easily kiss her if he chose. He longed to most desperately, but did not; for something inside warned doing so would only increase her power over him. Despite his passion, Elwood did not forget the Queen was preventing him from finding the Eye of Ogin, and Granashon, and a way back home.

He decided to let her lead for the moment, but in the meantime he had to say something. "I don't want to be without you either," he began.

They were startled by a voice at the tent flaps. It was Nemoor, poking her head into the darkened room. "Queen, it grows very late," she said, clearly interested in the way they sat so close, holding hands.

"I know, cousin," answered Ainathuai. She squeezed Elwood's hand and said in a voice that gave him a warm shiver, "Until I see you again tomorrow—good night."

* * *

"We have *got* to get away," whispered Drallah. "We've been here too long." Gathering warmth from the fire and talking, she and Elwood were lying under their blankets head to head. It was after midnight, and they were both exhausted. Elwood had just recounted his talk with Ainathuai, and Drallah was deeply unhappy with him for revealing the truth about himself to the Queen.

"Elwood, you're her slave! You should *not* have told her. It's the thing that's different about you that interests the witch so; that's why she keeps having you visit the tent."

"Oh, really?" said Elwood, rankled. "So it's Nemoor who has me to their tent every day, not Ainathuai?"

"I know, I know," she said quickly, mindful of hurting his pride. Even though she saw the Queen as a little girl spoiled by power she had not earned, and would not forgive her for forcing them to be her slaves, for Elwood's sake Drallah was touched by what was happening between the two of them. She was also glad her friend's affections had turned to someone other than herself.

"I told Ainathuai the truth because I know that if I can just make her understand how important it is, she'll let me go."

"But after you told her, she said just the opposite—that she couldn't let you go."

"She will. I just need another chance. I know I can convince her."

"And if you can't?"

"Then Granashon will help us somehow. We just need to be ready when she does."

* * *

When Elwood awoke, dully glowing embers were the only light. Drallah was shaking him gently, and whispering in his ear.

"Wake up! We're leaving."

Out of the dark a canine face appeared and hovered over him. He thought it was Slukee until the eyes caught the ember light and for a moment glowed a pale catlike green. Elwood saw then that the muzzle was longer and sharper than the dog's, and the ears more triangular. The face looking down at him, he realized, was Tornonk the truan's.

"What?"

"Be quiet and get up. Tornonk is taking us away."

It was the middle of the night. Thinking he was probably in a dream, the boy rose bleary and shivering to his feet. Tornonk handed him a bundle. Hefting it, he recognized his pack, quiver, and bow. He peered into the dark at Drallah as she shouldered her own gear, which the Queen had given back to her after the Great Hunt. Booj paced nervously at the Winharn girl's feet, his shining black feathers smudged with the embers' orange glow. Slukee stood watching Elwood eagerly, eyes and ears alert for a command.

Silently they followed the white tip of Tornonk's big tail out from under the pavilion and into the surrounding trees. He led them on a winding course through the tall pines, and they met none of the vigilant sentries who ringed the Queen's pavilion. After walking in the dark for a soundless, circuitous hour, Tornonk suddenly stopped and turned to face them.

"I am willing to guide you safely out of Ashawda," he said very softly. "Where do you wish to go?"

"Why—" began Elwood, but Drallah silenced him with a touch of her hand.

"If you would guide us to the River Gaulatash, where its flow marks the southwestern edge of Ashawda, we'd be grateful."

Flexing his long whiskers, the fox truan looked at her with curiosity and perhaps a little surprise. Then he turned and, taking not a moment to get his bearings, began to lead them in a different direction.

They walked all night. Tornonk kept them moving swiftly despite the dark, and by morning they had left the Queen's pavilion far behind. The farther they went, the more desolate Elwood became. He would never have left Ainathuai without saying good-bye, if that were possible. He felt it was too cruel to have found her and in such short order be forced to leave her. He trudged along after the fox truan's white-tipped tail, feeling very sad and sorry for both himself and the Queen.

The day came bright and frigid out beyond the tops of the trees, but under their boughs it was dim and not as cold. The fox truan called a rest, and they spread their blankets on the ground and sat down. Looking into his pack, Elwood found not only all his old belongings, but new ones as well. It had been filled with parcels of corn wafers, candied squash, and dried venison, just enough for several days of walking. As he and the others broke their fast, Tornonk began to speak.

"By now the Queen and her cousin know you are gone, and that I have taken you. They will likely send hunters, but without me they have no one on hand who can track at night. So, we will walk night and day, rest little, and outstrip them. This is better than trying to shake them off our trail. If I were alone, I could lose the Queen's hunters with ease, and soon circle back if I wished, and hunt *them*. But with you four along it would not be so easy."

"In how many days do you plan to reach Gaulatash?" asked Drallah.

"Seven or eight, if we are not hindered."

She nodded grimly. She, Slukee, and Booj could go so far in so short a time, but she feared Elwood could not.

"Tornonk?" began Elwood tentatively. He expected Drallah still did not want him questioned. "We're grateful for all your help—but why are you doing it?"

"I was the Queen's willing servant, not her slave."

Elwood waited for Tornonk to continue, but the truan seemed to have said all he was going to. Feeling Drallah's eyes upon him, he left it at that.

When they finished eating, Tornonk all but commanded the companions to rest until it was time to move again. The humans rolled themselves in their blankets, Slukee curled up tight against Elwood, Booj flapped to a branch overhead, and with the fox truan watching over them, they slept. Exhausted, Elwood sank into a deep slumber, into which came a strange dream. He was at the front of a classroom in his world, and Ainathuai was with him. The room was full of students, and the attention of all was focused on Elwood and the Queen. He gave a kind of presentation to the class, explaining to them who Ainathuai was. Turning to her, he saw the bear's claw around her neck. Then a booming, terrifying voice behind them spoke Elwood's name. In the place where the teacher's desk should have been sat a giant bear, and stuck upon each of four of his terrible claws was a doll's head, the body no longer attached.

The boy awoke heavy with regret for having left Ainathuai. He wondered how she reacted to the news that he was gone. "If things go the way they're supposed to, you'll never know," he told himself as he and the others prepared to set out again.

* * *

Much of the rest of that day, and all of that night, and for days and nights more, Tornonk led them onward through the great pine forest of Ashawda. Always he avoided human habitations, which were many, for Ainathuai's land was populous and thriving. News of his disloyalty to the Queen could not have spread so soon, but Tornonk did not offer any other reason for traveling in secret. He was almost always mute, interrupting his silence only to softly announce it was time to move again, or to remind the companions they must make haste. Elwood's desire to know why Tornonk helped them was kept from boiling over by weariness, for their daily rest amounted to only half as much as he was used to. The first two marches were the most difficult, but, determined as he was to equal Drallah, he persevered, and even grew a little stronger and hardier each day.

At the end of the third night after their escape, as they climbed the side of a low-swelling hill, Tornonk stopped them in the midst of a fallow clearing. Facing back toward the rising sun, the fox truan stood silently turning his head this way and that for some time while the rosy orange of a cloudbank deepened on the horizon. The others waited quietly for their guide to speak or move. Finally he said, "Even if the Queen's hunters follow, we have left them far behind. They will not catch us now."

"How do you know?" asked Elwood, but Tornonk only shrugged and led them on over the hill.

After that the fox truan let them light campfires and rest more of the daylight hours, but they continued to walk all through the nights. He also became more talkative, and as they were stopped and he sat weaving fresh pine boughs into his jacket, or simply staring into the depths of the fire, Tornonk would sometimes tell them an interesting story or piece of lore, usually something associated with the locale they were passing through at the time.

But as they were camped one morning in the lee of an immense pine, the fox truan, squatting on the pads of his feet with his bushy tail wrapped around them, began softly to sing in a language completely strange to the companions, and oddly beautiful. Even though they could not understand a word, in different ways the song, which was long and full of changes, caught and held the imaginations of each of the four friends. As he sang they forgot the campfire before them, and Ashawda, and the horde that would soon attack Winnitok. Following the roaming melodies of Tornonk's song, each slipped into a waking dream.

"A family story," said Tornonk when he had finished. His audience stirred and gazed at one another in mild surprise. For some reason turning and looking beyond the tree at his back as he spoke, Tornonk continued, "It is the tale of my clan's first mother and father; how they met in this world, long ago."

Slowly he rose to a crouch, his muzzle wrinkled and his teeth showing as he breathed in through his nose and mouth. The companions, who did not hear or see anything untoward in the forest around them, remained where they sat, perched, and lay. Each of them had been carried far from the fireside by Tornonk's song, but now all watched and wondered what he would do. Slowly and lightly the fox truan stepped away from the fire and placed a hand on the ancient pine, his neck stretching forward and his tail stretching back. Then he darted out of sight behind the bole of the tree, and the companions heard fierce growls and scrabbling in the earth. A few moments later Tornonk reappeared clasping a plump fox in his arms, her eyes wild and her teeth bared as futilely she tried to squirm free.

Tornonk put the fox down by the fire. Pinning her there with one hand, he threw a blanket over her with the other. Full of wonder, the humans, the dog, and the raven regarded the fox truan and the fox in silence. Still pinning her to the ground, Tornonk spoke softly to his captive.

"I know you, vixen. Now show your true face!"

The fox ceased struggling, and after a few moments something strange began to happen. The air above the blanket began to stir, its movement visible like a faint bow of color-tinged heat rising from sand. The lump of the fox beneath her shroud expanded upward, and suddenly a woman stood where the fox had been. Wearily she drew the blanket around her bare, plump shoulders. It was Nemoor.

The four friends were so stunned none of them moved or spoke, but if Tornonk was surprised he did not show it.

"Why do you follow us?" he asked in Wohmog.

"I told you once why I would follow you, if ever you left," answered the witch, her voice faint with exhaustion.

"You say, then, that it has nothing to do with this human boy?"

Nemoor looked at Elwood, then turned back to Tornonk and smiled. *"Wamomo,* all of Pahn has to do with this boy."

Tornonk's tail twitched. "You may rest by our fire a while before you return to the Queen."

She nodded and sat down cross-legged among them. Their offers of food she silently refused, accepting only water. This she gulped down in long drafts, as though she had had none for a long time. When she had quenched her thirst she fell to staring into the heart of the fire, and her eyes grew blank. Silent as well, the companions wondered what her appearance might portend, and what her exchange with the fox truan might have meant.

"Her shape-changing has left her weary and weak," said Tornonk. Nemoor did not seem to hear him.

"Will she try to take me back?" asked Elwood as he stared wide-eyed at the unheeding witch.

"She may, but not by force. I think she has come to trade with us—for something else."

Not even blinking as she stared into the fire, Nemoor sat motionless the rest of the morning and all that afternoon. The companions slept, but often throughout the day they woke from fitful dozing to see that their unexpected guest was still with them, and had not moved. They did not see Tornonk sleep at all. Toward sundown he roused the companions, and even as they were shouldering their gear for another march Nemoor continued to sit as she had for hours, eyes still upon the same point in the fire, which was now just a pile of smoldering coals. Finally, as Tornonk separated the coals with a stick, the trance ended. Nemoor looked up at the fox truan and smiled as if at a new day, but Tornonk's response was cold.

"We leave now. You must gather your strength and fend for yourself."

Rousing herself further, Nemoor answered him in Ashawnk, but Tornonk continued to speak in Wohmog.

"You know well why."

Again the woman replied in the language of her people, this time at length. Her words, or perhaps her impassioned tone, appeared almost to agitate the fox truan. When she finished he replied in Ashawnk, and the two began to debate in earnest. Tornonk paced back and forth as they talked, while Nemoor remained cross-legged on the ground. Elwood listened awkwardly, deeply curious about what was being said but also conscious of the intrusion. Slukee had no such qualms, and eagerly attended the exchange. Drallah, patiently awaiting a resolution, stood and looked off into the trees. Of the four, only Booj had some idea—Ashawnk being one of many languages he knew in bits and pieces—of what the fox truan and the woman were saying to each other. He listened from his perch atop Drallah's pack with head cocked first to one side and then the other, his big beak working as though he were silently repeating all that they said.

They talked on for some minutes until Nemoor rose and, turning to the companions, spoke to them in Wohmog. "Please, we won't be long," she said.

The four friends walked away from the camp through the darkening forest. Out of sight and hearing of the woman and the fox truan, they stopped at a stump covered in faintly glowing moss, and Booj lit upon it.

"Well? What were they saying? Did she say why she followed us?" the humans eagerly asked the raven.

"Several reasons," croaked Booj. "First: she loves the fox truan!"

Drallah gasped. "Loves?"

"But the truan said that's one reason he left the Queen's service."

"He doesn't love her, then," said Elwood.

The raven closed and opened his opalescent eyelids. "I'm not so sure."

"So she's not after me at all, then?"

"I think she is. She wants Tornonk to let her come with us. She told him you're 'an arrow waiting for a bow,' or something like that."

"What about Tornonk, what did he say?" said Drallah.

"He *says* he doesn't want her on this journey. He's angry with her about the Queen's dealings with the Graycloaks and treatment of the woogans. And about the *Suntawantus,* and other things. He said the Ashaws forsake their ancestors. He's weary of it."

"Do you think he'll let her come with us?" asked Elwood, his feelings mixed. He feared and distrusted the witch, but also hoped she might share news of her cousin the Queen.

"Maybe, I don't know," croaked Booj with a shrug.

"Did she mention how long she's been sneaking around our camps?" asked Drallah.

"She said she's been trailing us since the afternoon after we escaped, but only caught up with us this morning."

"What about the Queen?" Elwood asked. "Did she say what the Queen did after we left?"

"No. But the witch did say she advised the Queen it was no use sending hunters after us."

Elwood shook his head. "I don't understand the love part. I mean, how would they . . . "

"I know," said Drallah. "But it's different for them. Truans and witches both live sort of on the border between the flesh and blood lands and the spirit worlds. Sometimes bodies are not so important to them. And of course, Nemoor can change shape. But Booj," she added thoughtfully, "do you think she really loves him?"

"I don't think she is false—about that. And besides, with care she could've done him in. She wants more than whatever she sees in Elwood, I'd say."

"The raven heard the truth," said a voice out of the dusk. It was Nemoor, who, with Tornonk beside her, had approached the companions unnoticed. "Tornonk and I walk the same path. I knew it before we met, when I was still a girl studying with the great witch Gall, in the land of Magua.

"I was infatuated with a man in Gall's service. As girls do, I longed to learn by magic whether or not he was my love, my soul's companion, and I begged Gall to teach me the dream-spell by which I could know for certain. The spell sends the caster to sleep, and in her dream she is visited by the one she seeks. I persisted, and finally Gall taught me the spell as a reward for my skill and excellence in the craft, for I was the best student she had ever taught.

"I cast the spell, and slept. But the soul who came to me in my dream was not the handsome young man I had hoped to see, but a fox truan I had never met.

"His soul haunted me, and I forgot my girlish infatuation with Gall's servant. Five years later, when I went to live in the House of my uncle King Meituai, I found Tornonk there, and we met for the first time in the lands of flesh and blood—but not for the first time.

"All the years since, I have spent trying and failing to convince Tornonk our paths through the spheres are one; he agrees now to walk with me a little while. For reasons other than love, of course."

All eyes turned to Tornonk, who after a pause spoke directly to Elwood. "She will not try to return you to the Queen. She has promised."

"Good," said Drallah. "But do you mean you want to let her come with us to Gaulatash?"

"And Migdowsh," said Nemoor.

"No!" said Drallah, startled. Then, in a tone that would permit no argument, "We go on our own from the river—we will go on our own now."

Reaching into Tornonk's small bag as though it were her own, the witch drew out a bundle of dried meat. Then, hunkering down and leaning back against the stump, she unwrapped it and began to eat.

"I must have food while we talk," she said between mouthfuls. "I am famished from the changing, and the trance, and the long trail."

"You've kept us too long in this land already," said Drallah. "We don't have time to talk. Tornonk, we can find our way from here. Thank you for all you've done. We won't forget it. Farewell."

At that Drallah turned and strode off. On top of the green stump, Booj gave a little *crark?* and then launched himself after her. Elwood and Slukee followed in the girl's wake, the boy mumbling thanks to Tornonk over his shoulder as they walked away.

"Hear us before you forgo our help," called the fox truan.

They stopped, and Drallah took a step back toward him.

"You journey to a perilous place," Tornonk continued. "We could help you."

"I don't see why you should want to help us."

"We know what you seek and why you seek it. Even before Elwood told Ainathuai, and Ainathuai told Nemoor, we guessed your purpose."

Elwood looked quickly at Nemoor. "Yes," she said. "The Queen told me your story the morning we discovered you were gone. She was distraught; she fears you will die in the Swamp. She begged me to bring you back. Do not be angry with her: there was very little about your purpose we did not already know."

"Of course, when we captured you and searched your gear," continued Tornonk, "we found the copy of Ingagil's map with its note on the Ogin, the seeing-shell that Nentop the Nohar made long ago. And news of Granashon's disappearance had come to Ashawda from your land. It was not difficult to put the two together, and guess you were on a hunt for the Eye, to use its power to find the Nohar. Remember, the Eye belonged to Mobb of Ashawda. The tale of the Eye of Ogin is well known to the Ashaws.

"And I saw there was more behind your hunt than the foolhardiness of youth: Elwood Pitch and Slukee were not born in Ehm, and I did not need a witch to tell me so, or to see the wallet, and the strange papers and pictures and metals, that he brought with him from his world. And with the sense of his strangeness, there is also something that hints of great purpose."

"But why do you want to help us?" repeated Drallah.

"If Winnitok can be conquered, then so might Ashawda, and Urnutok, and Baggatok: the whole of Pahn. The Ringish have always meant to possess it all. Their numbers grow in the south, and they have a powerful master in the sorcerer Egode Vallow. He would move quickly to overrun our lands, given the chance.

"But Winnitok would not fall if Granashon the Nohar were found, and if she once again wielded her power. Then the yug horde would fail, and so would the Ringish sorcerer. I helped you escape the Queen, and would help you find the Nohar, because I do not want the Ringish to conquer these lands. And because I believe we might succeed, since powerful magic goes with Elwood Pitch."

"And Nemoor?"

Tornonk twiddled his whiskers and said softly, "Her reasons are not so clear, even to herself. But she is a strong ally, and has sworn not to hinder you in any way."

"My reasons are clear enough," said Nemoor. "I understand now it was a mistake to keep Elwood Pitch a slave. I too fear what will befall these lands."

Drallah mulled. Tornonk she trusted, for even the wickedest truan was honest. Nemoor, however, she did not trust, and she could see that Tornonk's faith in the witch was limited. But after all, she thought, the fox truan was shrewd, and knew Nemoor, and had agreed to let her join him in offering the companions help. With the aid of two such allies, their chances of finding the Eye would doubtless increase.

"Thank you," she said finally. "We welcome your help."

"Good!" said Nemoor. "Then may we return and rebuild the fire? I've exhausted myself catching you, and need more rest."

*   *   *

While Nemoor slept and Drallah and Booj remained with her, Tornonk, Elwood, and Slukee walked several miles to a village. Rousing some of its people, they bought for Nemoor a blanket, buckskins, moccasins, and other things the witch could not carry while she took another shape. They also acquired for her a long knife and a short broad-bladed sword, so she would not be armed with magic alone. By the time they returned the night was half gone; since Nemoor needed rest, they did not set out again until dawn arrived, gray and cold. With the sunrise came a fall of heavy snow. It continued all that day, collecting upon the trees until boughs drooped beneath its weight. Then the snow would slide and plummet to the forest floor with a whoosh and a thump.

The next day in the early afternoon they came to a town on the bank of the meandering and long Gaulatash River; the western boundary of Ashawda. The evergreen forest had given way to bare cottonwoods, affording the travelers longer views. Some while before they saw the town itself, they saw many pale gray trails of smoke rising into the paler gray sky.

The people of the town were astonished to see the Queen's cousin and the Queen's greatest scout among them, and there was a rush to welcome the travelers. Tornonk quickly set about bargaining with gold coins for two fine canoes, four paddles, and fresh supplies. Once he had gotten these, they immediately put the canoes in the waters of Gaulatash. Tornonk and Nemoor climbed into one, and the four companions took the other. With scores of curious Ashaws standing on the bank to watch them depart, they paddled out upon the river, and the flow carried them away from Queen Ainathuai's land.

"WHAT ARE THE SEEKERS SEEKING?"

The Gaulatash River was at that place a wide stream, slow and deep. As it bore the canoes along, the blanket of snow on either bank thinned gradually until it was all but gone, and the ancient forest dwindled into much younger woods. Like Oldotok, much of the lands south of Ashawda had been cleared and peopled by the Ringish, only to be abandoned after the wars. On the River's banks the travelers saw many empty ruined farms and towns deep in the process of being absorbed by thicket and wood. For miles and days, all they saw that was human in the land was dead.

Tornonk warned the rest it was dangerous country they were passing through, and so they kept the canoes to the River's middle as they paddled south. They were nearing the Burnt Hills, a place that for countless generations had been cursed with barrenness. Despite their lack of green life, or possibly because of it, deadly wicked things were drawn to the Hills' hollows and caves, and Tornonk warned that these sometimes wandered up the banks of Gaulatash. So the travelers were wary, especially after the sun went down.

Knowing what they now did about the two of them, the companions could not help but watch Tornonk and Nemoor with a certain curiosity. Away from Ainathuai and her court, Nemoor had lost her imperious air, and her behavior in Tornonk's presence was more like that of devoted follower than Queen's right hand. Twice or thrice when Elwood and Drallah's canoe drew even with the fox truan and the witch's, when the latter was paddling in the aft seat, they noted an expression of longing on Nemoor's face as she gazed at the rusty-furred back of Tornonk's head. At night, in the warmth and light of their campfires, they watched as Nemoor paid many little attentions to Tornonk, who, when some response was necessary, without fail— but always respectfully— rejected her.

They paddled by day and camped when night fell, landing the canoes just before dark at places where the deserted riverbank sloped gently down to the water. Once ashore again, some of the travelers hunted for a sheltered spot in which to build a fire, while the rest gathered wood for fuel. Searching a thicket for the latter on the third evening of their journey down the River, Elwood, Slukee, and Nemoor discovered a long-since fallen tree lying in a low cave-like hollow.

"It won't be hard work to keep warm tonight," observed Nemoor as they set about breaking up branches and throwing them in a pile. Since her one brief admission of wrongdoing days before, the witch had not referred to Elwood and Drallah's recent enslavement. Nemoor seemed to ignore or forget that she and her Queen had but lately held them in thrall, treating them instead like they had never been anything other than good friends since the day they met. Elwood was somewhat resentful of this, but not enough to matter. He was too impressed by Nemoor's charm, beauty, and closeness to Ainathuai to hold a grudge.

Elwood yanked distractedly at a stout branch. There was something on his mind, a question he had been wanting to ask Nemoor for days. Intentionally he had refrained from asking among the others, but now, having the chance for a private word, he could not bring himself to speak of it.

"Tell me," she said, arching an eyebrow with a smile and glancing his way. She could see, he had a feeling, right into his thoughts.

"What?"

Nemoor's smile grew yet more kind, deepening the dimples in her plump cheeks. She took a step toward him.

"Tell me what you want to know, so I can tell you."

Though he knew he should be wary of trusting her too much, it was impossible for Elwood to look upon her smiling face and doubt her motives at the same time. He sat down on the trunk of the fallen tree and asked, "Why did you make those dolls? I mean, of Slukee and me?"

"Because the Queen bid me to."

"Why—did she?"

Still smiling irresistibly, Nemoor sat down beside him and put a hand on his shoulder.

"It would've been best to ask her that yourself. Why didn't you?"

"I was going to, but we left before I had the chance."

"Why do you *think* Ainathuai bid me make her dolls?"

"I don't know. What is the magic in them? I mean—do they have power over us?"

"Ah. You fear she wanted to use you somehow. . . ."

"I didn't say that," Elwood objected quickly. "I just don't under-stand what they are, what they're for. And I didn't think a girl like her would . . . you know. She's Queen, and she's so pretty."

The witch tilted her head and said with mock-sternness, "Do you not know what a handsome young man you are?"

The boy blushed, too surprised to respond.

"Don't worry," Nemoor continued. "There's no magic of that kind in Ainathuai's dolls; there is no such tie between the dolls and those they resemble."

"But there *is* magic? What kind?"

"A kind that makes them much more wonderful than lesser dolls. You see, I give Ainathuai's dolls a little vision-magic. When she wants, she can make them come alive for her, and be alive with them. In a way, it's like any child with any toy. But with my dolls—with my dolls it's much more . . . real."

Trying to imagine what this might mean, and what Ainathuai's Elwood and Slukee dolls might do when they came alive for her, the boy got up and resumed gathering wood.

"But it's not my place to answer your question," continued Nemoor. "I'm not even sure of the answer. If you want to know why Ainathuai bid me make those dolls, you'll have to ask her yourself."

He nodded and wondered if, should he ever have the chance to ask her, she would even hear him: he had, after all, run away from her in the middle of the night, without a word, just hours after they had bared much of their hearts to one another. But it was all idle wondering; he was traveling farther and farther away, and could not reasonably expect his path, strange as it was, to cross hers again.

* * *

Before sleep that night Tornonk stirred from his thoughts and said, "Tomorrow we will reach the rapids called the Teeth. They are impassable; we'll have to leave our canoes behind and walk. We would have to give them up soon anyway—Gaulatash is narrow through the Burnt Hills and flows past a thousand ambushes. We must go another way."

As Tornonk had said they would, the next afternoon the travelers came to the Teeth: a narrowing shallow place in the river strewn with jagged upthrust rocks. The cold brown waters churned and boiled, quickly becoming hazardous. They landed on the eastern bank, and carried the canoes out of reach of any flood. Briefly they discussed hiding them for their return journey, but soon agreed it was not worth the time it would take to do so properly. So they left them upside-down, paddles underneath, amidst a stand of beeches.

The fox truan led them on a pathless way through the river-wood, out of sight of Gaulatash but not beyond hearing of its rushing waters. On the ground were scabby crusts of snow. The day was gray and mild, and everywhere were signs and glimpses of creatures going about their affairs. But as they walked farther and the sun sank low, the number of such signs and glimpses grew fewer, the ground became uneven, and the river-wood thinned. They were nearing the barren margin of the Burnt Hills. The travelers stopped for the night before it was dark and before leaving the concealing woods entirely.

To be safe they passed the hours of darkness, which were completely overcast, without a fire. Fortunately it did not grow too cold, and wrapped in their blankets they were warm enough to sleep. Drallah was the first guard; after two hours had passed, she gently shook Elwood awake. Wordlessly he rose, and likewise without a word she lay down on the spot he had made warm. Drawing deep breaths to clear his head of sleep, Elwood squatted and scratched behind Slukee's ears. While he did so the dog continued to lie where she had been sleeping by the boy's side, though at the changing of the guard she had propped herself up on the elbow of one foreleg. The boy and the dog stood and stretched, and then stepped silently away from the spot where the others were sleeping. Feeling his way with hands outstretched, Elwood found a tree a few feet off to lean against, and Slukee curled at his feet.

Opening his ears the way Drallah had taught him, Elwood began to listen. The first thing he heard was the gentle breathing of Nemoor as she slept. The others were silent: Tornonk never made a sound in his sleep, Drallah had perhaps not yet drifted off, and though he had known him occasionally to snore, at the moment Booj too was resting silently. Searching for some sound of the raven on his perch above, the boy observed that a meek south wind was visiting the branches over his head. He became aware of Gaulatash chattering in its rocky bed a quarter of a mile away. He began to hear furtive movements of night creatures, sounds he did not yet have experience enough to identify. His eyes adjusted to the dark. Though the light of the high-riding sickle moon—filtered and deflected as it was by the cloud that covered the world—was all but imperceptible, still it was enough for him to discern shapes close at hand.

After a time Slukee, who had fallen back to sleep, began to whimper at a dream. Stooping, Elwood lay a hand on her shoulder. She shifted position, then suddenly leapt up. As he straightened again in surprise, the boy was alarmed to hear a strange noise coming from the vicinity of the river. *Wind? Wolves?* he wondered, straining all his attention toward the sound. Then with an odd shiver of fright it came to him: people were singing.

Returning quickly and lightly to the others, Elwood and Slukee found Tornonk crouching over the spot where he had been asleep, his sharp muzzle pointing at the sky. Drallah too woke and sat up, and so did Nemoor. Booj stirred in the branches.

"Who are they?" whispered Elwood.

"Listen!" commanded Tornonk.

The eerie song was growing clearer. More than a few people were passing near their camp, singing as they went. Their voices were shrill, yet unmoved. They drew nearer, and the travelers could hear that they sang in Wohmog. Soon they could distinguish every word.

What are the seekers seeking?
Where is the smoke now it's gone?
It is beyond the world of worlds.
It floats with marrow in the bone.

What are the seekers seeking?
What will they become?
They hunt ashes on the wind.
They will be hidden from the sun.

What are the seekers seeking?
Where is the smoke now it's gone?
Off beyond the world of worlds
Where everything is gone.

After a silence the song began again farther off, a distant sound fading away to the south. When Elwood's ears could no longer separate the singers' voices from Gaulatash's, Nemoor spoke.

"They're a danger only to themselves."

"What are they singing about?" asked the boy, a chill on his heart. He had an unfounded, uncanny dread the answer was the travelers themselves.

"Who knows? Maybe they're 'the seekers.'"

"They follow the riverbank to the Hills," said Drallah, restraining a shudder.

"And to their deaths."

* * *

In the pearly twilight of dawn, while the others were breakfasting on cold cornbread and dried apples, Tornonk slipped down to the riverbank to examine the signs left by the passing singers. Shortly he returned and told the rest what he had found.

"There were about twenty human-folk; some wearing Mowan-made moccasins, some nothing. All their marks are uneven and light—they carry no burdens, and I think they are sick and hungry."

"They'll stir up all the monsters in the Hills, the way they're going," said Drallah.

"Yes. Their presence here is bad for us," replied Tornonk.

No nearer to knowing what possessed the singers to behave as they did, the travelers set out. Soon they left the last of the woods behind them. They crested a rise, and saw the other side descended into a wide, barren land that spread to the southern horizon: a land of parched tors like great blistering boils, and of undulant ridges like giant worms half-buried in the ashen earth. The few bare trees were stunted and isolate. Otherwise, as far as the eye could see, nothing grew but nameless gray weeds. To the southwest here and there could be seen stretches of the Gaulatash River, its nourishing waters seeming to have no effect on the barren waste they passed through, save to increase by contrast the travelers' sense of the land's utter desolation. The Burnt Hills were well named.

Booj took to the air to reconnoiter the way ahead, and the rest hurriedly began to descend the long exposed slope. Tornonk angled their path toward the mouth of a shallow defile between two ridges, the low ground of which cut like a broad groove north and south through the Hills. Once the defile was reached, its sunken position concealed them from any far-off unfriendly eyes that might be watching, and they walked more at ease. In land so bare, with Booj scouting from above, they would learn of any danger well before it was upon them. Also, there was no cave or hollow Tornonk was unaware of, no potential ambush along the way he did not know. The fox truan knew the Hills so well that, though he had looked at Ingagil's map, he did not need to consult it to find the Breathless Gate. Past journeys had taken him there, and his memory's map was drawn in much greater detail.

The raven returned from the south with news. "I have seen the singing humans. They still walk the riverbank, a few miles farther down. Vultures follow them. Otherwise, nothing moves in this whole *kon-n-nk*–blasted place."

"They do not rest much," said Tornonk. "Maybe not at all. The riverbank is rocky, hard walking. How many miles?"

"Five?" shrugged Booj.

"If they rested since they passed us in the night, it was not for long."

"I wonder what drives them," said Drallah.

Through the day they continued to follow a line parallel with Gaulatash, keeping to the low ground as much as possible. At times their southward course made it necessary for the travelers to scale hills and ridges, their heights commanding deeper, wider vistas not had on the low ground. They moved quickly over the barren earth, and by afternoon the great gray humps of the Hills lay in every direction. Toward the river, high up in the sky, floated and circled a growing number of big turkey vultures.

Booj, returning from another scouting flight, swooped down out of the sinking sun to his perch on Drallah's pack. "We've come even with the singing people; now we'll pass them. They can barely walk anymore, I think."

Tornonk stopped. "I want to try to see them."

At that moment they were descending a ridge that lay northeast-southwest, and he now turned and led them along just beneath its summit in the direction of the river. Finding the ridge ended in the base of a somewhat conical hill with a flat crown, they climbed its eastern side. When they reached the top, the humans and the fox truan crawled on their bellies to the hill's western rim, and looked out toward Gaulatash.

The opposite slope rolled downward in rounded steps to meet the river, grown much narrower since the rapids, less than half a mile off. Shielding their eyes from the brilliant sun and its dazzling reflection off Gaulatash, they scanned the riverbank. Quickly they spotted a group of figures, tiny with distance, making their way slowly along it. They walked in scattered file, and their steps were so faltering that even from afar the travelers could see they were near collapse. In the sky above, the vultures saw as well.

Tornonk turned to Booj, who was standing between his head and Drallah's. "Would you go down—carefully—and ask them where they are going?"

With a quiet whoosh the raven was in the air and gliding down to intercept the band of strangers. The others continued to lie flat on the crown of the hill, watching.

"These dying folk might not concern us," said Tornonk, "or they might. Maybe he can find out."

Nearing the strangers, Booj suddenly broke from his long, graceful glide. Wheeling sharply, he started back toward the hilltop. The strangers seemed to have noticed him, and came almost to a halt.

"Something's wrong," said Drallah.

Like a small black bolt of lightning, Booj, keeping his distance from where they lay watching, shot past the travelers and out of sight behind the hill. A few moments later he reappeared on the hilltop, on foot and from the east, in such haste he waddled. "Ambush!" he croaked. "They're walking into a yug ambush."

The others turned their eyes back to the riverbank as Booj rejoined the travelers' lookout. No longer scattered straggling along their way, the strangers were now walking slowly onward in a close group.

"I saw a green face looking out from behind that rock—that one like a table, where the river bends away. I called to warn the humans."

They watched the strangers approach the place Booj described. A long flat rock, almost indiscernible from the riverbank at that distance, lay at a right angle to the river just a few yards from its edge. All around it were scattered more boulders, some large enough to conceal a number of crouching ambushers.

"They know it's a trap—why don't they run away?" said Elwood, his heart beating so hard and fast it hurt.

"They have no weapons," rasped Booj. "Why don't they heed my warning?"

A swarm of yugs detached themselves from the distant jumble of rocks, the low sun flashing bloodily on the tips of their javelins. Ferociously they set upon the humans, who did not run or even try to defend themselves.

"Let's help them!" cried Drallah, jumping up and casting off her gear.

"They will all be dead before we could get there," said Tornonk. "Get down, Winhar! We cannot reach them in time."

"They sought death, and they have found it," said Nemoor.

Even as she spoke the slaughter ended. The corpses lay on the ground in a heap that the killers, plundering, clambered over. It did not require long to take from the dead what they would. Once finished, the yugs, apparently considering what to do next, fell to milling around.

"I could tell them now what they'll do, though they won't decide themselves until nearly dark," said Tornonk with disgust. "They debate where to have their feast: whether to bear their prey back to their lair, or to stay the night where they are. In the end they will stay where they are. They are yugs, and yugs always choose whatever takes the least work."

"Let's go," said Drallah, seeing Elwood's face had turned as ashen as the hills all around. "There's no advantage in staying here." She shouldered her pack and bow, and with the others crept back to the eastern side of the hill. They slid over the rim and down into the defile below, then struck out toward the south once again.

THROUGH THE
BREATHLESS GATE

Having led them on well into the night, Tornonk at last called a halt at the edge of a round pit-like depression in the base of a hill. Weary to the bone, the three humans climbed within, wrapped their blankets around their shoulders, and threw themselves to the ground to sleep. Slukee curled up tightly against Elwood's side, and lacking a tree to perch on, Booj settled on Drallah's pack. Tornonk slipped up the hill to take the first watch.

The air was mild, and across the sky was a veil of cloud so thin the stars shone through. Elwood lay on his back gazing up at the pulsing, scarlet light of the Coyote Star, in a part of the western sky not blocked from his view by a ridge. His body felt half dead with exhaustion, but his mind, unable to call up anything but the massacre they had witnessed that day, would not rest. Try as he might, he found he simply could not close his eyes. While he lay sleepless, light from the rising moon entered and began to fill the dark hollow. His horror at the memory grew with the light, as though nourished by it.

He was startled by a voice. "You must put it away from you for tonight, Elwood," it whispered. It was Nemoor. Turning his way, her beautiful round face was illuminated by the blue-green moonlight. "You need to rest," she continued. "And so do I, but I cannot while your trouble is flying around."

"I'm sorry, I didn't realize you could—tell." He had forgotten she always seemed to know when his heart and head were in turmoil.

"That's all right. What if I found out why those people are dead? Would that give you peace?"

"We would all be glad to know," said Drallah, who was also unable to sleep.

"How?" asked Elwood.

Nemoor loosened her blanket and propped herself up on an elbow. "Their spirits may still be near."

"You mean . . . "

"I'll go out from my body to find them, and see if the spirits will tell me their story. I'll be back before the sun. Whatever happens, do not disturb my body. I may seem in trouble, or cry like I'm hurt, but you must not touch me nor speak to me."

"It's dangerous, Nemoor," said a soft voice over their heads. It was Tornonk, just come silently down the hill; with his big keen ears he had heard their talk. "It's dangerous, parting body and spirit before death. And if yugs come while your spirit is away, what then?"

"You will defend my body until I return, I hope."

"I will. But I might fail." The others noticed something unusual in the fox truan's voice, an uncharacteristic hint of earnestness, and guessed that it was fear for Nemoor.

"This is in my power, Tornonk. I won't be long, and I won't come to harm."

She cast off her blanket and sat up, crossing her legs before her and letting her head hang over her lap. She began to hum or sing murmurously; a faint, hypnotic sound that in turn chilled and warmed the hearts of the others. Then she was silent again.

It seemed to Elwood that half the night had gone by when Tornonk, who had left the pit some time before, reappeared, crouching at its edge. The moonlight shone on the tips of his fur. "She has gone," he said, but did not explain how he knew. "Remember, whatever happens: do not touch her, do not speak to her."

The companions remained sleeplessly awaiting some change in Nemoor, and Tornonk returned to his watch on top of the hill. The moon sank, slowly withdrawing its blue and green rays from the pit. Nemoor's strange venture diverted Elwood somewhat from the memory of the massacre, and he found himself yawning. Still the witch did not move, or make a sound.

He awoke with a start from a dream of some distant place. His mind had at last succumbed to his body, and he had fallen asleep with his back against the wall of the pit. It was still night. The sound that had awakened him came again: a quiet moan out of the pitch dark a few feet away. As she had warned she might, Nemoor was reacting to whatever was happening in the world of the spirits. Elwood was too frightened to move.

"If she gets any louder," he heard Drallah whisper in the dark, apparently to Booj, "things will start coming out of their holes to look for her."

Abruptly the moaning ceased, and they heard Nemoor draw a deep gasping breath. In moments Tornonk, his vision unhindered by the dark, was back in the pit and at her side.

"Are you all right?"

The voice that replied was small, and it trembled. It was Nemoor's, but much changed from earlier. "All right, yes."

"Tell us what you learned, before it fades and you forget."

In a voice not much louder than a whisper, Nemoor began. At first her speech was hesitating and broken, as if her tongue and lips had been long out of use, but soon her words began to flow. However, these were so strange that the others understood nothing of what she said.

"There was a face in the fire under the breakfast. Only the girl the sun touched saw. A drinking mouth, he says. The flow's gate, the mouth's tongue. Oh, hurt! Burned—peeling—breath—*hurt*. A mouth opens to drink fire, water, to drink snow-skin, leaf-skin, sun-skin dripping on the hills. . . . Oh, the dogs howl in the river; the fire smokes, they breathe. The curse from the mouth—"

They waited to hear more, but she did not speak again that night. As dawn approached she began to breathe slowly and heavily, and they knew she had fallen asleep. Since sleep was needed by all, they remained in the pit through the morning, each taking a short turn at watch. Nemoor, however, they did not disturb, as her journey to the spirits had left her much wearier than the rest.

A little after noon, anxious to be going, Tornonk finally roused Nemoor from her sleep. The others were climbing out of the pit beneath the hill to prepare for another march; looking back, they noted how gently he knelt by her side and woke her. The two remained in the pit talking quietly for several minutes while Nemoor ate. Then they emerged, she seeming returned to her normal state of mind, refreshed, and ready to set out.

Though Elwood and Drallah would have liked to question her about her time among the spirits, they both sensed Nemoor was not yet ready to speak of it, and so all that afternoon they waited and wondered as they walked on through the ashen Hills. Other than the endless gray ranks of weeds and the rare forlorn tree, they saw nothing living. Even Booj, returning from his farseeing flights, reported no being afoot. They pressed on, stopping after dark in the lee of a hill. Before Nemoor took the first watch, Drallah finally asked her what, if anything, she had learned among the spirits of the dead, repeating to her her strange words of the previous night.

Out of the darkness came the sound of Nemoor breathing something between a groan and a sigh. It had been her idea to seek the spirits, but she had not imagined learning from them news as dire as she now had to tell.

"The spirits of the dead showed me ... things I never expected to see. Their journey and ours are ... " Before continuing she shook her head roughly, as if dispersing a fog. "I know now where the Ringish sorcerer Egode Vallow is to be found: he dwells in secret in Migdowsh."

"Are Vallow and the Otguk allies?" interrupted Tornonk in a voice much sharper than the friends had yet heard him use.

"I do not know. The spirits spoke only of the sorcerer. It was he who worked a curse from afar that destroyed their village. They were from the land of Mowan, to the northeast. All was well with them, until one day they woke possessed by an awful madness. Neighbor slew neighbor, and families set their own homes on fire. The ones who did not die were driven south, on and on without rest, by the madness of the curse. It was Egode Vallow who drew them; it was Egode Vallow who did this to them—all to provide food for his yug soldiers. His yugs are many, and they are hungry. All who dwell near these Hills are in great danger. The sorcerer calls them to their deaths.

"That is the reason for the slaughter we witnessed. That is what I learned walking the cold plains beyond the lands of flesh and blood."

There was a stunned silence. Finally Elwood said, "Vank-mul. General Fienoth. That must be where he was heading—the Swamp."

"On some errand to his master," said Nemoor. "I wonder if the scouts we sent to follow him are still alive."

"And I wonder," said Tornonk, "why the Otguk allows Egode Vallow to dwell in his domain. It would be strange and terrible should those two have joined in common purpose."

* * *

Eventually Nemoor moved off to keep watch, and the others lay down to sleep with darkened thoughts. Their second night in the desolate Hills was cloudless. A chill western wind was blowing, but as the ground where they lay was protected by the hill, few wisps of wind-driven cold could reach them.

Elwood awoke feeling he had only been a moment asleep, though it had been hours. A hand with a palm that was coarse like the pads of Slukee's paws was gently shaking his head as it grasped and covered his mouth. A soft voice whispered a single syllable in his left ear.

"Yugs."

Tornonk released his mouth and stole away into the darkness without another word. Elwood sat up. The thin moon had already come and gone, but by the light of the stars he could see the vague shapes of the others rising and gathering themselves. No one made a sound. He strained his ears, but could hear only the wind blowing through the hills.

The fox truan returned, and with hand signals told them to don their gear. They were ready in a moment. Then he gestured in the direction they had come from, and the rest understood it was toward the yugs he was pointing. His green eyes gleamed in the starlight, and he whispered a single word: "Haste."

He turned southward and set out at a stealthy trot, and the others followed. As they went they spread into a single file; Nemoor after Tornonk, then Elwood, then Slukee, then Drallah in the rear. Booj glided here and there across their path, and occasionally they glimpsed his silhouette against the stars overhead.

They had been jogging thus for only a few minutes when a wild cry sounded among the hillsides not far behind. It was quickly followed by dozens more, all from the vicinity of their resting place. The yugs had found their camp.

"Sounds like a lot of them," muttered Drallah, unconsciously grabbing the grip of her knife.

Now Tornonk abandoned the winding way of the low-ground, instead pushing straight up, over, and down the hills and ridges in their path. As they were scaling one of these, Booj glided low over their heads.

"They're catching up!"

Not stopping, the fox truan looked back. With his excellent night vision, he could see what the humans could not: more yugs than he could quickly count were pouring over the top of the ridge the travelers had just come down themselves. Like Tornonk, the yugs saw by night as well as by day, and in the moment he looked back those in the lead spotted their quarry. Whooping and hollering at each other, they began to run. Elwood turned in the direction of the fearsome sounds, but to his night-blind eyes the yugs looked more like a landslide, a denser darkness gushing down the dark ridge.

Cursing in Ashawnk, Nemoor stopped and turned to face the yugs. Elwood, Slukee, and Drallah hurried past her, then paused to see what she would do. Tornonk also stopped, and Booj lit on Drallah's pack.

"Cover your ears," the witch muttered.

They saw the upper half of her form against the starry fields just above the horizon; beyond her lower half the yugs were swarming on toward them. Under the yugs' wild cries, they heard a low steady hum growing deep inside Nemoor. As it grew she slowly raised her open hands, then suddenly flourished them high over her head. At the same time her mouth stretched wide, and the low hum building within her came forth as a crashing thunderous cry that made the others cower and cover their ears. Dozens of yugs caught in the cry's powerful cone were thrown backward and dashed to the ground. There they lay stunned, while the rest turned and hustled back over the ridge, whimpering and calling out to one another.

Tornonk shook the shout's lingering effects from his ears, surveyed the felled and fleeing yugs, and turning to move again said, "That's given us time. Now come!"

They obeyed, Nemoor swaying a little as she went. Tornonk set the pace at a cautious run. Though he and Slukee could negotiate the dark ground at any speed without risking a fall, the three humans could not, and he knew that a twisted ankle now would mean the end.

Before long the eastern horizon, seen from hill- and ridgetop, began to pale. For some time a dullness had been creeping over the stars in that region of the sky. Their purple-black backdrop faded to violet, which was soon overtaken by a growing soft orange-rose. As the light of the world increased, so did the travelers' pace.

"Happy dawn," cried Drallah to Elwood. "Light to run by—and shoot by."

"*Cren-n-nk!*" called Booj as he swooped down along their file from high above. "They're after us again!"

Tornonk slowed them to a trot and called up to the raven, "I thought there were close to forty. What's your count?"

"That, or a few more."

"Many more than were at the riverbank. Maybe they were joined by another band, or more than one." Half to himself he added, "While we spent yesterday morning at rest."

The fox truan began to run again, and the rest matched his pace. As he ran he constantly studied the terrain. Several times, when their way passed over high ground, he stopped and scanned the hills in all directions. The morning was not far advanced when, pausing on one such height, he sighted the pursuing yugs descending a hillside in the distance.

"We are just a few hours' walk from the Gate on the map, but there come Vallow's soldiers. We cannot allow them to follow us into the Swamp. But they are too close to lose in these hills."

"What should we do?" asked Elwood, looking back with the rest at the trailing yugs. They were still too far away to pick out individuals from the mass.

"Climb," he answered with decision, pointing to a high, steep-sided tor adjoining the ridge they stood upon.

When they reached its pocked narrow summit a few minutes later, they found the far side of the tor, though still a formidable incline, was less steep than the side they had come up by. From this high point, they could see more of the Burnt Hills all at once than they yet had. Nothing moved beneath the blue winter-bright sky, so deeply contrasted by the dull dying gray of the earth; the yugs, for the time being, were hidden beyond a chain of hills.

Elwood, Drallah, and Tornonk set about stringing their bows and readying arrows. Slukee stood watching the north with flashing eyes and ears aloft, staunchly thrusting the cascade of white fur down her front in the direction of their danger. Booj minced back and forth over the hilltop, occasionally spreading and snapping his wings in agitation. Nemoor sat with legs crossed and eyes closed on the hill's highest point, her short sword across her lap.

After studying the land in every direction for a time, Tornonk pointed to a trio of squat hills to the southwest and said, "The last encounter in the Battle of the Burnt Hills was fought there."

But as he spoke, Slukee growled, and the first yugs came over the ridge that ended in the base of the tor. They ran steadily in a tight group of two and three across; at that distance, as more and more streamed into view, they looked to the travelers like a giant green snake slithering swiftly toward them.

"Tornonk," began Drallah with a rare note of uncertainty in her voice, "are you sure this is wise?"

"According to such wisdom as I have. We could not lose them: they are too close, and these sickly weeds cover all the ground; even a light step leaves a lasting sign. And if we allowed them to chase us into Migdowsh, they would raise the Swamp against us. Better to fight these yugs here than the Otguk himself in his lair.

"It will take them time to get up this hill, as it did us," he continued, testing his bowstring and eyeing the yugs' approach. "We will have plenty of shooting before they reach the top. If they do close with us, we three will stand in a triangle around Elwood and Slukee."

The morning was only half gone when the yugs reached the tor, and without pause began to climb. The greater number swarmed together on the northern slope, but many spread to the eastern and western faces. As they climbed, some of those waiting above made a count.

"Thirty-six," croaked Booj, nervously tearing apart a weed with one foot.

Haunted to distraction by the memory of the riverbank massacre,

Elwood nocked an arrow with trembling hands. Barely seeing them, he looked over the yugs, who had now drawn near enough to pick out details of their appearance. The majority bore short javelins with cruel hooks at the base of their long heads, the rest tomahawks. They had covered themselves with what seemed to be the dried inverted husks of some big water plant, with holes cut to admit the arms and neck. Their green feet were bare, and on their heads they wore a variety of caps, helms, or crowns that appeared to be fashioned of dried flora as well. They were too far yet for him to see the red of their eyes.

"Granashon, I hope you're watching this," he muttered under his breath.

Tornonk barked directions. "Drallah, on my right; Elwood, left. Use every arrow well!"

Each chose a spot at the summit's edge and took aim. Nemoor, still sitting cross-legged on the very top of the tor, called to Booj. The raven perched on the blade across her lap, and the witch began to stroke his feathers and whisper in his ear.

The twang of a bowstring was heard, followed by a strangled cry from below. Tornonk's was the first shot. His bow was small, but shooting from above extended its range. Drallah was next: a second yug cried out, fell, and rolled lifelessly back down the slope. Before Elwood could shoot even once, they both struck a second time. He did not want to waste an arrow on a shot he could not make, but now the yugs on his side of the tor were drawing within range of his skill. Because the incline was steep, and because their backs were hunched, the yugs were climbing on all fours. They drew nearer, and Elwood could see their yellow tongues hanging from their mouths. Eight pairs of crazed blood-red eyes were fixed upon him. He aimed at the heart of the nearest, imagining, as Drallah had taught him, his arrow already piercing that precise spot. He saw this very clearly in his imagination, then realized he was seeing it in reality: he had let go the arrow almost without knowing, and the arrow

226

had flown true. The yug, shot through the heart, made no sound. His upward progress ceased. He stood and wavered a moment, then fell flat on his back, slid a short distance down the slope, and lay still.

Elated by this success, Elwood set another arrow to the string and fixed on a second target. Again he let go the arrow, and again it arrived precisely where he intended it to. This yug wailed in agony before falling on his face, dead.

For the moment Elwood's fear was gone, and his only thought was to avenge the Mowanish villagers. He shot a third arrow, and another yug fell. Though he was practically delirious with rage, somehow he had more control over his body than ever before. With newfound swiftness he grabbed another arrow and drew it smoothly back to his ear.

The girl and the fox truan also persisted in raining one well-aimed arrow after another down on the ascending yugs. As the foremost neared the top, the dead and dying of almost half their number lay strewn across the face of the tor and piled at its base. But it seemed the yugs were too crazed to balk under the deadly fall of arrows, and they were about to reach their prey.

Before they were able to, the sky was blotted out, and a vast blackness swept over the archers' heads. Drallah gasped in disbelief: it was Booj, by an illusion of magic appearing to have grown as big as the tor. He produced an illusionary hurricane with a mighty flap of wings, and with giant feet clawed at the yugs. *"Cron-n-nk!"* he cried, and the hills shuddered at the sound. Overwhelmed, the yugs flung themselves shrieking back down the steep slope. Even as they fell the sky returned, and Booj, his natural size again, glided back to the top of the tor.

Rising from where she sat to better see the effect of her magic, Nemoor stood beside Tornonk. After the last one, she would not have the strength to produce another shout for some time. This brief illusion of a giant Booj, however, served just as well: the yugs were dazed and scattered across the lower slopes far below. Many had lost hold of their weapons, and all anxiously watched the sky for the giant raven's return. When after several minutes he did not reappear, they gathered themselves and started the assault over again.

Slukee stepped somewhat timidly over to Booj, who was swaggering proudly at Drallah's feet, and questioned him with her nose. The raven replied with a friendly croak.

"Yugs would not normally brave another attempt," said Tornonk. "They are in the sorcerer's power. Remember! Use your arrows well."

The yugs seemed to climb even faster this time. As they neared once again, Elwood could feel his ecstasy ebbing away. Still, he gritted his teeth and muttered dark curses on the yugs as the first one drew within range. He released his arrow, but it fell somewhat short, impaling the yug's foot. He whisked up another from his dwindling store on the ground beside him, and took aim again. This one missed entirely. He nocked another, counting as he did his remaining arrows. "After this," he thought, "only three left." He also counted six pairs of red eyes coming up his side of the hill, all of them locked on himself. He prepared to shoot.

That arrow struck near enough to the mark, though not on the mark exactly, and another yug was down. As Elwood drew his third-to-last arrow, he felt a slight return of the ecstasy with which his aim had been so deadly before; but he reached out for it too greedily, and released the arrow too soon. It flew wide of the yug he had meant it for, who was now very close. The second-to-last also went off target, wildly so, and did the boy's enemies no harm.

He grabbed up his last arrow as the foremost yug was climbing over the summit's edge. His marvelous mastery of himself and his bow had gone, and been replaced by intense doubt of his own skill and strength. As he fumbled with the arrow and the yug was upon him, he glimpsed Nemoor darting forward with sword in hand. Slukee was at his side, growling viciously. In the yug's gnarled green fist swung a long tomahawk, which he raised over his head to strike the boy. Unable somehow to shoot in time, Elwood desperately raised the bow to block the falling blade. He succeeded, but the yug made a second thrust with the tomahawk's blunt wooden haft. It struck Elwood sharply on the temple just below his cap, and he fell to the ground as the fight began to whirl around him.

* * *

Elwood woke to a throbbing pain in his head, and a moist, soft tongue gently licking his temple and cheek. He opened his eyes. Slukee's face was immediately above his own, blocking out half the empty blue sky. In a moment Drallah's appeared beside the dog's.

"You were hit hard. Just be still."

"Is everyone all right?"

"You're the only one hurt."

"The yugs?"

Drallah tried unsuccessfully to keep her excitement and pride out of her answer. "Dead, every one—and six of us against thirty-six! You should've seen Tornonk fight. He probably killed a dozen with his sword alone."

"Six," corrected the fox truan softly. He and Nemoor were hunkered down just beyond Drallah, who knelt at Elwood's side.

The boy threw an arm around Slukee's neck and sat up. He winced, gingerly touching his head. The place he had been struck was swollen.

"Don't move," warned Nemoor, "the wound may be deep."

"We cannot stay here, so we must hope it is not deep," said Tornonk. "But rest for the moment, Elwood. Drallah, will you tend to him?"

While Elwood, Slukee, and Drallah remained on the tor's summit, Tornonk and Nemoor moved among the yugs retrieving arrows, insuring all were dead, and rolling the corpses down the slopes. While they undertook this grim work, Booj flew off in a great circle to learn if any further trouble was at hand. As the minutes passed,

Elwood decided he was not badly hurt, both his vision and his thoughts being clear. He looked around at the battlefield: on three sides of the tor's crown, lifeless green shapes in gray husks were ranged chaotically as they had fallen.

Without moving he looked at the yug closest to him. It was flat on its back staring sightlessly upward, a grin of agony on its face. On the ground beside it, a pool of yellow blood was drying brown. He thought of the vengefulness that had so suddenly possessed him, and was just as suddenly gone. He had not known he was capable of such wrath, or such deadly skill. Wondering where in himself these things lay hidden, he regarded almost admiringly the vegetal green of the yug's skin. Recalling and pondering what Noshkwa the herb witch had said about the yugs' maker, how he had created the yugs in part as a kind of cruel joke, Elwood turned his outward attention to the empty sky.

In less than an hour, the raven came back to say that nothing stirred save the wind for many miles. But he had bigger news: from high above the Burnt Hills, he had spied the hazed brown edge of Migdowsh. While the companions were talking in excited tones of this, their far-sought and now imminent destination, the fox truan and the witch returned with a sack containing all the arrows they could find that had not been broken.

"Gaulatash bends near here," said Tornonk after he had heard Booj's news. "On the way we can stop and cleanse our arrows and blades. Elwood, are you well?"

To indicate that he was, the boy stood up.

"Good. There's no time to hide the yugs; but at least on the low ground they can't be seen from afar. Now: let's get away from here, and reach the Swamp as quickly as we can."

Proceeding south from the tor, they found the terrain at times very gradually descended as though toward a shallow but vast valley bottom. The hills and ridges became denser, forming mazes between them. Through these they jogged, Booj acting as lookout high overhead. Elwood's pain worsened, but he steeled himself against the discomfort and pressed on, uncomplaining. They kept to the low ground, and the sun was hidden behind the summits of the western hills, leaving them among shadows. Still its rays illumined the gray heights, and the sky remained a bright though deepening blue.

They turned into a long natural corridor between two great humped ridges; the weeds that covered it, they noted, had been crushed down by many passing feet. The corridor stretched for half a mile to a pair of stony beehive-shaped hills that stood side by side like monuments or sentinels. Above and between them hung a thick umber haze. Though they were there for the first time, Elwood and Drallah recognized these hills from Ingagil's map: they were Gutt and Gatt, the Breathless Gate.

Tornonk slowed them to a trot while Booj flew ahead, circled the twin hills, and flew back. He had seen no apparent danger, and so glided silently to his perch on Drallah's pack. Cautiously they proceeded along the corridor between the ridges. As they neared its end Tornonk halted them, and went forward alone. Like a red shadow he vanished between the hills. In a few minutes he reappeared, beckoning to the others. Going to him, they all passed through the Breathless Gate, and the companions saw the Great Swamp at last.

SEARCHING

With their first steps into the narrow gap between the hills, there was a great change in atmosphere. Behind it was windblown and chill, but walking forward the air quickly turned stagnant and warm, filling their nostrils with an extraordinary stench of rotting vegetation. At the same time they began to hear a distant, steady hum. On the other side of the Breathless Gate the level of the land dropped sharply, and what they saw spread out below them was more like some measureless nightmare realm than any country of the waking world. The sun, lingering just above the western hills, suffused the haze over the Great Swamp with a crimson light. Beneath this thin shimmering veil, the last rays shone like blood and fire upon countless labyrinthine pools, streamlets, and bogs. All across the watery land, bending and doubling under their own decaying weight, stood multitude upon multitude of giant swampland reeds and ferns edged red by the sun. The Swamp stretched into the distance as far as the eye could reach—from the travelers' high vantage, very far indeed—and gave them such an awful impression of the infinite that Elwood and Drallah were struck dumb. Remembering why they were there, Elwood felt like fainting, and his head seemed to swim in circles around the throbbing bump on his temple.

"Somewhere down there lies the Eye of Ogin," said Nemoor with a dramatic wave of her hand, then added matter-of-factly, "maybe."

"But doubtless the Otguk and the sorcerer *are* down there," said Tornonk. "We should not stand in the open."

Beginning where they stood, a rocky tongue of land plunged sharply to the level of the Swamp. Tornonk leading, they began to descend. Looking east and west, they saw that the sides of the last hills were practically sheer, and stood as a natural rampart along the Great Swamp's edge. The gap between Gutt and Gatt was the only one to be seen in all the miles their position commanded.

As it neared the level of the vast buzzing Swamp, the tongue widened and finally at the bottom split in two. The halves ran off in opposite directions, forming a thin, level margin of rocky earth along the base of the Hills. Seeing that grasses and ferns trying to grow on this strip of solid ground were well trampled, they did not doubt it saw much coming and going of Graycloaks and yugs.

Without pausing, Tornonk strode down into the giant twilit ferns of the Swamp, and the rest followed. Instantly the wide world became narrow, and the dry earth moist. As they pressed forward, they disturbed a pair of herons who, taking flight, called alarms of *"fronk! fronk!"* to one another. In response, the surrounding hum of swampland noise, a steady and immense chorus of countless, mostly tiny creatures' voices, grew louder and higher in pitch. The travelers took a few more steps into the ferns, and the fox truan turned to say, "Follow me closely; even here at the edge there are quicksands, disguised pools...."

Finding it too warm and close in the Swamp to wear them, the humans paused to shed and pack their blankets. That done, they all crept farther away from the Breathless Gate. As the very last of the twilight faded, Tornonk settled them in as dry a place as could be found to wait out the dark hours. After a cold meal and a little whispered conversation, the other travelers lay down to rest while Drallah stood first watch. As the night took hold, voices faded from the swampland chorus. Soon noises became fugitive and irregular: the

squeak of bats hunting their breakfast overhead; the splash of a creature jumping into a pool; other sounds, harder to identify. Once,
the travelers were startled by a squeal of fright and pain that tore
across the Swamp and was followed by silence. But far more disturbing was the singing of frogs that began in the middle of the
night and continued for several hours. As she kept watch, Drallah
wondered about their size: if the depth and volume of their voices
were any indication, they were big even for bullfrogs. Though their
song consisted solely of the phrase, *"brob-BWA, brob-BWA,"* in monotonous repetition, something told her there was more to the frog's
music than its simplicity suggested.

"The Otguk's children, probably," she said to herself, touching
the grip of her knife.

In the morning, the returning sun was hidden beyond a heavy
cover of grayish-brown and yellow cloud. The Swamp began to hum
and buzz again, and some of the creators of the noise began to whir
and blunder around the travelers as they broke their fast. They were
mostly green flies as big as Elwood's thumb, but dragonflies, their
long indigo or fuchsia bodies shining like new metal in spite of the
dulled sun, darted among them also. The green flies rapidly became
intolerable. Not quite in time to prevent one from giving Elwood a
bad bite on the back of his neck, Drallah unpacked the little pot
Noshkwa had given them. Gently she pried open its dragonfly-
embossed lid and hastily dabbed some of the thick oily jelly she
found inside on the skin, fur, feathers and clothes of each of the
travelers. It smelled faintly and not unpleasantly of some substance
no one but Nemoor could identify, but she refused to tell the others
what it was.

"It is secret," she declared as Drallah dabbed her forehead. "I will
say; the herb witch gave you a gift more precious than you know."

The mysterious jelly worked well. The bugs that had begun to
swarm around them withdrew, and the travelers were able to discuss in peace how to begin the search.

"Ingagil wrote," said Drallah, "that when he and Pruck followed the yugs into the Swamp, their signs led due south from the Breathless Gate, and they trailed them for five miles before they turned back."

"So we will walk as far that way, and begin the search in those parts," said Tornonk.

As they went, the humans and the fox truan each cut a tall dry reed to test the ground with. Stopping on the way, Tornonk showed the others the reeds' usefulness, and how deceiving appearances in Migdowsh could be: prodding its center with his staff, a patch of what had seemed firm, moss-covered land sank like a carpet into a pool of thick brown water that was lying hidden just underneath. Below the surface, the sunken moss closed around the end of Tornonk's staff, and he had to struggle to draw it out again.

Slukee sniffed at the edge of the exposed pool. "Walk with me!" said Elwood, anxiously waving the dog to his side.

Such hidden dangers, and the wateriness of the land, made the going very slow. By the time they walked five miles, the sun had already reached its peak beyond the cloud ceiling. They had come to a series of water fields divided by patches and peninsulas of boggy land. In the shallow waters stood sparse groves of death-bleached trees, all stripped bare of limbs and bark but still standing. After some searching, they found a little mound that rose like an island above the standing water. It was as suitable a place to camp as they were likely to find, so they stopped, shed their gear, and unpacked a meal, while they ate discussing what they would do.

"As usual, we'll need to rely on you and your wings a lot, Booj," said Drallah. "You're much better equipped than the rest of us for this hunt."

"Booj will not be the only one with wings," said Nemoor. "Nor will he be the only raven."

"You're going to change shape?" asked Drallah. "We were hoping you might have some kind of seeking power—some magic that could lead us to the Eye, or something."

"Because it is such a powerful object, I may be able to sense it; but the Eye of Ogin will probably have to be nearby before I can. The more ground I cover, the better."

"For those who will remain on the earth," said Tornonk, "I fear the denizens of the Swamp. We who do not have wings to fly away should hunt together."

They decided to begin with a circle two miles across, their camp at its center. Booj was to fly over the eastern half, Nemoor the western, while Elwood, Drallah, Slukee, and Tornonk explored the same ground on foot in an outward-moving spiral. Once this plan was agreed upon, Nemoor went off to the far side of the island-mound to make her transformation.

She did not take long. As Booj foraged for bugs a few feet from where the rest waited and watched the Swamp, a plump raven suddenly appeared beside him and, without a word, began also to probe the muddy earth with her beak. He hopped backward for caution's sake, and eyeing her with suspicion rasped, "Is it you?" She laughed. Once Booj had briefly examined her new shape and expressed his wonder at her change with a mild *crark,* the pair joined the others, who were dividing up the witch's belongings and adding them to their own bags.

It was a long, dismal afternoon for the four earthbound searchers. Most of the ground within the circle was under as much as three feet of murky brown water, which, because it rendered their eyes of little use, obliged them to search with the ends of their reed staffs and the bottoms of their feet. It was not long before their moccasins and britches were soaked inside and out, and Slukee's fur was plastered to her ribs. There were constant fears of sinkholes, water snakes, yugs, nahrwucks, and worse, as well as a wearying struggle against reason: they plainly saw that in the more than two hundred years since the Eye of Ogin was brought to that place, it could very well have sunk deep into the mud of the Swamp, so deep that no amount of hunting would ever uncover it. And that, of course, was merely one of numberless ways the Eye could be lost forever.

Though Elwood and Drallah had told themselves from the start that they understood and accepted the all-but-impossible nature of their quest, until that afternoon of wading through the perilous water fields—while facing the prospect of untold days spent in the same way—they had not actually grasped the hopelessness of the undertaking. Over the course of their long journey to Migdowsh, whenever they considered the minuscule chances of finding an object the Eye's size in a place as immense and dangerous as the Great Swamp, both had imagined Granashon would, once they arrived, show them the way somehow—with another vision maybe, or a sign. But now, having arrived, and so far lacking any such guidance, the hunt seemed very different from their imagining of it, and reason began to shake their faith in the wisdom of what they had come to do.

She's shown us the way all along—she won't stop now. So Elwood told himself a hundred times as he slogged on through the thigh-high water, testing and searching the soft submerged ground without any real hope the effort might result in success. If they were going to find the Eye, he was certain, it would have to be with Granashon's help.

Through the afternoon, Booj and Nemoor came to them several times to report. They saw nothing of the Eye. They did, however, see a crooked swamp-tortured road that led roughly south toward the heart of the Swamp. It consisted in places of causeways of raised mud, in others of narrow planks. Judging by its state, they said, it was still used, though the raven and the witch had not seen anything moving on the road.

"The Graycloak's way to his master," said Tornonk. "Either the Otguk is dead, or he and the sorcerer have some kind of arrangement. The monster would not allow a road to be built through the Swamp otherwise."

*   *   *

Evening came, and they selected a bar of relatively dry ground on which to spend the night. They had been as thorough in their afternoon's search as they were willing to be considering the shortness of Winnitok's time, the vastness of the place, and the hopelessness of finding the Eye in the way they were attempting to; so they planned to move on to a new area in the morning. Farther south was the obvious choice of direction, since that was the way the yugs who stole the Eye had fled. Exhausted, wary, and wet, they passed an uneasy night.

Continuing to search the Swamp by the same method, they spent three more days without success or major event. Nemoor kept her raven's shape throughout. As the winged travelers needed less time to explore areas the rest took half the day to cover, the pair, always searching for a glimpse of the Eye glowing in the mud, flew farther afield. The ravens were ever on the lookout for gray-cloaked men marching green-skinned soldiers up the Swamp road, or, lurking in a pool or slime-pit, the dreaded giant shape of a frog.

In the middle of the travelers' fifth night in the Swamp, the song of the frogs, which had followed them each night since the first, altered suddenly. The pace of the incessant *brob-BWA, brob-BWA* jumped, becoming faster, almost frenzied. Then a cold drenching rain began to fall, and the frogs' song abruptly ended.

More than one of the travelers groaned loudly at the rain. There was no cover to be had, and their already wet blankets were quickly soaked. They had been hounded by fear, wet, and noise every night since they entered the Swamp, and were miserable for lack of sleep. With the rain they despaired of getting any rest at all before dawn, when they had to begin again their hopeless search.

"What are we going to do?" Elwood cried, sitting up and casting off his sodden blanket. Tornonk warned him to be quiet with a hiss.

"We're going to be wet," answered Drallah in a low voice.

Lowering his own, Elwood said, "I don't mean about the rain. I mean, what are we going to do here? Keep looking for the Eye for the rest of our lives?"

No one responded for a time, during which the loud spattering of rain on mud was the only sound. Finally Drallah answered him.

"What are you saying? You don't believe any more that the Nohar guided us here?"

"Why won't she show us the way now? What if she didn't guide us here?"

"Then you should give up; leave. But I will stay."

Elwood said nothing to this, and there were no further words that night. They huddled silently and sleeplessly in the rain until dawn, and each rose under the weight of exhaustion doubled by waterlogged garments, feathers, or fur.

It was still raining, though only fitfully. After they had all eaten a little of their dwindling supply of food, Booj and Nemoor shook the raindrops from their feathers and labored up into the sky, while the rest wearily set out across the Swamp on foot. Reaching the center of the next search circle, they once again began their slow, spiraling hunt. They found in that area the Swamp was less water-laden, giving way to boggy but drier ground.

"We're not far from the road here—only two or three miles," warned Booj as he flew low over their heads, then on across the Swamp.

As they searched a wide field of ankle-deep water, Elwood silently shadowed Drallah. He was ashamed of his faithless, weak words of the night before, and hoped she was inclined to forgive him. Drallah guessed as much, and could tell Elwood would like her to speak, but was determined that he would be the one to break the silence. Toward mid-morning he finally decided to make an apology.

But as he opened his mouth to deliver it, Tornonk, who was a few paces ahead of the others, abruptly stopped. Stretching his neck and muzzle toward a colony of giant skunk cabbages rotting at the edge of the water field, he sniffed the air. He glanced quickly around the sky for Booj and Nemoor, but they were nowhere in sight. His eyes on the gray, man-high wall of leafy plants again, he stepped back to stand with Elwood, Drallah, and Slukee.

"There is a scent from up ahead—it may be human."

They all tried with the fox truan to penetrate the cabbages with their eyes, but could see nothing. "What do you want to do?" whispered Drallah.

Before answering, Tornonk scanned the sky again. Seeing neither Booj nor Nemoor, he cursed under his breath. "I can't be sure; the cabbages are too strong. Now I don't smell that other smell. Stay here, and I'll go and see."

The fox truan handed his staff to Drallah and walked to the edge of the cabbage colony, but did not immediately enter it. The ground beneath the cabbages was slightly higher than the water field, and almost dry in comparison. Tornonk crouched for a time studying the ground at the line where the land rose, then disappeared from view among the giant leaves. After a minute or two Elwood, Drallah, and Slukee began to follow slowly in his wake.

They had almost reached the water field's edge when Tornonk reappeared. Bolting out from between two cabbages, he nearly collided with Drallah.

"Graycloaks," he growled, and it was as if he summoned them with the word. From out of the leaves directly behind him burst a pale man shrouded in gray bearing a long spear, followed closely by another, and then another. Swiftly turning and drawing his sword, Tornonk crouched and sprang on the first, stabbing at the man as he flew through the air. Drallah dropped the staffs she was holding and gave Elwood a shove away from the oncoming men. Whipping the knife from her belt, she moved to help Tornonk.

Drallah had only meant to direct him away from danger, but her shove caught Elwood so off guard it nearly knocked him down. Regaining his balance, he remembered he was carrying Nemoor's sword. It was out of reach behind his back, though, held in place by a pack strap. He threw down his staff and fumbled desperately with the pack's buckles. Beside him Slukee was barking short, ear-splitting barks.

In a few moments Tornonk and Drallah had beaten back two of the men; the third lay in the mud. "There are more," barked Tornonk as he turned to Elwood, who was still struggling with his pack. Then, after a split second's consideration, the fox truan said, "We run," and with that went splashing off along the cabbage border, the humans and the dog following. They had gone only a few paces when another Graycloak rushed into the open, sword swinging at Tornonk. The fox truan parried the blow, then struck one of his own, dropping the man face down in the ankle-deep water. Looking back as they ran on, they saw that one Graycloak after another was emerging from the cabbages in pursuit. Their numbers were approaching a dozen when Tornonk and the companions crossed over a spongy bar of land and into a new water field.

Elwood found himself in swamp up to his knees. The ground all around him was treacherous, he knew, but there was no time to tread cautiously. He splashed onward heeding only their pursuers, obliged by the water's depth to haul one leg above the surface then jump with the other. With each jump the landing moccasin sank in the mud and required strenuous effort to yank free. A few feet to his right, Slukee progressed by a four-legged version of the same technique, her motion a little like a salmon fighting its way upstream. Drallah and Tornonk had to slow themselves so as not to leave the boy and the dog behind, and it was plain that they could not all cross the water field faster than the long-legged Graycloaks.

Yelping in dismay, Elwood felt one of his feet plunge deep into the mud. He brought his other foot down to catch himself, but that too failed to find the bottom. The next instant something grabbed his legs and pulled, submerging him entirely. He tried to cry out again, but instead swallowed a great gulp of swamp water. Then he was lost in the dark.

Among the Brawbwarb

The floor on which Elwood lay glistened with water drops, and smelled a little dankly—though not unwholesomely—of moist, deep earth. Upon it were shining gentle alternating lights of chill blue and warm orange. The only sound was a faint *drip, drip*.

He woke and began to cough up the portion of the Swamp he had swallowed. While his lungs and throat were clearing, and his nasal passages were smarting with the water that had gone up his nose, he became aware in a vague way of his surroundings and state. He was alone in what seemed an entry-less, windowless chamber, his waterlogged clothes clinging to his skin. His cap was gone. He could recall sinking in the mud as he and the others ran from the Graycloaks, but not how he had come to this place. Then he remembered that, as he sank, something had grabbed him by the legs.

He heard another sound: *sploosh, sploosh*. Turning toward it, he saw that the floor sloped almost imperceptibly down to a pool at the far end of the chamber. There was no telling its depth from where he lay propped on one elbow, but that was not his first concern; emerging from the pool, the shifting blue and orange light shining upon its dripping skin, was a giant frog. Elwood watched in terror and amazement as the creature pulled itself out of the water with long, splayed fingers. Then it sat or squatted on its big hind legs, folded its hands over its round pale belly, and looked at Elwood out of huge orange eyes set in salient bumps at the top of its head.

The Otguk! Elwood's thoughts screamed. *The Otguk's got me!* On hands and heels he scrambled a few feet farther away from the frog, frantically looking around the room for some escape.

Something spoke to him then, with words he heard not in his ears but in his thoughts. He could not say what language was used, though he understood it perfectly. It seemed to come from somewhere deep beneath the surface of what he thought of as language; as though it emerged whole from some seed, some core from which words grow. Translated into speech that mouths make, it said:

"Don't fear me, please!"

His terror was momentarily replaced by surprise. The voice of another, as well as his own, was sounding inside his head. He looked at the frog, who still sat regarding him. Through his confusion and fright he put a question to it. "Did you—say that?"

Again the thought-voice spoke. *"I cannot understand you that way. Think to speak."* At the same time, the frog bobbed its head in what Elwood was sure was a species of nod, and an answer to his question. It *was* the frog's voice inside his head.

Rising to a crouch, Elwood looked around him. Piled against a wall were his swamp-soaked pack, bow, and quiver, as well as Nemoor's sword. Beside them, on a hump raised of the same earthen material as the floor, was set the source of blue and orange illumination. Its tones, brightening and dimming alternately and ceaselessly, poured from holes cut in the thick rind of a large round vegetable. Other than these, and the boy and the frog, the room was empty.

"No harm will come to you among the Brawbwarb, if you bring no harm to us. You wear secret jelly. Are you a friend?"

Several things occurred to Elwood in quick succession. Though undeniably a giant among frogs, the creature before him was not much larger than himself, and nowhere near the Otguk's reputed size. Also, he could somehow tell by her thought-voice that the frog was female; the Otguk, as everyone knew, was male. But most importantly, after the shock of first seeing her passed, the frog no longer seemed so threatening. If she were the Otguk, he would be in her stomach by now, he was sure. Relieved but still cautious, he closed his eyes and concentrated hard on answering her in thought-speech.

"Yes, a friend. But where am I? And who are you?"

He thought in his own language, but as his words were received they were translated, and a reply flowed back into Elwood's mind from the frog's.

"I am Jum, of the Brawbwarb. Your kind call us frog truans. We are beneath the Swamp, in a city of my people. I carried you here, to guard you from the Gray Ones."

"What about the others, my friends?"

"I brought you below, and saw no more. But I can take you to a place nearby where some of those who've been watching you strangers are meeting. They will know about your friends."

Elwood looked with misgiving at the dark water from which the frog truan had emerged. *"That way?"* he asked, wondering how well she understood his need for air.

With a thought Jum showed him what lay beneath the surface of the water. The pool dropped into a network of flooded passages. After a very short distance, one of these passages led to a part of the city that was not flooded. If Elwood would allow her to carry him, Jum would quickly take him there, and then guide him by a mostly dry route to the place where they could get news of his friends. Seeing the length of the watery tunnel in his mind, he believed he could hold his breath until they reached air at the other end.

As he shouldered his things and hung Nemoor's sword from his belt where he could reach it, he realized Jum must have removed them while he was unconscious. He glanced at her splayed, seemingly jointless fingers with surprise: he would not have guessed them nimble enough to work the buckles of his pack and quiver. As soon as his gear was secure on his back, Jum took up the light in the crook of her left arm and wrapped her right around Elwood.

He shrank a little from the frog truan's touch, involuntarily recalling a bullfrog he had seen long ago. It had been a dark spring morning of heavy rain when he was seven or eight years old. One of the Pitches' neighbors had a gazebo, and it was there, waiting for the school bus, that Elwood had seen the creature. As big as a football, it crouched comfortably in the torrential rain just outside the pavilion, sucking into its mouth a big earthworm. Disgusted and fascinated, Elwood had watched the worm slowly disappear like a thick piece of spaghetti.

Jum was looking at him with her huge orange eyes. He could not read her expression, and wondered if she had seen his thoughts. Hoping she had not, Elwood took and held a deep breath. Together they hopped into the dark water of the pool.

He was surprised to see that Jum's strange vegetable remained alight even underwater. Its blue and orange beams illuminated a very tall, wide passage, along which they were swiftly swimming. The walls and ceiling were completely covered in an elaborate series of relief images, the floor with a circular relief pattern. Skillfully fashioned scenes depicting frog truans and other swampland races—some of which Elwood could not even identify—told stories of such length their beginnings and endings lay beyond the reach of Jum's light.

Almost immediately he felt a desperate need to breathe again. After a minute underwater, he was glad indeed to see the frog truan's powerful legs had carried them to a place where the passage curved upward. A moment later they surfaced and stood dripping on an otherwise dry floor. Gulping air, Elwood saw both the passage and the stories continued beyond the water.

Jum walked on long bowed legs, her ever-changing gourd of light cradled in the crook of one arm, her broad webbed feet slapping the floor lightly. Seeing her stand for the first time, Elwood noticed she wore a kind of belted skirt around her lower middle. Dangling behind her from the belt was a short curved sword with a blade that was broad like a cleaver, and a bag fashioned from a single large leaf. She did not appear to carry anything else.

As they walked, the frog truan filled Elwood's thoughts with an account of her people. The Brawbwarb had always shunned the world outside their own, and were almost completely unknown to the rest of Pahn. Sequestered for countless generations in the forbidding Swamp—which to them was not forbidding, but as ideal a land as they could wish for—Jum's people had been numerous, prosperous, and strong. All that ended with the coming of the Otguk, whom they called *Zaw*, a Brawbwarb name for death. Zaw nearly destroyed them, but they resisted stubbornly, surviving for many years on the edge of extinction. They lived in hiding, in parts of their ancient cities the monster could not penetrate, watching and waiting for some chance to win back their land.

Then, some seasons ago, the human soldiers in gray had come, and green-skinned yug soldiers, led by a sorcerer. Strangely, Zaw had let them in, allowing them even to dwell in his lair in the ancient city of Cromgo, beneath the center of the Swamp. The newcomers had built a road over the Swamp to Cromgo, and attacked the Brawbwarb at every opportunity. Because the sorcerer and his soldiers were under the protection of Zaw, the frog truans did not dare drive them away, so survival had become more difficult still.

When the travelers arrived, like all strangers they were watched by the Brawbwarb with suspicion from a safe distance. But then they put on the bug jelly, and there was a tremendous stir among the watchers. Normally they would have avoided Elwood and his friends at all costs, but Noshkwa's gift, which they could smell wafting off the strangers even at a distance, made them deeply curious: such jellies were a great secret of the Brawbwarb, and it was a source of much wonder to them that strangers had come to have any. Though they did not need protection from bugs themselves, for the benefit of those rare friends who were not of their race, the frog truans had concocted repellents like the jelly since ancient days. Because the bugs of the Swamp were one of their best defenses against invaders, the secret of the jelly's making was carefully kept. And so, though it was now winter and they would normally be taking to their beds underground, Jum and others had stealthily followed the travelers' progress with hopes of learning who they were, why they had come, and where they had gotten the jelly.

The boy wondered at all of this, but more than anything else his thoughts were driven by fear for the others, and especially Slukee. He understood the frog truan had only meant to help him out of trouble, but wished intensely she had not taken him away from his friends— who, Elwood realized, if still alive, probably thought he was dead.

As he walked beside his new friend, Elwood looked around with awed interest at what her light revealed of the ancient city. The passage leveled soon after they left the water behind; from it branched many other ways, leading he wondered where. Occasionally they passed through grand halls, and he imagined them as they must have been in former times, filled with light and crowds. In spots throughout the passages and halls were peculiar remains, shapes sculpted of the same hardened-mud material as the rest of the city, now fallen and broken. In those that were not too damaged Elwood sometimes recognized shapes from the natural world, but more often they appeared to have been symbols of some kind. A thought from Jum told him how the sculptures had come to be ruined: they were smashed long before by the Otguk, as he passed that way hunting her people.

"He comes here!" thought Elwood, alarmed.

"Oh yes, oh yes. Zaw comes here sometimes. But soon we will be at Rounder Sink. He cannot go there."

Though Elwood could not know—his sense of time and distance not being what they were beneath the open sky—they had traveled more than five miles underground when they came to an old cave-in, a place where, long before, the mud overhead had fallen in a great mass that seemed to block the passage ahead entirely. Since falling, the mud had hardened again, preserving the chaotic semiliquid contours of its soft state. Coming to a halt facing the obstruction, Jum raised her light so its gentle beams shone high up the wall of mud, revealing at the very top a small irregular opening.

With a sudden jump she was perched on an outcropping halfway up the cave-in. She motioned him to follow, which, due to the irregularities of the wall, was not difficult. As he climbed she jumped again, this time landing just below the opening. For an instant Elwood was startled by the sight of another giant frog peering out of the hole at them, but then he realized it was one of Jum's people and a friend. The two truans spoke to one another, he guessed, but because they did not direct any of their thought-speech to him he could not know what was said. Reaching the top of the wall, he was scrutinized by another pair of spherical orange eyes.

"Sometimes Zaw tries to dig down into our Sinks," said Jum, explaining the cause of the cave-in. *"But he doesn't have skill with the mud like we do. We know the art of turning the mud from hard to soft, and soft to hard. When he starts breaking through the hard mud, we make it too soft to clear but too thick to swim through. After he gives up and goes away, we turn it back."*

"We don't always succeed, though," said the second frog truan. *"We've lost some sinks to Zaw—and many of our people."*

The rough opening that bored through the cave-in was so low Elwood had to crawl on his hands and knees. Like the frogs they resembled, the truans moved with hands and feet on the ground, Jum having hung her light-gourd from her belt to free both arms. The tunnel ended just below the ceiling of a big open space. Looking out upon the chamber, the first thing Elwood noticed were many blue and orange gourds piled in the middle of the room. Then he saw that there were more than a dozen frog truans in the chamber, some gathered in and around a pool in the corner, some looking out from recesses in the walls, a couple just entering through one of several entrances. All stared up at Elwood.

With a thought of reassurance from Jum, he scrambled down the side of the cave-in and into their midst. They gazed at him silently, but their voices filled his head. Addressing all present, Jum explained that Elwood had not come to harm the Brawbwarb, and needed to find his friends.

"*But why have you come to the Swamp, you and the others? And where did you get jelly?*" asked several thought-voices.

Frightened, and unsure how to make his thoughts heard in more than one mind, Elwood began tentatively, "*We're looking for something—something that was lost.*"

"*What? What was lost? What's it got to do with the jelly? What?*" The frog truans formed a close circle around him, and their minds pressed in on his. He tried to answer them all at once.

"*A magic sea turtle shell—Noshkwa the Oldhar gave us the jelly.*"

"*We're frightening him,*" said Jum. "*Let just one talk.*"

"*Jum is right,*" said an elder female frog truan. "*We won't harm you, so don't be frightened. Why do you look for a turtle shell?*"

Elwood realized with sudden hope that the Brawbwarb might know of the Eye—maybe even where it could be found.

"*It's an ancient magic shell; the Eye of Ogin. My friends and I need it, to find someone. Do you know about it?*"

"*It's news to us. What makes you believe it's here?*"

"*It was stolen by yugs—a long time ago—and they ran away with it into the Swamp.*"

"*Before Zaw, or after?*"

"*About two hundred and fifty years ago.*"

"*That was before Zaw came. The yug-people were not permitted to walk Migdowsh then. If the Swamp did not get them first, then the Brawbwarb did away with them.*"

"*But then the Brawbwarb would have the Eye. Are you sure no one here knows about it? It glows with magic, it's always shining.*"

But none of the frog truans had heard of such a thing. Neither had they heard of strangers possessing the precious secret jelly, a matter that plainly was of greater interest to them. The elder female questioned Elwood about it again. He told her of Noshkwa, and she replied, *"Many hatchings ago, when the Brawbwarb still lived in peace, there was an herb-user we called Tut who came from the land called Oldo-tok. She was a Brawbwarb friend; they say for a human she was very wise. She may have learned from our people how to make jelly. Your Noshkwa may have learned it from her."*

"Noshkwa told us the mothers in her family have all been herb-users. Maybe that was her grandmother, or great-grandmother. But please: doesn't anyone know what happened to my friends?"

"Yes, yes. The other human and the fox man were captured by the soldiers. They take the road to Zaw's city, in the heart of the Swamp. The Brawbwarb called it Cromgo: the city around the sacred Pool of Aw. Life-spring of the Swamp, and the Brawbwarb.

"A few of our people watch the soldiers still, but the fate of your friends is certain. They will be taken to the Pool to be fed to Zaw. It was by a corruption of the Pool's power that Zaw, who once was one of us, made himself a monster."

"What about my dog? And the ravens? Weren't they with them?"

"None of us saw what became of them."

Elwood hung his head. "Slukee!" he breathed. With a great effort of will he rallied what hope he could find. *Maybe she got away,* he said to himself. *Drallah and Tornonk are alive, for now. And Booj and Nemoor are free.* His first impulse was to return to the scene of the Graycloak ambush to look for Slukee. But while he did not know her situation, he did know Drallah and Tornonk would soon be dead if no help came to them. Asking the elder female how much time there was before the Graycloaks and their prisoners reached Cromgo, he learned the journey would take them about two days.

"Can we save them before they get to the city?"

The thoughts of multiple frog truans grumbled remonstratively among his own, though more than one argued against the rest. For the sake of their very survival, the Brawbwarb did not openly defy the Otguk.

"The less we defy Zaw, the less he hunts us," said the elder frog truan. *"To rescue your friends, we would have to reveal ourselves to him. He is terrible. The Brawbwarb cannot help."*

"But please, can't you just take me to them? It's all I ask."

The frog truans debated. Most argued the best they could do for Elwood was to teach him the way to the road. Jum pleaded with them to think of his youth and position, alone as he was in a perilous country. Several wondered if the strangers, since they possessed the secret jelly, should be treated as Brawbwarb friends. The debate went back and forth, and finally it was decided three of the group who were willing would accompany Elwood in an effort to find his friends. However, they would not try to rescue them, and by no means would they enter Cromgo. Grateful, Elwood thanked the frog truans and begged them to help Slukee if they found her. Then he and his three guides set out from the big chamber in Rounder Sink.

"The Brawbwarb hope you find your friends, and your turtle shell," said the old frog truan as they departed.

"Thank you," replied Elwood, desperately hoping the same.

The three who guided him were Ongon, Moikoik, and Elwood's friend Jum. From the debate he gathered Ongon and Moikoik had volunteered because they despised Zaw more than they feared him. As for Jum, she simply felt responsible for Elwood, and wished to help him.

The four quickly left Rounder Sink behind by way of another cramped tunnel, and were soon jogging down wide image-covered passages like others Elwood had seen in the city. Though he had had no opportunity to study a single series from beginning to end, he started to recognize episodes he had glimpsed before, and guessed that some stories appeared over and over again. He would have appreciated the distraction of talking with Jum about them, but none of the frog truans were speaking, and he did not care to be the one to break the thought-silence. At first he had feared he might unintentionally bare his mind to them—or worse, be vulnerable to its exploration—but as he grew used to their thought-speech, he began to understand that, unless his thoughts were especially intense, the Brawbwarb could only know of his mind what he offered.

After an hour they stopped at a branching of the way. The passage on the left was about fifty feet high and as many wide. It sloped downward, and was rough and bare compared to the rest of the city. The passage on the right was much narrower and climbed very gradually. Though its surfaces were also bare, they were very smooth.

"We have to make a choice," said Moikoik, raising Jum's light-gourd so that it shone down each way. *"The left-hand is the Old Cromgo Road. The right goes up to the outside. The Old Road is much straighter than the highway the soldiers and your friends take. If there were no trouble, it would be the fastest way to catch them. But much of it lies half underwater, and in parts at this season the water reaches the ceiling. No matter to us Brawbwarb, but Elwood Pitch needs air at all times. And—there is Zaw. He uses the Old Road."*

"Let's go outside, then," said Elwood.

"But we are not safe from him out there either. Nor from the soldiers, and worse things too. And going that way we wouldn't have much chance of catching them before they reach Cromgo. We have to move in secret, while they march on their highway careless of whether they're seen or not."

"What do you think we should do?"

"The greater risk for the better chance," said Ongon.

"Yes, the Old Road," said the other two. *"It will hide us, and we can move fast. And Zaw won't come, perhaps."*

"What about the water? I need to breathe!"

"The tunnel is not full for long distances—usually. I will carry you, and swim very fast," said Jum.

With more than a little doubt, Elwood consented.

They took the very high and wide tunnel on the left, which after a short distance leveled and became half filled with mud-dark water. The frog truans waded in without hesitation, and Elwood followed.

At Jum's request he threw an arm around her back, and she sank into the chill liquid until only her eyes and the boy's head and shoulders remained above the surface. With a kick of her powerful legs she went knifing through the water, Elwood in tow. Ongon swam on her left and Moikoik her right, their shapes oddly lit by the underwater glow of the gourd hooked on Jum's belt.

Seeing what swift and tireless swimmers the frog truans were, Elwood's hopes began to rise. They must be moving five or ten times faster than they would up above, he thought. If they could just continue unhindered, they were sure to catch up with the Graycloaks and his friends. He tended his hope, but the exhaustion that had been put off for a time by his recent spell of unconsciousness was returning.

The tunnel continued on through the mud beneath the Swamp. It was like a dream to Elwood: his weariness, the ceaseless glide of the giant frogs, and the restless blue and orange light shining in the water made him doubt he was truly awake. He struggled to continue clinging to Jum.

They had come a very long way when the frog truans finally glided to their first halt. The ceiling of the tunnel before them sloped down into the water, and it was this that had stopped them. With a *sploosh-sploosh* the big paired bumps of Ongon's and Moikoik's eyes sank below the surface, and their forms passed out of the gourdlight and down the tunnel. A few minutes later they returned, and with their thoughts showed Elwood and Jum what lay ahead: the tunnel was completely submerged for several hundred feet, followed by a short space which was not, and then another water-filled stretch. After that the tunnel returned to its usual level, with plenty of space between water and ceiling.

Elwood could see it was a long way to hold one's breath; but Jum was incredibly fast in the water, and there was no other way to go but back. He tried to expand his lungs with a few deep breaths, then took in as much air as he could, held it, and thought to Jum, *"Ready!"*

She pulled him close in the crook of one strong arm and dove into the liquid murk. Underwater, Elwood did not open his eyes, but focused solely on holding his breath. The air trapped in his chest felt like a powerful animal bent on escape, which it did, with a roar, when they burst from the water at last. The pocket of air they had reached was just high enough for Elwood to tread water without bumping his head on the roof of the tunnel, and they paused there briefly while he regained his breath for the second stretch. When he was ready he told Jum, and again she pulled him close and bore him away under the water.

When they emerged into the air this time Elwood's head was spinning, and in his eyes the dark tunnel was bright with careening stars. He could barely keep an arm around Jum. As his senses recovered, the longing for some dry place to lie became so desperate Jum heard it in her thoughts. A short way ahead, she reassured him, was a dry tunnel up to the surface where he could rest.

He could not remember getting there when he awoke. Jum's gourd had been placed near at hand, and he was lying in a relatively dry level space at the bottom of a steep, narrow tunnel. A few feet from where he lay, the tunnel ended in some larger space; above, it climbed into the darkness beyond the ever-shifting glow of the gourd. Sitting up, he found he was strong enough to go on. Having been so constantly wet in recent days, he hardly noticed he was still soaked.

"Jum!" he thought into the dark, then tried calling her softly. After a few moments she hopped into the light from up the tunnel.

"We are here. Are you refreshed? The sun's at its peak; you began to sleep soon after it rose. We should go."

She picked up the gourd and stepped to the lower end of the tunnel. The light showed something of the wide watery space beyond, and Elwood recognized the Old Cromgo Road. As he shouldered his gear, Ongon and Moikoik came bobbing up from the dark water below. With a hop and a splash Jum joined them, while Elwood carefully lowered himself from the tunnel's lip.

They went on in the same fashion as before, Elwood clinging to Jum's back in the center, Ongon and Moikoik on either side. The Old Road continued roughly straight, level, high, and wide, just as it had for so many miles. The frog truans swam as vigorously as when they first set out, having either rested during the halt, or not yet needing rest; Elwood could not say which. Along with their strangeness, his utter dependence on them made him reluctant to question his guides.

From his low vantage hanging off one side of Jum's back, he stared ahead into the unchanging darkness beyond the water-shaded light of the gourd. He thought of his friends somewhere in the Swamp above, and wished impatiently for the long dreary journey underground to end.

When a large wave came flowing toward them from out of the darkness ahead, he thought it a trick the light was playing on his tired eyes. But it came on, overwhelming the little opposing wave that preceded the frog truans. The three swimmers immediately stopped. For a moment there was near silence as the disturbed water stilled, and then, from somewhere up the tunnel, a rumble like a cave-in came rolling their way. Before Elwood knew what was happening, they were turned around and fleeing back the way they had come.

The rumble sounded again, and much closer. A poisonous stench filled the tunnel. Elwood could hear terror in the minds of his guides, and knew they could hear it in his. He saw that they were caught in a long, long trap, the only possible escape from which was the tunnel to the surface where Elwood had lately slept. It seemed a faint hope, though: they had left it more than a mile behind.

"Throw away the light!" thought Elwood to Jum, believing her gourd betrayed them.

"Useless! Zaw sees just as well in the dark."

The rumbling became continuous, and its source rapidly drew near. Elwood looked back and choked on a cry. A gigantic mouth had appeared at the edge of the sphere of gourd-light; a maw so wide it seemed to rival the tunnel itself. Above and behind the mouth, the light flashed in black onyx-colored eyes that were huge and round, and glared down at the boy and the truans from fleshy nests atop the head. Elwood also glimpsed giant frog-arms cutting through the water, and saw the monster could very nearly touch both sides of the tunnel at once.

Suddenly the steady rumble broke into a bellow of rage and pain, the great eyes glowing in the dark disappeared, and there was an awful thrashing in the water behind them. Moikoik still swam beside Jum and Elwood, but Ongon was nowhere in sight. *"He turned to face Zaw, so we might escape!"* wailed Moikoik. The sound of struggle soon ceased, and an ugly, angry grunting echoed down the tunnel. The remaining swimmers pressed on.

Again they heard the Otguk's rumble, and knew by the sound he was catching up. *"Not much farther,"* said Jum, showing Elwood a mental image of the space that remained between themselves and the tunnel to the surface. It was close indeed, but looking over his shoulder the boy saw the enormous mouth was again bearing down on them. Feeling the monster so close behind, Jum and Moikoik both threw the last of their strength into their leg-strokes, increasing slightly the distance between them and him. But Zaw kicked harder also, and soon would be close enough to bite at the frog truans' webbed feet. With his free arm Elwood reached for Nemoor's sword, but as he was drawing it from its sheath Moikoik grabbed him around his middle and threw him into the air.

He landed on hands and knees in the bottom of the familiar, steep shaft to the surface. The frog truans leapt from the water after Elwood, and each grabbed the boy by an arm to drag him up and away from danger. Even as they did, Zaw reached the opening of the shaft, which was far too small for him to enter. He cracked open his giant maw and spat out a long, split tongue. Jum and Moikoik threw themselves and Elwood to the floor of the tunnel. The tongue snapped to its limit in the air directly over the boy's head, then flew back to the bottom of the Otguk's mouth. Enraged, the monster smashed his face against the wall. Chunks of mud broke and fell away, but the wall held. The frog truans and the boy jumped up and ran on.

Momentarily thwarted, the Otguk watched them climb out of sight. Then, intent on following them up to the surface, he turned his great bloated body around and swam back down the Old Cromgo Road.

THE CROOKED HIGHWAY

S lukee lay curled in a tight, heartsick ball, her eyes fixed on the spot where she had last seen Elwood. She was a few yards away, in a nest she had flattened for herself where the reeds grew thick, and where she could see without being seen. It was noon: over an hour since Elwood vanished, and the Graycloaks overpowered the others and took them away. During the struggle, two men had chased Slukee into the reeds, but when a third yelled, "Damn it, forget the dog! Help over here," they let her be. Hiding, she had watched in terrible distress as they surrounded the girl and the fox truan—who had stopped when they heard Elwood's cry, just as he disappeared—took their weapons, and led them away to the south. She watched them go: she would not leave there without Elwood. As soon as they were gone, she waded to the spot where he had sunk into the mud, and searched the ground beneath the water with her paws. She found the mud unusual in texture, but much too firm to sink through. When she tried to dig she got nowhere, though, as the mud constantly slid back into the hole. The watery earth would not let her in, and there was nothing else she could do but watch and wait.

The clouds above Migdowsh began to thin, and the sun shone waveringly through. Two faint shadows passed over the water field. Looking up, Slukee saw Booj and Nemoor high in the air, and hailed them with a bark. They glided down to a decaying tree hard by her nest.

"Where're the others?" croaked Nemoor, who had taken the voice of a raven as well as the shape.

In answer, Slukee splashed to the place of Elwood's disappearance, pointed down into the water with her nose, and looked back at the two birds.

"Oh, no!" rasped Booj.

Nemoor shook her beak. "If they went down there, why isn't the dog sinking?"

She flapped over to Slukee and, hovering just above the water, tried to see what lay below the surface. But the water was too dark with mud to discover anything, and she quickly returned to her perch. "I wish I was in my own shape—I could feel what's under the water there. But as soon as I change back I'll need rest, and water, and clothes...."

Having a thought, Booj tilted his head sharply to one side. "Try asking her about each of them separately."

"Slukee," began Nemoor, "Tornonk?"

The dog turned away toward the south and back again quickly.

"Drallah?" asked Booj. Slukee's reply was the same.

"Elwood?"

Whining, she again pointed into the water before her with her nose.

"I don't understand it," said Nemoor. "She does mean that exact spot, but it's no sinkhole—she couldn't stand there if it was. What could have happened to Elwood? And why would Tornonk and Drallah leave her behind?"

"The road isn't far from here, and it goes south. Maybe they're captured."

"And we've hardly been in sight of it all morning.... Let's go quick and see."

"What about Slukee—and Elwood?"

"She must come with us. When we find Tornonk, he can tell us what happened, and then we can find the boy."

"She'll have to be persuaded. She hides in the reeds hoping he'll come back here."

Booj flapped to a point just over Slukee's head. Hovering there, he croaked, "Come, Slukee! We're going to find Elwood."

He and Nemoor glided off toward the south then, looking back at the dog and calling to her as they went. But Slukee was not convinced, and remained standing in the water where they had left her. She stared after them with a long, anxious face, her wet tufty ears aloft.

"She's not coming," crarked Booj as he turned back.

"Let me try something," said Nemoor, following him. She lit on the ridge of Slukee's back, and pressing her beak gently into one of the dog's ears, whispered a few strange words. "All right?" she croaked, leaning far to one side in order to meet the dog's eyes with her own. She took off again, and this time Slukee followed.

Picking her way through the treacherous water fields, the dog followed the ravens as they wheeled in slow circles a short distance before her. Soon they came to a narrow walkway of rotting planks laid end to end: the road they were seeking. Impatient for some sign of the others, and having promised Slukee to return quickly, Booj and Nemoor flew off southward along its line as fast as their wings would carry them. The dog followed at a run, her paws beating a rhythmic *thrump-thrump, thrump-thrump* on the swamp-chewed planks.

* * *

Drallah walked with a straight back and a blank face, but she was wretched. She had not been looking in Elwood's direction, had not seen him go under the water, but knew very well what a sudden disappearance in the Great Swamp likely meant. Still, she reasoned silently, she could hope for his survival: she did not know for certain what happened. But she did know he was probably dead, and that it might have happened differently if only the Graycloaks had not prevented her from coming to his aid. Her pain was made even worse by the memory of her last words with Elwood, that they were angry and unkind. She dearly wished Booj and Slukee were there, and to a lesser degree Nemoor too. She barely noticed her weariness and long-drenched state.

Their hands bound before them with rope, Drallah and Tornonk were being marched south along the makeshift road of planks and embankments. As they went, the talkative captain of the Graycloaks, a fat yet hungry-looking man called Gamitch, explained what was in store for the prisoners. He and his men were bringing them to a place the captain called the Garrison, in the center of the Swamp. His chatter soon revealed what they already suspected, and greatly feared: that the Otguk and Egode Vallow had formed an alliance of some kind.

"You two trespassers will be a special treat for our master's Big Friend," he said. "You know who his Big Friend is? The frog devil who rules this accursed muck-hole, that's who. But as far as I care, your lives will be for my two trooper boys—that's how it ought to be. But, one way or the other! The B. F.'s always hungry, you know, and doesn't care for yug meat. I wish he did; when there's nothing else, the master sometimes lets him have one of our own...." There was dark resentment in the fat Graycloak's tone as he trailed off.

It was clear that he and the other men did not like to take their eyes off Tornonk. Fear, curiosity, and suspicion were all apparent on their faces. Though she did not understand the Ringish they used among themselves, Drallah heard their captors speak his name, and realized they knew or guessed who he was. This was no surprise, as Tornonk was famed for his skill in the woods and his prowess in combat; and he was the only fox truan in the lands west of the Mossheads known for dealing with humans. Drallah wondered if Tornonk had seen some of these Graycloaks before—as they were passing through Ashawda with Vank-mul, for instance—

but if he recognized any of them, he gave no sign.

Drallah did not doubt that, unless catastrophe had struck them as well, Booj and Nemoor would soon find her and Tornonk. Hopefully by now they had found Slukee, and Elwood, alive or dead. With the raven and the witch's help, she speculated, they should be able to escape the Graycloaks. But unless they killed them all, news of the travelers in the Swamp would soon reach the Otguk—and if he were to hunt them, small was the hope they would live to find the Eye, and Granashon.

They tromped noisily down the road of wood planks throughout the afternoon. The Graycloaks moved fast, those behind the prisoners regularly jabbing them in the back with the butts of their spears. Toward sunset, they came to a steep-sided causeway raised over a swath of bog, a ridge built up between two vast water fields. Soon after mounting the embankment, they spotted another party of six cloaked and hooded troopers approaching from the opposite direction. The two groups met in the middle of the causeway.

"Well, Captain Gamitch, what goes on?" called the man at the head of the new party as they came near.

"Wrongful capture of friends of the Queen of Ashawda, General Fienoth—or do you prefer Vank-mul?" said Tornonk in Wohmog, before the captain could answer.

Coming to a halt a few paces from the fox truan, the Ringishman drew back his hood from the long-snouted reptile skull he wore on his head. "What brings you down this way, *Mis*ter Tornonk?" he sneered. Then, eyes full of recognition but not surprise, he turned to Drallah.

"And you. Why the devil are you here?"

Drallah thrust her chin forward, and said nothing.

"Caught this morning, sir, if you haven't already heard," said Captain Gamitch. "East of the Road. The lad went down a sinkhole, and the dog ran off. The beast killed Blissen and Arche before we got him under control."

General Fienoth scanned the sky over the captain's head. "What about the ravens?"

"Haven't seen them, sir."

Fienoth considered for a moment and said, " It is nearly dark; our parties will camp here. And I will question the prisoners."

As the last of the sun reddened the Swamp between them and the western horizon, the troopers built two campfires atop the raised road, then gathered around one to rest and eat. The prisoners were made to sit by the second fire, General Fienoth commanding two men to bind their legs, free their hands, and give them food. While this was being done, Captain Gamitch brought Drallah and Tornonk's gear. Seating himself before the prisoners, Fienoth rummaged through their things, starting with Drallah's.

"What's this, I wonder?" he said, drawing from her pack the blue pot of bug-jelly and prying open the lid. Waving the pot under his nose, he look pleased. "Better stuff than ours, for certain," he said half-aloud as he slipped the pot into his cloak.

Continuing his investigation of Drallah's pack, he found her copy of Ingagil's map in the waterproof bowstring pocket. He unfolded the paper, and with his face half concealed behind the skull of the dead reptile, proceeded to study it. Drallah silently cursed herself for bringing this telltale copy along instead of committing the map to memory.

Fienoth looked up and fixed his crag-browed eyes on the girl. "So—a treasure hunt?"

Resolutely silent, she stared into the fire.

Fienoth pulled from the pack the bundle of Nemoor's buckskins and moccasins that Drallah had been carrying for her. "Ashaw-made ..." he observed, unraveling the bundle. Holding up the shirt by the shoulders, he looked past it at the Winharn girl, then back. "A little short for you, isn't it?" Then he seemed to catch a scent, and his brow bore down heavier still upon his eyes. "What?" he muttered, and pressing the leathern shirt to his face, inhaled deeply the particular fragrances of Nemoor's hair and skin that lingered there. Laying the shirt down, he rose and stood leaning over Drallah, sniffing her hair and neck. Taking the shirt up again, he waved it in front of her.

"I know this smell. It isn't yours. Where did you get these clothes?" His eyes flashed. "Answer me, girl!" he demanded, raising his open hand to strike.

"I praise your nose, Fienoth," said Tornonk blandly. "You are right: those were the Queen's cousin's. I borrowed the clothes from Nemoor, so my friend here would have a second set for the journey."

Fienoth wheeled to face him. "And what was your journey?"

"A treasure hunt, as you guessed."

"And what does a beast care for the beauty, the power of riches? Nothing at all—unless it's something very special?"

Tornonk shrugged. "No matter what I say you will throw us to the monster. There is no advantage in talking."

"The advantage is this: if you do, your last hours won't necessarily be filled with pain."

"Torture us if you want. But I've already told you: we are looking for Mobb's lost heirlooms."

"Heir*looms?* Not one in particular? And what have two children come all the way from *Winnitok* got to do with it? Why do you hunt with them, rather than with Ainathuai's best scouts?"

"I keep what company I wish."

"It happens I . . . saw this girl several weeks ago, beyond Imwa," said Fienoth, turning back to Drallah. "What was your business in Oldotok?"

"It's quite simple," answered Tornonk, continuing to speak for her. "When you saw her, she was on her way here, to Migdowsh, from Winnitok. I met them passing through Ashawda. They showed me their map, and I decided to join them."

"Pshaw!" spat Fienoth, and, spinning on his boot-heel, stalked away from the fire. Gamitch and the two other troopers remained, limiting any exchange between Tornonk and Drallah to meaning-filled looks.

"Captain," Tornonk asked, "how far is it to the Garrison?"

"We'll get there late tomorrow, unless the B. F. meets us halfway—which he might."

Then the captain leaned toward them and spoke in a lower voice. "I'll tell you a secret. Master Vallow has a big, wonderful bowl—magic, you know. He fills it with water, and in that water he can watch what's happening anywhere he likes, anywhere at all. Did you wonder how we knew you were in the Swamp? His seeing bowl, that's how. And if his Big Friend gets back to the Garrison before we do, my Lord will tell him all about you. Perhaps the B. F. won't wait for his feast to come to him, haw haw!"

In spite of themselves, Drallah and Tornonk turned to one another in unguarded amazement. It all fit into place: how the Graycloaks had found the travelers in the Swamp; how the general and the captain had known the makeup of their group in advance; why Fienoth had not been surprised to see Tornonk and Drallah. Egode Vallow possessed the Eye of Ogin, and through its magic eye had been watching the travelers. *"If you haven't already heard,"* Gamitch had said to the general when they met. And the phrasing of Fienoth's questions after he saw Ingagil's map—and the Eye mentioned thereon—had hinted at what the Graycloak already guessed: the purpose that brought the travelers to Migdowsh.

Misreading the looks on their faces, the captain believed he had succeeded in frightening them. *Ah, they'll talk for the General now,* he thought to himself.

Quickly regaining his stoic demeanor, Tornonk said, "A magic bowl, eh?"

I saw his weakness, and now the beast's trying to save face, thought the captain as he said aloud, "Yes; ancient witchery, very powerful. My Lord's been watching you in it for days."

"Have you—seen the bowl?"

"I've seen it, certainly! Master Vallow often has me in his chambers to discuss his affairs. I'm one of his main men, you know. Not that I've ever looked into the bowl."

"What does it look like?"

"Like 'normous fine jewels all stuck together, each with its own shine. The shape is strange—like the shell of a sea turtle. But beautiful, you know. The sight of it takes the breath from you."

"Will we see it when we get to the Garrison?"

"What does it matter to you?" said the captain, narrowing his eyes. "You're as good as dead. Anyway, you won't see it. If you live so long, you won't get any farther than the Deep Pool. That's where Vallow meets with his Big Friend, and feeds him his dainties, you know. It's in the chamber beyond that—"

"Gamitch, what the devil?" interrupted Fienoth, stomping back into the firelight.

"Just seeing if I could get them to talk, General," blurted the captain. "Now that you're back, I'll order the night's guard."

"Sounded like you were the one doing the talking," the general growled as the fat trooper scuttled off to the other campfire. Then he removed his bone hat, spread a blanket on the opposite side of the fire from the prisoners, and threw himself down.

"I've thought on it, and I don't care why you came, Mister Beast," he said. "There's no profit in trying to understand why animals and savages do anything. Your kind and hers—through all the years the Ringish have tried to make something of these lands—have harried us and hindered us, and for what? Ignorance and spite. Riches for the taking on every side, but you let them lie—until people who understand their value come along, and then you snarl and bite and make certain none profit.

"I came over when I was a lad, but I remember Ringune well," the general continued. "That is a country where men understand the value of the world—even these lands of waste and darkness. I tell you, a change is come. I have been in the struggle many long years, and I have seen the way fortunes change. The Ringish who would tame this hell have not had a leader the like of Egode Vallow. His wits and his power will take us far. This time the animals and the savages will not prevent us.

"No, Mister Beast, I don't care at all why you're here. But I'm glad you are. You'll be dead soon; and first chance I get, I'll pay our friend the pretty witch a visit."

The darkness beyond the fires had been deepening and was now complete. Night-creature noises replaced the throbbing hum of insects. Fienoth commanded two Graycloaks to stand guard a few feet from where the prisoners sat, and spoke no more. Nearly dry at last, Drallah pulled her blanket around her shoulders and lay down, but Tornonk remained seated and staring into the fire. For a moment their eyes met again, sharing a hint of what each was feeling in the wake of the evening's revelations.

Wrapped in her blanket, Drallah silently wept. From what the captain had said to Fienoth, she knew the Graycloaks had actually seen Elwood swallowed by a sinkhole. She had to accept that he was gone: for someone to emerge from such a trap was unlikely in the extreme. It was utterly miserable that his long journey, begun in another world, should end without achieving what they had ardently believed to be its purpose—yet had come so close to doing so. For the Eye of Ogin had been found, and it was near. Drallah had no joy of the news, as she would if Elwood was still with her; only sorrow. But joy or sorrow, she thought, her responsibilities remained: to try to find the Eye and Granashon, that the Nohar might protect Winnitok once again.

Just minutes after Drallah's heavy heart and weary limbs at last surrendered to sleep, her rest was disturbed by a distant, terrible noise. From somewhere far in the dark north and east, the bellow of a monstrous frog came rolling over the Swamp. The watery land was suddenly very silent and still. Also awakened from their rest by the noise, the troopers stirred and spoke among themselves in fearful whispers. Still stretched upon his blanket on the other side of the fire, Fienoth spoke.

"The Otguk is abroad."

A second bellow rumbled across the Swamp. Drallah prayed Slukee and Booj were safe, wherever they were, and Nemoor too—though she did not worry so much about the witch. The Otguk bellowed a third time, now sounding a little farther to the north. The girl took heart: at least the monster was far from the Eye of Ogin and the Garrison, which lay to the south; it was still possible he did not know the travelers were in the Swamp. If the Otguk was not there at the Garrison when they arrived, then only the sorcerer and his soldiers would stand between her and the Eye. But whether there or not, it seemed to her less and less possible that she and the others could avoid meeting the monster.

* * *

In the darkness just before twilight, Tornonk, sleeping with one eye open, observed a strange occurrence: the pair of guards set to watch the prisoners laid down on the ground, and judging by the snores that followed, fell asleep. After a few moments a figure crawled laboriously over the rim of the causeway, paused by one of the guard's unconscious bodies, then slowly, as though against a tide of weariness, proceeded toward the fire's dimly glowing remains. The figure stopped at Drallah's pack, which lay where Vank-mul had left it, and began to search through its contents. Then, spying Nemoor's buckskin shirt, britches, and moccasins strewn on the ground nearby, it abandoned the pack and crawled over to them. The figure, whom Tornonk could see was Nemoor herself, pulled her clothes on, then crawled to where the fox truan lay near the embers and ashes of the fire. With the knife she had plucked from the belt of the sleep-enchanted guard, she began to saw at the rope around Tornonk's ankles. He sat up, and the witch smiled weakly into his green cat-eyes. He returned her smile, took the knife, and quickly cut the rope.

Moving over to where Drallah lay asleep, he silently woke her and cut the rope that tied her ankles as well. The three crept toward the same side of the embankment by which Nemoor had climbed up.

Twilight came stealing over Migdowsh, and there was a stir as creatures of the day began to wake. As the girl, the fox truan, and the witch were nearing the edge of the causeway, their movements were noticed by a swamp sparrow darting overhead. Suspecting they were predators, the little bird gave a loud *tcheep!* of alarm.

Instantly Fienoth was awake, on his feet, and after the prisoners. He flung himself headlong upon Tornonk. The two came together, cursing and snarling, and wrestled one another to the embankment's edge. There Fienoth pinned and began to choke Tornonk, the truan's large red ears sticking out over the steep descent. Trying to break his grip on the fox truan's throat, Nemoor jumped on the general's back. Grabbing him by a shoulder, Drallah also tried to haul him off. Feeble from working her magic transformation, the witch could not budge the big Graycloak; her weight on his back only helped to anchor his strength, and as a result the girl could not move him either. Roused from their sleep by the noise, the troopers snatched up their blades and came running, the two Nemoor had enchanted waking also.

Booj, who had been waiting impatiently in the swamp below for Nemoor to free the prisoners, shot into the air and flew at Fienoth's face. There he hovered, clapping his wide wings about the Graycloak's ears and jabbing at his eyes with his thick beak. Unable to fly to her friends' aid like the raven, Slukee dashed from the stand of giant fiddleheads in the causeway's shadow where she and Booj had been hiding themselves, and began to scramble up the almost sheer side of the embankment.

Fienoth cast Nemoor from his back with a shrug. Releasing his grip on Tornonk's throat, he threw up his hands to shield his face from the raven's attack. Despite their situation, Drallah shouted with joy when she saw Booj. Even as she did, two Graycloaks grabbed her by the waist and arms and dragged her away from Tornonk and Fienoth. Two others took hold of Nemoor, who had grown too weak to struggle, and many more pressed in around them. Using the distraction provided by Booj, like a red eel Tornonk wriggled out from under Fienoth. A dozen hands reached to grab or strike him. Dodging and dancing, the fox truan wrested a sword from one, and with a spinning, sweeping stroke drove them momentarily back. Wheeling toward the men who held Nemoor, he stabbed the nearer of the two dead, then was beset by a furious shower of blows. With the back of his hand, Fienoth smacked Booj squarely in the breast, throwing the raven into a stunned spiral that ended at the base of the causeway.

Rising and turning, the Graycloak saw Nemoor was there. Amazed, he made a quick study of her as she was dragged from the fray by one of his men: her body was limp, and her face was stricken with fear as she watched Tornonk fighting a crowd of foes. It occurred to Fienoth that she had been one of the ravens traveling with the fox truan.

"Hold!" he roared. His troopers obeyed, cautiously backing away from the fox truan. His guard still up, Tornonk looked queryingly at Fienoth. Nemoor also turned her eyes to him, but the Graycloak did not look her way again. There was a grim smile on his face as he glared back at the fox truan, and all understood he desired to kill Tornonk himself, unassisted.

As Fienoth opened his mouth to speak again, with a bound Slukee gained the causeway's summit just behind where he stood. She sank her teeth deep in the thigh above his knee-high boot. He roared again—though differently—and, grasping and lifting Slukee off the ground, tried to pull her from his leg. All looked on as the general and the dog struggled; then, astonished, he released her, for suddenly it seemed to be hailing giant frogs.

From both east and west of the causeway, each with a single arcing leap, their long graceful legs dangling almost straight down as they flew, nine frog truans launched themselves from concealment in the waters of the Swamp. Landing amidst the Graycloaks, with cruel heavy swords they hacked and hewed. Taken by surprise, several troopers, including the captain and the two restraining Drallah, fell without even raising a hand to defend themselves. The rest fought desperately for their lives.

Beyond wonderment at the frog truans' unlooked-for arrival, and seeing that they attacked the Graycloaks only, Drallah grabbed a Ringish sword from the ground and rushed to help Slukee, whose jaws remained locked on Fienoth's leg. Tornonk quickly positioned himself over Nemoor, defending her where she lay. Down below, Booj had recovered most of his senses; with a beat of his wings he was soaring over the fight, looking for the point where he was most needed.

"Let go, Slukee," called Drallah as she charged, sword raised to strike, but still the dog would not release her grip on the general's leg.

Ignoring the dog hanging on his thigh, Fienoth set his feet and hands to meet the girl's attack. As he did he looked around him, and saw that if he stayed there it would be his death. Already more than half his troopers had fallen, and now those that remained were outnumbered. It was a rout: the frog people, whom he had always judged weak and cowardly because they lived in hiding, had taken him and his men completely by surprise.

His decision had been made. Sidestepping the swing of her sword, he sent the Winharn girl reeling backward with a punch in the jaw. Turning then, he leapt from the top of the causeway to the swamp below. Slukee nearly went with him, but let go her grip on his leg at the last moment. Some of the Graycloaks who remained in the fight saw their general flee, and quickly did the same. The rest followed. Those who could leapt as Fienoth did, or slid down the side of the embankment. The frog truans chased them, and in moments only the travelers—along with numerous dead, and nearly all the soldiers' gear—remained on the causeway.

Tornonk and Booj joined Drallah at the embankment's edge, where she knelt with an arm around Slukee. As the dog licked her bruised jaw, Drallah watched the chase on that side of the causeway unfold. Five Graycloaks were spreading out across the wide water field that lay below, struggling through waist-deep water toward the east. Each was followed by a frog truan who, with long precise jumps, tested and harried them. As the travelers watched, one of the frog truans landed squarely on his foe's shoulders, driving him under the water. After a swing of his sword the frog truan hurried on, and they did not see that Graycloak again. Farther away than the rest, and in spite of the limp that Slukee had given him, Fienoth was loping off across the northeast corner of the water field. Reaching a hump of mud at the end of a brambly peninsula dividing that field from the next, the general checked behind him for any pursuit. He sighted Drallah and Tornonk watching him from atop the causeway, and before disappearing into the brambles, cupped his hands in a horn to his mouth and shouted across the water, *"I'll set the hounds on you, you stinking fox!"*

Without visible reaction, Tornonk watched him go. Then he said, "We'll carry Nemoor to a hiding place, somewhere she can rest. Now—get your things."

The Graycloaks had piled most of the travelers' gear together, and so it did not take long to gather their supplies and weapons. They were able to retrieve all but their scant provisions, which, being superior to theirs, the Graycloaks had eaten the night before, so the travelers helped themselves to the troopers' food and water. Remembering Noshkwa's bug jelly, Drallah went to the spot where Fienoth had slept and found the pot where he had left it, wrapped in his cloak. After stowing the jelly in her pack, with morbid interest she picked up Fienoth's crown of bone, which the Graycloak general had been obliged to abandon as well. She turned the skull over in her hands once or twice, then flung it into the waters of the Swamp.

As Tornonk buckled on his sword, one of the frog truans dropped from the sky and landed before him with a wet thud. She had an ugly wound in her shoulder, and a cut under one of her bulging eyes. While the rest watched curiously, the two truans of different kinds stood facing one another, but did not speak. There was a cry like a muted trumpet call from out in the Swamp, at which the frog truan quickly turned, jumped from the top of the causeway, and sped away in the direction of the call.

"We must hurry," Tornonk said as he joined the others. "I'll tell you as we go." Kneeling, the fox truan gently lifted and threw the half-conscious witch over his shoulder. Then, setting out briskly despite his burden, and with the rest following, he explained his meeting with the frog truan. "They are thought-speakers; we were speaking to each other with our thoughts. There was no time for the questions I wanted to ask her, though. She left the chase to warn us: the Otguk is drawing near, and can smell spilled blood miles away. She showed me how get to a place where we can hide and rest—from the monster at least, for now. There's nowhere we can truly hide from Vallow, and the Eye of Ogin. She and the others will silence the rest of the Graycloaks, and conceal the fallen and their gear as best they can."

Soon they had left the scene of the fight behind, and Tornonk had related what little he had learned about the people called the Brawbwarb. Following the image the frog truan had placed in his mind, after a mile and a half Tornonk led them off the road to the west, into a reedy bog. Taking care not to leave a trail, they found hidden amidst a dense surround of tussocks the entrance to a narrow hard-mud tunnel. Entering this earthen mouth, the travelers disappeared beneath the Swamp.

THE HEART OF OGIN

"*There is the road, Elwood.*"

"*And you're sure my friends couldn't have come by here already?*"

"*The Old Cromgo Road runs straight, and this way is crooked. We went a long way very fast in the Old Road. I doubt they have passed by already.*"

Elwood and the two frog truans were crouching in a fern bog and looking to the west. It was mid-afternoon; they had encountered Zaw two hours earlier. The monster, they knew, was making—perhaps had already made—his way to a passage up to the Swamp's surface, a particular one that the frog truans knew was wide enough to admit his bloated vast bulk. Once in the open, it would not be long before he reached the upper end of the tunnel they had escaped through—the location of which, Jum assured Elwood, Zaw knew precisely. From there, his powerful senses were certain to pick up their trail.

"*Then I'll go north to meet my friends now,*" said Elwood.

"*Taking different ways is our best hope of escape,*" mused Moikoik.

"*Yes,*" said Jum. "*But there is a short time yet before Zaw comes. I will go with Elwood a little farther.*"

Moikoik assented, wished them well, and, with Elwood's thanks sounding in his thoughts, jumped away to the southwest. Keeping the highway in sight but never straying from cover, the two that remained moved cautiously north, Elwood watching all the while for his friends.

They had been creeping through the bogs for an hour when Jum laid a long-fingered hand on his arm, and they halted. Seeing no movement in the direction of the road, and every moment expecting the appearance of the Otguk, Elwood feared the worst. But after a moment of stillness, he was relieved and surprised to see it was a group of Jum's own people, as first the eyes, then the heads, then the rest of three of the frog truans arose from a green-scummed pool directly in Elwood and Jum's path.

"These three were watching your captured friends!" exclaimed Jum. Staring curiously at Elwood, the newcomers hopped from the pool, and the five met at its edge. Briefly explaining how she had come by Elwood's company, Jum warned the other frog truans that Zaw was on her trail and the boy's. They in turn told of the fight on the causeway that freed the strangers from the Graycloaks, which the three had taken part in. When Elwood heard that his friends were alive and together still, he became so excited he forgot to speak to the frog truans with thoughts.

"Where are they now?" he cried.

"I talked with the fox man," said one with a gashed shoulder. *"I warned him that Zaw is near, and that the road is dangerous. I showed him the way to the nearest path beneath the Swamp. They were going there to hide and rest; by now they have moved again."*

"But did he say which way they're going?"

"Yes, yes. They are following the crooked way to Cromgo, the fox man said."

"But that is just where the humans were taking them," cried Jum. *"They escaped. Why go to Cromgo?"*

"I was called back to the fight before I could ask what they do. They have come to kill Zaw, maybe. That is our hope; that is why we risked defying him so openly. That, and they wear the jelly, like Brawbwarb-friends from long ago."

"They left the highway. I missed them," pondered Elwood. *"But I know where they're heading."*

"There is no secret now: Zaw knows we have aided the strangers," said Jum. *"If your friends challenge him, I want to help. I'll show you the way to Cromgo."*

Quickly realizing the strange human boy and Jum would not be persuaded to do otherwise, the three frog truans bid hasty farewells, and each taking a different direction, disappeared into the surrounding swamp. Wasting no time themselves, Elwood and Jum turned and struck out toward the south. Through the clouds the setting sun shone a pale and ghostly gray-red. By the time it rose the next morning, and if they lived through the night, they would be in Cromgo, the Otguk's city.

* * *

"The frog truan also told me that the place the Ringish call 'the Garrison' is an ancient city beneath the Swamp," said Tornonk to Nemoor. The witch had recently come out of trance, and was eating hungrily as he related all she had missed. "It is their base, and the monster's lair. She could not stay and tell me more, but the captain's loose talk may suffice. If we can find the 'Deep Pool,' we'll find the Eye."

"And the sorcerer waiting for us."

They were sitting in the very dim light of a hard-mud shaft that slanted steeply up to the surface, the same they had sought after the fight on the causeway. It was near twilight in the Swamp above, and they had been hiding underground for hours. Nemoor had largely recovered from her magic transformation, enough at least to move again. Having also benefited from the much-needed rest, the others were readying themselves for the dangerous journey through the nighttime swamp.

"A good thing for us the frog people of Migdowsh live here still," said Nemoor, taking a last bite of stale Graycloak bread. "Most Ashaws think the Otguk drove them from the Swamp long ago—if they believe they ever existed at all."

"They have been watching us closely since we arrived," said Tornonk. "It is their song that we've heard each night. I've said nothing—it would have done no good, frightening you all more than you already were—but for days I was concerned they served the Lord of the Swamp."

Soon all were ready. From his perch atop the pile of gear, Booj announced he would take a look at the world above before they started. Spreading his wings, he hopped into the air and disappeared up the shaft. A moment later, the others froze at the sound of the raven crying out in astonishment and fright. The cry was followed by a tremendous splash of water and rumble of earth; then the tunnel filled with a terrible bellowing. Drallah leapt to her feet and started toward the surface, but Tornonk, catching her by an arm, restrained her. He motioned with his free hand for silence, and for a long minute all was still.

The eyes of each of the travelers strained toward the distant circle of dimming sky that marked the tunnel exit. Her form and features rigid, Drallah hardly breathed as she stared upward. Then darkness entered the circle, covered it, and she could see nothing at all. At the same time, the silence was broken by a shriek as Booj, falling more than flying, returned, his feathery body careening off the hard mud of the shaft's rounded sides. Though she could not see him in the dark, Drallah happened to stand in his way, and bodily put an end to his wild flight. Kneeling, she gently took him in her arms.

"I'm all right . . ." he said in a shaky whisper, "but the *monster!*"

Laying a hand on a shoulder of each, Tornonk silently directed Drallah and Nemoor farther down the tunnel. The girl still held the raven, and Slukee followed at her heels. Shortly the shaft became level. The fox truan whispered, "Stay," then went back for their gear. Once he returned and their things were distributed, he led them deeper into the dark. They walked on for some minutes, until

Tornonk believed they could whisper without risk of being heard by the one who lay in wait above.

Somewhat recovered from his fright, Booj hopped up on Drallah's pack and told his story: as he emerged from the tunnel-mouth, he had been lashed at by a giant, forked tongue. Dodging, he was spared by a hair's breadth. His first attempt to catch the raven having failed, the immense frog—who, Booj assured them in an awed, affrighted whisper, was much more immense than they had ever imagined—snapped his long tongue back into his mouth and propelled himself into the air with a mighty jump. As Booj shot away, the Otguk soared after him, his maw stretched wide enough to engulf scores of ravens. The monster fell short, but only just, landing in a water field with an enormous splash. Booj flew on with all speed as the Otguk's bellow of frustration resounded across the Swamp. Safely away, he looked behind and watched the monster creep back to his ambush at the tunnel-mouth, no longer heeding the escaped bird. Booj climbed high into the sky, aimed himself like an arrow at the hole in the earth, and shot downward. But the Otguk was only pretending to ignore the raven, and took a snap at him as he whizzed by. Poor Booj had another narrow escape, actually feeling the feathers of his wingtip brush the great horrible lips.

"We can't go up now," said Drallah. "And he may wait there for days."

"Maybe this tunnel leads to another exit," suggested Nemoor.

Tornonk looked thoughtfully down the passage. "And maybe it leads eventually to the ancient city itself," he said. "It is a city beneath the Swamp; a road to the city may lie beneath the Swamp too."

At the thought of this possibility the travelers grew more hopeful, and Drallah said, "We'll follow you and find out."

* * *

The thin moon rode high over Migdowsh. Though it dulled as the morning twilight grew, still it shone brightly enough for Elwood and Jum to mark its crescent in a pool of black water. They were hiding in a stand of bulrushes some twenty feet away, watching the pool and discussing what they would do next.

"The way under the pool soon leads to a hall, the northern entrance to the city," said Jum. *"All ways out of the north go through that hall; if your friends come, they will come that way."* Earlier she had explained to Elwood that the Brawbwarb kept memory-images of Cromgo, and of all their ancient lands, which each hatching passed on to the next. Though she had never been to Zaw's city, she had memories of the way it was hundreds of years before; meaning that, as long as they were not changed, Jum knew the tunnels below almost as well as those she had grown up in.

"How long will we be underwater?"

"The passage of the pool is like this," answered Jum, placing in the boy's mind a picture of a vertical shaft like a well, which at bottom connected with a series of openings and tunnels.

With a groan, Elwood took in a deep draft of air to stretch his lungs, for he saw he would once again need to hold his breath a long time. Unslinging his pack, he checked his bowstring. Finding its special pocket remained watertight, he shouldered his pack again and declared his readiness to Jum, who was making sure the light-gourd was secure in the bag that hung from her belt. They stole to the edge of the black pool. Elwood took and held a deep breath, Jum grasped him about the waist, and together they plunged into the cold water.

When at last they reached air again, Elwood could not instantly tell what kind of place they had come to. He burst from the water and fell on his hands and knees gasping, his dripping forelocks plastered over his eyes. Before he had a chance to recover his breath or push aside his hair, something hit him on the side of the head, knocking him flat. As he lay stunned, big hands grabbed him roughly by the arms and stood him on his feet.

Elwood looked about him. He was surrounded by Graycloaks in

a room or passage bright with torchlight. Jum was stretched on the floor. A pair of the pale gray-shrouded men, having taken away the frog truan's sword, bag, and belt, were busy wrapping her in a cocoon of thick rope. While several pairs of hands stripped Elwood of his own waterlogged gear, another of the men stooped to bring his face up close to the boy's.

"And just what're you doing here?"

Still gasping, Elwood did not reply. The Ringishman laid a heavy hand on his shoulder then, and began forcibly to steer him through the crowd. The other Graycloaks parted, allowing them to pass, and Elwood found himself being pushed through a large gang of ghastly figures, all hunchbacked and green-skinned. Several human voices swore at them and shouted, "Make way!" The yugs shuffled aside, baring their teeth and looking Elwood up and down with red eyes. Twisting and craning his neck, he tried to get a glimpse of Jum. With difficulty he saw that, for the purpose of carrying the frog truan, they had slung her bound, helpless form from the long haft of a spear, which two men at either end bore on their shoulders. *I guess I'm not worth the bother of tying up,* Elwood thought.

His hand still grasping and driving the boy irresistibly on, the Graycloak who appeared to be in charge spoke in low tones with another at his side, and the rest trooped around them. They moved down a grand image-decked passageway very like ones Elwood had seen going to and from Rounder Sink, though the circumstances and the torches the men carried made it seem very different from those. There was also a difference in the air, which was tainted with a foul vapor that caught in the nose and throat. It was the same poisonous stench that had enveloped Elwood, Jum, and the others as they ran for their lives from the Otguk in the Old Cromgo Road.

As they marched, the torch-lit troop came upon new openings, passages, and halls with growing frequency, but Elwood did not see anyone anywhere other than their captors. The men found their way without hesitation or talk, and without seeming to heed the endless succession of strange cracking images that shone red in their torchlight. The yugs hung together at the rear, almost beyond the light's reach.

They moved fast, and before long reached the chambers the Gray-cloaks sought. Having passed through a kind of antechamber, they entered a space larger by far than any Elwood had yet come upon underground. It was a perfect circle, with a high-domed ceiling and four equidistant openings in its one continuous wall. The wall was covered from floor to dome's edge in the remains of especially elaborate and beautiful relief images. In many places these were crushed and crumbling, as though an enraged giant had repeatedly hurled himself against them, and they were often cracked from holes made to receive the many torches that burned all around the chamber. From its outer edge toward its center, the floor was level for only a few yards; it then began to descend in a slimy slope to the surface of a wide, circular pool about a hundred feet across. A fetid fume hung over the pool and filled the dome. Struggling not to swoon, Elwood realized he was standing hard by the center and source of the foul reek that filled the city: once the Brawbwarb's sacred Pool of Aw, now Zaw's watery lair.

Within the grand Chamber of the Pool, the troop turned to the left and marched between wall and water to the next opening. This they entered, and Elwood found himself in a smaller space lit by four torches. Most of the party halted there, but the men with captives in hand continued on with them through a further passage. Marching down its short length they entered still another chamber, and there they stopped.

This place was almost empty. A curious many-hued glow emanated from its center, casting light upon everything. The source of the colorful light was a large object, in shape like a deep platter or long shallow bowl, set upon a low tripod of wood. But the illumination was not cradled in the hollow of the thing; rather it was set within its very substance, like the light in a hot coal. Its appearance was so wonderful, so marvelous, for several moments the question of just what he might be looking at did not occur to Elwood. He simply stood gazing, enchanted.

Then he realized it was the shell of the magic turtle; it was the Eye of Ogin.

He wanted to shout. His thoughts raced with his pulse. Here at last was the end of his long journey and search—but he had been caught, and could do nothing.

The Graycloak gripping Elwood by the shoulder said something loudly in Ringish. An answer came from the other side of the Eye, and the boy realized a man had been standing there since they came in. The Eye's dense rainbow light fell on him as it did on the wall behind, obscuring his outline; but now that Elwood had spotted the man, he was able to study him. He was not tall, nearly bald, and his thick, aging features were clean-shaven. In the glow of the shell, his dark red robes were nearly black. His head was bowed, and his attention appeared to be directed down into the hollow of the Eye. The boy could guess who he was.

"Fine, Captain Curwen," Egode Vallow answered, speaking in Wohmog. He did not look up. His tone struck Elwood as very businesslike. "The other trespassers will reach the Pool very soon," he continued. "And *he* will return imminently. There is only a little time. Bring the boy closer."

Captain Curwen shoved Elwood forward and stood him beside the glowing Eye. Still the man on the other side did not look up. Holding his breath, Elwood stole a glance within. The Eye was filled with glimmering water that seemed too wholesome to have come from the Pool. The thick, notched rim also glowed with colorful light, but the hollow was dark.

"Do you know what this is?" asked the sorcerer.

Elwood looked at the toes of his waterlogged moccasins and did not answer.

"It is an old, old power. Or a part of one. It is an eye—and a channel. It was lost in the Swamp long ago. By my art I found the hole where it had lain for centuries. I drew it from the muck and made it mine.

"Here in this water I watch the world. Here I first saw you and your friends. One day, not long ago, I noticed that many of my green helpers were lying slain in the Hills. I asked my men: who would do such a thing? Casting about, I found you and your party searching the Swamp. My General Fienoth knew you; he did not, however, know what you were looking for.

"Searching, searching through the Swamp. *What can they be searching for,* I wondered. But your friends and the ... *Brawbwarb,*" (the sorcerer seemed to find the name distasteful), "slew all the men I sent to find out—all except Fienoth, I think. We have been lax. We should have exterminated the frog folk long ago. Then my men would still be living, and your friends would have arrived by now. But, of course, you would like to see your friends. Why don't you take a look?"

Elwood hesitated a moment, then leaned over the Eye and gazed into the shimmering water. It was opaque and glassy still. At first he saw nothing but his own reflection, but presently he noticed an odd kind of movement beneath the surface. Then, like mist blown by the wind, the water disappeared. As it did, a living picture was revealed. It was blurry, but he could make out a group of figures walking along a tunnel by torchlight. The picture then became very clear, and his heart leapt. He could plainly see Tornonk leading, Nemoor holding up a torch, and striding along with Booj perched on her pack and Slukee trotting at her side, Drallah. It was so real, so like looking through a window, Elwood could barely resist the urge to call out to them.

"They are less than a mile away," said Vallow, his eyes fixed on the water in the Eye. "My men are seeing to it they find their way to the chamber of the Pool. While we await them, tell me ... what were you searching for in Migdowsh?"

Watching his friends walk into the same trap that he and Jum had, Elwood remained silent. Captain Curwen boxed his ears with such force they rang, but still he would not speak.

"If you do not want to . . . *die* before they arrive, my boy," said the sorcerer, "you will tell me instantly what the savages and the beast man want in Migdowsh."

Still Elwood gazed silently into the Eye. Slukee's coat looked in bad shape, he thought, but otherwise she seemed well. Maybe Drallah's back was not as straight as—suddenly the picture vanished. The sorcerer had thrust a hand into the Eye, and with a violent splash the hollow was filled once again with simple glimmering water.

"Tell me what they want!" he shouted. Raising his eyes from the banished picture, Elwood saw that Vallow was looking at him directly for the first time. His businesslike air was gone; in his staring eyes were sparks of rage, and the light on his angry face was like paint for some ill-purposed ritual. Still glaring at Elwood, he drew apart his robes, exposing an ornate medallion-like circle of bright metal on his chest over the heart. Squinting his eyes against the confusing glow, Elwood realized the medallion was not suspended from a chain, but set directly in the sorcerer's flesh. Skin growing up around the edge of the metal circle held it in place.

Elwood recalled the rumor Tuthwoy Glim had heard about the sorcerer. *So it's true,* he thought. *He traded the heart in his chest for power.* Repulsed, he turned his eyes away from the old man.

The sorcerer laid a hand over the medallion, and his rage seemed to subside somewhat. "Fienoth tells me you and the girl have come all the way from Winnitok. And that you saw my army on the way. Look there!" With a wave of his hand over the water in the Eye, a new picture appeared: endless columns of yugs trickling steadily through a wild wood. "The invasion has begun. They are crossing the river into Winnitok."

Elwood looked on in horror as the horde advanced. He and the others had come too late. Even if they found Granashon tomorrow, how could they prevent the land from being overrun? Watching hints of these thoughts pass across the boy's face, Vallow chuckled humorlessly.

"You and your friends chose an inconvenient time. Having to monitor your movements even as my invasion begins . . . is irritating."

With a deep breath Elwood tried to will the water in the Eye to show him Granashon; but he did not know how to do it, or did not have the power, for the picture of the yug horde remained. Unconsciously he clenched his teeth and let go the focus of his eyes, repeating the Nohar's name continuously in his mind. The picture in the water did not change. The sorcerer asked again what search had brought them to Migdowsh, but Elwood barely heard him. Then Captain Curwen struck the back of the boy's head with an open hand. Elwood lurched a little to one side; the picture in the Eye wavered and disappeared. His reflection returned, and then he saw something.

Another face—was it a reflection, a living picture, or something else?—overlapped his own in the glimmering dark water. An ageless feminine face, wild, wise, and beautiful, with flecks of fiery green floating in the deep brown of her eyes. Fearing the sorcerer saw her too, Elwood held his breath.

Looking intently into his eyes, like one of the Brawbwarb she spoke a picture in his thoughts, and he understood what he must do. Quickly Elwood glanced around the chamber. In a corner, a tall feathered spear was leaning against the wall. He darted a look at Egode Vallow, but the sorcerer did not seem to see the face of the Nohar. When he looked in the water again, she was gone.

"Oh, never mind—the witch and the beast have arrived," said the sorcerer. With his robes flowing after him he swept from the chamber, and the Graycloaks quickly followed with the prisoners.

Elwood began to hear an awful noise that grew louder the nearer they drew to the Pool: a roar of shouts and laughter that echoed through the underground spaces. Still following in the sorcerer's wake, the group entered the enormous Chamber. They halted before the top of the slimy slope down to the water, and Elwood saw what the noise was about.

Across the water, standing in a close group with weapons drawn, were his friends. They were trapped. The Pool lay on one side, the wall curved on the other, and scores of foes stood before them and behind them. Some of these had driven the travelers into the Chamber of the Pool, where others had been waiting. The Graycloaks and yugs were keeping a distance of several yards, and though many bore spears and javelins, for the time being they hurled only insults and jeers.

None of his friends had yet seen Elwood, who was mostly hidden from view behind the sorcerer's wide robes. He hoped they would not: their only chance lay in his being forgotten. At the same time, he craned his neck and hungrily took in the sight of them. Drallah's brave stance—knees slightly bent, arms half-raising knife and tomahawk—filled him with familiar admiration. She stood shoulder to shoulder with Nemoor, whom Elwood could see was busy within herself preparing magic. They both stood back-to-back with Tornonk. The fox truan stood in a half-crouch, his sword before him and his big tail bristling out behind. Perched on top of Drallah's pack, Booj's wings were spread menacingly, and he had ruffled his feathers to make himself appear twice his true size. Standing beside Tornonk, with ears flat and lips pulled back to show her teeth, was Slukee. The sight of his dog facing death without him was more than Elwood could stand.

Egode Vallow turned and spoke a word to Captain Curwen. In response the man released Elwood's shoulder, raised his hands in the air and shouted, "Silence!" Immediately there was quiet throughout the Chamber. Elwood ducked back behind Vallow's robes. Turning in the direction of the shout, all eyes fell on the sorcerer. The silence lasted several long moments before he spoke.

"Why have you come here?" he asked in a curiously practical-sounding way, as though he was conducting uninteresting but necessary business.

The water of the pool carrying her words across the great chamber, Elwood heard Nemoor answer, "Let's talk of it, you and I."

"Yes, witch, let's," replied Vallow dryly. "But we must be quick, for the lord of this land is nigh. He does not talk. Ah, he comes!"

As the sorcerer spoke the center of the wide Pool began to bubble, and then to boil. All over the Chamber, Graycloaks and yugs shifted their feet uneasily, inching back from the Pool and glancing toward the exits. Moving with the captain and the two men bearing Jum, Elwood found himself at the back of the group. With pounding heart, he saw that all eyes were on the roiling, reeking Pool. It was the chance he needed. He ducked unnoticed into the smaller empty chamber close at hand, then broke into an all-out run to reach the Eye.

He found it as they had left it: aglow, filled with glimmering water, unattended. Before going to the Eye, he rushed to the tall spear he had seen leaning in the corner. Taking it up with both hands—it was much taller than him and heavy—he saw the spear's polished haft was of a dark wood he did not recognize. The long broad head looked keener than a cougar's claw, and three hawk feathers trailed by a cord from its base. The wood of the haft made his palms tingle inexplicably, and though he saw not the slightest scratch, he sensed somehow this weapon was older even than Cromgo.

Bearing it to the Eye, he raised the spear with both hands over his head and plunged its blunt end into the dark glassy water. Immediately he felt something beneath the surface grab hold, and the water began to shine with a golden light. A big hand emerged from the light and grasped the rim of the shell. Another hand followed the first, for a moment grabbing the spear-haft, then the rim of the shell opposite where the other had taken hold. Elwood withdrew the spear, and a figure hauled itself up out of the shining water and sprang to the floor.

To Elwood she seemed taller than any human he had ever seen. Her unbound black hair reached past her middle, she was dressed in simple buckskins, and over her shoulder was thrown a blanket of sky blue. As she emerged from the Eye, the chamber filled with a mossy, smoky, drowsy fragrance of winter earth. Elwood was not prepared for the unmediated sight of her skin, burnished from the inside by immortal health, or her brown and green eyes, which had gazed on long ages, gazing now directly into his own; even the extraordinary whiteness of her teeth as she smiled down at him: in her kind there was almost more life than a mortal could bear. He stared dumbly up at her, where they were and what was happening completely forgotten.

Granashon looked around her. Then, kneeling beside Elwood, she grasped her spear in one hand and laid the other on his shoulder. She spoke, and her voice was like the horn of a deer: deadly hard, but dressed in velvet.

"You have freed me at last, Elwood Pitch. Where is Egode Vallow?"

* * *

The Pool was churning violently. From atop the slimy slope down to its poisoned waters, through the emerging vapor-filled bubbles, Drallah and the others could see a gigantic splayed frog-shape rising slowly to the surface. Across the Pool from where they were trapped, the Ringish sorcerer looked on with hands clasped over the medallion in his chest. The scores of Graycloaks and yugs blocking their escape were also transfixed by the monster's approach. The Chamber itself seemed to hold its breath. At last the massive eyeballs, and the gulch that lay between them, broke the surface. The water stilled. Like an island filling half the Pool, the Otguk regarded the sorcerer Vallow.

"My friend," said the Ringishman; so he had addressed the monster for years, since the day he tamed him. "The trespassers we sought are here."

Slowly paddling his massive hands, the Otguk turned to face Drallah and the others. Whatever they were feeling in their hearts, the two humans and the fox truan faced him stolidly; but Slukee, nearly overcome with terror, cowered and looked sideways at the monster. Still perched on Drallah's pack, Booj hid his face behind one of his wings.

Drallah marked the baleful black light in the Otguk's eyes as he greedily looked each of them over. Swallowing the terror welling up in her throat, she hefted her tomahawk and whispered to the others, "The eyes; try to hit the eyes ... " The monster began to gather himself for a leap.

Just as she was about to send her tomahawk spinning toward a giant eyeball, a swift movement on the opposite side of the Chamber made Drallah hesitate. A tall figure she thought she recognized, followed by a short and slight one she knew very well, came running in through the entrance behind the sorcerer. Slukee, seeing them too, gave a sharp yelp; not of terror or despair, but of overwhelming surprise and delight. The dog yelped once more, and bolted off toward the new arrivals.

The Chamber was thrown into chaos. Death-cries resounded as, with her great spear, Granashon felled Captain Curwen and the two men bearing Jum. The Otguk rotated swiftly to face the Nohar, his giant webbed feet thrashing the water. Turning and seeing Granashon had escaped her prison, Egode Vallow made a sign over his head and vanished. Panic-stricken yugs and Graycloaks clogged the exits. Slukee dodged through their legs as she raced around the Pool toward Elwood, who was drawing a dead man's sword from its scabbard. Drallah, Booj, Tornonk, and Nemoor followed the dog, with blows cutting a path through the amazed soldiers.

"Stay back!" cried Granashon, waving them away. "He comes now, and there is nothing you can do against him."

Lunging mightily, the Otguk reached the edge of the Pool, and with a great disturbance of foul water leapt to the top of the slope.

The Nohar strode to meet him. With one giant hand the monster snatched up a yug who was attempting to escape the Chamber, crushing him with a quick, slime-fisted squeeze. He hurled the broken green body at Granashon, who sidestepped it easily. The Otguk caught a second fleeing yug with a flick of his forked tongue, grabbing hold of him with a hand as he drew him kicking back to his mouth. This one he threw alive, screaming. Granashon brought her spear to bear, impaling the yug upon the blade.

As the Nohar withdrew her weapon from the green corpse, the Otguk hauled himself close enough to reach her with a fully extended swing of one foreleg. But Granashon dove clear of the giant hand, and stabbed at a finger almost as long as herself as it swept past. The monster's skin was like armor, and even her powerful thrust could not pierce it. Still, the blow was enough to cause him pain, and he drew his hand quickly back and shook it as though he had been singed by fire.

Granashon moved to follow that stroke with another, but stopped in mid-step. Her shoulders jerked strangely, her arms dropped to her sides, and the head of her spear rested uselessly on the floor. Her tall form trembled as she strained to move, but could not.

Looming like a hill above her, the Otguk stared down at the helpless Nohar. The black light in his eyes flashed and glittered. All who remained in the Chamber were silent as a rumbling issued from deep within the monster's belly. The Otguk was laughing.

Elwood watched in disbelief as Granashon stood unmoving before the Lord of the Swamp. He saw that some sorcery had taken hold of her body, and that she was defenseless before the monster. With both hands gripping the sword he had picked up, Elwood took a step toward her. As he did, the Otguk's laughter trailed off, and Elwood heard another sound that was almost as chilling: from somewhere near at hand, a whispering voice.

"Yes, yes! But don't gloat too long, my friend," it said.

Turning to see who spoke, Elwood saw something uncanny.

Among the battered pictures on the wall near where he stood, one of the frog truan images had a human face—and the face was alive. The eyes blinked as they concentrated on the battle in the Chamber, and the lower lip trembled. It was the face of Egode Vallow.

When the sorcerer vanished at the battle's outset, Elwood realized, he had hidden himself among the images in the wall of the Chamber. From this magic hiding place, he had cast the spell over Granashon that would allow the Otguk to kill her.

Elwood raised the sword over his head and hurled himself at Vallow's face. Seeing the boy coming, the sorcerer rapidly blinked his eyes and vanished once again. Elwood's sword struck the wall where the face had been an instant before, and did no harm.

But the sorcerer's hold on Granashon was broken: as the Otguk bore down on her with his enormous mouth stretched wide, the Nohar suddenly leapt into motion again. Driving her spear up into his descending jowl, she sent the monster lurching backward.

Pressing him, Granashon followed the monstrous frog, her spear aimed up at the great lumps of his eyes. The Otguk jumped backward and away from the oncoming Nohar, landing with a mighty crash on the slime-coated slope down to the Pool.

Granashon halted at the top of the treacherous slope. Because the monster had come to rest below her, their faces were nearly level. They regarded one another for a moment, and then the Nohar spoke.

"Come back up, demon. We are not finished."

The black light in the Otguk's eyes danced. Gesturing to her to come down the slope, he raked the giant tips of his fingers through the slime.

Granashon laughed. The sound was wonderfully free and clear amidst the poison atmosphere of the Chamber. "No," she said. "I've only just escaped a trap, and will not fall into another."

The monster continued to watch her, but did not move. Brandishing her spear defiantly, the Nohar said, "If you wish to fight, come back up!"

The Otguk spat out his long tongue with terrible speed and accuracy. Its forked tip struck Granashon, clutching her middle. Yanking her off her feet, the tongue hauled her irresistibly through the air toward its nest in the gigantic frog's mouth. But as she flew, she leveled and extended her spear before her, aiming it at the back of the monster's throat. With all the might of his own tongue, the Otguk drove the head of the Nohar's magic weapon deep into his own flesh.

Having over the course of his long life crushed innumerable armed foes to death in this way, the Otguk was accustomed to having the inside of his mouth pricked; but none had ever had the reach, the skill, and the courage to truly hurt him until now. As his tongue pulled the Nohar in, an intolerable shock of pain went through the whole of his gigantic bloated body. He tried to bellow his agony and fear and rage, but the only sound that came was a choking, which soon ceased. The baleful black light in his eyes went out, his tongue loosed its hold on Granashon, and the dead mass of the Otguk began slowly to slide into the waters of the Pool. As it did, the remainder of Egode Vallow's soldiers who were still able fled the Chamber.

Seeming very small within the monster's wide-open maw, with a great pull Granashon drew her spear from his flesh. As the Pool swallowed the carcass she leapt clear, and with the spear's help carefully mounted the slope. At the top she found Elwood kneeling on the floor, with Slukee dancing in circles around him. Then Drallah reached them, and her happiness was so great she neither spoke nor moved, but looked from Granashon to Elwood and back, her weapons hanging forgotten in her hands. Finally she dropped them, and kneeling beside the boy, put her arms around him. Booj lit on her pack just by her head. Nemoor and Tornonk, awed by the Nohar and the feat they had just witnessed, stood close by.

"Zaw is dead," Granashon said in thought-speech as she deftly cut Jum's bonds with the tip of her spear.

Jum rose slowly, amazed. *"Who are you?"*

"Your people know me as Broon, but I am called Granashon in the

land of my heart." Then she said aloud, "The attack's begun. I must go to the Eye of Ogin."

They followed the Nohar to the chamber of the Eye. On the way Elwood introduced his friends to Jum.

"It was Jum who grabbed me when we were running from the Graycloaks," he said. "She—wanted to save me. She brought me down into one of their old cities, and her people helped me find you again. One gave his life for us."

"We also owe her people much," said Drallah. Then she nodded her head in Granashon's direction and asked in a hushed voice, "But where was *she?*"

They stepped into the chamber. "There," answered Elwood, pointing at the glowing Eye of Ogin. Beholding at last the wonder they had come so far to find, no one spoke. As they looked on, Granashon leaned her spear against the wall and stood with hands open over the Eye, chanting words of power and gazing into the water. The distant echoing cries of fleeing men and yugs had ceased, and the passages and chambers of the city were silent. At last Granashon spoke to them again.

"Come and look," she said, and they all gathered around the Eye, Elwood holding Slukee in his arms so she too could see. Within was a living picture of a river winding through a wood. They saw the land from high above, as though through the eye of an eagle, or a window set in the sky. For a mile and more, the riverbanks and the river itself were in turmoil.

"Lilikit!" cried Drallah.

The view descended to just above the tops of the bare trees. On either side of the River, countless green yugs in iron caps, and a few Graycloaks also, ran here and there, or crawled on the ground like worms driven from the soil by heavy rain. On the right bank it seemed there was a Winhar behind every other tree, and their deadly arrows were taking a grievous toll. Over on the left bank, brawny woogan fighters were cutting more of the invaders down as they ran away to the west. In the River itself, scores of yugs and Graycloaks clung desperately to big rafts as though tossed by the winds of a hurricane, and many attempting to swim back across were drowning.

"Vallow's force is far bigger than the defenders'," observed Tornonk. "Why do they retreat?"

"Because, with the help of you all, Elwood Pitch freed me from my prison, and my power is no longer cut off from the land. It flows once again up through the roots, and pours out the branch tips all around Winnitok."

"The Dread of Granashon," said Nemoor, awed and humbled by power far greater than her own.

Apparently in response to some silent invisible manipulation by Granashon, the view in the Eye moved closer still, until it was below the bare treetops and they could see the faces of those nearest at hand. It passed over the River from the right bank to the left, and the companions cried out as they caught a glimpse of Kwog NiKwog and Tuthwoy Glim in the thick of the one-sided fight. The woogan and the man appeared unharmed and to be much delighted about something—probably the turn the battle had taken. The Eye moved on, rising again and following the River north. As it passed over the land, they saw the invaders were being turned and routed at two other points along Lilikit. Everywhere they looked, yugs and Graycloaks were fleeing or fallen.

Granashon stepped back from the Eye and declared, "Egode Vallow's horde is defeated."

"But what about Vallow?" asked Elwood.

"Gone—for now. Everything the Falseheart was trying to accomplish has failed. Now he will hide, and start again. It was a mistake not to have killed him before he was aware of me."

"Granashon," began Drallah after a deep breath, "where have you been?"

Grinning archly, the Nohar turned to her and said, "A question I am often asked, and seldom answer. But you have freed me, and saved Winnitok, so I will tell you. I was a prisoner of Vallow. Some of us have been hunting him for years; the Falseheart is too dangerous to live free in Ehm. Two summers ago I got word he was in the Great Swamp, and the Otguk's guest. I came fast when I heard, knowing that with the poisoned magic of the Pool, which was the monster's strength, Vallow would do much worse than he had yet done.

"When I arrived in this city it was silent; it seemed abandoned. I found my way to the Pool unchallenged, and though I could feel that he the Brawbwarb call Zaw was near, he did not show himself. I entered this chamber and saw the Eye, the lost turtle's shell my cohort Nentop took from Ogin Island long ago. I understood a lot then; how Vallow was able to oversee all his works in different parts of Pahn. Then I looked through the Eye."

The Nohar clicked her tongue and smiled ruefully.

"Which was foolish. Vallow had set his trap well; it dragged me in like a whirlpool. I could hear him laughing as it took me away. I was carried to the cave in Ogin Island, and there I was a prisoner— just like Nentop was. I soon understood my power could not reach Winnitok from within the Island, and that that was Vallow's hope in sending me there. My Dread would fail, and keep him from my land no more.

"But I also learned the turtle's shell is always at the heart of that place, whether the hard *thing* is a thousand miles away or there in the cave. Vallow knew it too—he used that tie to send me to the Island— but there were things he did not know. In the cave, I also could look through the Eye—from the other side. And in the cave, the Eye does not always look on this world alone.

"So that is where I have been, Drallah Wehr. Now, I have been underground long enough. Who wants to go above?"

Elwood opened his mouth to speak, but Granashon stopped him with a raised hand. He was unsure, but thought he saw pity in her eyes as she looked down at him.

"Not here, Elwood. You've waited a long time to know some

things; now wait a little longer. The monster's reek is foul. Let's go above."

So saying, she poured the water on the floor, tucked the Eye of Ogin under her arm, and, as she would a staff, took up her spear. Then, by the shell's glow, quietly chanting in rhythm with her long, long strides, the Nohar led them out of the dark city that was Zaw's no more.

A Choice of Worlds

By long sloping ways they climbed to the surface of Migdowsh. Sometimes they glimpsed wary, affrighted men or yugs, but all fled before the face of the Nohar. Since they did not threaten to attack she let them go; but hide and flee as they might, none of those Egode Vallow left behind that day lived long afterwards. The Great Swamp and the Brawbwarb made certain of that.

Above ground they found it was not long after noon, and Elwood was amazed to realize they had only been a few hours in Zaw's city—many fewer than it had seemed. A cold rare wind they could not have welcomed more was blowing across the land from the west. For the first time since the travelers passed through the Breathless Gate, the sun was shining freely in a blue sky.

"The Swamp is glad of the monster's end," cried Nemoor, arms spread wide to catch the wind.

"There is change already," said Granashon. "Maybe we will see Jum's people, and tell them why."

They started north up the crooked highway in the bright afternoon light, Elwood and Drallah giddily trading accounts of the two days since the Graycloak ambush as they went. Booj, Nemoor, and Tornonk interrupted with questions and remarks, and frequently Elwood paused to tell Jum in thought-speech all that was being said.

"It never occurred to me," said Drallah, almost singing, "that

Granashon was guiding us to the Eye because she was actually *in* it—or through it, I mean."

Elwood grew quiet at this, for it reminded him of the ominous expression on Granashon's face when he started to question her. He had also begun to think of how, if the Nohar was able to help return him home, he and Drallah would soon be saying good-bye.

As darkness was descending they met a band of frog truans stealing along the roadside toward Cromgo. Guessing the cause of the great change but cautious still, they had set out to learn if Zaw was actually gone. The moment Jum saw her people she leapt into their midst, and after a few words and images in thought-speech they all began to bellow and caper with joy. Granashon and the travelers looked on as they rejoiced at the end of generations of exile in their own land; then the frog truans were all around them, showering the monster-killer and the rest of their liberators with thanks and praise.

Most of this band went hastily away to bear the good news back to their people, but several remained to accompany their guests to the nearest place of comfort beneath the Swamp. Like Rounder Sink, it could only be entered by ways too narrow to allow the monster access, and so it had been a valuable haven while the Otguk ruled Migdowsh. In spite of their narrowness, the entrances led to a number of chambers, some quite large. As well as tunnels, a series of pools and streams interconnected the chambers, and in those subterranean waters grew huge floating water lilies the Brawbwarb called roog. From these the place got its name: Roog Sink.

Soon a continuous procession was passing through the chamber where the travelers, Jum, and Granashon supped and rested in the blue and orange glow of many light-gourds. As they passed, the frog truans thought-called promises of lifelong gratitude and friendship to each of them. From a neighboring chamber, a joyful song was growing louder as it was joined by one deep frog voice after another. All the Brawbwarb were gathering in the Sink to celebrate Zaw's end.

The celebration was still growing when, taking up the Eye of

Ogin, Granashon led Elwood and Slukee off to a chamber a little apart from the people and the noise. They sat down by a still pool, upon which floated the thick pads and ghostly flowers of four roogs. Scattered around the cross-legged boy and Granashon as they talked were two luminous gourds, the reclining dog, and the glowing turtle shell.

"In the cave at the heart of Ogin Island where the sorcerer imprisoned me," the Nohar began, "I found a strange and wondrous thing: there is an eye in the air just below the ceiling of the cave, in size and shape very like the eye in this magic turtle shell. And like this eye, the one in the cave allows you to see whatever place you wish. Wondering at this, I grew to understand the Eye of Ogin is a thing of two sides, and one side always remains fixed in the heart of the Island from which it comes.

"After I was taken, for many long months there was nothing to do but look on as Egode Vallow's plots unfolded across Pahn. One day I looked in the Eye but did not command it; instead, I let the Eye show me what it would. I saw a strange land, stranger even than the Ringish countries beyond the Sea. I saw an endless city, and roads crossing and covering up half the earth, and the countless— *machines*. I am not a judge of worlds. But there amidst the city I saw a little place of young woods, and it was a flower in the desert to me.

"As I looked, a boy and a dog came walking there. They went down into a hollow under a pair of oak trees, and as I watched I began to have a strange realization: that the divide between me and what I saw through the Eye was not what it usually was; that I might actually be seen, heard, or felt by those I saw. I watched as the boy, who was you, Elwood, sat in the hollow. And then I knew you could feel that I was there."

The moment in the hollow came back to Elwood as Granashon spoke of it. Vividly he saw the tiny pool fed by the trickling stream, and smelled the scent of new-fallen leaves. He remembered well the particular moment of longing for his old home, and the sudden certainty that someone else was there.

"None before had ever been aware of me as I watched them through the Eye. I realized if I could communicate with someone beyond Ogin, that one might help me escape. I continued to watch as you walked on, reaching out to you with my will. Then ... the view through the Eye changed. Half became another place, my place, the Glade in Winnitok, while in the other half I could still see your world and you. Then I saw the path between the worlds.

"I knew I was being given power to reach you through the Eye. And I knew, if only you were in Ehm, I might find a way to tell you where I was. So I showed you the path, Elwood."

Because Granashon was so tall and they were sitting close together, Elwood had to lean back to meet her eyes. "You were able to do all these things," he said. "You showed me the path, and the tale of the Eye in the *Noharitt*. And you sent the poison ivy smoke to save us in Oldotok—I even saw you then. So why couldn't you use the Eye to tell anyone else where you were, what had happened to you?"

"The little I was able to do within the cave, through the Eye, I was able to do through the tie between you and me. I do not know why, but my will could only reach *you*. And so when I realized I could do it, I had to show you the path—though I wasn't able to tell you what walking it would mean."

"But why me?"

"That is a mystery I have often wondered on as the days passed and I watched you draw closer to the Eye. Perhaps it was chance that brought us together, a stroke of fortune amidst the ties between worlds. Or perhaps it was Tehm the god taking pity on me, like he did Nentop when he was a prisoner in the cave of Ogin. Though breaking the Island open again seems more practical than this.

"I did not choose you, Elwood, nor was I given a choice. But had I been, I could not have chosen better. You have braved hardships and dangers far beyond your years. You have rescued me, and saved my land.

"And now I fear I must ask you for something more: your forgiveness. For in bringing you to this world from your own, I could give you no true choice. Though you chose to walk the path, you had no way of knowing where it would lead, the full round of what you were choosing: to leave your world, and yourself."

Elwood was silent, afraid to learn what she meant. "I didn't leave myself," he said finally.

"To leave your*selves*—some of them—is closer to what I mean. When you took the path between the worlds, you divided. You left another Elwood Pitch behind."

Elwood did not understand her at all. In spite of the great reassurance that was her presence, he was growing alarmed.

"There are selves within selves, Elwood, just as there are worlds within worlds. You've noticed that this world and your world have a lot in common. The oak trees of your world, the oak trees I first saw you under, are very like the oaks of Ehm. Your dear companion Drallah is human, just as you are. And you have seen countless other things that are alike between our worlds."

"Yes, I know. But there's a whole lot different. . . ."

"Yes: they are also very, very different. And for the same reason, the path you took between the worlds was not for all the Elwoods that are. Only for some of them."

"What are you saying?"

"That when you left, an Elwood Pitch remained in your world, where you and he were born as one. But now, he is not you, and you are both whole unto yourselves."

Not believing what he was hearing, Elwood dug a thumbnail into the hard mud of the floor and asked, "Slukee too?"

"Her too."

"So my mother, my father," he choked, his eyes welling. "They don't know I'm gone?"

"No, Elwood. They never knew," she answered quietly, wrapping a strong arm around his shoulders. "I am sorry. My land was in peril, and I had to take the chance I was given. I will do all I can to mend the wrong I have done you. I do not think it wise, but if you wish it, I will take you back to my Glade, and return you and Slukee to your world."

"You *can* send us back," he cried, for a moment hopeful. "But then what? I've wanted to get home all this time—" He stopped, unable to imagine doing so now, unable to say *But there would be two of me.*

Granashon looked at him a long time, her ageless face full of pity. Then she knelt beside the pool and filled the turtle shell with water. Crossing her legs once again, she balanced it on her knees and looked within. She had been searching the water just a short time when she said, "Look."

He leaned forward on his knees and gazed down into the Eye. As he looked the water turned misty, as he had seen it do before; then the mist was drawn aside like a curtain, and he could see a living picture of young winter woods at dusk. He recognized the two oaks standing over the little hollow where Granashon first found him, and knew he was looking at the wooded park in his own world, near his own house.

"The Eye is yours to control, Elwood," said Granashon. "It will show you what you want to see."

He thought of his family's house less than a mile from the hollow, and the Eye instantly began to pass its unblinking gaze over the woods in search of it. Very slowly it moved, and Elwood realized it was responding to a reluctance within him. Although he longed to see his mother, father, and sister again, he did not want to see the one who was himself and not himself.

Finally the Eye left the woods, crossed the road, and looked down on the house from a little distance above. It was almost dark, but there were no lights or other signs of life within.

"No one's home," he said. Granashon nodded, but said nothing. He lingered a few moments, staring at the blank bedroom windows on the second floor. Then a wash of light passed over the front of the house, and his father's car pulled into the driveway. It came to a halt before the garage. All four car doors opened at once, and his father, his mother, his sister, and one other all stepped out. With a twinge in his stomach, he saw that this last was the other Elwood. His father went around to the back of the car and opened the trunk, and he and Ellen began to gather up shopping bags that were stowed there.

Responding to his desire, the Eye descended to a point just above their heads and looked down on Elwood's mother as she moved around to the back of the car to supervise her husband and daughter. She was wearing her big blue coat against the cold, the same one she had had for years. Her attitude at the moment was one he knew well: she always became especially focused and efficient just before dinnertime.

"Oh, Mom," he said, beginning to sob. Watching him worriedly, Slukee softly whined.

His mother smiled at his father as she took one of several bags off his hands, and turned to go into the house. Laden with groceries in plastic, he followed her. Elwood glimpsed his face close up before he too turned, and saw he had begun to grow his mustache and beard again.

Then, strangely, Ellen looked up into the air over her head and seemed to stare directly at Elwood. His heart jumped. Forgetting he could not be heard he called through his sobbing, "Hey, Ellen!" But she only turned and followed their parents up the walk toward the front door. He realized she must simply have been looking at something in the sky, which was filling with dim stars.

Reluctantly he turned the Eye toward the front walk, and saw the other Elwood where he stood on the porch. He watched as the boy unlocked the front door and knelt to greet the other Slukee, who had been left at home, as she swarmed out of the house. One by one his mother, father, and sister passed the two and went inside. While Slukee shot off to the bushes under the living room window, Elwood marked the great difference between her and the Slukee by his side: the dog he watched through the Eye was well fed, and her coat was sleek with regular brushing—very different from the skinny, scraggly dog who had just walked hundreds of miles with him through great peril and suffering. Turning away from the water in the shell for a moment, he kissed the fur of Slukee's head.

His weeping subsided, and he brought the Eye close to the other Elwood. His hair was trimmed short, and he seemed pale. He did not look like he could survive a single day of the kind Elwood had been living for so many weeks. All the same, Elwood was racked with jealousy, and longed to be in his place. The other Slukee ran back into the house. He watched as the other Elwood also went inside, and closed the door behind him.

He did not direct the Eye to follow his family within, but watched as lights appeared in windows all over the house, shining out on the deepening dark.

"Home," he whispered, not realizing he spoke aloud. "Show me home."

The Eye shot away into the west, sweeping over mile upon mile of cities and fields, rivers and mountains, traveling so far so fast it caught up with the passing light of dusk. After a time it slowed, and Elwood recognized by a line of low snow-clad hills the land where he had been born. The Eye descended as it approached. He saw in the last of the light the steaming noses of Holstein cows poking out of their stalls at Mason's Dairy, and the Fishlocks' house and barn. He looked hopefully for someone he knew, especially one of his friends, but all the people seemed to be indoors or away from home. Then the Eye passed over the Pitches' old house. At the sight of it, so familiar and dear, his heart ached anew with love and bitterness.

A boy several years younger than him was digging in a snowdrift under the eaves of the garage. Elwood did not know him, but remembered hearing the family who bought the house had a young boy. He watched him—yet another who had taken his place—carving a fort out of the snow, the only person stirring in the whole neighborhood, it seemed. Gray smoke began to rise from the house's chimney. Taking note of it, the young boy turned expectantly toward the front door. It opened a little, and it seemed he was called to, for he jumped up, brushed the snow from his pants, and ran inside. After his departure all was still, all except the chimney smoke rising into the twilight.

Elwood sat back and turned his gaze from the water in the shell. Twice before, his life had changed utterly: once when he and his family moved from their old home, and again when he found himself in another world. Following those changes, there had at least been hope his life would return to the way it had been. But now that he knew he had become two separate people, everything was changed once again, and there was no such hope.

After a long silence he said half to himself, half to Granashon, "At least they haven't been thinking all this time that something bad happened to me. I guess I should be glad."

Drallah appeared at the entrance to the little chamber, Booj hopping and strutting behind her. She stopped short at the sight of Elwood's tear-smeared face, then rushed to join him where he sat.

He barely knew how to begin to tell her what he had just learned. "I split in two when I came here," he said, deadness in his voice. "I don't understand it, but Granashon does. There's another me in my world. I saw him."

Drallah slowly shook her head and stared at him.

"When he took the path between the worlds," said Granashon, "only a part of him could come. That part became his whole self, and left another whole behind."

Dragging his sleeve across his face Elwood said, "Drallah, she can send us back."

"But that's great news . . . "

"I can't go back. It would be too strange, too . . . unnatural. It would be too hard for the other me, and my whole family. Things like that don't happen in my world. There's no magic there. No one would understand."

Drallah began to object, but Elwood continued.

"And they don't need me. I'm still there; I always have been—as far as they know. They never knew I left. It's like I died, and—and nobody knows."

Beginning to understand, Drallah cried out, "Oh, my friend!"

"It is true that if Elwood returns, his life in his own world would be most strange, and difficult," said Granashon, "for both himself and his other, and everyone around them. It would be so in any world; in Ehm as well. I feel very certain that once such a dividing has been done, it is better for the halves never to meet again. But I will send you and Slukee back to make the best of life in the world you were born to, if that is what you want. It is your choice, Elwood."

"It doesn't seem like much of a choice," he replied desolately. He almost said, *It's a little late for you to offer me a choice, isn't it?*

"You and Slukee have us, here in Ehm," said Drallah, taking his hands in her own. "We're your family, Booj and I. My uncle Mithloo will have you in his house, gladly. My mother and father will welcome you too. All of Winnitok will welcome you for returning the Nohar to us."

He thought of the unwitting sacrifice he had made, and of the land he had saved. He remembered all he would let go, and all he would keep. He thought of not having to say good-bye to Drallah, and of one day perhaps seeing Ainathuai again. With all of this in his mind at once, with Drallah, Booj, Slukee, and Granashon surrounding him and waiting to hear what he would say next, Elwood cleared the tears from his throat and said, "Then we'll stay."

* * *

The next morning, Jum and a jovial escort of several dozen frog truans joined the travelers as they continued north, walking with them, and jumping and swimming too, all the way to the Breathless Gate. There, beneath the rampart of the Burnt Hills, with many promises of welcome and return, the Brawbwarb and the travelers said farewell.

"*Thanks, Jum,*" said Elwood, taking in his hands some of her long fingers.

"*Thank you. We saved both our lands at once.*"

For a moment taken aback, he said, "*Yes ... my land is Winnitok.*"

"*And you always have a home in the Swamp.*"

For years afterwards the Brawbwarb were a less hidden, friendlier people than they had been even before the monster, welcoming in their reborn cities visitors from all over Pahn and Magua. Their numbers slowly grew as they reclaimed all Zaw had taken, and the harm the monster had done was healed.

Some things would not heal. So poisoned were the waters of Aw that the Brawbwarb had no choice in the end but to seal the Chamber and the Pool, making them Zaw's tomb. All the same, memory of the Pool before the coming of the monster was passed on to each new-hatched generation, and in that way the place was not utterly lost.

With provisions from the Graycloaks' supply in Cromgo, the Nohar and the travelers left the vast humming Swamp behind and walked on into the Burnt Hills. Subdued after the Otguk's death and the flight of Egode Vallow, the denizens of the Hills did not trouble them, and they made good time northward.

At the northern edge of the Hills they came to another parting: Tornonk and Nemoor were continuing up the Gaulatash River to Ashawda, while Granashon and the companions were turning toward the Gulf of Pahn and a sea canoe to Winnitok. Knowing what they did of his motives for helping them escape Ashawda, the companions were surprised by Tornonk's decision to return there. They could only suppose it had something to do with Nemoor, who was convinced the Queen would pardon him for his disloyalty. But the fox truan was closemouthed as usual, saying nothing of the reason for his change of heart.

One reason Nemoor believed her cousin would forgive Tornonk was his role in the recovery of a long-lost heirloom of her House: the Eye of Ogin. As they were leaving Roog Sink, Granashon had handed the Eye, which she had wrapped in big roog-pads to hide its light, over to Nemoor. "This was stolen from your ancestors, and you should take it back to your House," she had said. "Don't let it be stolen or lost again, and don't forget how its theft long ago might have ended in the ruin of Pahn." Shooting the witch a piercing look she had added, "It is a great power. Nentop was not wise, giving it to a human. He did, though, so I honor the right of your Queen to keep it. It would be better if you did not try to master its secrets. But if you must, look into it seldom. Do not misuse it."

"Can I not convince you to return through Ashawda?" asked Nemoor as, standing on the stony eastern bank of Gaulatash, the two groups prepared to say good-bye. "The Queen will be disappointed when she learns you might have, but did not." This last she said directly to Elwood, who had been quietly inclined to follow the witch's suggestion the several times she made it.

"No, I am heading straight to Winnitok," said Granashon. "My power has returned, and again protects the land; but I have been a prisoner, and want a rest at home. You all do what you like."

"I will tell her the tale, then," continued Nemoor, eyes still on Elwood though she addressed them all, "and her people will hear it too."

Handing the witch a makeshift leather envelope, Elwood asked, "Would you please give this to the Queen?" With an ink quill and a scrap of parchment from the Graycloaks' supplies, as well as help from Drallah writing in Wohmog, he had composed a note to Ainathuai which read:

Dear Queen Ainathuai,

*I want you to know I was sorry to leave. I had to go,
though. You know why. But all that's done now, and it turns
out I won't be going back to my world. I am going to live in
Winnitok.*

*There are a lot of things I want to say to you, but I don't
know if you want to hear them or not. Maybe you could
write to me and let me know. I can be reached in the house
of Shonah and Moodin Wehr, in Ohrimo.*

I hope some day I'll see you again.

Elwood

Taking it with a smile, Nemoor said, "She will get it."

Drallah handed Tornonk another letter, this one addressed to
Tuthwoy Glim and Kwog NiKwog. "Would you get this to our friends
on Mount Kulenumpt?" she asked. "We promised to let them know
when we'd done what we needed to, but I don't know when we'll
go that way again."

"Yes, I will see to it. Next time you come back over the Mountains, look for me." Then he stepped close to Elwood and Drallah, and
grasped them both by a shoulder.

"I have hunted with many remarkable people in my life. But you
two exceed them all in the greatness of your hearts, and the honor
I was done joining you. I will not forget."

"Nor will we," returned Drallah. "All would have been lost without Tornonk. And Nemoor," she added hastily.

They parted; the companions and Granashon walking east,
Tornonk and Nemoor north. As Elwood and Drallah turned to wave
a last farewell, they saw Nemoor, tiny in the distance, with both
hands raise the unveiled Eye of Ogin high over her head, where it
shone against the wintry gray of Gaulatash like a rainbow within a
star. Then she returned it to its wrappings, slung it back in place
over her shoulder, and followed the fox truan out of sight.

* * *

In the following weeks Granashon guided the companions through
a dry hill country, over a low mountain pass, and down to the Gulf
of Pahn. During the last stage of the journey to the Sea, they sometimes saw it lying blue and gray and green across the horizon: Elwood
and Slukee's first glimpses of those deep salt waters that endlessly
flowed around the east and south of Winnitok, and on the far, far
shores of which lay the countries of Lindilune and Ringune.

At the Gulf they procured a long broad-bottomed canoe with a
single short mast, and set sail for Winnitok. All through the days of
their ocean voyage, Granashon kept up a steady stream of talk and
song, occupying the companions' minds while their bodies had little to do. To be in the Nohar's company so long had a wonderful
effect on the companions, and it seemed that simply being close to
her immortal vitality and strength helped erase the weariness and
pain of their perilous journey. She could not, however, touch the
change that was made in Elwood on the night he saw his other, the
self he had been parted from.

When they were nearing the shores of Winnitok at last, Booj flew
ahead to Drallah's home in Ohrimo, just above the place where the
River met the Sea, and told her astonished mother and father she
would soon be arriving with Granashon. The news quickly spread,
and they were met in Ohrimo Bay by many boats filled with joyful
people who had come to welcome the Nohar, and the companions
who found and freed her, home to Winnitok.

* * *

It is told elsewhere how, in the years that followed, Elwood Pitch and Dral-lah Wehr became scouts of great mastery and courage, renowned through-out Pahn and beyond for their deeds on the trail, in the hunt, and in war. Drallah Wehr was a woman of wisdom and prowess, and a leader of her people. But the heart of Elwood Pitch was always haunted by the self he left behind, the other who lived on in the world of his birth. This led him through terrible darkness, and was the cause of much sorrow.